# Maggie's Going Nowhere

# Maggie's Going Nowhere

ROSE HARTLEY

MICHAEL JOSEPH
*an imprint of*
PENGUIN BOOKS

MICHAEL JOSEPH

UK | USA | Canada | Ireland | Australia
India | New Zealand | South Africa | China

Penguin
Random House
Australia

Michael Joseph is part of the Penguin Random House group of companies whose addresses can
be found at global.penguinrandomhouse.com

First published by Michael Joseph in 2020

Cover photography by Dutch Scenery/iStock (caravan); Winterling/Depositphotos (wine
bottles); The Corner/Depositphotos (vintage pattern); Serkucher/Depositphotos (cat)
Cover design by Lisa Brewster/The Brewster Project
Typeset in 12.25/17 pt Goudy by Post Pre-press, Australia
Printed and bound in Australia by Griffin Press, part of Ovato, an accredited
ISO AS/NZS 14001 Environmental Management Systems printer

A catalogue record for this
book is available from the
National Library of Australia

ISBN 978 0 14379 548 3

penguin.com.au

MIX
Paper from
responsible sources
FSC® C009448

*For Kiki and Tim*

# Chapter 1

Wedding dresses have a special kind of perfume. The one my best friend Jen was squeezed into smelt like rotted hair, mothballs and musk, but that was because the dress was one hundred and three years old and had been stored with the meticulous care that old ladies take of their broken dreams and bitter memories. The light filtering through Jen's bedroom window fell upon her cleavage, which rose like two pale boulders over dangerously stretched lace. One sneeze and –

'It doesn't look right,' she said, twisting around to see the back. 'Does it?'

My mother poked her eager face around Jen's bedroom door. 'Can I see?'

'Come in, Valerie,' said Jen. 'You're filling in for Mum, so you have to tell the truth. What do you think?'

'Um,' said my mother. She cocked her head to one side, looking doubtful.

She wanted badly to be a cool mother figure to Jen, the golden child she was supposed to have had instead of me. She wanted to assuage Jen's fears about the wedding, the choice of groom, and whether she would look pretty while making the biggest mistake of her life. But all my mother could say was 'um' because even she couldn't convince herself that Jen looked like anything except a raw chipolata in a white tourniquet.

A seam popped as Jen turned back to look at me in desperation. 'Maggie?'

Who was going to tell her that the dress did not flatter her? Who would have the gall to imply that the family heirloom, the exquisite mass of vintage lace that four generations of women before her had worn down the aisle to begin their disappointing marriages, did not fit her? That, in fact, it looked fucking heinous?

'It looks fucking heinous,' I said.

'Maggie!' my mum snapped. 'It looks beautiful, darling. It just needs to be taken out a little.'

'It can't be taken out. There's no room in the seams,' Jen said. 'I'm too big for it.'

'*It's* too small,' I said. 'It's made for miniature Italian women who eat nothing but tomatoes.'

'What will I tell Mum?'

'Just send her a picture,' I said. 'That'll tell her everything she needs to know.'

Jen took out her phone and snapped a selfie in the mirror to send to her mother, who was on a cruise in Europe, or maybe Antarctica, who knows. Jen's mother spent her life on cruise ships to avoid confronting Jen's father, who liked to philander in hotel rooms on 'business' trips. Jen's two older sisters lived in London and Abu Dhabi respectively, so I, with occasional help from my mother, was acting as a fill-in family member while Jen planned her dream wedding to Jono, the worst man in the world. The man who once ordered buffalo wings because he thought they were made of buffalo and he 'liked eating endangered species'.

Mum was elated to have been invited to witness Jen trying on the heirloom dress. She kept shooting me sideways glances as if to say, *See? This could be you one day, if only you'd keep your legs together and learn to cook.*

The wedding planning was having a strange effect on Jen. It had made her more anxious to please than usual; she'd already bowed to her parents' emailed demands that she recite her vows in a church even though Jono wasn't Catholic, and specified to the gram how heavy the invitation cardstock should be. Yet at the same time she exuded a palpable sense of relief, as if she was anticipating a time in the near future when she could finally relax, not from the stress of the wedding but from the stress of waiting to be settled. Her relief sat uncomfortably with me, like an old man with slightly crazed eyes who stands too close. Marriage was what she wanted, but no one except Jen and my mother thought that marriage to Jono would make her happy.

Just as I thought Mum was about to crack and admit that the dress needed a slight adjustment, such as being tossed onto a fire, Jen's mother called. She must have been by the pool, prawn cocktail in hand, bad tan lines showing above her beach dress. At least, that's what I imagined everyone looked like on cruises.

'Hi Mum,' Jen said.

I heard the tinny sound of her mother screeching down the phone but couldn't make out the words.

'It's too small,' Jen protested.

More screeching.

'No, I can't do it up at the back. My bust. I – okay. Okay. Okay. Uh-huh. Oh. Okay. Thanks. Love you, Mum.'

Jen hung up and burst into tears.

'She says I have to lose weight to fit into the dress. It's a family heirloom. She says I can't be the first one in the family to walk down the aisle in a polyester fright from China. She's sending me a diet book. It's called *Food-Free At Last: How I Learned to Eat Air*.'

'Oh, Jen.' My mother patted her on the shoulder. She shot me a look as if to tell me this was all my fault.

'I. Look. Horrible.' Jen heaved with sobs.

Jen was a saint in my eyes: a nurse who would give her last hot chip to the sorry-looking dog at the cafe if it so much as nudged her knee. So if she must marry the man who was once hospitalised for sticking his cock into a vacuum cleaner on a bucks' night dare, I'd be damned if I was going to let her walk down the aisle looking like a sausage.

Something had to be done.

I stepped up behind Jen. Grabbed the delicate antique lace at each shoulder. Pulled down, hard. God, that tearing sound was delicious. Buttons popped and flew across the room. Priceless Edwardian silk shredded and gave up the fight. The dress was ribboned, split from shoulder to waist. There would be no rescuing it now.

'Maggie!' my mother screeched, and grabbed at my hands. I thought she might hit me. 'Maggie, what have you done?'

Jen's mouth was open as she stared at me in the mirror. Tattered lace slid slowly down pink flesh, exposing her strapless bra.

'Oh my God. *Maggie*.' She picked up a piece of dead lace and caressed it, pale with horror. Bits of the dress were hanging off her shoulders like frayed string. 'You realise this was all done by hand a hundred years ago. You can't get lace like this anymore. They don't make it.'

I shrugged. 'Tell your mum I did it. Tripped and grabbed you to steady myself. Or that you looked so beautiful I murdered the lace in a jealous rage.'

Jen's hands slowly went to her mouth. She screeched with laughter. 'My mother is going to die of horror. You bitch, you've killed my mother!'

My own mother put her head in her hands. 'Oh my God.'

Jen reached towards the ceiling, and the ruins of the family dress slowly crumpled to the floor, leaving her clad only in her bra and undies.

'I can't believe you just did that.'

I opened my palms. Innocent, I swear. 'Hey, now you can find a dress you actually like.'

———

It might appear that I spend all my days tearing up irreplaceable wedding dresses and bitching about my mother, but there are other things I enjoy, too.

Country music. Sex. Bitching about my mother.

Most of my energy, however, is devoted to avoiding hard work. In my view, the human race invented work for no good reason, and now that we're technologically advanced enough to make most jobs obsolete, we could be sitting back and letting the robots take over. Yet people around me insist on striving harder and spending more time at work than ever. I can't understand it. I've been doing the same commerce degree at Melbourne University for ten years and am no closer to graduating than I was five years ago. I know what happens when people graduate from commerce: they become accountants. My mother is one. That's a kind of hell I'd do anything to avoid.

On the evening of the dress-tearing incident, Jen and Jono held their engagement party at a bar around the corner from

Jen's house called The Fainting Chair, a fine establishment with wood-panelled walls that hosts good alt-country bands. The surly owner winks at me above his long sideburns every time I walk in. The party was a great opportunity for endless numbers of old high school and uni acquaintances to improve their self-esteem by asking me about my degree. When are you going to finish? What will you do afterwards? How many subjects did you fail this year? To the last question I always reply, 'Only three,' so they can giggle and wait for me to join in laughing at myself. Which I always do, because I'm not an idiot. I have some social graces.

Jen's parents had offered to pay for the party, but only if she held it at the Melbourne Club and invited all their friends. She declined in favour of The Fainting Chair, saying she just wanted to put some money over the bar and let the guests buy their own dinner. Her parents were so annoyed they didn't bother coming back from their respective overseas trips to attend.

I doubt Jen would have had the guts to refuse her parents if I hadn't been around to egg her on. That's how we work, Jen and me. I'm the dark-haired, round-faced one with eyes the colour of overcooked peas, who stole bottles of rum from behind the bar when we were fifteen. She's the one with angelic blonde curls who distracted the bartender while I did it. Most of the time she's a people-pleaser, a dutiful daughter. But every now and then someone, usually one of her parents, pushes too far – asks her to hold her engagement party at the Melbourne Club, the domain of the illuminati – and she turns to me for advice, knowing I'll say fuck 'em. Then she spends six months in purgatory, apologising to her parents as they remind her over and over about that time they bought her a house.

At The Fainting Chair, a four-piece alt-country outfit were

playing in front of the old piano. The music was good and the slide guitarist was abominably sexy. Jen stood by the bar, tapping her fingers out of time, looking nervous. She was wearing a poufy 1950s dress, pink with white flowers, cut low at the neckline to show off her perfect rack. Her curls spilled over her shoulders. I knew she'd spent hours making it look like she'd hardly tried. She was clutching a cider and talking to a cute guy with dirty blond hair and irresistible dimples. One point of the collar on his red plaid flannelette shirt was poking up adorably.

I caught the cute guy's eye, flicked my hair back as sexily as I could, and shambled over in my battered black heels.

'Maggie, this is Dan,' Jen said. I shook the guy's hand and he smiled, showing those dimples. 'He's friends with Biyu's boyf—'

'Why haven't I met you before?' I asked.

Dan laughed nervously.

'How's Lisa?' Jen cut in. 'Lisa is Dan's *girlfriend*, Maggie.'

'Uh, not anymore,' he said. 'We broke up.'

Jen flushed red. 'Oh Dan, I'm so sorry. Oh my God.' She put a hand up to her cheek.

'It's all right,' he said.

Jen stammered something about the band.

'The slide guitarist is good,' I said, ever helpful.

Dan followed my gaze. 'Interesting tatts.'

The babe on the slide guitar did have interesting tattoos. Prison tattoos, in fact, done in biro. I could make out a clumsily written 'memento mori' on his wrist. I wondered if he'd actually been to jail or if he'd just got really drunk and let a friend loose with a pen.

'Interesting tatts, interesting life,' I said.

Jen dragged me further along the bar, muttering about getting me a drink.

'I'm so embarrassed,' she whispered when Dan was out of earshot. 'I can't believe I didn't hear about Dan and Lisa breaking up.'

'Are you going to obsess over a totally imaginary offence all night? Because I don't think Dan cared.'

'I can't help it.'

The unpolished wood bar was rough beneath my fingers as I tried to catch Surly's eye to get a drink. Jen's friends were clustered in small groups, wearing suits and glittering jewellery, and I thought I detected the scent of superiority in their aftershave and perfume. They were studiously avoiding Jono's friends, a group of mining bros who were a little louder and a lot drunker. The suits looked out of place in the dingy bar. I overheard a man muttering contemptuously about the Elvis pictures on the walls.

'Your friends suck,' I told Jen. 'Except me.'

Technically, some of Jen's friends were my friends too, but over the years, as they'd landed corporate jobs and bought houses and talked about getting engaged while I still wore my trackies to class and sat next to nineteen-year-olds in lecture theatres, I'd started thinking of them as her friends, not mine.

'Honestly, maybe I should have had the party at the Melbourne Club. Everyone's weirded out.'

'No way.'

'No one likes it here.' She wrapped her hands around her cider glass and looked about, her face scrunched up in worry. 'But I wanted to have it somewhere I felt comfortable. Jono isn't helping at all.'

'Of course he isn't.'

Jono worked as a fly-in-fly-out rigger on a mine in South Australia. When I first met him I thought he was a handsome, sexist fool who wore deep V-neck T-shirts, drank Canadian

Club and ate up the 1980s rock that FM stations fed him. But he turned out to be sly, spending his days off living rent-free in the house in Collingwood that Jen's parents had given her.

Jen had been working on her Pinterest wedding board for a long time, but getting Jono to propose had been the hard part. They'd been together for six years and Jen had been dropping hints like sledgehammers for three of them. A month ago she broke down over breakfast at a cafe and confided to me that she'd secretly booked a wedding venue last year after she and Jono bought tickets to Paris, because she had been certain he was going propose in front of the Eiffel Tower and if she didn't reserve Fairy Lights Winery straight away they'd have to wait a whole eighteen months for another warm-weather weekend to become available. Two couples got engaged in front of them during that visit to the Eiffel Tower, but Jono showed no sign of even noticing, let alone dropping to one knee. When they got home she panicked, stuck her head in the sand and pretended she hadn't paid a deposit for a wedding that wasn't happening.

'What should I do?' she'd asked, hyperventilating. 'Fairy Lights keep emailing to ask me for final numbers and to decide on a menu. Their florist asked if I want classic or deconstructed arrangements. I told her I want peonies! Oh my God.'

'Well,' I said, 'you can either forfeit the deposit, call it a life lesson and dump Jono – which is what I suggest you do – or, if you're set on the peonies, you can tell him what date he's getting married.'

She went for plan B. She informed Jono they were getting married on the twelfth of December and suggested he buy a ring.

He'd shrugged. 'Okay.'

So now she had three months to organise a wedding.

Jen is methodical. At the beginning of Year Twelve, she

outlined her plan. Finish school, study nursing, meet a doctor. She did meet a doctor in her first year at university, but he was so unbearably arrogant she had to dump him in her second year. She revised the plan on the fly and met a miner instead. Somehow Jono was even more arrogant than the doctor had been, but Jen didn't seem to mind it in him. His main attractions seemed to be muscles and a high salary – although I never saw him share any of it – and Jen claimed he was wild in bed.

Jen and I have been friends since the second day of Year Eight. I had already been at Wodehouse Catholic School for Girls for two years when she arrived. My mother had packed me off there in a mission-brown and orange uniform before I finished primary school, as she'd decided I needed more discipline than what was on offer at the local public school. Of course, the only lesson that truly sank in was the one the Year Sevens taught me when they showed me how to practise giving blowjobs on a banana.

When Jen first turned up and sat next to me in our English class, I suspected she was boring. Her face was too smooth and pretty, eyes set too wide – the picture of innocence. More importantly, I didn't like how her silver pencil case matched her pens. At lunch I decided to psych her out by announcing I was going to flash the gardener. The school's gardener was only twenty-one and, though his monobrow prevented him from being thoroughly cute, he was the only male under thirty in the entire school and therefore the object of our collective teenage fantasies. My friends and I had memorised his daily rounds, so I knew he'd be passing by the window during art class. Jen turned to me and said – the only words out of her mouth so far – 'I dare you.' I was outraged. How could she, the angelic new girl, call my bluff?

An hour later we were sitting by the window, paintbrushes in hand, as the gardener approached to rake the leaves from the path outside. My pride would not allow me to back out. Jen quietly observed as I undid a button, knocked softly to get the gardener's attention, flipped out a single boob and pressed it to the glass. He turned in alarm at the sight of my pale tit, squashed against the window like a sponge, and hurried away. It was highly likely the man lived in fear of some student's teenage horniness getting him fired.

'You did it,' Jen whispered, and beamed. 'Awesome.'

I think she was the first person who'd ever expressed pride in my actions. We've been inseparable ever since. Outwardly, the only things we have in common are our unbearable families and our taste in music. But we have kindred souls.

Throwing up her hands in laughter when I tore up her great-great grandmother's wedding gown was, in hindsight, a predictably Jen reaction, though no one but me would know that. Most of the time she lives vicariously through me, pretending to discourage me from behaving badly but secretly relishing the tales I have to tell afterwards. And I always linger on the juicy parts.

Her favourite story is the one where my date and I were busted in the act by three generations of a family, who were having a Mother's Day picnic in the Botanic Gardens on a sunny afternoon. Turns out Moreton Bay fig trees don't give quite the level of privacy you think they will. Still, it was worth it for the wink I got from the ninety-year-old grandma in a twin-set as I darted past in an unzipped dress.

After my cider arrived I turned back to find Jen still wringing her hands, alternating between mortification at not knowing about Dan's break-up and choosing the wrong venue for her

11

engagement party. I was almost grateful when Sean walked
through the door, late as usual, and swaggered over to kiss my
cheek.

'Hey, hot stuff.' He slapped my butt.

'That's original,' I said.

Nobody could believe I was dating Sean. Or, more accu-
rately, nobody could believe that Sean was dating me. Honestly,
sometimes I could hardly believe it. He was tall and broad-
shouldered, with dark hair and eyes, and eyelashes as long as
a horse's. He'd gone to uni with some mutual friends and Jen
introduced us not long after he moved into a house a block away
from hers. There'd been a teeny tiny scandal at the beginning of
our relationship, in the form of his ex-girlfriend, a model named
Masha, who'd objected rather crudely when he had chosen, of
his own free will, after approximately ten drinks at the Leinster
Arms, to trade her in for me.

Sean's nickname among friends was The Stal, short for stal-
lion, which Sean – and I, at first – thought was because he had a
way with women. Recently, however, his friend Con confessed to
me that the nickname was conferred on Sean by Masha because
when you get in bed with him the race is over before you know
it's begun. I took great offence to that. Sean was, in my view, an
excellent boyfriend. He'd hardly complained when I moved into
his house without asking a year ago, never expected me to clean
or cook – he had a cleaner, and we ordered in most nights – and
I still got a little thrill whenever he walked into a bar and every
woman's eyes followed him. In return, I overlooked his tendency
towards excessive speed in the bedroom and encouraged him to
attend every single Hawks game during the footy season. I was a
model girlfriend.

Lately, though, I'd felt uneasy. A few months ago, Sarah

Stoll had started working at the same ad agency as Sean, and tonight he was bringing her to the party. Sarah is possibly my least favourite person in the world. She's been dogging my heels since high school, where in Year Nine she threw a pair of brown-stained underpants over the fence of the neighbouring boys' school after carefully sewing a label with my name on it into the seam. She isn't evil, exactly – I once witnessed her rescue a duckling stranded in a swimming pool, so she can't be a complete psychopath – but she possesses an overdeveloped sense of schadenfreude. Especially when given the opportunity to be the architect of another person's misfortune. Especially if that person is me.

Sarah was a copywriter and Sean was an account coordinator on the same team, and a few weeks ago they began exchanging texts after work and on weekends. Sean insisted they were friends and that I was unfairly holding onto old grudges.

'Hiii.' Sarah had trailed Sean into the pub. I envisaged her face popping out after an axe through the door. She looked the same as when I last saw her a few months ago, a pretty face painted Oompa Loompa-orange, hair as blonde as a Swede's, eyes lined as black as a university fresher's. She'd had eyeliner tattooed on her eyelids when she was nineteen, in fact. In her short gold glittering dress and stiletto heels like steel cigarettes, she was lethal.

Sean put a warm hand around my waist. Sarah immediately began talking shop.

'Oh, Sean, remind me on Monday, we've got to blue-sky that Libra ad.' She was practically purring as she brushed Sean's arm with one finger.

'Yeah, let's take a helicopter view on it,' he said, and they both laughed. Were they talking in code, I wondered, because how else did they manage to make adspeak sound like sex talk?

Sarah turned to me. 'So, Maggie, how's the life of leisure treating you?'

'It's great,' I said.

'It should be, with me paying the rent.' Sean turned to Sarah. 'She's been doing commerce for ten years. They had to make a special allowance for her at uni to let her keep going, because there's a cut-off and she'd flunked too many subjects.'

I'd heard that speech before from my mother, but not from Sean. There was a note of satisfaction in his voice, as if my failures gave him triumph. I stared at him for a moment, startled, then took the bait.

'Because being an account coordinator at a mid-level ad agency makes you a genius,' I said.

'Genius enough to have a job.'

He had a point, but so what? He was my boyfriend. He wasn't supposed to cut me down in public. That was my mother's department. Making lists of my failures was her favourite pastime.

'So, Sean,' I said, 'do you still think breasts are genitals?'

'They are genitals,' he said.

'Nope. They still aren't.'

He turned to Sarah. 'If I grabbed your boobs at work, you'd be able to do me for sexual harassment. Therefore breasts are genitals.'

'Do you? Maybe I'd do you, but not for harassment.' She laughed, showing a set of implausibly white teeth, and put a hand on my arm. 'I'm only joking, Maggie. Just jokes.'

Through unhappy coincidence, Sarah and I had also wound up at the same residential college, Barff, for the first two years of university, where she once took up-skirt photos of me while I was passed out on the common-room coffee table. For a few years she used to bring the photos out as a party trick to show to any man who expressed the remotest interest in me. So I know what her idea of a joke is.

Sean winked at her. 'Maybe I should start harassing you.'

An arrow of dread to the stomach. Sean was not the sharpest tool in the shed, but he wasn't usually mean. Had working with Sarah imbued enough cruelty in him by osmosis to flirt with my sworn enemy in front of me, or did he always have a nasty streak that I hadn't noticed because we'd never had a reason to argue?

In general, I have a long fuse. I endured ten years of my mother telling me I should stop acting like a tramp before I told her, with as deadpan a look on my face as I could muster, that she was a lonely, nagging witch who was jealous of my sex life because she'd probably never had an orgasm. That happened a year ago, and she threw me out of home. Luckily, Sean was there with a cute little rented house in Collingwood that I could move right into.

My fuse was burning now, but strangely I didn't feel like screaming. I felt like sinking my head into a bucket of wine. This was Sarah's forte: non-confrontational public humiliation, the kind you suck up with your pinot noir. Most people don't know how to handle it. They just find a seat at the bar and watch their relationship implode from a distance. Not me, though.

'Wow, your banter is infectious.' I shook a jaunty finger at Sean and Sarah. 'In fact, I think it just gave me chlamydia.'

'Oh, you probably picked that up in high school.' Sarah smirked. 'I hear it can go undetected for a long time.'

Sean laughed uproariously and dropped his arm from my waist.

Sometimes it's what people don't say that hurts the most. For Sean to laugh at Sarah's chlamydia joke but not at mine was like an icepick to the heart.

He and Sarah looked at each other like they were waiting for me to leave. And Sean's aftershave was making me queasy. I walked away, trying not to succumb to feelings of defeat. I am a proactive person, I told myself. I am not a victim.

The band had finished playing their first set and the handsome guitarist approached the bar, waiting to order. I straightened my shoulders. Sean wasn't the only one who knew how to flirt outrageously. Or at least, he wasn't the only one who knew how to say inappropriate things to attractive people. The guitarist was a touch older than me, well into his thirties, with the beginnings of silver in his stubble. He leant against the bar while all around him people talked, gestured, flirted; the still point in a fidgeting room. I took in his size: a compact man, not tall but not short. Inked on his left forearm were those navy-blue ballpoint pen tattoos, while on his right were hummingbirds in full colour. Those were professionally done, and lovely. He had a slight frown on his face, as if his mind was somewhere else.

I gently inserted myself between him and the bar.

'I'm Maggie.' I stuck out my hand and he looked at it.

'Hi Maggie.' His voice sounded like rocks rattling in a tin.

I took my hand back, undeterred. 'I need to ask you something. Do you think breasts are genitals?'

See? Two can play at this flirting game.

His expression remained inscrutable as he lowered his lashes, but to his credit he didn't drop his gaze to my tits.

'Why?' he asked.

'I had an argument about it with someone just now.'

'Huh. No, breasts are secondary sex characteristics, I'd say.'

'That's what I said.' That's what I'll say next time, anyway.

The bartender handed him a pale ale without being asked, then raised an eyebrow at me because the words, 'What would you like?' were more effort than he could be bothered making. I ordered a cider and took it with both hands. A drop of condensation slid down the glass. The guitarist's fingers were close to mine and the warm crush of bodies pressing around us was a good excuse to lean into him a little more. He was wearing a simple grey T-shirt and his body looked nice and firm. I turned to search for Sean and Sarah: they were facing each other, barely an inch between them, and neither had noticed that I was talking to a hot guy. Sarah was smiling up at Sean like he'd just told her spray tans were half-price this week. Wait, did Sean just reach out and brush some hair from Sarah's face? Touching her face was beyond the pale.

I turned back to the bar, drank half the cider in one go and put the glass down, my hand shaking a little.

'This is a bit forward,' I said to the hot tattooed guy, 'but would you be interested in having sex in the bathroom?'

Okay, maybe that was a slight overreaction to a face touch.

He didn't blink. 'With you?'

'Yes.'

There was a pause in which I began to regret my choice of words, but I kept my smile firm and alluring. At least, I hoped I did.

'Does this have something to do with the breasts or genitals question?'

'No, this is unrelated.'

'So you just want to have sex with a stranger?'

A hot stranger. A hot stranger who played a mean slide guitar, who wasn't my traitorous boyfriend.

'Yes.'

'Why?'

A man behind me leant over my shoulder, breathing bourbon all over me. 'I'll have sex with you, love.'

'Piss off.' I didn't turn my head or remove my gaze from the guitarist's eyes.

He smiled ever so slightly. His eyes had freckles in them, brown specks dotted over green irises, like lily pads on a pond. He took a sip of his drink and stood up straight, making me stumble a little as I lost my leaning post.

'Good luck with your mission,' he said, and walked off.

My cheeks burned, but there was relief mixed in with the embarrassment. I might have been in a tiny spot of bother if he'd said yes.

Jen had seen me.

'Cut it out,' she hissed, grabbing me by the upper arm and dragging me into a dark corner. 'Don't do this again. Not at my engagement party. You. Have. A. Boyfriend.'

'He's sleeping with Sarah Stoll.' I pointed. Sarah was rolling her eyes at something, both hands resting lightly on Sean's jacket lapels. 'He's probably giving her a mussel-rustle every day in the supply closet at work.'

'They're flirting. It doesn't mean anything.'

'It does. You didn't hear them earlier. They're sleeping together, I know it. And look at that!'

'What?'

'Look at his pants.'

'What about them?'

'There's a bulge.'

'That's because Sarah is rubbing against him. Okay, so maybe he's attracted to her. It doesn't mean they're sleeping together.'

I gave Jen a look.

'Fine,' she said. 'You think your relationship is about to crash and burn. So what? You can't help but go down with a flourish of shame?'

'Ouch, Jen. But yes. Exactly. Sex in the bathroom at The Fainting Chair is a story for the grandkids.'

'Sex in the *bathroom?*'

'Don't tell me you've never done it.'

'At home. In my private en suite. With my fiancé.' She pressed her glass to her pink cheeks and sighed. 'God, I sound like a wanker. I'm just jealous. I'd kill to pull some guy into the bathroom and screw him senseless.'

I gave her what I hoped was a sympathetic look. 'Jono's still avoiding the old in–out?'

She whipped her head around to see if anyone had overheard and lowered her voice to a whisper. 'We haven't done it at all since he's been back. I mean, he's away for ten days and back for four, I deserve at least . . .' She waved a hand. 'Three boinks. But nada.'

'If it makes you feel any better, you probably won't have sex after you're married either.'

Jono was only the second man that Jen had slept with. Me, I'd lost count. I had a little problem remaining focused. But I hadn't cheated on Sean. With him, things were serious. At least I thought they were.

Jen and I ordered tequila shots from the barman. I drained mine, ate my lemon slice and adjusted my dress. 'All right, I won't drag anyone into the bathroom. But I am going to make Sean see that he's making a terrible mistake.'

'How?' Jen asked.

'Dunno. Parade by with some guy, make sure he's seen me.'

'Seems like an . . . undergraduate technique,' Jen said.

'I *am* an undergraduate, remember? Anyhow. Watch me.'

I headed back to the bar, avoiding the bourbon-breather, who was still leering. He had booze-ruddied cheeks and wore a wedding ring. Around the other side of the bar, the blond guy with dimples was talking to a guy in a suit. What did Jen say his name was? Dan. I approached breezily.

'Nice flannie,' I said.

Dan's shirt was red and blue plaid flannelette with pockets at the top, and his jeans were old and worn. He looked down at his pockets and smiled.

'Thanks.'

'Bit hipster, isn't it?' the suit guffawed, elbowing Dan.

'This is Collingwood, mate, it's uniform,' Dan replied.

'Have you checked out the Elvis paintings?' the suit asked. 'I've counted three man buns tonight.' He waited for me to laugh.

I wanted to roll my eyes, but refrained. Men like him tended to break out in honking laughter at the slightest provocation, and I didn't feel like being the object of fascination for a middle manager who worked on Collins Street. I wanted him to leave so I could talk to Dan, so I tried reverse psychology.

'Your suit is great. It reminds me of this guy I see in Myer all the time, he's a total dandy. He has these massive sideburns and wears a necktie and a little dandy cap. He carries his dog with him everywhere. It's a shih tzu. But personally I think you'd do better with a French bulldog.' I shoved my glass at him. 'Would you mind getting me another cider, sweetheart?'

The suit's face fell a bit, and he muttered something about being delighted to get me a drink.

Dan was smiling into his beer. 'I've seen that dandy guy in the Dumpling House, I think.'

'Ooh, I tried those dumplings last week. I didn't feel sick at all afterwards.'

Dan laughed. 'The waitresses are great, aren't they? They don't even pretend not to hate you.'

This was going well. 'Let's get another drink,' I said.

'What about the guy you just sent off to get one?'

'He'll find something to do with it.' I pulled him towards the bar, far from where the suit was straining to get Surly's attention, ordered another cider and necked it.

'I'm a builder,' Dan said during a quiet moment. 'What do you do?'

'I'm a children's author,' I said. 'Picture books. I'm having a meeting with my editor tomorrow.'

'That's pretty cool. What's your book called?'

I swallowed and searched frantically among the posters on the wall for inspiration. My gaze settled first on a vintage *Karate Kid* poster, and then on a bull's skull. '*Karate Cow*,' I said.

After ten more minutes of chat, I took him by the hand. 'Hey, come with me for a second, will you?'

I led him through the crowd. We weaved through the front bar, past film posters for 1950s B movies and the Elvis paintings hanging on the wall above Sarah, who was now holding the palm of her hand up against Sean's as if to measure the difference in size. I caught a strain of laughter and the fragment of a sentence, something like, *it's so big*. I tried to swallow the humiliation. Sarah was a sadist, and I would not give her the satisfaction of knowing that seeing her with Sean hurt me. But it did. I coughed loudly as I passed to make sure Sean saw that there was a guy with me. An undergraduate technique, like Jen said. I slowly and theatrically pulled open the door, making sure the bell jingled.

On the footpath, a lone smoker puffed away at one of the wooden tables facing the side street. A few hundred metres away, police cars, taxis, fixed-gear bicycles and tottering drunks would be crawling Smith Street, savouring the aromas of lamb and garlic sauce coming from the Souvlaki Palace. Faint sirens whined and blue lights flashed in the distance. The cold air hit my face but my body was warm and buzzing from the cider. Dan followed me out of the bar, looking around.

'What are we doing?' he asked.

'We're gonna make out,' I said.

'Okay.'

I pushed him against the wall, making sure the smoker had his back to us.

'What's your name again?' Dan asked.

'Maggie.'

The brick wall seemed to be moving, or maybe I was swaying. We kissed like high schoolers, urgent and pestering. My dress rode up a little around my hips and I pulled away from him for a second to adjust it, checking to see if anyone had popped their head around the corner. My hands shook a little. Hardly thinking, I grabbed Dan's crotch firmly with both hands to stop them shaking.

'Oof,' he said. 'You've got some grip.'

He had a good smell about him, a hint of maple syrup. I wanted to tell him he smelt like a pancake, then giggled as I imagined his confusion. Dan must have thought I was trying to take his pants off, because he unzipped. Shit, now he was waiting for a hand job. I had made a slight error of calculation. I wanted Sean to see another man hitting on me; I didn't really want to be caught with my hand down the other man's pants. My plan, if you could call it that, was for Sean to see me cosying up with some guy, drag me away, and then rediscover his passion for me on the couch later. Although, now that I was here, Dan was feeling pretty fine to me, warm and firm. Somehow, the next second – I swear it was automatic, a reflex – my hand was inside his underwear.

'Ouch,' Dan said.

'Sorry. My heel got caught in the drain.'

'We could go back to my place,' he suggested.

'Better not,' I said, 'I—'

The noise of a lighter catching made me turn my head. Behind us, the guy I'd ignored as a solitary smoker was tucking a silver lighter back into his pocket. Next to him, Sarah Stoll leant companionably against a table, a lit cigarette dangling from her fingertips, watching me with a triumphant smile. All of a sudden, I felt the cold.

# Chapter 2

Sarah's eyes roved from my hand, still firmly wedged in Dan's pants, to my rumpled dress, to my mouth, which was probably smudged with pink lipstick. I removed my hand and smoothed the folds of my dress while Dan re-zipped his pants. Even through the cider haze, the stupidity of my entire plan came barrelling home to me. I had just handed Sarah an ace.

'I was helping Dan fix his fly,' I said.

Sarah took a puff of her cigarette. 'Uh-huh.'

I beamed at her and then brushed past to get back inside. No point lingering. My heart hammered in my chest. It was uncomfortably crowded and I kept my head down as I weaved among people. Dan caught up with me at the bar, flushed and breathing heavily.

'Can I have your number?' he asked.

'Are you serious?' I looked at him, incredulous. 'I just gave you half a bad hand job and you want my number? What are you gonna do, call me?'

He smiled. 'Tomorrow morning I want to look into my phone and know that this really happened.'

I put my number in Dan's phone and waved goodbye.

'Half a bad hand job? Sounds like you made someone's night.'

I turned to find the tattooed guitarist I'd tried to drag into the bathroom earlier grinning at me from the next barstool. He raised his beer glass.

'Shut up,' I said.

———

Every life has the occasional lucky instant. For some, good luck is just avoiding something bad when it happens, like missing the plane that goes down over the ocean and later insisting to the cameras that God was watching over you – too bad for the two hundred poor fuckers who caught their flight. For others, it's an impulse that turns out to be a good decision. Staying for one last drink after you catch a glimpse of longing on the face of someone you thought was too good for you. Or reaching your boyfriend at the bar before Sarah Stoll could press her lips to his ear and tell him she saw you in the alleyway with your hands down another man's pants.

Sarah was detained by her radar for gossip; Jen and Jono were arguing and she paused to watch, taking in their contained, jerky gestures with eagerness, lips open as if the sight of an engaged couple arguing gave her true pleasure. One hand was resting on her collarbone, the other held her glass close to her shiny orange face. Behind her, the owner of the bar eyed Jono with distaste, slowly wiping a tea towel over the counter. Jono had probably insulted him, or said something explicit to one of the pretty bartenders. But I couldn't afford to waste time helping Jen. I had to get to Sean. I elbowed my way through the crowd to reach him.

'Hey, Big Bum,' Sean said, hooking a hand under my butt cheek.

'Wanna go? Looks like the party's gonna be over in a second.'

—

I woke up around eleven, the sheets in a tangle around my legs, the soft but persistent tapping of a paw on my left cheek. A grey blur passed across my vision as my cat Dot shoved a wet nose in my ear and then took off out the bedroom door, yowling. I rolled over and felt a twist of anxiety in my stomach. I had got Sean home without incident, but in the cold light of day I realised two things: either he was cheating on me with Sarah, in which case my relationship was already over, and in the worst possible way; or he wasn't, in which case I'd been caught by Sarah making out with some stranger without cause.

Either way, I was screwed. And besides, what did I think Sean would do if he had seen me with Dan, even if we had only been flirting? Rush over and drag me away? More likely he would have shrugged and started talking to Dan about football. Sean never got jealous, because it never occurred to him that he might be inadequate. He was Gaston with a Toorak accent.

With my trackies hanging low around my hips I shuffled into the living area to find Sean flicking through television channels, a plate of bacon rinds in front of him. The designer stubble across his perfect jawline was a fraction darker than last night. He settled for a moment on the news, where a woman with frosted coral lips was reporting that more asylum seekers had died in detention this year than had been resettled in Australia, then he shrugged and bounced to a morning program hosting a battle-of-the-sexes debate on the weighty topic of 'Does leopard print make a woman look slutty?'

'Hey.' He didn't turn his head from the screen.

Fear rose in my throat. Had Sarah already told him?

'Morning,' I said.

'How're you feeling?' He sipped his coffee and I sensed no seething fury under the question. Relief washed over me. No one had told him yet, which meant I had time to think about how to argue my case when he inevitably found out.

'Hungover.'

I moved to the kitchen, pulled more bacon out of the fridge and greased up a pan. Bacon fried in butter is an excellent hangover cure.

'Yeah, you crashed out hard,' he said.

'Mmm, and how were Sarah's caresses last night? Lingering? Coquettish?'

It's a fact that infidelity does not make a person less prone to jealousy. The more unfaithful a lover is, the more they suspect their partner of the same behaviour.

Sean didn't answer. Instead he took a sip of coffee and asked, 'Why didn't you do the washing-up yesterday?'

'They're an art installation.' I jerked my hand at the pile of dishes in the sink. 'It's a narrative piece on my life. I call it The Tower of Mediocrity.'

He shot me a sarcastic look. 'Just wash them, will you? I did them all last week.'

I poured some coffee and poked at the sizzling bacon with a spatula. Sean waited for me to respond. When I said nothing, he prodded further.

'Think of it like exercise.'

'Don't,' I said. 'Don't say anything more, if you value your life.'

He turned back to the television. 'I'm just saying, it wouldn't hurt.'

I looked for something to throw at him. Coffee? Too hot, might burn him. Bacon? Can't waste it. Cat? Animal cruelty, plus she'd scratch me. I settled on Sean's mobile phone, which lay on the bench, an unread text message on the screen. I pitched it with my left hand while still grasping the spatula in my right. It hit his shoulder with a satisfying thud.

'Fark!' he shouted. 'Jesus, Maggie!'

Too late, my hungover brain realised whose name I'd seen on the message notification. Sarah. Sean picked up the phone, shaking his head. Then he read the text message. His face turned white, then red, and his nostrils flared.

'Maggie.' His voice was thick and strained as he looked up at me, stunned and yet oddly triumphant. 'Sarah says you hooked up with some guy last night.'

The bacon popped, and I discovered I was no longer hungry.

'What?' My voice cracked. 'Sorry?'

'"Sorry". Is that it?' he said in disbelief. 'So you don't deny it?'

'No, no, no. Wait. This is ridiculous. I was just getting some air and—'

'While rooting some guy in an alleyway?'

'It wasn't a root. She's mistaken. It was probably someone else. It wasn't what it looked like. I was really drunk. Sarah was really drunk, I mean.'

He stood up. I put down the spatula. He thundered into the bedroom and I followed him, shaking. He began pulling my belongings out of the wardrobe. Tired student clothes – leggings and frayed T-shirts and oversized woolly jumpers – sailed onto the floor like autumn leaves.

'Sean, wait.'

'Get out of my house.'

'What, so you can move Sarah in? I only made out with him because you're obviously sleeping with her!'

'I'm not sleeping with her,' he said.

The smell of burning bacon wafted into the room. Sean kept throwing my possessions over his shoulder. I dodged a flying shoe.

'You know, you'll change your mind about this when you realise what a horrible person she is,' I said.

He swivelled to face me. 'I'll change my mind when you get off your arse, cook a meal for once in your life and get a fucking job. So never.' The smug tone in his voice was rehearsed, as if he'd been wanting to say it for months. *Had* he been wanting to say it for months?

He grabbed my clothes and stamped out the front door with them, throwing them onto the street with a flourish. Unpleasant rays of sunlight bounced off the neighbour's white fence. A young hipster couple paused at the bundle of clothes before detouring around it, smirking. I covered my face with my hands while Sean disappeared into the house, returning with my favourite lamp, followed by my mother's teapot, some books and utensils, a Depression-era chest of drawers made from fabric-covered fruit crates, and finally the cat. He dumped all of it next to my clothes, except for Dot, who clawed him in the chest when he tried to drop her on the bundle of student rags, so he shoved her at me. She lay tense and poised in my arms but for once didn't scratch me. She must have known it was serious.

Sean went back inside and slammed the door.

'Sean!'

The small Victorian houses lining the street stood still as sentries and a gentle breeze ruffled my cheeks. I scratched Dot behind the ears and she began purring. My meagre possessions, the only signs that I'd lived twenty-nine years in this world, were scattered over the footpath. My mother's teapot had rolled into the gutter and broken, the fragments of green and pink china pointing sharp edges upwards. I closed my eyes.

The door behind me opened and Sean stepped out again. Maybe he'd changed his mind? I opened my mouth to say something pitiful and he threw my favourite cushion at my face. It was the one purchase I'd made since I moved in with him, and was covered in rainbow-coloured splotches like a watercolour painting. The cushion landed in the gutter, which made me angry.

'Enjoy looking at Sarah's orange face for the rest of your life,' was the only insult I could come up with.

'I hope you get swine flu,' he said.

It was the most intelligent comeback that had ever come out of his mouth. I wished I'd thought of it.

—

Unbidden, the memory of a trashy magazine cover from a year or two ago rose in my mind. It was after a pop singer who shall remain nameless broke up with her boyfriend and gained half a kilo. The headline screamed 'FAT, SAD AND ALONE' and below it was a picture of the poor sad sack chomping into a meatball sub. I'm not unattractive, I told myself. I'm fine, given the right lighting and angles. I have shiny hair and a nice face. I'll find someone. Maybe I'll even find someone who likes country music and buys treats for my cat. I definitely wasn't going to cry over Sean. My eyes were definitely only wet because the harsh morning light was pricking at them, and my hands were definitely only shaking from the hangover.

I walked across the street to my car and dropped the cat and my cushion on the passenger seat. Dot was not happy. Cats do not like to be moved, and Dot has been moved several times in her life. Each move made her more ornery. She shot into the back seat and stood on her hind legs, pawing at the window and meowing.

My car is a beautiful early 1970s sea-foam-green Holden panel van, which, after Dot, is the joy of my life. Dad left it in the garage after he jumped ship, and I claimed it immediately. It has charm and style, and starts most of the time. Today it didn't. I put the key in the ignition and turned it. Nothing but a hacking cough from the engine.

With nothing better to do, I called my mother.

'How could you betray that nice boy?' There was a peal of desperation in her voice. 'You can't go five minutes without sex.'

'You're just jealous because you've been fifteen years without sex.'

'Hmph.'

When I was younger, my mother wanted me to marry a great man. Now she'd settle for anyone with a job and no inclination to violence. When I showed up with Sean a year and a half ago she was ecstatic. His looks would have been enough, but when he opened his mouth and the accent of a Scotch College boy rolled out, she nearly keeled over with joy.

'I was trying to make him jealous. I didn't *mean* to cheat on him.'

'Old habits die hard, eh?'

I scratched my legs. 'Can you please just pick me up? The car won't start.'

'I'll be there soon.'

She hung up.

I rested my head on the steering wheel. When I looked up, I saw a man in a stained tracksuit pawing through my possessions, most of which were still on the footpath outside Sean's house. His long, grey beard nearly reached the top of the rusted shopping trolley he was pushing.

I opened the car door as he picked up the lamp.

'Um,' I said. 'That's mine.'

'It's on the footpath.' He put the lamp in his shopping trolley. 'Public property.'

'No it isn't.'

I jumped to my feet, strode over and snatched the lamp out of his trolley, then immediately felt mean. The little pile of junk on the footpath wasn't much, but it was more than he had.

'Fine, take the lamp.' I shoved it at him.

He took it without looking at me, too intent on bending over to inspect the Depression-era chest of drawers. He drew a finger through the dust on the top.

'You can't have that,' I said. 'It cost me fifty bucks.'

He sniffed, unimpressed. 'Fifty bucks? Looks like it's covered in dish rags.'

He put the lamp back in the trolley and tootled off, wheels squeaking and jerking over pebbles on the footpath. A sudden foreboding washed over me. I pictured myself pushing my own shopping trolley down the streets of Collingwood, picking up hard rubbish to pawn for booze money.

Never, I thought. My mother will always take me in. Family's family.

I carted the rest of the gear into the back of the panel van and sat in the driver's seat to wait for Mum. She took her sweet time, giving me plenty of opportunity to mourn the beautiful little house I was about to leave. Sean lived in a single-fronted Victorian cottage with original lacework, a bronze hanging bell for a doorbell and tessellated tiles on the verandah. It radiated cute. The pot plant out the front needed watering and I considered giving it a drink from my water bottle but decided against it. Sean would have to water it now. He'd lift the watering can with his perfect muscled arms, then maybe tip it up to splash some cool water over his pecs, glistening in the sun . . . goddammit, there's nothing worse than being horny and dumped.

When Mum pulled up beside my panel van in her thousand-year-old Ford, she was shaking her head before she even applied the handbrake. The windows were down. She looked over at Sean's house with a sigh. Then she whipped her head back to me, eyes narrowed.

'Is that my teapot in the gutter?'

# Chapter 3

Watching my mother behind the wheel is a painful thing. She is alert, stretching forward, straining her head this way and that, like a pelican watching for fish guts to be thrown its way. She waits exactly five seconds after touching the indicator to change lanes, and she tuts and shakes her head when someone cuts her off.

'Bloody geriatric,' she says. Then she stretches her head even further forward to get a better look at the culprit and bears her disappointment in silence when they turn out to be her age.

I grew up feeling like a foreigner in my own home. I don't know why, really. My mother came from money; she inherited the big house in Camberwell. My dad was a gambler, a philanderer and a drinker. I should have felt right at home with the illicit sex and the money that wasn't ours, but I didn't. My mum wanted a daughter who got married at twenty-five and repeated all her mistakes. My dad wanted someone to rant to when the divorce got ugly. My brother wanted to get the hell out of there and make shoes in Brussels. I just wanted to have sex on the couch and listen to good music.

The trees in Camberwell are huge. Beautiful plane trees that shade the wide streets and provide cover for men stepping out of their Mercedes and women coming home from their cosmetic surgeons. I used to count the spaces between the shadows thrown by the leaves while I walked home from school, debating which water polo player I should try to sleep with next. Often, I would skip dinner at home altogether in favour of hanging out at Jen's place, where her mother and father were equally awful but at least they weren't mine.

We pulled up to the front gate. Mum parked at the kerb and yanked the handbrake up without a word. She put a hand to her hair, brushing flat the flyaway greys, and got out.

'Wanna help me with my stuff?' I called after her. No answer.

My mother's house always has the sensation that someone is in the next room. It's dark, a poorly built 1920s fright with haphazard additions and a deep backyard. The floorboards creak even when no one is walking on them, and there's always the sound of a tap dripping in the laundry or kitchen, or the flapping of sheets on the line in the side courtyard. Mum likes to leave the television on at night, which drives me mad. Always somebody talking.

I gathered up the clothes from the back seat of the car and carried them into my old room, where the bed was already made. Dot wandered in and promptly sat on the pile of clothes, which I'd dumped on the floor.

'Good choice, Dot. No need for me to put anything away, 'cause I'll be outta here soon.'

It was a lie, unless I found a new boyfriend in record time.

Here's the thing. I was on Centrelink. I got student support of around 200 bucks a week. 'Earning' 200 a week, with no rent to pay and hardly any bills, I could just squeak by. The catch was I either had to live with my mother or find a boyfriend who was too nice to make me pay rent. But even the tiniest, rat-and-asbestos-infested studio apartment on Easey Street cost 300 a week. If I paid rent on my own apartment, I would have had approximately negative 100 bucks a week.

I turned to find Mum standing in the doorway, hands on her wide hips.

'Family meeting in the kitchen,' she said.

'Family meeting?' I looked around. 'What, is Harry here?'

'No. He's still in Belgium.'

'So you mean, you and I sit at the kitchen table? Is that a meeting?'

'Five minutes. We'll be discussing your downward mobility.'

She left, and I sighed. With my brother permanently stationed in Europe, I was the recipient of an unfair amount of my mother's wisdom.

Five minutes later, I was seated opposite her at the round kitchen table.

The Tudor-style kitchen was cavernous, full of cupboards that wouldn't close and holes hidden by the fridge. A mouse's paradise. Sure enough, I saw a mouse trap on the floor, the kind that the mouse runs into with a little door at the back to shut it in without killing it. Mum couldn't bear to kill mice. She'd let them out at the end of the street after dark when the neighbours couldn't see, and they'd run right back in again a few days later. Dot would sort that out.

Mum fixed a pair of glasses to her snub nose. Her cheeks were flushed. Before her on the table lay a lined notepad with a long, illegible list written in pencil.

She cleared her throat.

'First, there was Billy.' She looked up. 'He used to bring you chocolate frogs after school, remember? And drink cups of tea with me. He was so sweet. And you went and bonked that flabby water polo player from Melbourne Grammar and broke Billy's heart.'

I was dumbfounded.

'Remember?' she pressed.

'Yes, it was tragic. And that water polo player was mean. Whatever his name was. What's this about?'

'And then there was Salvatore.'

Salvatore, the gruff country boy who cracked terrible puns. I went out with him for the first two years of my degree, then two weeks before exams I cheated on him with a tall, goofy accountant I met in a bar, with whom having sex was a little like wrestling a live deer.

'Salvatore had a heart of gold,' she continued. 'You told me he used to cook you potato gems whenever you were feeling sad. Or hungover.'

'Well, he put them in the oven,' I said. 'Mum, is that a list? Have you written a list of people I've dated?'

She ignored the question. 'Then there was Jock the grey-hound breeder.'

'The guy who thought feminism ruined society, yeah.'

'And Gary the amateur football player.'

'The compulsive masturbator. Seriously, Mum. You've written a list.'

'And Johan the unemployed musician. He used to write you love songs.'

'And took my Centrelink money.'

'Not to mention the ones I never heard about. And you

cheated on all of them! I thought Sean would be different, but you're just like your father. No conscience.'

Dot wandered into the kitchen and sat down at Mum's feet, licking herself in unspeakable places. Then she rubbed her face against Mum's legs. Mum bent down to coo and pat her, the precious only grandchild, then sat up again, her expression serious.

'All except Jeremy,' she said.

'What?'

'Jeremy. From Grade Ten. You didn't cheat on him.'

'Yeah, I know I didn't cheat on Jeremy, what's your point?'

'Well.' She folded her hands over the ridiculous list. 'Didn't he cheat on you?'

My first love slept with Isobel Cartagnon, the prettiest girl in my year at school, less than a month after my father was busted rogering my science teacher, Mrs Moleskin. I was fifteen. It was a rough year.

'So?'

'So, do you think perhaps all your cheating has something to do—'

'No! Fuck Jeremy. Jesus, Mum, go back to night school if you want to become a psychologist, don't practise on me. You're hopeless. Anyway, I did cheat on Jeremy.'

'You told me you didn't!' I could almost feel the hot blast of maternal outrage.

'I lied.'

'You cried for weeks. I let you have two days off school. You lying toad!'

Toad?

'Well, it's karma,' she continued. 'Losing your home is karma, and you deserve it. You stole Sean from someone else, you cheated on him and now you've lost him. Karma! You're not a good person, Maggie.'

'Mum, that's pretty rough. What, you like Sean better than me? Sean, the autonomous human being who *chose* to leave his beautiful infomercial-model ex-girlfriend for me because she was going on a six-week holiday to Japan? Why don't you just disown me and go drink your fat-free bloody Jarrah with him!'

'I bloody well will!' she yelled. 'That's exactly what I'm going to do. I'm cutting you out of my will. You're not getting any more cash from me, even after I die. And before you ask, no you are *not* moving in here.'

I sat back in my chair. 'What? But Mum—'

'Yes?' she spat.

'Renting in Melbourne is impossible on student payments. What will I do?'

I didn't think much of her threat to write me out of her will – as if she'd bother with the paperwork. But I knew from experience that booting me out was serious, and this time I didn't have a boyfriend's house to go to. I was like a soccer WAG whose credit card had been cut off, facing the prospect of choosing between her manicure and her spray tan. I didn't know anything about getting by on my own.

Mum leant forward, a look of dark determination on her face.

'You want to live the high life in Collingwood, floozying around, you can damn well get a job.'

'Look, if this is about that thing I just said . . . I was getting a rise out of you. I didn't cheat on Jeremy.'

'It not about Jeremy. You're twenty-nine.'

'I'm aware.'

'What about my future grandchildren?'

'You'll have to wait.'

'You'll end up bloody barren.'

'Oh, come on. Barren?'

'Sean was a handsome man with a good job. You could have had a good life with him.'

'A good job? Sean's been an account coordinator for eight years. It's a job for twenty-two-year-olds out of ad school. He was on forty-five grand!'

'Oh, and what are you on, moneybags? What's Centrelink pay you? Ten grand a year?'

I said nothing.

She sighed. A long, slow puffing billy of a sigh to let me know I was endlessly useless. Suddenly she looked older. Mum had been beautiful when she was younger, with long dark hair like mine and heavy-lidded eyes. Now she had a lunch lady's haircut and a soft middle that was actually very nice to cuddle on the rare occasions she felt like hugging her children. She scrabbled beneath the papers in front of her and pulled out an envelope that she'd clearly already opened. It had the University of Melbourne insignia on the front. I still had most of my mail directed to Mum's house, since I tended to move often.

'What's that?' I asked as she handed it to me.

'It's time to get a job.'

I unfolded the letter.

Most of the time, you've got eight years maximum to complete an undergraduate degree. I'd had two official extensions to finish mine, but apparently now the university was as fed up as Sean: after ten years, they were booting me out. Instead of a Bachelor degree in Commerce with a major in accounting, they were bestowing on me a Diploma of Accounting.

I could almost taste the subtext: *We hope to never hear from you again.*

—

I lay on the bed in my childhood bedroom. The walls were still as Smurf blue as they were when I was a kid and there was a new crack in the ceiling that looked a little bit like a penis. I contemplated it for an hour or two. So my mother didn't want me living with her, and the university didn't want me taking up space in their lecture theatres anymore. That meant the flow of Centrelink money would stop. There was always the jobseeker's allowance, but it was harder to get and they made you work for it. A gazillion job applications a fortnight, Work for the Dole after six months. On the other hand, the prospect of applying for an accounting job was so painful that I pushed the whole catastrophe out of my mind and thought instead about what my mother had said. I didn't know exactly how much money I was supposed to inherit, but my mother was an only child and my grandparents had been pretty loaded. There had been a beach house in Portsea and a farm in the Southeast that my mother sold after they died, when I was six or so, and I had memories of my grandmother wearing a lot of diamonds. I didn't believe Mum was serious about cutting me out of the will. It was just another attempt to harangue me into marriage. You'd think the world's most vindictive divorce would have put her off the whole institution, but no.

My mother has made many mistakes in her life, but her marriage was the worst one. Her second-worst mistake was to have children. Children – even rewarding ones like myself – were noisy leeches who needed feeding. Her third-worst mistake was to get a job, but she had to because no one else was going to pay her kids' private school fees. The relentless grind of responsibility warped her into a nagging buzzkill. The curious thing, the part that I always wondered about, was why, if she wanted a life so stable and dull, had she married a man like my father, a man who spent his weekends at the greyhound track and kept a packet of condoms in the glove box for his curious children to find?

Mum was the only one who didn't see the divorce coming. Dad had never held a job for longer than six months, so he had a lot of free time on his hands, which meant a lot of affairs. The night Dad left for good, he packed his things into Mum's car, a four-wheel-drive, so that he could take his favourite chair with him, then cheerfully said goodbye to my brother and me.

'Probably see you in a few weeks,' were his parting words. Yeah, right.

Mum stood weeping at the kitchen sink, as if she didn't want to cry onto any surface she'd have to wipe clean after. Two months later, when it was clear he wasn't coming back, she gave me his panel van. Eventually she stopped saying his name.

Poor Jeremy couldn't cope with me crying in his arms every afternoon. We'd stopped talking about him and his plans. I was interrupting his homework time and he had ambition, places to go, scholarships to win. I think he slept with Isobel just to shake me off and get his homework hours back. As an exit strategy, it worked.

I guess I learnt it from him. Now when a boyfriend returns from a late night out and seems a little evasive about what went on, or starts getting texts from attractive workmates, I simply pull the eject lever. A make-out session in the alleyway outside The Fainting Chair. Professional relationship sabotage. No going back.

Compared with my father, Sean was the world's most responsible man. I wondered if I really came down with swine flu, would

Sean feel so guilty he'd take me back? I made a mental note to ask Jen how to get infected with swine flu.

My phone rang. It was a private number, and I debated whether to answer. Could Sean be calling from a hidden number to tell me that, upon reflection, hooking up with some guy in an alley was a totally reasonable response to his flirtation with Sarah? Probably not. I answered anyway.

'Hello?'

'Hi, is that Maggie?' The voice was male, and nervous. Telstra, I thought. First-timer, obviously. Being monitored for quality control purposes.

'Yep, who's this?'

'Uh, it's Dan.'

For a moment, I drew a blank. Who the hell is Dan? My brother's ex-girlfriend's sister's husband, right? The plumber?

'From last night,' he added.

'Oh, Dan!' Of course. Why was he calling me? Surely he wasn't looking for another awkward tug behind The Fainting Chair?

'Um, how's your day going?' he asked.

Well, Dan, I burnt my bacon, got dumped by my boyfriend, scratched by my cat, thrown out of university, and now my mother is threatening to cut me off. Also, I'm pretty sure I ate some sour yoghurt earlier because I've farted thirty times into the doona and now my cat won't look at me.

'Fine, thanks.' I tried to remember what he looked like. Cute and slightly cuddly; cherubic, perhaps? 'So how are you, Dan? How did you pull up this morning?'

'Yeah, not too bad, bit worse for wear.' He sounded relieved that I was making normal conversation. 'How did your meeting go?'

'What meeting?'

'With your editor?'

'Dan, I have no idea what you're talking about. What line did I pull on you?'

'You said you were going to have a meeting with your book editor.'

'Did I?'

'You said you'd, uh, written a children's book? *Karate Cow*?'

That got a laugh out of me. More like a cackle. God, I'm sounding more like my Year Seven maths teacher every day. She had a cackle like a duck on MDMA. I wondered when I had told him I was a children's writer. On the way to attacking him in the alleyway, probably.

'Dan, I was having you on. I'm not a children's author.'

'Oh.' He sounded disappointed. 'I suppose you're not twenty-two, either?'

'I'm twenty-nine.'

'Oh.'

I decided to continue ruining his day just for the hell of it. 'I've also just been kicked out of home. And I'm on Centrelink.'

He was silent. Digesting the bile of his disappointment, I suppose, and wondering how to get off the phone quickly without seeming like a jerk.

'Sounds like you need a drink,' he said.

What?

'And dinner,' I said, wildly optimistic. 'Really need dinner.'

'You live in Collingwood, don't you?'

Er, sort of. I decided not to explain. 'Yeah.'

'How about I take you to T-Bird Thursday night?' he continued. 'The noodle place on Wellington Street.'

Was he kidding, or just desperate?

'Are you kidding, or just desperate?' I asked.

'Jeez, that's a bit rough.'

After I hung up I lay on the bed for a while, trying to hatch a plan. My last thoughts before I fell asleep were that unemployment was a moral stance, a form of passive resistance to avoid giving the government tax money to imprison refugee children on Nauru, and maybe Dan would have a cute Victorian cottage that I could stay in just for a little while.

—

I woke up the next day around lunchtime and waltzed into the kitchen to boast to Mum that I already had a date.

'Why are you still in your pyjamas instead of looking for a job?' She plunged her hands into a sink full of soap suds, rattling the pots, while I made a toasted cheese sandwich. 'Heartless moll,' she muttered.

'Excuse me?'

'Well, I don't see you mourning your break-up.'

The vinegary sting in her words brought back the memory of Sean touching palms with Sarah in the bar. I was, in fact, feeling pretty low, but there was no way I'd give Mum the satisfaction of knowing it. I helped myself to a Lucozade, taking gulps between spilling sandwich crumbs onto the dull brown tiles as I ate my toastie.

'I am a Strong Woman,' I informed her through a mouthful of grease.

'Good. Then you'll easily be able to manage your own life from now on.'

She took her hands out of the suds, wiped them with a tea towel, and shoved a piece of paper in my face.

'What's this?'

'A budget.'

'A what?'

The handwritten lines were grainy from being photocopied. She must have already filed the original away in the 'loser' drawer. There were lines for rent, food, clothes, utilities, phone bills, dental, doctors' visits, credit card repayments, health insurance, contents insurance, car insurance, petrol, car servicing and registration, vet visits, internet, and a tiny column for 'dining out and entertainment'. Each 'i' and 't' was jauntily dotted and crossed in the spirit of helpfulness and generosity.

'I'll talk you through it now, and then you can go and wash off your panda eyes,' she said.

I rubbed the bags under my eyes and my fingers came away with flecks of black. I must have forgotten to wash my mascara off. This was too much the day after a break-up. I handed the piece of paper back and she took it in her tired, arthritic hands. I couldn't remember a time when my mother didn't have knobbly knuckles like a farmer.

'Mum, I can't deal with this right now.'

'Don't talk American to me. You sound like one of those awful reality TV teenagers.'

'Whatever.'

'There it is again! *Whatever*,' she mimicked. 'I don't care if you *can't deal right now*, you're damn well going to. You're taking over all these bills from me. All of them. I'm not paying your mobile phone bill, or even your health insurance.'

I licked melted cheese from my index finger. 'You're the one who took out private health cover for me. What if I get arthritis like you and need a knee replacement? I'll be on the wait list for years, hobbling around with a stick like a gypsy. You hate gypsies. Would you really do that to me?'

She said nothing, just stood with her arms folded across her faded shirt with the mismatched buttons.

'You know I'll never call you if I have to pay my own phone bill,' I said.

'I don't care. I'll call you.'

'I won't answer.'

'You will or I'll clobber you. Anyway, you'll be needing your weekly meals from me once you enter the real world.' Mum set her mouth in a determined line. I recognised her expression as one I wore often.

'Jesus,' was all I could say.

'Don't swear.'

'It's not a swear word.'

'Well, don't say it. I've calculated that if you don't eat out or drink alcohol, you could break even on $43,000 per year before tax. If you want to have a little fun on your weekends you should try to get a job earning fifty grand, just to be sure. It's unfortunate you didn't get your Commerce degree because PricewaterhouseCoopers probably won't take you with just a diploma, but I've done some googling and took the liberty of sending your résumé to a recruitment agency in Abbotsford. You've got an appointment with them at three pm.'

'You did what? Mum, I don't even have a résumé.'

'Well, I took the morning off work to make you one.'

'You impersonated me? That's a pretty crazy effort to go to just to make me pay some stupid bills.'

'Some stupid bills?' Mum's face darkened. 'I've been paying your stupid bills for almost thirty years. *I've* been working so that *you* can bludge through uni, pay for your worthless cat's dental work, and go on boozy nights out where you cheat on your boyfriend and humiliate me as a mother!'

I was angry. She not only wanted to throw me out into the seething waters of the world without a life jacket, but to tie a lead weight to my foot and chuck me into the shipping lane in front of an oncoming tanker. And she was making me feel guilty.

'Fine!' I shouted. 'I'll become a stripper. Would you like that?'

She laughed. 'Go ahead and try. They'd throw you out on the first night. You have to be fit to be a stripper. You'd fall off the pole!'

She was still laughing when I stormed into my room. I looked around. Blue and white bedsheets. White wardrobe. Chipped dressing table with a teenager's girly mirror. Bronze spoons for coming third – always third – in high school swimming competitions. I didn't want this stuff. A house in the suburbs. A respectable job. Children. A divorce.

Mum must have felt guilty for laughing at me, because she followed me into the room after a few minutes, the budget replaced with bank notes. No matter how tough her words were, she always caved. Mum was like gravel-coated butter.

'Here's the deal,' she said. 'You can't live here, but if you attend this appointment with the recruitment agency and make a real effort to get a job I'll let you stay for a month while you look for a new apartment. I took out twelve hundred dollars. It's an advance on the bond you'll have to pay. It's the last money you're getting from me, and I mean it this time.' She smoothed down the doona. 'What do you say?'

I saw no way out.

'Fine,' I said. 'I'll go to the appointment.'

'Good.' She turned to go, then stopped. 'Oh, and I didn't mean what I said about Dot. *She's* not worthless.'

—

I took a taxi to Sean's house to pick up my car after lunch. The blinds on his front window were drawn and the plant on the verandah still hadn't been watered. My car was where I had left it across the road, and this time the engine turned over without any protestations. I drove to the recruitment agency, which was on a weird, quiet lane off Victoria Street populated by twisted wattle trees and boarded-up houses, and one weedy vacant block protected by a long, tall fence with 'No Trespassers' signage stapled to the wire. There'd probably be mid-rise apartments going up there soon. I parked and got out, regarded the chipped decal writing on the dark glass window – Superior Recruiting – and wished I'd bothered to look at the fake résumé Mum had written. Supposedly, this agency would help falsify my qualifications to the point that someone might be duped into hiring me. I checked the time and as I returned my phone to my pocket I accidentally rubbed the slippery bank notes Mum had given me. Probably not the best idea to carry $1200 around in your pocket on the way to Superior Recruiting.

Just as I was about to cross the road, a woman emerged from the building and leant against the wall. She took her phone out and made a call, then lit a cigarette. She looked to be in her early forties, in a suit and dark stockings, with that family-court-dad shoulder hunch. A waft of smoke curled about her head and dissipated in the breeze. As I got closer, I overheard her conversation.

'No typing speed test this time,' she was saying. 'But I'll get some temp work next week, they think. Reception.'

A shudder ran through my body. There was only one job I dreaded more than accounting, and that was reception. Having to actually talk to people and be pleasant. When I thought of getting an office job, Mum's face the night Dad left rose in my mind, the shock that turned her white. That look that said, *I did everything right and now what?* It kept circling until I was seething with anger. Who said I had to live like this? Who said I had to have a job and live in a house and pay taxes? This is the system we are born into and we have no choice in the matter.

Maybe I choose not to be part of it.

It was strange that the people who liked me the most, like my mother, approved of my choices the least. How could it be that the people who wished me well actually wanted me to spend my days in an accounting firm? On the other hand, people who disliked me, like Sarah Stoll, seemed overjoyed that I'd never had a job or a steady place to live. I took a walk around the block to clear my head. My appointment wasn't for another twenty minutes.

On Nicholson Street, I saw the caravan for sale.

It was small and squat and sat low to the ground, shaped like a triangle with the tip cut off. It was made of corrugated aluminium, silver with a green speed stripe all the way around. Sea-foam green, in fact. The same colour as my car. The hand-written sign leaning against one tyre was asking for $1100.

And I had $1200 cash in my pocket.

# Chapter 4

The caravan's owners were named Wayne and Sheila. They were both inside having a cup of tea when I knocked. Wayne wore his pants hitched up to his nipples. He ushered me in. It was tiny and cramped and the windows were dirty, letting in a brownish filtered light at both ends of the van, which were only ten feet apart. On the left were two brown vinyl seats with a laminate table between them. Directly opposite the door, the kitchen had a sink and gas cooktop with wood veneer cupboards above. To the right was a brown vinyl couch that folded out into a bed, and behind me, opposite the sink, was a slender built-in wardrobe. The faded curtains still showed a hint of 1960s floral glory. I could just stand up straight at the caravan's highest point, in its centre, but Wayne had to duck his head slightly.

'Well, this is it,' he said. 'The pump tap doesn't work. You just get those boxes of spring water. But you can get a gas bottle for the cooktop, that works good. This window here is busted out, we never bothered to get it fixed, but you can get new Perspex made to fit.'

A strange feeling came over me. I was standing in the tiniest, crustiest piece of shit ever to be slapped on a set of wheels and called a caravan, and yet it felt . . . cosy. It had character. It suited me.

It felt like home.

Wayne showed me how to put the jacks up and down and connect the caravan to my panel van's tow bar.

'Just put a rock behind a wheel whenever you're parked and you'll be right,' he said.

'Great,' I said. 'Thanks.'

Sheila wiped away a tear and rubbed her hand on her track-suit pants. 'I'm going to miss this old girl, but we need the money for our kid. She's having chemo.'

'Don't worry,' I said. 'I'll take good care of the van.'

I counted out the money and handed it over. Wayne took it and nodded.

'Ta.'

After they had taken one last look at their beloved and disappeared inside the little tumbledown house it was parked in front of, I connected the caravan to my car. If I went back to the recruitment agency now, I'd only be fifteen minutes late. They probably wouldn't mind. But going to a recruitment agency to get a job was living in the *future*. I wanted to live in the *now*.

I towed the caravan to my mother's house. On second thought, I parked it further down the street and unhitched it from the car. No point asking for trouble just yet.

—

Mum got home from work at 6.30 pm and stomped into the kitchen, irritable from dealing with inferior clients. She'd been an accountant for thirty years, the last ten of which she'd spent in a small magazine publishing company that just couldn't seem to stay in the black financially. She always came home grumbling.

'Did you see that piece-of-crap caravan down the street?' she said as soon as she'd put her bag on the counter. 'I asked the neighbour, he doesn't know whose it is. I bet some bloody gypsies have moved in. I'm calling the police.'

She grabbed the phone and started dialling the local police station. Goddammit, why hadn't I parked it further away? I'd spent fifteen minutes disconnecting it from the car so Mum wouldn't know it was mine but hadn't considered that she'd take offence to its very existence.

'Mum, don't do that. It's probably someone's holiday home.'

'Like hell it is. It's ten feet long and looks older than I am. In Camberwell, we don't buy caravans, we buy beach houses. It'll be full of layabout hippy travellers. They'll be breaking into houses before you know it.'

I heard the sound of ringing down the line and sighed.

'It's my caravan.'

She paused. A tinny voice on the other end of the line asked for her name.

'You're joking.'

'No, I'm not.'

She hung up the phone. 'It's not yours.'

'It is.'

'When did you buy it?'

'This afternoon.'

Clouds of fury formed on her face. 'And how much did you pay for it?'

I swallowed. 'Eleven hundred.'

She stood silently for a long minute, while the clock above the kitchen bench ticked, counting down the seconds until my doom. Suddenly she lunged for something in her handbag and I flinched. With trembling hands she held out the document she had seized, and I realised it was the budget she had so carefully written out for me. I took it from her. It felt heavier and thicker than it should have, so I lifted the top sheet.

Underneath the budget was a thick wad of paper, official-looking, covered in legalese and stamped with the insignia of a lawyer's office. It was my mother's will.

'I told you that was the last money you'll ever get from me.' Her wet-eyed look caused a strange lump to grow in my throat, and I realised there was something else in her expression, fear maybe, as if she could hardly believe she was doing this. 'I told you I was cutting you out of my will. I hope you don't regret buying that caravan, because it's the last purchase you'll make with my money. No more bond money, or bail money, or what-ever else you want next time.'

I flipped through the pages of the will, stunned, but couldn't see my name anywhere, only my brother Harry's. 'Is this perma-nent, Mum? Because, you know, I plan to live a long time. You might change your mind.'

She paused, angled forward, jaws clenched like a pit bull's. 'I might. If you can prove to me that you're capable of being independent.'

I swallowed. 'Define "independent".'

'No moving back in here with me, or moving in with Jen, or sponging off some poor man that you use up and dump. If you can prove to me that you're capable of living on your own and taking care of yourself – earning your own money – I'll write you back into the will. You've got . . .' she considered, 'six months to prove it to me. You've already spent the bond money I gave you on a caravan, so I suppose you'd better go live in it. Just like that awful whining country musician you go on about all the time who lived in his car.'

I cleared my throat. 'You know, that awful whining country musician you speak of is David Allan Coe. He's an unhailed genius.'

She threw up her arms. 'An unhailed genius! You told me he wrote a song called "Eff—Effin' in the Butt"!' she spluttered.

'"Fuckin' in the Butt",' I corrected her. 'Not his magnum opus, I concede, but it has its merits.'

Her face turned red as she pursed her lips so tightly they resembled the very anus about which the great David Allan Coe so eloquently wrote his ode.

'Get out! Get out of my house!' she shrieked.

'Okay, Mum.'

I started to back out of the kitchen slowly. At the last second I veered towards the fridge, pulling the door open so hard the jars rattled in the shelves, and grabbed a bottle of chardonnay that was cooling in the fridge door.

'Oi!' Mum shouted.

I slammed the fridge door and sprinted out of the house, bottle in hand. On my way through the front yard, I collected Dot, who hung limp in my arms with the resignation of the defeated.

—

I towed the caravan back to Collingwood.

A pit of fear opened in my stomach as I rumbled down the freeway. I had not actually planned to start living in the caravan right away. I had planned to deck it out and maybe sleep in it a couple of nights a week when it was parked on Mum's street to give us both a bit of breathing space. Now that it was clear she was serious about cutting me off there were a few things I had to think about. Number one concerned a bathroom. The caravan didn't have one. Number two concerned water. The taps in the caravan didn't work. Number three concerned electricity. I could have gone to a caravan park and had the use of bathrooms, running water and electricity, but caravan parks cost money, were too far from Collingwood and were full of holidaying families, cabins on stilts and screaming children brandishing water pistols. And since I wasn't a holidaying family, I suspected I would be an object of suspicion, or worse, pity.

I had no real answers with which to reassure myself, so with one hand I opened the bottle of wine that was resting on the passenger seat and swigged it, after checking the side mirrors for cops. I thought about moving in with Jen and then remembered what Mum had said about not moving in with Jen. Swigged the bottle again. When I reached my old street I slowed the panel van down to idle in front of Sean's house. The light was on in the front room but the curtains were closed. I kept going until I reached Charlotte Court, which was a laneway directly behind Jen's house. It was a tiny, quiet cul-de-sac with a small apartment block on one side and three houses on the other. The car spaces had no time limit, so I backed into one of them. Wayne had showed me how to reverse the caravan, but I was no master at it and the caravan ended up pretty crooked in the parking spot. I put the handbrake on, sat back in the driver's seat and with silent determination emptied half the bottle of wine into my gullet, before unhitching the car and parking it one spot over.

The pink of the sky was beginning to fade to darkness when I tottered out of the car and opened the caravan door to look inside. It had a tinny, unfamiliar smell about it, like unwashed clothes in the laundry sink. Dot followed me through the door and coughed up a hairball on the floor in protest before jumping onto the table and meowing for dinner. I would have to buy cat food from the supermarket, since I had not thought to steal any from Mum's house, but first I lay down on the hard vinyl bed with a jumper rolled up as a pillow. The room spun.

# Chapter 5

Outside, the sun was coming up. Magpies called to each other over the low hum of cars on the Eastern Freeway, three streets away. I was thirsty and needed to use the toilet, but there wasn't one. No food, because I had not thought to buy anything except chocolate and cat food when I went to the supermarket at 8 pm the night before, and I'd already eaten all the chocolate. No fridge to use even if I had food, and no electricity to power the fridge I didn't have. I had no sheets, no towels and no spare clothes.

Perhaps I had not thought this through.

I walked to Centrelink in Richmond, ducking into a service station along the way to use the facilities and buy a bottle of water. Now that I was kicked out of uni, my student payments would stop. I figured the rumpled dress, mascara-stained cheeks, pasty hangover skin and greasy bed hair would ensure I looked as incapable as possible and make the transition to the dole easier.

They paint the walls of Centrelink in bright colours, purple and yellow and green. It's supposed to have an uplifting effect. I guess that's why everyone looked so happy.

I took a number and sat down to wait in the queue among polite pensioners, parents carrying snotty children, and the woman in the long leather coat who I saw every time I came to Centrelink. I looked for bleached hair and long faces, friends in low places, but found surprisingly few of my people. Maybe it was too early for them.

When my number was called I rose and shuffled to a floating desk near the middle of the room. The open-plan virus had infected Centrelink. I didn't know how anyone could concentrate in that human zoo. My legs were heavy and there was a bad taste in my mouth. My luck had come back, though, because I got a nice young guy with pimples on his cheeks who didn't seem too jaded yet. I informed him that I was no longer a student and thus needed money from a different source, namely the Newstart Allowance. He looked through my file and then tried to make me fill out some job-seeking forms online.

'Are you serious?' I said. 'Do I look capable of holding down a job?'

'My brother with Down Syndrome has a job. I'm sure you can manage.'

'Look, buddy, I can't fill out these forms. I live in a caravan. I don't have a shower. I don't have internet. Next week I probably won't have a mobile phone. I can't fill out the forms.'

He eyed the black smudges under my eyes and fiddled with a zit on his cheek.

'Okay. No problem. Maybe I can help.'

'Yeah?'

He tapped on the keyboard. 'If you volunteer at a registered not-for-profit for twenty hours a week you don't have to apply for jobs or do the Work for the Dole program.'

'Really?'

'Yeah.'

'Twenty hours volunteering.' That was nearly double my university contact hours, but presumably a charity would be a laid-back place to spend the day. 'And then I get paid?'

'Yeah. You do have to show up and log your hours online, but the place where you volunteer will be able to help you with that.'

The guy obviously thought I was a basket case. I let him think it. Stared at him.

'Okay,' he said eventually. 'How about I make a phone call for you?'

'That would be great.'

'Okaaaay.' He tapped a few more keys. 'So, what would you say your skills are?'

'I can add. Subtract. I did well in macroeconomics.'

'So you have a university degree?'

'A diploma. In accounting. But I do not want a goddamn accounting job.'

'Administration assistant okay?'

'Yeah, fine, as long as I'm not the receptionist.'

He picked up the phone. 'Yeah, hi Agnes, this is Jake from Centrelink calling about your application for volunteers. I have a Maggie Cotton with me who is interested in the administration assistant position. She has a diploma—'

He looked up at me and I shook my head.

'Er, she has several years at . . .' he mumbled, 'the University of Melbourne. Christian?' Jake flicked a look at me. I shrugged. 'No problem, no problem at all. Yes, of course, she's very sensitive towards the homeless. Really interested in social justice.' He paused. 'Milo?' He placed his hand to cover the phone receiver. 'Do you like Milo?' he whispered.

'Huh?'

'She's ambivalent about Milo,' he said into the phone. 'Great, great. How's nine am tomorrow? Wonderful. Thanks, Agnes. Bye-bye.' He hung up.

'Milo?'

'That's what they fired their last administration assistant for. Stealing Milo tins.'

'Who did?'

'It's a charity called the Nicholson Street Angels in Abbotsford. They're a very nice bunch and they do great work. The office you'll be working in is responsible for raising money for a church that runs a homeless shelter, and there's a women's shelter nearby that they run also. Next door there's an op shop where they sell donated clothing. Part of your job will be to organise the roster of volunteers who work in the shop.'

Telling other people when to work: a role I was born to do.

'Cool,' I said.

'Okay, you've got an interview tomorrow, but it's just a formality. Do you . . . uh . . . do you have other clothes you can wear?'

'I'll borrow some from a friend.'

'Great. Your interview is at nine.' He wrote down the address. 'And, uh, look, I'm not supposed to directly arrange these volunteer positions, so if anyone asks, you went through our job agency, all right?'

'Sure.'

He wrote down the address, his cheeks flushed with the pride that comes from helping the Unfortunate.

—

Jen was sipping a coffee in her terry-towel robe when I knocked, her blonde curls foaming around her head like a halo. Her work shifts usually began mid-afternoon, so she must have been having a lie-in. She looked me up and down, a lost fawn on her doorstep. In one hand I held the almost-empty bottle of chardonnay. I still had on the wrinkled dress from yesterday, since until I picked up my clothes from Mum's place I had nothing else to wear.

'What have you done now?' Jen asked.

'I dunno.' I walked inside and she shut the door after me. 'But I feel pretty good.'

Jen's place was the holy grail of Collingwood: four bedrooms, painted weatherboard, Victorian ceiling mouldings, large back-yard with a pair of lemon trees and a passionfruit vine. The two front rooms housed a spare bedroom and an office, while the back two rooms Jen used as a bedroom for herself and a library and exercise room, to house her yoga props and books on gardening and architecture. It was a dream house and she'd owned it since she was twenty-four.

I sat in her sunny kitchen at the cute laminate table with orange vinyl chairs while she made me a coffee.

'Do you mind if I have a shower here?' I asked. 'And borrow some clothes?'

She raised her eyebrows. 'That bad, is it? What happened?'

'Let me finish my coffee and I'll show you.'

Jen threw on her trackies and walked with me to the lane behind her house. The caravan glinted in the sun like a spaceship.

'My new home. All ten feet of it.'

Jen put her head in her hands. 'Oh my God. What did you do?'

'You wanna see inside? There's no bathroom, unfortunately, but it's pretty cute.'

'No. Later.'

We walked back past Jen's corrugated-iron back fence and

sat in her kitchen once more, where I glossed over the details of what had happened between her engagement party and this morning.

'Okay, here's what we do,' she said. 'You shower and eat at my place. You sleep in the van. You can't move in here, sweetheart. I'm getting married soon and I refuse to bunk with my bestie for the rest of my life. No offence, I love you, all that. But no.'

'I didn't ask.'

'You were going to.'

I might have, if my mother hadn't threatened to cut me off forever.

'God, I can't believe you slept in that thing,' she continued. 'Does your mum know about this?'

'Yeah.'

'I'm going to take a wild guess and say she's not happy about it.'

'Does the Pope shit in the woods?'

'So she's kicked you out again.'

'Yep.'

'Kicked out of home twice in one week. Is that a record?'

I shrugged.

'You want me to call her?' Jen asked. 'Maybe I can talk her round.'

'I don't think she can be talked round this time. She cut me out of her will. And you know what? I kind of like the caravan.'

Jen's eyes widened. 'She cut you out of her *will*?'

'I have six months to prove to her that I can be independent, and if I fail it's forever. So I couldn't move in with you even if you wanted me to. That's part of the deal.'

Jen shook her head. 'I'm going to make you some scrambled eggs.'

She fussed about in the kitchen with butter and eggs. When she put the plate of toast and scramble in front of me I started shovelling it into my mouth.

'Mmm, delicious. Hey, what happened with you and Jono the other night?'

'Hmm?' She was already scrubbing the pan.

'Your fight. At the engagement party.'

'Oh that? That was nothing. He wanted to put more money over the bar. But it's kind of annoying, because he still owes me for electricity.'

'Huh.'

'He says he shouldn't have to pay the bill because he's not here most of the time.'

'So he just pockets all his earnings and lives at your place for free.'

'Well, it's not like that. It's our money, and all that.'

'Sounds like it's his money.' I held my breath, hoping she wouldn't point out that I'd done the same with Sean. Luckily, Jen was too nice to mention little things like that.

———

It was a strange day. I bought supplies for the caravan with the last of Mum's cash, but I still could not think of a way around the problem of electricity. The wind picked up in the afternoon and the caravan wobbled gently, the curtains blowing about like sails because of the broken window. People stared at the van as they passed and a group of drunks coming home from the pub in the late afternoon banged on the door, shouting. I didn't open it. I put a torch beside the bed in case I needed to sneak into Jen's house during the night to use the bathroom. Just before I went to sleep, lying on a set of sheets I'd borrowed from Jen, light from the streetlights pouring in through the open curtains, a frowning middle-aged man in gold-rimmed spectacles knocked on the door, introducing himself as my neighbour from one of the apartments above.

'Hi,' I said.

'Hello. Just wondering how long you'll be parking your caravan here?'

'Indefinitely.'

He coughed. 'You can't stay here. It's illegal.'

'It's not,' I countered. 'Check the City of Yarra website. It's perfectly legal.' It was true, I had checked.

I closed the door in his face and discovered that my hands were shaking.

# Chapter 6

On Wednesday morning I woke up, slipped into Jen's house, used her bathroom to get ready, and put on the job interview outfit she'd set out for me on the coffee table: black skirt, white shirt, red heels. Back in the caravan I ate stale bread with peanut butter and drank half a bottle of warm, flat mineral water. At eight-fifteen I drove to the interview.

The Nicholson Street Angels was just a hole in the wall, a glass door with bars across it in a rundown building, two doors down from what looked like a safe injecting room. A bell jingled when I pushed on the door. Inside, it was about what I'd expected: squiggle-patterned 1990s carpets, stained furniture and an empty reception desk with a framed photograph of a pristine coastline hanging incongruously above it. The place smelt faintly of mildew. After a moment, a middle-aged woman in silver-rimmed glasses and a drooping brown cardigan came hurrying out.

'You must be Maggie,' she said. 'I'm Agnes Sharaf. Come through.' She ushered me into a small, windowless room at the back of the office that smelt of fungi.

I'd researched the charity on Jen's laptop and knew vaguely what they did. Their website was awful, but I gathered that their main purpose was operating two safe houses: one was for teenage mothers and women escaping domestic violence, and the other was short-term accommodation for homeless men. The locations of the safe houses were a secret. The organisation was affiliated with the local Anglican church, and raised money via the op shop next door to the office.

I sat down before a jury that consisted of Agnes and another woman who introduced herself as Josephine Potts. Josephine had dyed black hair, powdered white skin and an air of New Age pseudoscience about her. She was wearing a fluffy cream jumper that looked like it had been knitted from somebody's pet bunny. I bet she's into crystals, I thought.

'What made you want to volunteer for the Nicholson Street Angels?' Josephine asked as I settled into my chair.

'I just love the work that you guys do,' I gushed. 'It's so important – you know, society's most vulnerable. I really want to get some experience in a charity.'

I had prepared a few phrases earlier. 'Society's most vulnerable' was one of them.

Agnes folded her hands before her. It appeared she could see through my drivel. My first impression of her had been of a pleasant but careworn woman, of Indian descent I guessed, with the breathless voice and rushed manner of a sweet, middle-aged motherly type. She had the sharp brown eyes of a keen observer, however, and she was watching me closely.

'Do you have any administrative experience?' Agnes asked.

'Not professionally,' I said, 'but I'm familiar with Excel, and time management is crucial in a university degree.'

I hoped they wouldn't ask why I'd been doing the same degree for ten years if I was so good at time management.

'Can you tell me about a time when you faced a difficult interpersonal situation?' Agnes asked.

I drew a blank. 'Er, can you be more specific?'

'For instance, have you ever had to defuse a situation when dealing with an irate or upset person?'

I immediately thought of my mother. 'Well,' I said carefully, 'I generally try to lower my voice when someone is angry. I find it has a calming effect. And then I explain my point of view in simple words, because angry people are generally not thinking right. And . . .' I thought of Jen's torn wedding dress. 'I like to solve people's problems.'

Agnes and Josephine nodded as if I'd said something intelligent.

'Wonderful,' said Agnes. 'One more thing.' They both smiled at me. 'You are aware this is a Christian organisation?'

'The Centrelink guy did mention something.'

'Now, you don't have to be Christian to work here, but you need to appreciate that our Christian values are very important to us. Is that okay with you?'

'Well, I am Anglican,' I said.

The words tumbled out before I could stop them. Why did I say that? Despite having attended a Catholic school, I wasn't religious. I'd never even been christened. Apart from a brief holy stint as a six-year-old when I played the donkey in my primary school's nativity play, I hadn't believed in God for a single minute during my lifetime. However, these words seemed to have a soothing effect on them both.

'Good, wonderful,' said Josephine. 'You're welcome to join us every afternoon at three o'clock for Prayer Time. It's optional, of course, but we find that connecting with God is a wonderful way to remind us why we do the work we do.'

'Great,' I said weakly.

Agnes looked at Josephine and then back at me. 'Could you excuse us for one moment?'

They left the room and I fiddled with my hair in the grey silence, vowing to buy a Bible and read it so that I wouldn't be caught out lying about my religion. The place was all right, I thought. Needed a few pictures on the walls and maybe a fan, but it wasn't too bad. The two ladies seemed okay as well. Agnes had her head screwed on, at least. The jury was still out on Josephine.

I'd hardly had time to start chewing my fingernails before they re-entered the room.

'We'd like to offer you the position,' Agnes said as soon as she'd sat down.

'Great!' I said. 'That's great. Thank you so much.'

'It's three days a week. You can choose the days you work,' she continued, 'but we want advance notice if you plan to change them. You'll be in charge of recruiting new volunteers for the opportunity shop – we don't go through Centrelink for those, we find it more effective to post ads locally, since the shop volunteers tend to be more . . . aged. You'll also be rostering the volunteers, interviewing candidates and doing general office administration. We don't get many phone calls but you'll be handling the filing system and be in charge of all compliance matters.'

I had no idea what compliance matters were. 'Great.'

'Can you start today?' Agnes asked. 'We've had some volunteers go AWOL and we need to find someone quick smart to come in to work the cash register tomorrow at the shop.'

—

I opened the door to my office. It was a small room directly behind the empty reception area, a drab rabbit hole with two desks facing each other, each equipped with an ancient computer and a phone. Both desks were otherwise empty, but underneath the one that Agnes ushered me towards was a grey filing cabinet so fat with files the drawer didn't close properly. I sat down.

'I'll get you the folders of prospective volunteers,' Agnes said, and left the room.

I opened the filing cabinet to see what was inside, and found newspapers. Just newspapers, and the occasional celebrity magazine. Whoever had worked in the office before me had simply shoved manila folders full of crap, and then filed them away. I imagined the Milo thief reading leisurely at their desk and then hurriedly stuffing magazines into the cabinet at the sound of Agnes's footsteps. I closed the cabinet again.

The smell of mildew was particularly pungent above my desk, and the window, which looked onto a filthy laneway, appeared to be welded shut. I tried to think optimistic thoughts. I could bring a desk fan to work. I could drink from a mug with a cute slogan. I could paint my nails green and watch them tap away on the keyboard like mossy pebbles. And if the job turned out to be as bad as I imagined jobs usually were, I could feign incompetence and head on back to Centrelink when I got fired.

Agnes returned, carrying a pink folder with the word 'reject' scrawled on the front in black texta.

'What does that mean?' I asked.

'It means these are applications we've rejected. It's unfortunate, but we have no time to advertise for new volunteers, so we'll need to choose one out of these.'

'Are the requirements for op shop volunteers . . . strict?'

Agnes looked around and lowered her voice. 'The only prerequisite for shop volunteers is that they aren't bat-shit crazy. If they aren't bat-shit crazy, they get the job.'

I was shocked. Agnes seemed like such a nice Christian lady. I hadn't expected her to be honest.

'So these people are—'

'Just find the applicant who's least alarming.' She adjusted her glasses and left the room.

I flipped through the applications, trying to find the least frightening volunteer. One had served a couple of years in Bindup Prison for armed robbery and assault, one wrote that she was 'looking forwerd to the free cloths' in the op shop, and one had written a fairly disturbing seven-page treatise on how he would 'straighten out the bums' at the Nicholson Street Angels. I tore the last application up and put it in the bin.

So far the one wanting free clothes was in the lead. I phoned the number listed. The girl who picked up sounded like Charlene from the golden years of *Neighbours*.

'Oh hon, thanks for phoning me back,' she said. 'But I'm waiting to hear from the Salvos first, they've got the best stuff. Do you mind if I get back to you?'

'We need someone to come in tomorrow,' I told her.

'Aw, well I couldn't anyway, love. I'm getting me acrylics done tomorrow.' She hung up.

Agnes popped her head in. 'Have you found someone?'

Jeez, give me five minutes, lady. 'No, not yet.'

'Chop chop.' She left.

Chop chop indeed. I could have turned up with Chopper Read and she wouldn't have cared. In fact, Chopper had lived near me in Collingwood, before he went to the great prison war in the sky. I used to see him shuffling down Keele Street in his trackies, his earless head grim, wearing an ironic expression as if he was prepped for smartarse remarks from strangers. Stuff it. Bindup was minimum security, wasn't it?

I picked up the phone and dialled the bloke who'd done time. It rang out. I hung up and sat back in my chair.

A second later, the phone rang. I picked up. 'Hello?'

'Did you just call me?' The man's voice was low and pebbly and vaguely familiar.

'Er, maybe, is this . . . Rueben Blackwood?'

'Who's this?'

'It's Maggie from the Nicholson Street Angels. I have your volunteer application in front of me.'

'You're the only one that's phoned me back. I've applied all over the place.'

'Yes, well, you sound, um, great. Have you ever worked behind a cash register?'

'I know how to work one.'

'Right, because you've robbed a few.' Best to get it all out in the open.

'Yes,' he said, with more than a hint of derision, 'because I've robbed a few.'

'Great. We need someone tomorrow. Can you come in?'

He said nothing for a moment. It sounded like he was scratching his chin. Or maybe his balls.

'Yeah, sure, I can come in.'

'Wonderful. And, um, no stealing stuff, please.'

'I don't steal from charities,' he said. 'I'm not a lowlife.'

'Glad to hear it.'

I thought I'd heard Rueben's voice somewhere before, but I couldn't place it. The only person I knew who'd been in jail was my uncle Ricko, who'd defrauded his employer of $500,000 and spent two months in low-security detention. Maybe I'd met Rueben through Ricko. It seemed unlikely.

'By the way, do you know my uncle, Ricko Cotton? He's been in jail too,' I asked.

'Oh yeah, Ricko and me have chai lattes together on Sundays.'

'Really?'

'No. See you tomorrow.' He hung up.

—

'I found someone,' I told Agnes, who was stirring a mug of what looked like very strong black coffee in the kitchen. There was no funny slogan on the mug, just a photo of a cocker spaniel. Good idea, I thought. I should get one made up with Dot's beautiful face on it.

'Wonderful,' she said. 'Well done.'

'His name's Rueben. He's got experience with cash registers.'

'Even better. Maggie, this is Christine,' Agnes said, gesturing to a woman sitting at a table eating a sandwich. 'Christine is our bookkeeper.'

Christine nodded. She looked to be in her sixties, small and dark, with glasses and a narrow, slightly pinched nose, like it had been squeezed in by a pair of pliers.

'Nice to meet you, Maggie.' Christine's voice was soft and quiet, with deliberate pronunciation. She smiled. 'I hear you don't like Milo.'

I liked Christine immediately.

'Maggie has already impressed us,' Agnes said quickly, shooting a disapproving look at Christine. She turned back to me. 'Next you'll be drawing up the roster and phoning volunteers to confirm their shifts in the shop for next week. It's very important to phone them, even though most of them already know their shift times. If they don't get a phone call, many of them simply won't turn up.'

———

The rest of the day wasn't too bad. I opened a spreadsheet with the roster history, set myself up with a work email account, and fiddled around with the roster according to who was available next week. I went through the list, phoning volunteers to confirm their shifts in the op shop and updating their personal records where necessary.

One volunteer, Margaret, sounded particularly ancient.

'Agnes, is that you?' her voice warbled down the line.

'No, it's Maggie. MAGGIE. I'm new.'

'Oh . . . oh . . . Maggie. Nice to meet you, darling. Via telephony, that is.'

'You too, Margaret.'

'Maggie . . . is that short for Margaret?' she inquired. 'The same as my name?'

'No, actually, it's just Maggie.'

'Oh, that's unusual. Quite unusual.'

Ten minutes later I was still on the phone to her and looking around nervously to make sure no one could overhear me wasting precious time on the telephone with one old biddy.

'You'll meet my daughter soon. She's a volunteer too,' she said.

'Oh, right.'

'She's very good. She's in the witness protection program.'

'Uh-huh.'

'We started volunteering after we shifted interstate. See, the Angels found us a place in their women's shelter, and of course after we got back on our feet I thought, well, I should really be giving back after all they've done for us. And they told us how

74

they needed volunteers, and I thought, it's a sign from God.'

'Oh, that was a good thought,' I said.

'Yes, it was. It was a pity we had to move, Karumba is a lovely town. But if I didn't move with my daughter I wouldn't have seen her anymore. Most of my friends have died now, so there was no point staying behind. You'll meet my daughter tomorrow. Her name's Belinda. Well, that's the name we have to call her now, but it's not her real name. Her real name is Bethany, but don't mention that to anyone. We can't call her Bethany anymore, even though the court case is over.'

'I won't say anything,' I said.

Fifteen minutes later I managed to hang up.

Josephine ducked her head through the door. 'Prayer Time!'

Her enthusiasm made my stomach sink. She'd refreshed her lipstick in a purple-red shade and it contrasted shockingly with her pale skin.

'It's a special one today,' she said.

Her words gave me the creeps, but I dutifully followed her into a windowless room where six metal folding chairs were arranged in a circle. Four people were already sitting there, including Agnes, who smiled when she saw me.

'This is Maggie,' Josephine said. 'Maggie, this is Boris, Bunny, and you've met Christine.'

Bunny, who looked about twenty-three, all perky breasts, heavy make-up and red hair teased so high you could use it for a ladder, gave a jaunty wave. Boris, a faded older man in a 1990s Rip Curl T-shirt and dad jeans, didn't even look at me but kept staring intently at the middle knuckle of his right hand. Boris was the only other volunteer; Bunny, Josephine, Christine and Agnes were all paid employees, though only Agnes and Josephine worked full-time.

'Since it's Maggie's first time, let's hold hands!' Josephine said. She held out a limp, pale hand for me to take. 'Does anyone have any words to share this afternoon?' She looked hopefully at me and I quickly dropped my eyes.

'I have something to share,' said Bunny. She was holding hands with Boris and Christine. I guessed Bunny was the one in charge of marketing, since I'd seen flyers asking for donations sitting on the ancient printer near the reception desk, and she looked like the sort of person who would add a second exclamation mark on the end of a sentence that read *Melbourne's most vulnerable need our help!!*

'I'm so excited we've got a new member of staff here today,' she said, 'because I have a special offering.'

'Go on, Bunny,' said Agnes.

I'd been wondering why there was an acoustic guitar lying next to one of the chairs, and praying to Buddha that nobody was going to sing. My stomach sank when Bunny picked up the guitar and began to strum it.

'I saw a woman on the street with her baby,' said Bunny. 'She was begging for money at the bus station. She looked so alone, so helpless, and I wrote this song to stand in solidarity with her, to tell her that God loves her and we are all one.'

Why didn't you just bloody tell her about the shelter instead of writing a song? I wanted to ask, but nobody raised the point and I figured it was best to keep my mouth shut on my first day. Josephine's smile was soft and understanding, encouraging Bunny to begin.

Bunny closed her eyes, strummed the opening notes and breathed in.

'*You think you are alone,*
*but I am with you,*

*you think you're on your own,*
*but I am here to say, we are one,*
*God is all around, we are on the ground,*
*you are not alone, for we are one.'*
Was I having an aneurysm?
*'We are lost, we are found,*
*don't be blue,*
*He is a part of you.'*

You could take thirty rejects from *Australia's Got Talent*, put them in a room together and force them to sing a Celine Dion song a cappella, and it would still be easier on the ears than this song. Bunny's lows were breathy, her highs plaintive. A hand went to her chest, pressing on her heart for soulful effect. I stared around the room. Agnes's face was still and impenetrable, but Josephine was nodding her head to the beat. Even Boris had closed his eyes, presumably in enjoyment.

After Bunny strummed the final note, Josephine wiped away a tear.

'God has given you such a talent, Bunny,' she said. 'You could go professional.'

Bunny nodded gravely. 'You know, I thought about it for a while. I could have got a record deal, but I just feel so much more fulfilled working in the not-for-profit sector. I can do so much more here.'

Agnes flicked me a small smile. 'Let us pray,' she said.

This was more bearable. Josephine read a prayer with only a few sighing pauses and creative flourishes, and my mind wandered off for a few minutes. As long as there wasn't singing every Prayer Time, I could handle this.

—

I was exhausted. Not being a natural talker, it took it out of me to spend so much time on the phone, even if most of the people I was talking to were sweet old grannies. By the end of the day, my voice was croaky.

'See ya, Agnes,' I said, as I put on my jacket.

'Bye, Maggie, and well done today.'

As I walked to my car I decided that, in terms of weird days I've experienced, it was about a six out of ten. Weirder than I had expected, but less weird than, say, the time I slept with the video game designer whose erection failed, so he began slapping his cock against my thigh in anguish, shouting, 'Come on, you bastard, come on!' and then sobbed that he didn't deserve blowjob privileges when I offered to help out. All things considered, I thought I'd be back in Mum's will in two weeks.

# Chapter 7

'So you didn't make fun of Christians, or the homeless?'
Jen was cooking me dinner to celebrate my first day of work. She loaded up two plates with steak, potatoes and greens and we took them outside to eat in her garden.

'Jeez, Jen, what do you think I am? I don't make fun of the homeless. I make fun of the Delta Goodrem wannabe who writes earnest songs about the homeless.'

'I'm sure you're incredibly sensitive.'

'I am! I can relate, because I live in a caravan.'

'Yeah, but give it six months and you'll be back in line for an Art Deco house in Camberwell. That's not relating, that's . . . "I pissed off my rich mum and now I'm in the dog house for a while."'

Jen's vegie patch was sprouting nicely. She had some kind of bean growing in an arch over our heads, and the grass was long around our feet. We sipped on cheap wine and watched the sun set over the corrugated-iron fence.

'So does this job mean you'll be able to afford an apartment soon?' she asked.

'First, I'm volunteering, so it's not technically a job. Second, Jen, I love you, but you know nothing about living on the dole. Centrelink payments cannot, and never will, cover renting on my own in Melbourne.'

She shifted uncomfortably.

'Don't fret,' I said. 'Just because your parents bought you a house doesn't mean you have to feel bad about it.'

'You should just sleep here tonight. Jono's not home. And your mum will never know.'

I waved my hand. 'Mum has eyes in the back of her head. She's probably spying on me. Anyway, it's only been two nights. I can't quit after only two nights.'

'I just can't believe you don't have a bathroom. This is all my fault. I should have stopped you from cheating on Sean at my engagement party.'

'It would have only postponed the inevitable. Speaking of which, when's Jono getting back?'

'Day after tomorrow. I haven't heard from him, though. They work so hard over there.'

'They drink so hard over there, you mean.'

Jono hated working on the mines, according to Jen, but the lure of the money was too strong for him to quit. Jen worried about him a lot. I didn't really know what to say; who knew what men got up to when they spent weeks at a time drinking beer and drilling into the ground?

At that moment, the sound of the front door banging made us turn our heads. Broad shoulders, a tanned face and luscious black curls sauntered into the kitchen and waved through the glass.

'Jono!' Jen shrieked, abandoning her steak in her hurry to run into his arms.

Usually Jen picked Jono up from the airport when he came home on his time off. He must have flown in early to surprise her. He moseyed to the living area, kicked off his shoes and plonked himself down on the couch, evidently awaiting his meal.

'The boss gave us all a couple of flexi days 'cause business has been good. Hey, babe.'

Jen sat on his lap to kiss him. 'I can't believe you didn't tell me you were coming back early.'

Kissy noises followed. I turned my back to give them some privacy, carrying our dinner plates to the sink.

'So, Maggie,' Jono said. He put one arm behind his head and the other around Jen's waist and leant back against the couch. 'I hear you finally fulfilled every girl's dream of becoming trailer trash.'

Jono had the swagger of a man who thought his dick gave him superpowers. He knew he was on to a good thing with Jen and yet it didn't stop him taking advantage of how much she adored him. The way he immediately flopped on the couch and expected dinner like she was his maid was particularly infuriating, but I'd been able to tolerate him for six years mostly because I hardly ever saw him. Something told me it was going to be harder putting up with his visits now that I was half-living at Jen's place, especially since he had been elevated to the status of fiancé and seemed to believe that it gave him certain extra privileges.

'Yep,' I said. 'I'm riding the new wave of minimalism.'

'Yeah, caravans are called tiny houses now,' Jen said. 'They're in. I'll make you a toasted cheese, babe.'

While Jen was gone, Jono and I sat in awkward silence, until he leant forward and I instinctively grabbed the remote control on the coffee table before he could get to it.

'You're not putting on *Alaskan Steel Men*,' I said. 'We're watching *The Bachelorette* and that's final.'

'You're a real pain in the arse,' he said. 'And it's not *Alaskan Steel Men* I wanted, it's *Dating Naked*.'

When Jen returned with the sandwich he grabbed her by the hips, swung her onto his lap and gave her a long, disgusting smooch. Jen squealed with laughter and upended the sandwich.

'Oh no!' She picked it up off the floor.

'Doesn't matter, I'll eat it. My girl keeps her floors clean.' He grabbed the sandwich and took a bite. 'So how long will you be using our place as a hotel?' he asked me, mouth full.

'Oh, am I getting in your way?'

Jen shot me a look, hearing the strain in my voice. 'You can use my place as long as you like, honey.'

It was generous of her to say it, considering I had already violated my promise not to take over her house. My hairdryer and shampoo were in her bathroom, my shoes were on her living room floor and less than an hour ago she'd lent me fifty dollars.

'Didn't mean it like that,' Jono said, though he clearly had. 'Just, you know. Living in a caravan. Really moving up in the world, eh, Maggie?'

'It's just until I get back on my feet.' Which might be never.

'Well,' he said, 'maybe Sean will take you back. Few blowies should do the trick.'

Jen punched him on the shoulder and he responded by squeezing her left boob. She slapped him over the head and he kissed her again, with tongue.

'If you're trying to make me leave, it's working,' I said.

By the time I left Jen's house I had a dozen eggs from her fridge, a packet of bacon, a loaf of bread, and a date set to help

Jen find a new wedding dress. She'd dropped strong hints that she'd also like me to find bridesmaid dresses that would suit me and both her stick-thin sisters and organise her hens' night within the next few weeks, but those things could wait.

—

At first I didn't even notice Agnes; the only person I saw was the lean, muscled man standing behind her with reddish stubble and intricate tattoos, the stillness of his stance oddly familiar.

I had spent the previous night waking up every two hours, dreaming repeatedly that someone was trying to get in through the broken window of my caravan, and hadn't got up for my second day at the Angels in time to shower. I'd rolled into work half an hour late and bleary-eyed, expecting a day of dull phone calls and typing into spreadsheets and maybe secretly recording Prayer Time on my phone in case Bunny debuted a Bob Geldof knock-off every day. But here was a handsome man with tattoos on his forearms, explaining to Agnes how to do something on her computer. He looked to be in his mid-thirties. The fact that I could not recall where I had met him was especially annoying given how hot he was. Agnes's lined smoker's mouth cracked a smile as she figured out whatever it was and she brushed away a strand of hair. She looked like a smitten teenager.

'Oh, Maggie,' Agnes gushed, when she finally noticed me. 'Rueben is wonderful.'

Ah, Rueben Blackwood. The man I'd hired. The ex-con who'd done time in Bindup minimum-security prison. How had he already made it into Agnes's good books?

'Did you know that he has a computer degree?' Agnes asked.

Rueben lifted his eyes to regard me evenly, and then it hit me. He was the guy who'd rejected me at The Fainting Chair.

The slide guitarist. And those tattoos on his forearms: intricately detailed hummingbirds on one arm, patchy blue scribbles on the other. I swallowed and felt my cheeks burn. A small smile lifted the corners of his mouth. *Please don't recognise me*, I thought feverishly. There was no way he would. Just another girl in a bar. That smile on his face now was just friendly, there was no flirtation in it. No sex at all in that smile. Definitely not. God, he was handsome. So, I'd almost had sex with an ex-con in a public bathroom. I frowned at him slightly, trying to pretend I wasn't blushing.

'That's great.' I cleared my throat. 'But I thought he was working in the shop?'

'Oh, I've called Margaret to come in for the day. Rueben is too useful here in the office. He already fixed my emails! Maggie, show him our electronic filing system, he says he can improve it.'

'Sure,' I said.

Anyone could improve it, because it was the worst filing system in the world. I guess that was irrelevant in the face of a 'computer degree'. I led him through to the back room and perched my bum on the desk while he looked around. The room was a touch small for two people, especially when one seemed to take up so much air.

Rueben. It was a good name. He was wearing the same grey T-shirt he had been wearing at The Fainting Chair and his hair looked unbrushed. The T-shirt was clean and unwrinkled, but he wore it as if he had no idea that it clung to his broad shoulders, as if totally unaware that the dip of neckline exposed a sliver of chest hair, that the line of his collarbone was so fine as to be like a wishbone. It irritated me. He lacked the self-consciousness of the film-star fox that he looked like. He made no gestures, keeping his hands by his sides as if he was a Zen master. Just watched me lightly.

'So, we spoke on the phone,' I said.

'We did.' He held out his hand to shake mine. It was warm and firm. A little shiver ran up my spine as I thought about his hand making its way up my thigh. *Focus, Maggie.* I sat down at my desk and Rueben pulled up a chair next to me.

'How'd you convince Agnes you were Christ reincarnated?'

'You weren't here yet and her emails weren't coming through. She came into the op shop and asked if anyone knew how to fix her computer. No big deal.'

'You know your way around Excel?'

'Among other things.' He smiled again in that sexy but irritating way and rubbed his nose. God, his nose was sexy. I hadn't even noticed it earlier because I was too busy staring into his lily-pad eyes, but it was smooth and flat and had the tiniest hint of a ski-jump at the end. He caught me staring and winked. Argh.

'Voila,' I said. 'Here's our filing system.'

He smiled in disbelief. 'This is literally a folder called Nicholson Street Angels Records. Without any subfolders,' he said. 'Saved to the desktop. Is there even any backup?'

'To back up, we print stuff out. Agnes has three filing cabinets in her office.'

'Have you considered creating separate folders for tax, employee, donor and volunteer records? And maybe signing up to a cloud-based backup system?'

'Oh, you're trying to take my job now?'

I don't know why I was being snarky but something about his calm gaze and self-assurance was throwing me off.

He shrugged. 'Just saying, it's not going to be hard to make improvements.' He got up, pushing a stray curl away from his face. His hair was thick and dark, with just a few streaks of grey at the temples.

'So when did they close Bindup?' I asked suddenly.

'Two thousand and nine.'

'When were you there?'

'A few months in 2001 and then a year in '03.'

'Two stints, eh? Must've been naughty.' I sorted out the pens on my desk, for lack of anything better to do. I wished he would get annoyed at my nosiness, but he just stood over me, gazing with his infuriating blank expression.

'Is that where you got your degree? While you were in prison?' I asked.

'No. I did a course after I got out. They're free for ex-cons.'

'Glad our taxpayer dollars are going to the people who need it.' Yeesh, I sounded like my mother. For some reason, this guy was really bringing out my bitchy side.

He smiled. 'You don't pay tax.'

'How do you know?'

'Because Agnes told me you got this gig through Centrelink. And you're a volunteer, too. So you don't pay tax.'

His calm, mocking smile was really starting to incense me.

'Eh. Details.'

'Look,' he said, 'I'm not here to take your job, although I could probably do it better.'

I huffed.

'I'm volunteering because if I don't, it's either Work for the Dole or clean toilets. I've done both for ten years and I'm tired of it. No one will hire an ex-con for a professional role unless he's got a reference from somewhere decent, and even then it's a long shot.'

I considered that. 'All right. If you don't muscle in on my job I'll give glowing feedback about you to Agnes so she'll write you a good reference.'

He smiled. 'I don't need you to do that. Pretty sure she already likes me.'

I rolled my eyes. It did seem that way.

The rest of the day was quiet. I showed Rueben our processes, which he mastered in less than an hour. Aside from a crazed volunteer in a purple tracksuit who burst into reception shouting that one of the other grannies had stolen her favourite jumper – a situation Rueben quickly defused by finding her another jumper next door from the racks of the op shop – the day was nothing out of the ordinary. I called volunteers to remind them of their shifts, updated the shop's records and inventory in a spreadsheet, and played solitaire on the computer when the internet went down, which happened at least once an hour. I discovered that at around 2 pm the sun would come through the window at just the right angle that I could discreetly sunbathe my lower legs by resting them up on the desk as I drank a cup of tea. Overall, the job was unexciting, but more tolerable than I had anticipated. Except that I couldn't help looking over at Rueben every now and then, clacking away on the keyboard and frowning at the screen. He had the kind of face that was broad and chiselled and yet somehow flat. It was beautiful to look at, and I found myself having to tear my eyes away from him to deal with the 'inspirational' emails from Bunny that were gradually filling my inbox with things like, *'I don't measure a man's success by how high he climbs, but how high he bounces when he hits bottom. – George Patton.'*

I'll hit *your* bottom, George Patton. I deleted the latest email and turned back to contemplating Rueben.

Why had he turned me down at The Fainting Chair?

At 5 pm on the dot I stretched, feeling the tired satisfaction that comes from a hard day's work, and packed up my desk. 'I have to shoot off,' I told Rueben. 'I have a date.'

He didn't look up from his computer. 'Who with, bad hand-job guy from The Fainting Chair?'

I stopped dead in the middle of putting my phone in my bag, heart thumping.

'You remember that?'

He raised those long, dark lashes of his to shoot me a look of pure amusement.

'Of course. Did you ever resolve your breasts-or-genitals dilemma, by the way?'

I swallowed. Nonchalance, Maggie. Practise nonchalance. 'Yeah. I broke up with the guy who thought breasts were genitals.'

'Uh-huh. That night, I suppose?'

'I like my relationships to go out with a bang.'

'In an alley.'

'That was a new method. But I would prefer you didn't mention that little escapade to anyone here.'

'Of course.' He smiled a secret half-smile, showing a hint of white teeth against light brown skin.

'Not a word. If you ever mention The Fainting Chair or alleyways again, you'll be outta here in five minutes.'

'You just mentioned it.'

'Well, that's the last and only time. We've never met.'

'And how exactly would you get me "outta here"? I didn't think volunteers had the power to hire and fire.'

'That's exactly my job,' I said. 'Hiring and firing, organising volunteers. So just you remember that.' I swung my bag over my shoulder, feeling Rueben's grin on my back as I breezed out.

# Chapter 8

My blood was pumping triple time as I got ready for my date with Dan. In Jen's bedroom, I flung on one of her dresses and twisted to check myself in the mirror. Recalling Rueben's eyelids lowered in amusement, the sexy half-smile when he revealed that he recognised me, seemed to carbonate my blood. There was only one way to calm my frazzled nerves.

'I need to root something,' I told the mirror.

I slipped on my shonky old high heels that I'd dug out from the back of the panel van and drew a line of red lipstick across my lips. In the living room, Jono was watching a game of soccer on television, holding a glass of whisky in his hand.

'You've hardly touched that,' I said. 'Do you even like whisky?' I grabbed the glass from him and drained it.

'Bloody hell, get your own drink.'

'Good idea.' I found his best bottle of aged Scotch in the pantry, cracked the lid and took a deep swig, to Jono's audible disgust.

I was ready to go.

—

T-Bird was a dingy-looking but famous Singaporean restaurant on a busy corner of Johnston and Wellington Streets. I burst through the door like a mongrel in heat, nearly colliding with the waitress. Daughter of the owner, I thought. Looked closer. No, wife of the owner.

'Got a booking?' she asked.

'No . . . I'm meeting someone,' I slurred.

She shrugged, not interested anymore. I walked past the ATM that slugged diners an extra fifty cents each time they took money out and into the warm, noisy dining area. It smelt of fried chicken and fish cakes. The place was cosy and familiar. I was mildly impressed that Dan knew about it; I had vague memories of him saying he lived in Richmond. I made a mental note to order the Hainanese chicken straight away before it ran out, as it inevitably would by 8 pm. An empty table looked inviting, so I sat down and picked up a menu, then remembered I was supposed to find my date first. I glanced up just as a cute sandy-blond guy reached my table and waved awkwardly. Dan.

'I'm over here,' he said, pointing to a spot two tables across. All cosy and sweet in the corner.

I inspected him closely. He was better looking than I remembered, though he had nothing on Sean. Or Rueben, for that matter. His dimpled smile was kind of adorable. Not that I was all about looks, of course.

The waitress approached. 'You went to the wrong table!' she said gleefully.

I looked at Dan. He seemed calm and unconcerned.

'Yes, I did,' I said. 'I'll have the Hainanese chicken, thanks.'

'None left,' said the waitress. 'It's very popular. You need to come earlier.'

Goddammit. I ordered the fried chicken balls instead.

Within an hour, talk turned to our exes. Dan filled me in on his recent break-up, which I figured out wasn't all that recent – a few months ago, at least. Some men take a long time to get over their exes.

'We were together for four years,' he said. 'Then she says she wants time out.' He swigged the last of his third beer. He'd brought four longnecks to the restaurant and had been averaging one every twenty minutes. Each time he took one out of its paper bag the restaurant staff would come running over to pop the cap for him. 'Five minutes later she's going out with some lawyer,' he continued. 'Some hotshot divorce lawyer.'

'Divorce lawyer,' I scoffed. 'Of all the evil, scummy professions.'

'Fuckin' tell me about it. He's all, fuckin', wearing suits, and'—he took another sip—'getting his hair cut, and—'

'Divorcing people,' I chimed in.

'Yeah.'

I was on my fifth wine, which made it approximately my seventh drink for the evening. I was heading up spew creek without a paddle.

'My ex was really handsome,' I said. 'I stole him off someone else. And then I cheated on him. With you.'

'She's just so beautiful,' Dan said, not listening to me. He had a little piece of noodle on his chin. 'She has this long, honey-coloured hair . . . it's like silk. And she was really nice to my mum.'

'My mum adored Sean. She disowned me when we broke up.'

Dan sighed and twisted his beer. We'd got in this state out of nerves, I suppose. He knew I was there for the free meal and I knew he was there for the free sex, and we were both trying to get drunk enough that we could pretend otherwise.

His face cleared for a moment.

'Wait a minute,' he said. 'Did you say you were still with your ex when we hooked up?'

'Er, yes.'

His eyebrows went up somewhere around his hairline. 'Jeez.' He sat back in his chair and looked at me, the noodle shifting up and down on his chin as he spoke. 'Speaking as someone who's been left for someone else, that's pretty poor form.'

'He didn't love me,' I protested. 'He was looking for a way out, and I gave him one.'

The truth hurts, even when you say it yourself. I was reminded that Sean had made zero effort to contact me since our break-up. It looked like he wasn't even going to bother picking up his beloved Hawthorn scarf, which he'd left in my car.

Dan narrowed his eyes. 'How do you know he didn't love you?'

'At first I was in denial about it. A while back he started comparing me to his idiot former girlfriend and I thought he was trying to make me jealous.' I waved my spoon. 'He kept saying things like, "She just really knew me, deeply," and sighing a lot. Over a girl who had breast implants at eighteen and told anyone who'd listen how she'd been in a Fanta commercial.'

'A Fanta commercial?'

'She didn't even have a speaking part! Just splashed around in a pool with her glistening fake boobs.'

'You watched it?'

'I found it on YouTube. But then I had to face reality when I realised he was having a fling – or about to start one – with Sarah Stoll.'

'Ah. I have met Sarah once or twice.' He sipped his beer.

'Enough said.'

'So you felt it was time to take a wrecking ball to the relationship.'

'Exactly.' I was sick of this date. And I was sick. I felt a little burp coming up. 'I have to go to the bathroom.'

—

Dan insisted on escorting me home.

'You're too drunk to walk alone,' he said, stumbling.

'Nah, nah, I'll see you round.' I really didn't want him to see the caravan. The shame spiral had begun and I needed to wallow in it on my own. I walked away from him, straight into a wall. 'Easy does it.'

'Maggie, you can't walk home like this.'

'Yes I can.' I tested myself, walking onto the road to balance on the straight white line while the breeze ruffled my hair and little Victorian houses seemed to watch from either side of the street. I put one foot in front of the other and promptly fell over. A car honked directly behind me.

Dan hooked an arm under mine and lifted me upright.

'All right. Which street do you live on?'

I sighed. 'Fine.' Guess I'd have to show him the caravan.

'You live near Jen, right?' Dan looked around as if Jen's house would be waving a flag for him.

'Yeah, just behind her house, actually.'

'That's so cool. You must get to see her all the time.'

'Yeah. It's gonna be different once she marries that jerk, though.'

Dan shot me a sideways glance as we passed a tumbledown stone cottage that was obviously a student share house, with a couch in the front yard and a vine that had eaten the entire verandah.

'You don't like Jono?'

'Have you met him?'

'I see your point,' he said.

'He's completely awful. He treats her like a servant.'

'Why is she marrying him?'

'The usual reasons. She loves him.' The growl of a motorbike cut the air. I picked a sprig of jasmine from a fence as we passed and waved it under his nose. 'Jen always looks at the world as a friend. She actually believes people wish her well, and the craziest thing is they do. Everyone except Jono treats her like a princess.'

'Maybe that's why she likes Jono. He's a challenge.'

'He's too dumb to be a challenge. No, he's familiar. I should have said, everyone except Jono and her own family treats her like a princess.'

'Didn't her parents buy her the house?'

'It's not the same thing.'

We turned into Charlotte Court. The caravan sat exactly where I'd left it, slightly askew in the car space. I spread my arms.

'Well, here we are.'

He raised his eyebrows. 'Wow, nice place.'

His gaze was fixed on the house behind the caravan, a beautiful modern wood-panelled two-storey feat of architecture.

'No, not there. There.' I pointed more firmly. 'The caravan.'

His eyes swivelled to the little silver turd. 'Huh.' The caravan's corrugated aluminium shone under the streetlight. Dan eyed me as if I'd said I kept my toenail clippings in jars.

'Isn't it cute?' I said. 'It's all sixties and trapezoid.'

'A caravan?'

'Yeah.'

'You bought this?'

'Couple of days ago.'

'I thought you were broke.'

I shrugged. 'Money comes, money goes. You want to see inside?'

Now that a bed was mere metres away, my vagina had taken over my thinking. I needed to get Dan on top of me. This could be the start of my new life. Free meals. Drinking and shagging all night. If my caravan's a-rockin', don't come a-knockin'.

Dan let out a short laugh. 'Hell, why not.'

I opened the caravan door and ducked my head to step inside, tripping on the top step. Dan followed me in. The streetlight shone in through the broken window, but it was still quite dark inside and since I had nowhere to plug in an extension cord to make the light work, I used the torch by the bed to illuminate the caravan. With an interior that was ten feet long and six feet wide, it didn't offer much room to move. We slid onto the tiny vinyl bench seats facing each other. Our knees touched.

'So, this is it,' I said.

'You've got no power?'

'I'll get an extension cord at some point.'

'And steal electricity?'

'Yeah, I guess,' I said.

He eyed the floral curtains and the sink. 'Is that a pump tap?'

'Um, yeah, I think. You can put a little water tank in below the sink.'

'Huh. Cool. Have you put one in yet?'

'No,' I said. 'I only bought it a few days ago, and I don't know how.'

'I could do it for you,' he said.

Was he trying to get in my pants with the offer of handiwork? I hoped so. There was a good buzz going on between my legs. Dan looked very fine. Tall and warm and smooth. Like he'd be heavy on me if we lay down. His full cheeks had a coating of blond stubble, which made them look less cherubic and more manly.

He frowned at me. Why are frowning men so hot?

'Why are you staring at me?' he asked.

It was warm in the caravan with the door closed. The heat spread to my cheeks. The caravan needed to be christened with a good, proper roll on the vinyl bed. With my right forefinger I traced the line of loosening linoleum on the tabletop. My left hand crept under the table and up Dan's thigh.

'What are you doing?' he asked.

I smiled at him. There was no way I'd stop now I'd started. He'd have to throw me off and run if he wanted to leave. I reached his zip and rested my hand there.

He stood up suddenly, hunched over so he wouldn't bang his head. Crap, he was going to leave. He looked at the door and I was filled with a deep rush of self-loathing. Then he cleared the distance between us, pulled me out of my seat and onto the table, and kissed me. He was not a bad kisser. No tongue, just pressure. I pressed my hands into his sides and squeezed my thighs against his hips.

I was just feeling some heat run down from my stomach to my knees when the fold-out table collapsed under the weight of my arse on it.

'Whoops.'

Dan lifted me up off the floor and led me over to the bed at the back of the caravan as if nothing had happened and laid me down. He pulled off my dress, pressed my knees apart and put a clumsy hand between my legs. He wouldn't make the top five of my lovers because of his lack of dexterity, but I predicted that he'd probably make the top fifteen. At least we weren't upright in an alley and I wasn't fumbling around with his zip and injuring him by accident. Compared with my sexual experiences of the past year – that is, Sean's style of lovemaking, which had earned him his nickname The Stal: hard and fast and grunty – Dan would almost certainly be the better option. When he pulled off my undies and lay down on me he was indeed heavy on me, in a good way.

We were lying together slightly squashed on the narrow bed, my naked butt resting uncomfortably on brown vinyl. His hard-on pressed into my lower belly through his boxer shorts as he kissed me slowly. The buzzing between my legs became more urgent, anticipation fixing my body taut. He pulled away.

'You're really horny, aren't you?' he said.

'Dan.' All tension fizzed out of my body. 'Do you know nothing of women? The word "horny" is about as welcome to my ears as the word "herpes".'

He grinned, unperturbed. 'You practically jumped me.'

I sighed and flopped my arm out to one side, hitting the caravan wall. What was his problem? He kissed my forehead and pulled his arm out from under me.

'Wish that happened to me more often,' he said.

'Well, why don't you just have sex with me then?' To my horror the desperation was clearly audible in my voice.

'To be honest, I'm kind of enjoying your frustration.'

'Well, screw you!'

'Nah, not tonight,' he said.

'Why not?' It was outrageous. There I was, naked and ready on a vinyl bed, and he didn't want to take advantage of the situation.

'You've had too much to drink, and I don't want to reward you for cheating on your boyfriend. I'm holding out in solidarity with Sean.'

'What, are you having trouble getting it up?'

'No!'

'You've got tickets on yourself, anyway,' I said. 'Like you'd be doing me a favour? From what I remember you're kind of clumsy.' Hopefully he'd forgotten that I was the clumsy one.

'That's not fair!' he protested. 'I was drunk.'

'Well, prove it then.'

'Prove what?'

'That you can screw properly.'

'Jesus Christ, woman.'

I raised my eyebrows at him. The sound of a drunk spitting in the gutter outside came through the busted window, and a breeze ruffled the faded curtain.

'Yeah, all right, just let me take a piss first,' he said. He looked around. 'Where do I go?'

'Uh, outside, I guess.'

He shook his head and rolled off me, arranging the boner in his boxers so it wouldn't stick straight out. He poked his head out the door before stepping out. The sound of splattering on concrete wafted in. It seemed to go on and on, like rain trickling down a gutter.

That must have been what lulled me to sleep.

—

The cold plywood wall was pressed against my butt cheeks when I woke. I was naked and furry-tongued, lying on my side, a headache splitting my forehead. Trying to move made it painfully apparent that the skin of my outer thigh was stuck to the vinyl bed.

'Ugh.'

Next to me, Dan was asleep with his mouth open. He was still wearing his boxers and his hair lay tousled over his forehead.

He stirred as I sat up. 'Morning,' he said, and stretched.

I tried to remember what happened.

'What did we do?' I asked. I was buck naked. Why hadn't we gone back to Dan's house, for God's sake? Why did we come back to sleep in my caravan? Dan angled his eyes slightly to the left, as if he was embarrassed to see me naked.

'I came back in last night and you were passed out.' Dan began putting on his clothes. 'I was gonna get a taxi home, but then I thought I'd just stay here and walk to my car this morning.'

'Huh.'

I hoped he would leave soon so I could sneak into Jen's house and use her bathroom. Dan was not in a hurry, however. He started opening the cupboards above the sink and inspecting handles.

'If you're looking for coffee, I don't have any. Or a kettle. Or electricity to power the kettle.'

'Nah, just checking the place out. It's well built.'

Great. I started pulling on my underwear, moving gingerly as a tight band of pain in my forehead throbbed with each movement. My mobile rang just as I hooked my bra together. I fumbled around on the floor, finally locating the mobile under my dress.

A disembodied voice introduced herself as Judy from Centrelink, inducing a shiver of dread that ran over me like a huntsman spider.

'Maggie Cotton? We've had a tip-off that you've been living with your partner for the last year,' she droned.

I could imagine the owner of the voice painting her nails purple and clacking her bangles on the desk as she cradled her phone in the crook of her neck. Just a feeling I got.

'A tip-off from who?'

'Sorry, I can't disclose that. Can you confirm that you have been living with a partner?'

'No,' I said. 'My boyfriend died.'

Dan's head shot up, startled. Dear God, why did I say that? Why hadn't I just said no, I was not living with anyone? Dan was staring at me in disbelief.

'It – it was a skiing accident,' I continued, trying to bring a little waver into my voice and hoping like hell it sounded genuine. 'It happened in New Zealand, a year ago.'

Crap, is there even snow in New Zealand at this time of year? Why didn't I just say it was a car accident? Dan's expression had morphed from disbelief to disgust.

'Well, that's interesting,' Judy droned, 'because I was just on the phone to one Sean Quinn and he sounded very much alive.'

'Wait, do you mean the tip-off was from him? My arse of an ex-boyfriend dobbed me in?'

Judy cleared her throat. 'I can't divulge that information. Mr Quinn's income means you shouldn't have been claiming the full amount of your study allowance for the past year. You'll have to repay the money and we may issue a fine. Are you aware that lying about your living arrangements is fraud?'

Dan brushed past me impatiently and buttoned up his jeans while Judy went on to inform me that I would be receiving a letter from them shortly, elucidating the exact amount of money I owed.

'Your repayments will be docked from your Newstart Allowance until the full amount is paid, or until you begin working full-time, at which time you'll have the payments docked directly from your pay. Once we've calculated the amount owed you'll be put onto a repayment plan.'

'What if I don't get a job?'

'The debt will remain until you do. Indexed to inflation. I suggest you get a job.' I detected a note of victory in her voice.

By the time I hung up Dan was fully clothed and fuming.

'By God, you can lie, woman. What was that?'

'That was Centrelink, and they didn't believe me.'

His eyes were burning through me, making me feel more naked than I was. I pulled on my dress.

'Why did you say your boyfriend had died?'

'Because I was trying to get out of paying a debt.'

'But you could pay for a caravan.'

'Well, now I never have to pay rent again.'

He rubbed his face. 'You're going to live in this thing? Here?'

'While I'm kicked out of Mum's, yes.'

'Oh, really? How? Do you need to go to the toilet right now? Eat, drink, shower?'

'I'm fine,' I said.

Now I just wanted him out. The full weight of terror from the phone call was beginning to sink in. I wasn't just out of an income, a university degree and a home. I had a debt, and a potential fraud case.

'Maggie, you are all kinds of weird,' Dan said. And then he left.

# Chapter 9

It was a hot, sticky night when I was arrested for public urination. I'd been in the caravan for two weeks and had bought candles and an extension cord. Each night after the houses that looked onto the laneway turned out their lights I snuck onto the front verandah of the fancy wooden townhouse and plugged the cord into its outdoor power point. Then I boiled the kettle (Jen's spare) for a cup of herbal tea and fried up bacon and eggs in the cheap electric frypan (also Jen's spare). I rarely used the light in the caravan so as not to call attention to myself, but when I did I closed all the curtains and read for a little while before bed. I had bed sheets (borrowed from Jen), a mug, plate, cutlery and a tea towel (purchased from the Nicholson Street Angels' op shop). I did my laundry at the laundromat on Smith Street. I kept an esky under the fold-up table and filled it with ice to keep my bacon, eggs and cider cold, and leant a hand mirror against the splashback, where I did my make-up and plaited my hair when it got greasy.

I was a little worried about Dot, who was still angry at me for dragging her out of Sean's cute little terrace house and Mum's cat palace. She'd left two long, vicious scratches down my left forearm and spent most mornings crouched on the laminate folding table, flicking her grey tabby tail from side to side and staring at me with hard yellow eyes. Sometimes she wouldn't come home all night, and I couldn't leave the caravan door open for her, so who knew whose verandah she slept on. She was probably getting feeds from the neighbours, who no doubt thought she was a stray, and would likely go feral soon.

My main worry, though, was the bathroom. It wasn't so bad while Jono was away in South Australia and I could use Jen's bathroom, but while he was home I found my options compromised. He tended to sit on the couch playing PlayStation for most of his time off, so I couldn't just waltz in and out of Jen's back door without him noticing. Tonight the problem was pressing. The caravan was a hotbox. I needed to pee and shower and eat something decent, but all I could do was lie on the vinyl and sweat. The telltale signs of Jono's presence were visible over the back of Jen's fence: a man's jacket draped lovingly over a chair in the garden, an empty beer bottle beside it. But I still had a key to Jen's place. I weighed it up. What was worse, peeing in the street or seeing Jono's face? The answer was obvious, so I went outside and squatted in the gutter in full view of my neighbours' windows.

I hitched up my jeans and darted back inside, flopping on the bed to think. My next Centrelink payment wasn't due until next week, so I had to make $12.87 last five days. There was only one way to do that without starving or listening to Jono talk about his new cock piercing. Stretched out on the vinyl, stomach rumbling, I called my mother. She answered on the second ring.

'What do you want?'

'Hi, Mum.'

'How's the caravan?'

'Oh, it's great, it's great . . . listen, how about we take a short break from our agreement and you let me come home for a few days? I started a new job recently and I think it will be easier at home until I'm all set up in the caravan. Plus I need to get some clothes.'

Mum paused. I felt her battle. She was divided between her fury at me for spending the bond money on the caravan and curiosity about my new job. I already knew which would win.

'What job did you start?' she asked finally.

'It's for a charity. Doing admin three days a week.'

That should put her in a good mood. A daughter with a respectable job working for a charity, that's something she could boast to her friends about. Never mind the living in a caravan part, nobody needed to know about that. I wouldn't tell her I was volunteering, either. And I would never, ever tell her about the Centrelink debt.

'No,' she said.

I nearly dropped the phone. 'What?'

'I'm glad you've got a job, but the answer's no. You can't come home. You spent the money I gave you on a caravan, so now you have to live in it. That's the deal.'

'Mum!'

'I – argh, shit.' Her voice went muffled.

'Mum?'

'Nothing, I just fell through the floor. Ow.'

'What, in the living room? The rotted bit?'

'No, in my bedroom. The floor's rotting out there too.'

I had a brilliant idea.

'Mum, I know a builder.'

'I don't need a bloody builder.'

'He'll probably check out the floorboards for free, and he'll give you an honest quote for what it would cost to get them fixed.'

She was quiet.

'Mum,' I continued, 'if you don't get those floors looked at you won't have a house to live in soon. You'll be sleeping in a termite nest.'

'Yeah, all right, bring him round. But you still can't stay here.'

'No worries.' I could pick up my clothes and begin the process of wriggling my way back into her good books. I hung up and lay on the bed, wondering how to convince Dan to check out Mum's floorboards.

The police officer, when he knocked, was young and hand-some and pink in the cheeks from the afternoon sun. He stood on the asphalt, blinking from the light that bounced off the aluminium when I flung open the door.

'Hello there,' I said. 'How can I help you?'

'Do you live here?' He straightened his shoulders in an attempt to look authoritative.

'Yes.'

'And,' he pointed to the gutter, 'is that your urine?'

I followed the direction of his finger. 'No. No, it is not.'

'We had a call from one of the neighbours, who witnessed you urinating in the gutter.'

'They must have had me confused with someone else.'

'Look, I'm not here to arrest you, as long as you move along. I'll write you out a warning.'

'I'm not moving along. I have every right to be here. The City of Yarra permits—'

'I'm familiar with the law.' His cheeks turned a darker shade of red. 'But you're causing a disturbance and if you refuse an order to move along I can take you down to the station.'

I stood silent. I knew my rights. Nobody could prove that it was my puddle, and nobody could force me to move.

'Well? What will it be? Do I have to arrest you, or will you move along?'

—

God, what is it with fucking vinyl? Everything in the Collingwood police station was green vinyl. Maybe the interior decorators thought that murky shade of green would soothe violent criminals, or maybe the vinyl was on special when they bought it. The pink-cheeked officer made me sit in a vinyl chair while he wrote me up for public urination, disturbing the peace and whatever the hell else he felt like. At least he didn't handcuff me. The blinking fluorescent lights reminded me of a documentary on CIA torture techniques that I'd seen on TV one time. As I sat there, it slowly dawned on me – a little late – that I'd be better off getting this pink-cheeked do-gooder on side.

'Look, buddy, sir, mate, if you're writing me a ticket, I don't have the money to pay it. I've got twelve dollars.'

'It's a little more serious than a ticket now,' he murmured, scribbling away on the piece of paper in front of him.

'Okay, look, what if I move the caravan a street away?'

He looked up from his piece of paper. 'You have to stop urinating in the street.'

'Fine.'

'Do you need to find a women's shelter?'

'A—' I was suddenly outraged. 'A women's shelter? Dude, I *work* for a women's shelter. I've got a Diploma of Accounting and a mother in Camberwell.'

'It's nothing to be embarrassed about. Plenty of people find themselves—'

'Haven't you heard of the tiny houses movement?'

He sighed, and I had a mad urge to grab him by the collar and explain that people who had jobs and kitchens and bathrooms and partners and children were almost always sad cogs in the capitalist machine, but I decided it wouldn't make him like me any more.

'Is there someone you can call? The mother in Camberwell, perhaps?'

A knot formed in my stomach. 'I already tried her. She's a little . . . irate at this moment.'

'A friend?'

'If my best friend comes to pick me up, you'll let me go?'

'With a warning.'

'Look, I could seriously just walk home right now. It's not far.'

'It's procedure. We need to release you into someone's care.'

'Someone's care?' I rolled my eyes all the way up to the shabby, probably asbestos-filled ceiling. 'I'm not a geriatric.'

PC Pink Cheeks folded his hands.

'All right, all right. I'll call Jen.'

Jen didn't pick up. It rang out and I dialled again. It rang out again. She was probably having sex with Jono, or discussing the wedding.

'She's probably working.' I put the phone down on the bench and realised I had no one else to call. My brother was in Europe. My other friends were just people I knew through Jen, who hung out with me and laughed at my jokes but could not be relied upon to rescue me from a ruddy do-gooder police officer and drop me back at my caravan without gossiping about

107

it to three thousand people. I did something I hadn't done in a long time. I called my father.

'Maggie!' Dad answered the phone immediately and his deep, rich voice sounded joyful, as if he was genuinely happy to hear from me. He must have found a new girlfriend.

'How's your tan, Dad?'

'Oh, tan's great, life's great, can't complain. New missus! She's dynamite. Blonde, curvy, forty-five. Goes off like a rocket.'

'Gross.'

'So what's up, love?'

'I've been arrested for living in a caravan. It's persecution.'

The policeman narrowed his eyes at me and I shrugged.

'A caravan! Good on you, love. I always wanted one, but your poor old mum never let me buy one when we were married.' Dad was always running out of money and moving house to avoid paying overdue bills, and like me he preferred living on someone else's dime, but unlike me he had a bent for luxury, so he'd probably hassled Mum to import a twenty-foot Airstream for eighty grand. 'What sort did you get?'

'A 1962 aluminium hand-built ten-footer. You can find it online. It's called the Periwinkle. People used to build them from instruction manuals.'

The policeman sat back in his chair, shaking his head and making a winding motion with his finger, as in, *Hurry up, lady.*

'Let me see.' I heard Dad tapping on his keyboard. 'Here it is. Oh, what a beauty!' He was practically roaring. 'What an absolute ripper. You don't sell this one, Maggie. You keep this. This belongs in *Classic Caravan* magazine. It'll be worth a bit. How much did you pay for it?'

'Eleven hundred.'

'Bargain! Hold on to it, it could be your retirement plan.'

Dad sighed. It sounded like he'd turned down his stereo. I braced myself for a deep and meaningful. 'Maggie, I'm so proud of you. In a caravan, you're beholden to no one. You're nobody's serf, working off a mortgage and giving birth to ungrateful kids who ask for iPads as soon as they can talk. You're free. You're living.'

'So, why don't you move into a caravan now?'

He laughed. 'I'm an ugly middle-aged man. It's all I can do to get women back to my apartment. If I lived in a caravan, no one would sleep with me.'

'Well, shit,' I said. 'No one will sleep with me either in that case.'

'All right, that's it,' the policeman leant forward, cutting in. 'Is he coming to pick you up, or what?'

'Can you pick me up from the police station?' I asked.

'Ooh, bad luck, love, I've moved to the Gold Coast.' Of course he had. 'Well, I've gotta go test drive this Beemer I found on Gumtree. Good luck, sweetheart.' He hung up.

'He can't come,' I said to the police officer, who was turning a delicate shade of purple. 'Turns out he moved to the Gold Coast.'

He put his head in his hands. 'Call someone else or I'll put you in a jail cell for wasting my time.'

I looked at my phone and willed Jen to call back. 'There's no one else to call.'

'Then I'm writing you up.'

'Wait. Wait.' I scrolled through numbers. Could I maybe call . . . ? I really didn't want to, but I sighed and pressed the button, scrunched up my eyes and half hoped for no answer.

Dan answered on the second ring. 'Well, hello. Is the trailer park wench hoping for another night of sensual snoring on the vinyl bed?'

'The trailer park wench is in jail,' I said. 'Or, almost.'

'Seriously?'

'Seriously. I need a favour.'

'What are you in for?'

'Doesn't matter. Can you pick me up?'

'Tell me what you're in for and I'll come get you.'

I sighed and shot the police officer my most mutinous stare. 'Public urination. Allegedly.'

Dan coughed to cover a laugh. 'Okay. Tell me where you are and I'll be there soon.'

—

After he signed me out of the police station, Dan took me for a cider.

'Now I need a favour,' he began.

'That's great, because I need a favour too.'

We were sitting on leather couches in Balloon Hour, a bar on Smith Street that was frequented by dope smokers and uni students and served soup made by someone's mum. It was quiet, dark and cheap. The candle on the coffee table between us had gone out.

'I just did you a favour!'

'All right, what's yours?' I asked.

Dan chugged his beer. 'She's engaged.'

'Who?'

He made a noise like he was trying to push the breath out of his lungs too quickly.

'Lisa. My ex. She's engaged to the divorce lawyer. She invited me to the engagement party.'

'What?' Someone in the back bar cheered wildly, and I thought I'd misheard. 'Your ex invited you to her engagement party?'

Dan nodded.

'Who does that? Is she trying to torment you?'

'No, no,' he said. 'She's a good chick. She wants to be friends.'

He knotted his hands a little, his eyebrows knitted like a pair of dirty blond caterpillars making love. Poor Dan. He had no idea of the depths of evil his ex-girlfriend was clearly capable of. She didn't want to be friends. She wanted to flaunt her success at casting him aside in favour of a more successful man. Dan's eyes were round and sad, like Dot's when I ignored her plaintive meows for more snacks directly after being fed.

'Will you come with me?' he asked. 'To the engagement party? The invite said I could bring a date.'

'You mean you're actually going? You want to go to this party and watch your ex moon over her new man? Why would you put yourself through that?'

'I just . . . I want to see for myself. If she's happy. And I can't turn up alone.'

I thought I understood. 'If you take someone, she might be jealous. And if she's jealous, she might realise she still has feelings for you? Dan, haven't you learnt from my mistakes? She's moved on.'

He smiled sadly. 'I love her.'

'Yeah, all right. But why would you ask me to be your date? Don't you know anyone better looking or more successful to make your ex jealous? Like, a stripper? Or a janitor?'

He fiddled with the label at the back of his T-shirt. 'You are good looking, Maggie. Anyway, I don't know who else to ask, and you seem to be a good liar.'

'I'm an awful liar. I am literally never believed.'

'Please?'

I wanted to stand my ground but was helpless against his pleading look and dimples. That and I really wanted him to check out my mother's floorboards so I could move back home. I felt a strange urge to pat him on the shoulder. I didn't, though. I just agreed to be his date for the torture session.

'Fine.'

'Thank you.' The depth of relief on his face was discomforting.

'But this is a way bigger favour than picking me up from the police station.'

He drained his beer and set it down on the coffee table. 'Okay, what do you want?'

By the time we left the pub, Dan had agreed to look at my mother's floorboards on Saturday, paid the bar tab and loaned me twenty dollars. Meanwhile, I had almost two weeks to prepare for Lisa's engagement party.

# Chapter 10

Rueben volunteered three days a week, like me. And, because Agnes decided she didn't want to have to repeat any instructions, she rostered Rueben and me on for the same days. So I was stuck in an office every Monday, Wednesday and Friday with the guy who not only knew my penchant for sticking my hand down strangers' pants but could do my job with his eyes closed if he wanted to, and who, with infuriating regularity, turned me on just by saying hello in his gravelly voice.

This morning, Belinda, whose mother, Margaret, had kept me on the phone for half an hour on my first day on the job, was being interviewed for a more senior role in the op shop. Agnes already trusted me to conduct interviews on my own, which I thought was a little optimistic of her, but I wasn't about to complain. Since we had no other candidates for the role, Belinda's interview was just a formality.

I closed the door and sat down opposite her in the tiny window-less room. She was in her late forties or early fifties, dressed in a pale pink pantsuit, with the most perfect Grace Kelly wave in her blonde hair that I'd ever seen. She had a lined, solemn face and heavy eyelids that drooped over her eyes like candle wax.

'So,' I said, 'you've been volunteering in the op shop for three months, I see. What makes you suited to the role of shop supervisor?'

'I have leadership skills. And I keep a careful eye on the shop.' She held up a dainty finger adorned with a long pink nail. 'When people come in and want things for free or get lipstick on the shirts, I know what to do. Firm but fair. And the older ladies in the shop listen to me.'

'Okay. Look, you've done pretty well so far and altogether we've had good feedback about you—'

'Have I shown you my scars?' she interrupted.

'Er . . .'

She stood up and lifted her shirt. All over her belly were deep red fissures, overlapping each other like cross-stitch. Some were deeper than others and still showed pinholes where they had been sewn up. She pointed to one.

'Here's where the knife went in first. It was a kitchen knife, semi-serrated, that's why it left a big crevice like that. Then he – my ex – took it over here, here and here.'

'Oh,' I said. 'Right. Jeez, that's nasty.' Nasty? Christ.

'All up, fourteen slash wounds and two stab wounds,' she said. 'They sliced some of my organs and I was in intensive care for a while.'

'Right. Yeah.' I fumbled, shuffling my papers awkwardly as though the interview was finished, hoping she would put down her shirt so I could leave. 'Okay, well, you've got the job, congratulations,' I said quickly.

'Thanks, sweetheart. Do you want to see my back as well? There are more scars on there.'

'Oh, no, that's all right. Maybe another time.'

She tucked her shirt back in and left the room, her suit pristine again. When I got back to my desk, slightly disorientated, Agnes came by to drop off some forms.

'How did Belinda's interview go?'

'Uh, very well,' I said.

'Did she show you her scars?'

I looked up but couldn't discern any particular expression behind the frames of Agnes's glasses. 'Yeah.'

'She always shows new people,' Agnes said. 'Her therapist encourages her to be open about her experiences, but I think she also does it so that other women will feel they can talk to her if they need to.'

She gave an enigmatic smile and went back to her desk. I headed to the kitchen to make a cup of tea. The kitchen door had a sign on it saying PLEASE KEEP DOOR CLOSED, so I opened it. The familiar sounds of Bunny's guitar greeted me. Bunny, Josephine and Boris were perched around the kitchen table. They twisted their heads to stare as I entered the room.

'*Jesus is my hero,*' they sang in unison. '*He guides me on my way.*'

They kept their eyes on me, still singing, as I made my cup of tea. I rattled tins and teaspoons to annoy them, pretending they were singing Justin Bieber at their desks.

'*He's my friend and my teacher, my family, my preacher,*' they sang. '*He lights up every day.*'

Just as I took my first sip of hot, weak tea, they burst into the chorus.

'*We all love Jeeeeeeeesus!*'

I choked on my tea, splattering a mouthful into the sink, and ran out of the room. The voices followed me out, high and clear and spirited. I reached my desk and leant on it, coughing with laughter.

'What is it?' Agnes asked me as she passed.

'Nothing. I was just thinking about Justin Bieber.'

She nodded and went on.

———

'He's so hot I can't concentrate on my spreadsheets,' I complained. 'Ridiculously hot.'

Jen was furiously scrubbing a lasagne dish over the sink, her lips pressed tight, curls shuddering with the motion. She seemed less than interested in what Rueben looked like, but I continued anyway. I'd spent the last few weeks alternating between wanting to strangle the calm smile off his face and wanting to screw his brains out.

'But the bastard always finds some way to slip in a reference to your engagement party.'

Jen stopped scrubbing. 'He was at my engagement party?'

'Haven't you been listening to me? He was the slide guitarist. He plays in an alt-country band.' I sighed with longing. 'He has excellent taste in music.'

I chucked a tea towel into a cardboard box full of food Jen was giving me, a homemade chocolate cake with hazelnut-chocolate filling being the biggest score.

'So he was the one you tried to sleep with first?' Jen said.

'That's the one.'

'Huh.' Jen went back to scrubbing. 'So does this mean you've lost interest in Dan?'

I'd lined Jen up to help me get ready for Dan's ex's party, which was just over a week away. She'd promised to make me look hot. Jen knew Lisa. She'd described her as 'a sweetheart, but crazy competitive', and said if I showed up looking like a reasonable replacement it'd drive her nuts.

'Dan's more of a back-up plan,' I said. 'Maybe when I get sick of the caravan I could stay at his place for a bit.'

Jen threw the sponge into the sink and turned to me. 'So you're going to throw yourself into another relationship? Do the same thing over and over?' She stomped into the living room and picked up a neatly folded set of bedsheets, which she was also giving to me.

'Dan doesn't want a relationship,' I called to her. 'He's hung up on his ex. I just need a nice place to sleep sometimes.'

It was true. Hiding out in the caravan after a long day of work, I felt somewhat like a budgie in a vintage hipster cage. It seemed like passers-by were staring even when they weren't. I hadn't moved the caravan following the incident with the baby-faced police officer; I was just hoping that if I didn't pee in the street he would leave me alone.

Jen stomped back into the kitchen. 'Sean didn't want a relationship either, remember? You talked him out of moving in with his girlfriend and then made the move on him yourself.' She threw the sheets into the box, tipping the whole thing over with a crash, then huffed and started picking up items that had sprawled over the floor.

'What, are you angry with me?'

'No, of course not.' She dumped the box onto the table and went back to the lasagne dish. 'I just think you need to learn to live on your own.'

'Living on my own sucks. Why are you murdering that lasagne dish? Is it me?'

'No.'

'Jono?'

She was silent.

'What, is he still not using his only God-given talent?'

She wiped a detergent bubble from her cheek. 'We haven't had sex in two months. I don't know what's wrong with him. Or me. I'm sorry, I didn't mean to be mean.'

'It's wedding stress.' I couldn't think of anything else to say. 'Hey, let's go dress shopping. This Saturday, after Dan looks at Mum's floorboards. But don't invite Mum this time. Let her think that by cutting me off, she might have annoyed you.'

'I would never blame Valerie for cutting you off.'

'Do it for me.'

'Oh, fine. So Dan's looking at your mum's floorboards?' She paused, as if to ask a question, then changed her mind. 'I can't Saturday. Sunday.'

—

Not long after I started the job, I got to know one of the Angels' clients, a woman called Hannah. She was as thin as a sapling, with inky eyes and a wide, sad mouth. A fresh scar curved out from her top lip and ended halfway up her cheek. Hannah was nice in a way that people who are bluntly rude to your face can be nice. She'd take me by the shoulder and shout in my ear, 'Girl, your skirt is too short! You look like a real slut!' and then she'd shake my shoulder with her thin, warm hand and laugh as if it was a compliment. And weirdly, it did feel like a compliment, like she was letting me in on some secret with her. She'd stare at Agnes and tell her she needed to smoke less, and Agnes's eyes would tear up because of the way Hannah said it, like she actually cared. Then Hannah would bum a cigarette from Agnes and pocket the lighter. But you could just tell Hannah's heart was so big, it almost hurt to think about it. She'd wander through the door of the office some mornings and ask what we'd got in stock. There were strict rules at the Nicholson Street Angels. All donations went straight to the op shop via the granny volunteers and nobody but nobody could walk in off the street into the office next door and demand to see the wares. Not only that, but the office workers, with the exception of Agnes and Josephine, weren't supposed to interact with the clients, to protect the privacy and safety of women who were fleeing abusive relationships. However, there were rules and then there were other rules. Hannah was allowed. She'd styled herself as something of a go-between – a representative, who informed us about what was needed in the women's shelter. As a show of appreciation, we sometimes held aside a particularly warm beanie or scarf for her. She'd kiss Josephine on the cheek and tell her she was a crazy witch.

'God loves you, Hannah,' Josephine would say. 'Peace be with you.'

'Oi, you lot,' she'd reply. 'I need a new shirt.'

Hannah was the only person at work who knew that I lived in a caravan. Everyone thought I lived with 'my friend Jen', because I didn't want things to get awkward if Josephine had missed the memo about the tiny house movement and decided she was harbouring a Vulnerable. But Hannah had lived in caravans, boats, tin shacks, on couches and the street, so I didn't mind telling her. She told me about her ex-boyfriend's caravan in Darwin, which had had no wheels, and how she'd worked on a sheep station in Western Australia as the only female shearer in a crew of thirty. I asked how she'd made her way to Melbourne and she shrugged.

'Looking for my daughter,' she said.

I almost asked if she'd found her, then didn't. I didn't want her to start crying or anything. We spoke in code about my caravan so that no one would figure it out.

'How's the cara?'

Everyone thought we were both into cars, because the words 'axle', 'jack' and 'tyres' popped into the conversation a lot. That is, until Rueben and I were both in the office on Friday morning.

'Hannah tells me you live in a caravan,' he said.

I was startled. 'Hannah told you that?'

Rueben spread his hands flat over a pink file. Everywhere he went, he found a place to spread his hands, as if the fingers always needed to reach for something, as if he was trying to make his palms larger by stretching them. It was a peculiar gesture.

'Hannah tells everyone that. But no one else figured out what a cara is.'

I swallowed. I didn't like Rueben knowing my living arrangements, and I was getting really sick of his constantly inscrutable face.

'And did you, er, mention this to anyone else?'

'Nope. Why, don't you want people to know?'

'Definitely not.'

'Well, I'll keep it to myself then. Though I don't see what's wrong with living in a caravan.'

'Nothing's wrong with it,' I said defensively. 'It's just that the police officer implied I needed help.'

'Police officer?' he asked, studying a spreadsheet on his screen.

'Never mind.'

Outside the office I could hear the kitchen singers starting up. Rueben and I exchanged a glance.

'Did you hear the one on Wednesday?' I asked.

'"We All Love Jesus"? Yes.'

I was a little awkward around Rueben. Not only had he witnessed the debacle that was my first encounter with Dan, but now he'd discovered I lived in a caravan. Meanwhile, I knew next to nothing about the guy, except that he was as cunning as a fox.

'So what was it like in jail?' I asked.

'What do you think it was like?' He didn't look up from the screen.

'Parties and butt sex?'

I fiddled about with some folders, turned my desk fan on and off again, thought about updating the volunteers spreadsheet, then opened an email from Bunny.

*Please have a think about one fact that you'd like to share about yourself for a special Prayer Time soon,* it said. *We're having a getting-to-know-you session, so it should be something that most people don't know about you.*

'There you go! Did you see Bunny's email? You can tell everyone how you landed yourself in jail.'

'Mmhmm.'

'So how do you get by money-wise, since you're a volunteer?'

'Same as you. Centrelink pays me Newstart to volunteer twenty hours a week. Still, I'm looking forward to the day I never have to deal with them again.'

My suspicions rose. 'So you want a permanent job here?'

'Here, or somewhere else.'

'You've got an IT degree. Surely you could do better than fixing computers for a second-rate charity part-time.'

He eyed me, a slight smile on his face. 'You think I'm angling to get a full-time job here, and you want it. You don't believe me when I say I just want to get Centrelink off my case.'

'I've been thinking that I could use a paid job,' I admitted. 'Those Centrelink rats have given me a debt because I didn't tell them I was living with my boyfriend, but they won't tell me how much it is. I've got a bad feeling it's going to be more than I can pay back on the Newstart Allowance.'

'How did they find out you were living with your boyfriend?'

'Bastard turned me in when we broke up.'

The lids of Rueben's eyes dropped slightly and I couldn't tell if he was amused or sleepy. 'That's low. I wouldn't do that to my worst enemy. It's the people united against the tax office, that's what I think.'

'Exactly!' I waved my arms. 'He got the house, he got rid of me, he was probably already screwing Sarah Stoll before we broke up, and yet he has the gall to ruin my life.'

Rueben looked like he'd only followed half of my outburst, but I guess he got the gist of it because he rubbed the stubble on his chin and offered to hack Sean's email for me.

'You want to get back at him? Find some dirt?'

'At first I wanted to get back *with* him, now I want him to suck a cactus.'

Rueben cracked his knuckles and a little thrill ran up my spine as he gently pushed my chair to one side so he could take over my computer. The muscles on his forearms pulsed as he typed. I counted seven tattoos, mostly of birds, flowers and pinup girls.

'What's his email address?' he asked.

'Did they teach you this at uni?'

He laughed. 'Not officially, it was a by-product. I used to hack into the lecturers' emails to find out what the exams would be about.'

After a few minutes of Rueben tapping keys to no avail, I grew impatient.

'Do you actually know how to do this?'

'Not really,' he admitted. 'The university system was a pretty easy hack. I've never tried Gmail. Can you guess his password?'

I thought for a moment. 'His Netflix password is "GoHawks99", try that.'

He tapped it in. 'Works. Pretty dumb to use the same password across different accounts.'

'Sean's IQ and his shoe size are about the same. He probably uses the same password for his online banking, too. In case that's of interest to you.'

He angled the computer screen towards me, frowning as he handed over the mouse. 'What kind of dirt will you look for? You gonna go the tax evasion route as well?' he asked.

I wasn't listening. I went straight to the instant messages from Sarah. There were over a hundred, starting from six months ago.

# Chapter 11

At first they were just chatty, complaints about work peppered with smiley emoticons.

*OMG did you see this cat meme, it reminded me of our stupid new boss, he is so lame.*

*You are so funny I can't believe you said that to Cindy!*

*Did u get that email from Con, what a loser . . .* generic, hardly worth reading.

Then the flirtation began.

Sean: *I thought I saw you at the MCG Friday night.*

Sarah: *I was at a wedding in Kyneton on the weekend. Wasn't me ;)*

Sean: *I know, it was just some other gorgeous blonde chick :)*

Two weeks later, Sean wrote: *I love casual Fridays for one reason. Your sexy as hell arse in those jeans.*

Sarah: *I'm glad someone noticed. They're new – so tight I don't know if I'll be able to get them off!*

Sean: *I could help you with that ;)*

It was a punch in the gut. Sean and Sarah were clearly an

item well before I'd blown things up at The Fainting Chair. It's not like I was an angel – I'd betrayed boyfriends with one-night stands plenty of times – but I'd never had an affair. I wanted to keep reading but couldn't. My eyes were hot with tears.

Rueben had generously moved away from me and was sorting through a filing cabinet to give me some privacy while I violated Sean's. He looked up when he heard me sniffle.

'You're dwelling on the personal stuff, aren't you?'

'Of course I am,' I said, trying to stop my chin from shuddering.

'All right, stop it. Let me take over. I'll find something incriminating in no time.'

'Don't bother. I don't care anymore.' I've never told a bigger lie in my life. 'I need an egg and bacon sandwich.'

Rueben came over and rolled my chair to one side. He logged me out of Sean's email account and leant on the desk. He looked me straight in the eye but his expression was kind.

'Go and get one,' he said. 'What's next on your list of jobs to do?'

'Gotta call the volunteers and fix their rosters for next week.' I wiped my eyes.

'I'll do it,' he said. 'Just show me their files and phone numbers.'

I nodded, handed him the files, and shuffled out of the office. The corner store had a filthy black-and-white chequered vinyl floor. Greasy egg and bacon sandwiches were kept warm all day in a bain-marie, just for times like these. The bread was white and heavily buttered, the rashers of bacon generous and fatty. I bit into a sandwich and felt my troubles recede slightly. I scoffed it in about three seconds and licked my fingers while I walked back to the office, thinking that Rueben wasn't a bad guy. Just a little unnerving, the way he looked people right in the eyes.

I guess it didn't help that he was my height. I was five foot nine and if we stood nose-to-nose our eyes would meet at exactly the same level. And God, those eyes of his.

Back at the office, I was still wiping my greasy hands on my jeans when Agnes popped her head in to say she had an important job for us. She seemed slightly breathless and kept adjusting her glasses.

'There's a very wealthy donor coming in to drop off some clothes to the op shop. There's a chance she'll leave a sizeable bequest to the Angels in her will so I try to deal with her personally whenever she visits, but today I have to take my dog to the vet.'

'What would you like us to do?' Rueben asked.

'Just keep her happy. She'll probably stay a while, wanting thanks for her Yves Saint Laurent or whatever she's dropping off today.'

'She donates Yves Saint Laurent?' I said in awe. I'd never even seen a piece of Yves Saint Laurent clothing up close, unless you counted the women on my mother's street stepping out of their luxury cars. I wouldn't have even known how to pronounce it if Agnes hadn't said it out loud.

'Yves Saint Laurent, Chanel, Christian Dior. We on-sell most of it to upmarket second-hand stores because they pay more than our customers can. She probably knows that, but don't mention it.'

'What's her name?' Rueben asked.

'Delia Fitz-Hammond. Call her Mrs Fitz-Hammond. Humour her. She's a little . . .' She didn't finish her thought, instead giving Rueben a sly look. 'I suspect she'll like you, Rueben.'

Agnes hurried out. *What about me?* I huffed inwardly.

Rueben and I walked next door in silence. He looked

particularly fine in his uniform of grey T-shirt and jeans as the sunlight bounced off his stubble, the dark hairs shining slightly auburn. By focusing on the delicately lilting planes of his face I could forget the humiliation of the emails I had read earlier, and pretend the burning rage thundering through my body was not because my ex-boyfriend had made a fool of me with a girl I'd hated since I was fourteen, but was, in fact, just sexual frustration brought on by being in close proximity to the most attractive man I'd ever met who wasn't interested in me.

Delia Fitz-Hammond was standing in the centre of the op shop commanding a middle-aged man who I assumed at first was her son, but later revised the assumption to her driver. He and the shop volunteers were bringing in boxes from a black BMW outside and arranging them about her feet as she waved an imperious hand. She was small and slender, dressed in black with platinum-and-diamond bracelets, and very severe in the face. From the smooth, taut skin of her cheeks I would have put her at a well-preserved sixty, but something about the bowed thinness of her legs made me think she was probably closer to eighty. She was a tiny lightning rod.

'Mrs Fitz-Hammond?' I said, recalling my best Camberwell accent. 'I'm Maggie Cotton and this is Rueben Blackwood. Lovely to meet you.'

She held out a delicate hand and I took her fingers and gave them a microscopic shake, worried she might break if I shook harder. She seemed to like my gentleness, probably taking it as a sign of deference.

'Maggie Cotton,' she said. 'I have some wonders of the world to deliver to your little operation today.' The driver hurried to open the first box at her feet. 'Not that one!' she barked. 'The big one.'

'We so appreciate your donation, and you coming in personally to deliver it,' I began.

'Maggie,' she interrupted. 'There is a social stratum.'

'Is there?' Was she going to tell me not to speak until spoken to?

'I am going to show you something from the very top.' She drew a mass of white, shining material from the box. Not another wedding dress, I thought. I looked closer.

'Is that an Elvis jumpsuit?' Rueben asked.

Held up to the early afternoon light, the rhinestones on the white polyester glittered like stars. It was a men's size large, too big for me. Delia Fitz-Hammond caught Rueben's eye and winked.

'This jumpsuit,' she said, 'symbolises the mating dance. The man who wears it, if he is of exquisite beauty or great talent, will render the suit a tool of attraction. However, if he is a fat, slobbering drunkard, he will render the suit and himself an object of ridicule. You!' She pointed at Rueben. 'Put this on.'

'I don't think that's part of my job description,' he said.

'Rueben,' I said, 'this great lady is a very important person and a valuable donor.' Delia Fitz-Hammond liked that. 'Try it on.'

'First I want to know if I'm a man of exquisite beauty.'

'Perhaps!' said Mrs Fitz-Hammond. 'But to find that out you must try it on. It is a test.'

'Just think,' I said. 'You'll never get this opportunity again. On your deathbed, you'll look up at the pressed metal ceiling of the poorhouse and lament, "Why, O why, did I not glory in thy holy glitteriness, Sir King? Why did I pass up thy greatest of offerings, thy spangled goodness, thy—"'

'All right.' Rueben shot me a dark look. He took the jumpsuit and disappeared into a change room. I thought I heard him muttering.

*Keep her happy*, Agnes had said.

'Where did you get that magnificent outfit?' I asked.

She smiled tightly. 'In another life I was a playwright.'

'And it's from one of your plays?'

'No, it's from the night I slept with Elvis.'

I didn't know whether to believe her or not. I looked at her sideways but couldn't make out her expression. Botox will do that.

'I myself cannot wear jumpsuits,' she said, gesturing to her stomach. 'My torso is rather long and they ride up in the crotch and separate my labia into little clamshells.' She pinched her fingers together to mime the separation of her labia. An enormous emerald ring sparkled under the lights.

'Camel toe,' I said.

'Excuse me?'

'That's what it's called when you get the clam shells.'

'Ah. How fascinating.'

From the change room, Rueben's voice floated over to us. 'I think I might be too short for this jumpsuit,' he called. 'I wouldn't want to disappoint you.'

'Come out, come out!' Mrs Fitz-Hammond shouted. She turned to me. 'I never waste time with men who refuse to lay bare their weaknesses in the name of art. The only truth is the raw truth, the truth that hurts, the truth that exposes our short legs.'

Suddenly she bounded over to the racks of clothing in the op shop, her spindly legs making her look like a young deer.

'Here's a jumpsuit for you,' she said, holding out a pair of 1990s sunflower-print denim overalls to me.

'I tend not to wear jumpsuits either,' I said. It was a lie. I loved jumpsuits – it was the childish sunflowers that deterred me. 'Bum's too big,' I explained.

'Big bums are a gift from Creation.'

'I tried to make mine smaller. Critical ex-boyfriend.'

'Never prune yourself to fit someone else's stunted notions of beauty,' she said. I took the sunflowers but didn't make any move to try them on. I was anticipating Rueben's emergence as a rhinestoney butterfly.

He didn't disappoint. The change room door was flung open and he stepped out, magnificent in the glittering white, slightly baggy jumpsuit, his shoulders held proudly back. The legs of the jumpsuit had been rolled up a couple of times. He'd slicked his hair back like Elvis's, and the resemblance, while not uncanny, was adequate.

Mrs Fitz-Hammond and I applauded.

'Bravo, bravo!'

Now will you hand over the Yves Saint Laurent? I wondered. I noticed the volunteers' hungry eyes on the boxes around us and realised I'd better sort through the donations myself to make sure nothing went missing.

'Stay like that, it suits you,' she told Rueben. 'It is time for me to leave.' She waggled a painted fingernail at me. 'I like you, Maggie Cotton.' She ferreted around in her Louis Vuitton handbag and drew out a small cream card, embossed with gold writing. 'Here's my address. When I die, come to my house and take my Chanel suits before my daughter pawns them for blow.' She blew Rueben a kiss as she left, her driver trailing after her.

I sent the op shop grannies on their break so Rueben and I could sort through the boxes. They left, grumbling, annoyed at missing the unveiling of Mrs Fitz-Hammond's donations. Rueben and I were alone.

'Aren't you going to put that on?' Rueben asked, nodding at the sunflowers in my hand.

'No, she just picked it out for me.'

'Oh, so I'm the only one who has to embarrass himself? Try it on.'

'All right, but brace yourself.' In the change room, I wriggled out of my jeans and into the sunflower overalls. I left my T-shirt on underneath to complete the preschooler look. Craning my neck in the mirror, I saw that the biggest sunflower luxuriated exactly over the spot where the sun didn't shine.

I burst out of the change room and did a twirl, wiggling the lewd buttflower ostentatiously. 'So,' I said as Rueben/Elvis clapped. 'Tell me again why you knocked me back that time?'

'What time?' he said, and I couldn't tell if he was trying to get a rise out of me or if women threw themselves at him in bars so often he genuinely couldn't recall one encounter from another.

'You know.' I shimmied over to baggy Elvis. 'At The Fainting Chair. How come you weren't up for a bit of vertical sexy times in the bathroom? Not that I want it now, I'm just curious.'

'Let's see what Mrs Fritz-Hambone has donated,' he said. He reached around me to pick a red spangled dress out of the big box the Elvis suit had come in. 'Nice. Very *Showgirls*.'

I opened another box and found a small, polished mandolin. Rueben plucked a string and a high, fearless note rang out.

'I think this is cherrywood,' he said. 'Beautiful.'

I couldn't concentrate on his words because his arm had gently brushed mine, making me shiver. Christ. My face must have broadcasted the mixture of alarm and longing I felt, because he half-smiled.

'It's just not my thing,' he said finally.

'What?'

He leant closer until I could feel the warmth of his breath on my cheeks.

'Oh,' I said. 'You mean sex isn't your thing?'

'I think I've found your Yves Saint Laurent,' he said. He even pronounced it correctly, the way Agnes had. It was a cream woollen dress, long and finely woven with black piping at the collar and cuffs. Beautiful. The upmarket second-hand shops could probably get five hundred dollars for it, meaning two-fifty for the Angels. He held the dress up against me, easing me gently against the wall of the change rooms. The cold bricks pressed into my back and Rueben's warm, hard body pressed into my thighs and belly. My breath left me and I willed him to kiss me as his lips came close to mine. One curl of black hair hung over his eye, resting against dark eyelashes.

'I didn't want to have "vertical sexy times", as you put it,' he said, 'that time at The Fainting Chair because I don't like getting intimate in bathrooms. They smell like cleaning products.'

'Makes sense,' I managed to say.

All I needed was a kiss; one kiss and I could forget the humiliating emails, the obscene sunflowers, hell, one kiss and I could forget my own name.

The sound of the door handle turning made us both jump. Rueben took a quick step back just in time as Agnes popped her head in.

'Oh look, it's Sunny the Clown and Elvis. Aren't you a handsome hound dog,' she said to Rueben.

Rueben and I stood awkwardly, waiting to be reprimanded for slacking off.

'I see Mrs Fitz-Hammond has got you trying on the wares, as

usual. I must say, it's nice not to be the one forced into a span-gled dress.'

So *that's* why Agnes took off for the vet. She probably didn't even have a dog. She winked at Rueben and dropped a box on the floor, turning to me. 'Someone just dropped these off at the office. Antique books, I think. Price them, Priscilla.'

—

That night, my mind shifted in a million different directions. Thoughts of Rueben and the heat of his lips muddled with span-gles and black-clad rich grannies. Dan and the mysterious ex whose engagement party I would be crashing. Sean, Sarah and denim sunflower overalls. Rueben again, and his long eyelashes. The only thought I could grab hold of for long before it skittered away again was the one that took root in my mind, squirrelling down to the dark, angry place where I nursed my grudges: that it might have been Sarah who orchestrated the Centrelink tip-off.

# Chapter 12

Mum is like those Dawson's bees in the desert. The male bees fight each other to the death to fuck the females, killing a few ladies accidentally in the process. After the mating frenzy is over, not a single male is left alive. My mother was like one of those male bees, only hers was a long, drawn-out frenzy of reproduction as she slowly exhausted herself raising my brother and me. What would she have left to show for herself when she died? Two inferior copies that at no point in their lives did what she expected.

The months after my dad left were the worst. Mum was as edgy as a cut snake and twice as venomous. She'd curl up on the couch in her dirty bathrobe after the chores were done for the night and cry silently, covering her face so Harry and I couldn't see. That only made it worse, because we couldn't approach to comfort her if we were not supposed to see she was crying. Once I made the error of hugging her anyway. All she did was press her face into the couch cushion and push me away with one hand. Her nails were long and sharp and left deep impressions in my upper arm. I never tried to comfort her again.

My brother had better luck, though he still wasn't allowed to hug her. Harry is eighteen months younger than I am, and Mum's favourite. Back then, he had Dad's thick ginger hair and button nose, and thin teenage shoulders. He used to hang off doorframes in the house like a monkey until one day he accidentally ripped off an Art Deco ledge in the kitchen. Anyway, Mum let Harry squeeze her shoulder from time to time when she was crying on the couch, but that was it.

The only creature that could hug her was our old cat, Zelda. Zelda was a tabby with a white moustache, an enormous bum and a purr like a truck engine. She'd curl up around Mum and nibble on her ear. Sometimes she tickled Mum's ear so much she even got a laugh out of her. I'd frequently find Harry and Mum huddled together at the kitchen window, feeding Zelda treats, patting her and saying, 'I love you, I love you, Zelda,' over and over again. It was the saddest day in the world when Zelda died four years later. Mum howled with grief when we buried her in the backyard. I think it was the first time in the history of our family that we could acknowledge how sad we all were. The cat was the only person none of us were embarrassed to love.

—

The old wrought-iron gate hung off its hinges. The rusted intercom no longer buzzed and the security-warning sticker was just for show. Many of the larger houses in Camberwell had security cameras and panic buttons that buzzed the local police station directly when there was an intruder. Mum's house had a shitty alarm that hadn't worked in years, and a nice little sticker pretending it did.

I was still on the footpath staring at the gate when Dan showed up in his work shorts with tool belt attached.

'I'm warning you. Mum can be temperamental.'

'Don't worry. Mothers love me.' He pushed on the gate.

'Not that way! Pull.'

Too late. At Dan's push, the remaining hinge creaked and snapped and the gate crashed to the ground. The noise brought a neighbour across the street shuffling out to watch. The broken gate lay on the ground like a dead bird.

'That wasn't a good start,' Dan said.

'Can you fix it?'

'It might need to be welded.' With a heave, he picked up the gate and leant it against the column. 'Sorry.'

'Not my gate. Let's go in.'

Mum had put on her best jeans to meet Dan, and had evidently blow-dried her hair. She opened the door before we had a chance to knock, looked at the gate and then from Dan to me.

'It just fell off all by itself,' I said.

Dan cleared his throat. 'I'm sorry, Mrs Cotton, I pushed on the gate instead of pulling it open.'

I stared at him. Why own up to it?

Mum's cloudy expression cleared. 'Well, that's all right. It was crumbling already. Dan, is it?'

Jesus Christ. If I had owned up to smashing her front gate, Mum would have thrown the garden rake at me. Dan confesses and she tells him it's all right? They shook hands, Mum beaming, and she ushered him inside. I followed, feeling like a third wheel.

'Watch the hall,' she said. 'It's nearly rotted out. I took up some of the carpet. Would you like a cup of tea, Dan?'

'Jeez, Mum, you should put danger signs around that.' A tear in the sagging carpet gave way to eerie darkness through which no floorboards could be seen. Like a sinkhole to suck you into an eternal Camberwell hell of tea and crumpets and botox.

Dan declined the offer of tea, saying he'd better just get to checking out the floors, and would she like him to look at the rest of the house as well?

'I used to work for a company that does a lot of renovations of old houses,' he said. 'I'm qualified to do building inspections.'

'Wonderful!' Mum gushed. 'And you must stay for dinner.'

I pulled Mum aside. 'What are you doing?'

'He's nice. Not as handsome as Sean, but still handsome.'

'Mum, I'm not dating him.'

'Why not?' she hissed. 'Is he gay?'

I poked my head into the hall to make sure Dan was out of earshot. He was pulling up more carpet around the sinkhole.

'He's hung up on his ex. And we don't . . . click.'

'Just because the sex isn't there right away doesn't mean it's not worth pursuing.' Gross. As if my mother was allowed to talk about sex.

'Don't be filthy, Mum.'

'I know what you're like. You place too much importance on sex. It goes, you know. The sex goes, and then you'd just better hope you're good friends with the man, because that's all that's left.'

'God, I hope Dan can wrap this up quickly. This is inhuman.'

'You should shave your legs,' she whispered, looking at the hairy pins sticking out of my skirt. 'You're going to seed.'

With my mother and me, there was no clear line between affection and insult.

A muffled groan shut us up. Mum and I trotted down the hall and poked our heads into the living room. Dan had pulled up the entire carpet and was staring in abject horror at what used to be floorboards beneath.

'Is it termites, or just rot?' I asked. The carpet had smelt mouldy for as long as I could remember.

'Looks like both. Have you had water damage recently?'

'The roof's been leaking for ten years,' I informed him.

Mum sniffed. 'Don't exaggerate, Maggie.'

'Eight years.'

He looked up at the ceiling. It was stained brown in places, and peeling.

'Okay,' he said. 'Any other rooms I should be looking at?'

'All of them,' Mum and I said together.

Mum followed him into the dining room while I took the opportunity to sneak next door into my old bedroom to bundle up some clothes into a duffel bag.

'I like men with tools,' I heard Mum say to Dan. I caught a hint of longing in her voice.

'I like tools with balls,' I called, but they didn't hear me.

'What's that you've got?' Mum asked. I moved to the doorway to hear better.

'It's a lenker rod,' Dan replied.

'A wanker rod?' This time they heard me.

'Maggie, go and put the chicken on,' Mum snapped.

I obeyed, dropping the duffel bag in the hallway. In the kitchen, I turned on the gas to heat the pot of Moroccan chicken, one of two dishes Mum always cooked.

'How's your new job going?' Mum had followed me in. She leant against the tiled wall.

'Fine.'

'Does this mean you'll be moving into an actual abode, instead of living in a caravan like a homeless gypsy?'

'Mum, gypsies aren't homeless. They deliberately move around, it's not the same thing. Besides, it's not a crime to be homeless.'

'Actually, I think you'll find there is a law against being itin-erant.' She took the spoon out of my hand and stirred the pot. 'It's called vagrancy.'

'I think you'll find the law's a dick.'

She slammed her hand onto the kitchen bench. 'Young lady! You can't come here and eat my food if you're going to talk like that.' Her hair was so neatly tucked behind her ears she looked like a schoolgirl.

'Come off it, Mum. You're being a dick, too. And no, I'm not moving into an "abode". My caravan is a perfectly legitimate dwelling.'

Mum raised her palms and looked to the ceiling as if to supplicate God. 'I've raised a daughter who calls me a penis,' she told the peeling plaster. She dropped her chin to look me in the eye. 'Why do you always talk about penises? What did I do wrong?'

'Nothing.' I lifted the wooden spoon to my mouth to taste the sauce. It was salty. 'The chicken's good.'

The sound of Dan's footsteps made us go quiet, even though we weren't talking about anything particularly secret. Maybe both of us wanted him to think we were a normal mother and daughter. He stuck his head through the doorway, face flushed.

'Mrs Cotton? Could I talk to you for a moment?'

'Of course, Dan.' She smoothed her hair and joined him in the hall.

My suspicions were instantly raised. I waited half a minute and then followed them out as quietly as I could. The floorboards creaked and the laundry door banged in its familiar way. I snuck through the sunroom and pressed my ear to the cold plaster to listen in. Dan's voice was low and muffled.

'. . . if you'd prefer I didn't,' I heard him say.

'Yes, best not. Maggie's not the sort of person who . . .' Mum's voice dropped, and I couldn't make out the rest.

Not the sort of person who what? I leant against the wall, arms folded, so they'd know I'd been listening when they came out. Mum looked a little pale and glum, but Dan just seemed embarrassed. He couldn't meet my eyes as he put his tools away in their box and adjusted his tool belt. He brushed a hand through the sandy scruff on his head and cleared his throat.

'Well, I'll be off, Mrs Cotton.'

Mum looked like she'd hardly heard him but automatically said, 'Stay for dinner.'

'Nah, I'd better be going. See you soon, Maggie,' he said to me.

After I shut the door behind him I turned to Mum. 'What, was he asking your permission to date me?'

Mum eyed me as if I was mental. 'Date you? Why the hell would he want to date you?' She shook her head and shuffled into the kitchen, shoulders slumped.

He definitely likes me, I thought. 'If you warned him off me, you've lost your marbles.'

'You need to stop drinking,' she called back. 'It's making your skin dry and your ego swell.'

Time to go home. I grabbed the bag of clothes and made for the door. Mum heard me walking down the hall and poked her head after me.

'What, aren't you staying for dinner?'

I stopped to consider the offer. Sit through her meddling in exchange for a hot meal or eat cold sandwiches in the caravan?

'Nah, I gotta go.'

'Fine, go. And take your mail with you.' She opened a drawer and took out what looked like six months of letters. 'When I was your age I was married with two children,' she called out, as I stepped around the broken gate.

'Yeah, and look how well that turned out,' I shouted back.

The ways a mother can harass her daughter are limitless. The ways a daughter can disappoint her mother are pretty cosmic as well.

—

Back home, I lay on the vinyl, kicked off my shoes and opened an envelope with a colourful Centrelink logo on the front. I unfolded the letter within.

They'd looked into my file. On top of not declaring my living arrangements for the past year, I'd apparently been receiving student payments entirely by mistake.

What?

I read the letter again. Input error. I read it and reread it, the words blurring with shock. You're supposed to complete a Bachelor of Commerce degree in three years. After that, the student payments are meant to stop, but mine hadn't. Administration oversight. I'd been unfairly receiving payments for seven years.

They were clawing back every dollar.

Seven years.

Ten grand a year.

I felt myself slipping down a rabbit hole, rank and dark, and reached for the nearest bottle of wine. It was empty. I lit a candle and held the letter above the flame until it caught, then dropped it in the sink to burn out. Could I just leave town? I had a caravan and no fixed address, who would find me in Darwin or Perth or Byron Bay and force me to pay back a debt? But no, that was no kind of life. Centrelink and the ATO always catch up with you. Besides, I couldn't leave Jen to deal with her wedding on her own. Rueben's face rose in my mind and I tried to push it back out again, because the little shiver that ran through me when I thought of leaving and never seeing Rueben again was somewhat frightening, and very surprising.

# Chapter 13

Sunday morning was ugly. The numbers in the Centrelink letter kept going around like a spinning roulette table. I couldn't even say it out loud to myself. How was anyone supposed to pay that back? My hands flailed about, as if to push the numbers away from my face. Denial was always the answer. A bottle of wine had washed down my cold, dry dinner sandwich the night before and left me with a screaming headache and the vague notion that I was supposed to go dress shopping with Jen.

It's best not to disappoint your closest friend within twenty-four hours of disappointing your mother, so I let myself in through the back of Jen's house, took a shower and dressed in the cleanest clothes I had, which was a polyester 1970s maxi dress in a print that would make the most flamboyant Pucci-lover's eyes water, and nothing else. The caravan wardrobe was filled with dirty underwear and even my bras were turning grey at the underwire from old sweat. I couldn't borrow one of Jen's bras because she was a double-D cup while I was a not-quite-C, and she was funny about lending undies. She'd lent me a pair or two over the years and never wanted them back even when I assured her I had washed them in scalding water.

So I'd be trying on bridesmaid dresses starkers. I just hoped that none of them were made of sheer silk.

Jen was in a low mood again. She shuffled out of her bedroom when she heard me get out of the shower, nodded in greeting and put the coffee on without saying anything.

'Ready to find a dress?' I tried to sound as cheerful as I could, but Jen appeared not to hear me. Christ, I never knew how much Jen's happiness relied on getting laid. At least, I assumed that was the problem. Jono's reasons for withholding sex were opaque, but it was just one more reason to hate him.

She poured the coffee and silently offered me a croissant. I took one.

'You want me to warm it up?' Her voice was rusty.

'Nah, it's fine like this.'

After I finished my croissant she wiped up the crumbs on the table.

'My mother's really angry'—she shook the crumbs into the bin—'about the dress.'

'What dress?'

She looked at me, deadpan.

'Oh, you mean her wedding dress? The one . . . ?'

'Yeah, that one.'

I opened my mouth to remind her that she hadn't minded too much about that, but saw the bags under her eyes and closed it again.

'Well, if it makes you feel better, my own mother's angry with me too,' I said, 'because I haven't shaved my legs.'

She pulled me into a tight hug. 'If my mother disowns me can I come live in your caravan?'

'Of course. We'll be a stationary Thelma and Louise.'

The bridal 'shoppe' on Glenferrie Road contained racks and racks of white, off-white, super-white and champagne-coloured dresses, all of which were hideous and none of which cost less than four thousand dollars. Jen tried on six and looked all right in most of them, but had it been my wedding, I would have rather worn my polyester fright than spend the equivalent of a trip to Europe on a generic dress I'd never wear again. However, I was slowly learning the value of keeping my opinions to myself. For five minutes, at least.

The change room had a French provincial theme. I was perched on the edge of a gold Louis XIV-style chair in the corner, while Jen stood before the mirror in a coffee-coloured lace tube dress with a slight fishtail. The overall effect was a little top-heavy, as her breasts spilled over the sweetheart neckline in an obscene show of cleavage. She looked amazing. Her face was flushed rosy pink and her hair was dishevelled from lifting dress after dress over her head and back off again. She turned carefully away from me, inspecting her backside in the mirror, as she asked, 'So Dan looked at your mother's floorboards?'

'Yeah. This dress is good, Jen.' I tugged on the train and checked the price tag. 'Four thousand six hundred. Still ridiculous, but one of the cheapest in here.'

'Did he say anything?' Jen asked.

'What?'

'I mean, is there anything going on with you and Dan?'

I shrugged. 'He didn't say anything to me, but he said something weird to my mum. Can't remember exactly what, but I think he was telling her he likes me.'

The shop assistant rattled the change room door before flinging it open, gasping at the sight of Jen's lace-clad figure with faux amazement that matched the faux French-provincial decor.

'It's bea-you-tiful,' she said. She tucked her hands into the sides of Jen's bosom to adjust the dress in a too-familiar way that would have made me slap her wriggling fingers away, but Jen allowed it. 'Stunning. This one is the last one of this cut in the shop, the display dress, so it's fifteen per cent off.'

'There you go, Jen. How about you get this one?'

'I have to think about it.' The shop assistant pressed her lips together at the doubt in Jen's expression and melted away again, saying she would come back with some more options. Jen's frown made me remember Jono, and that I shouldn't be pressing her to buy a dress since I didn't want her to marry the bastard. If I hadn't been so busy with my own problems I would have been more occupied with making Jen see the light before she married him and had millions of children.

Children. That was the heart of the problem. Children are an insidious evil in society. They inflict their selfish desires on innocent adults who only want to sleep in until nine in the morning and watch Netflix at night. Children corrupt free-thinking individuals and turn them into office slaves who fret about their mortgages and the chemicals in plastic milk bottles. Jen was really excited about having children. She didn't seem to understand the risks; she was not only excited, she was anxious to have them. She regularly mentioned that she was about to turn thirty and that she always thought she'd have her first child at twenty-eight. If I somehow managed to separate Jen and Jono, I'd have to find her a replacement man fast, and a clucky one at that.

The assistant slipped back into the change room with six more dresses, full-skirted white horrors encrusted with oil-slick shiny beads and tacky sequins.

'Just give me one minute and I'll be back to help you button up,' the assistant said, as she hung the frightful things on the hooks. 'I'll just go and find the matching lace straps for the one you've got on.'

Gah. Matching lace straps. Wedding dress shopping was the actual worst, but as yet I had no way to end it that didn't involve Jen purchasing a dress. I had to think fast.

'So what are you going to do about the sex problem you and Jono are having? Maybe you need pre-marital counselling,' I suggested.

Jen whipped her head around to peer through the gap in the change room door, checking if anyone had heard. 'Jono says he's just been tired lately.'

'You could buy a vibrator. Or you could, you know, not marry him.'

Jen turned red, clashing horribly with the coffee-coloured lace. I suppose I shouldn't have said that while she was trying on wedding dresses. But when your best friend is about to marry a donkey-brained loser you are obligated to go nuclear. I thought she was going to get angry at me, but instead she fiddled with her train.

'Do you think this is nylon lace, or polyester? I'd better ask the assistant.' It was a favourite trick of hers, to hide her anxiety by pretending to be busy.

'Is one preferable?'

'I need to call my mother,' she said.

'What?'

'And my sister. I can't decide on a dress and I don't trust you to be honest.'

'You mean you trust me to be honest but you don't trust my taste.'

'You'd send me down the aisle in a minidress and boots.'

'You'd look adorable!' I insisted. 'And I only suggested that once, after I saw the price tags.'

'It's okay,' she said in a soothing tone. 'You go get coffees and I'll dial up Spain and maybe Abu Dhabi to speak to my sister, too. I'll do a video call.'

She was trying to boot me out of the bridal shoppe, and I was glad to go. I ran down Glenferrie Road with the wind whipping into my face to find a cafe. While the barista filled the order I stared at the brown-brick feature wall behind her, and the hissing of the coffee machine lulled me into a passive state, enough to let the careful veneer of denial fall away. Words from the Centrelink letter came roaring back to me and I almost doubled over, clutching my stomach as the stabbing pain of panic hit.

'Are you okay?' the barista asked.

'Fine,' I gasped. 'Indigestion.' I took the coffees with shaking hands and, once outside, took a minute to gather my breath. No need to burden Jen with my problems.

My coffee run was pointless, though, because as soon as I returned, the shoppe assistant practically assaulted me trying to get the cups out of my hand.

'No food or drinks in the shoppe!' she hissed.

Jen looked exhausted and listless. She was on a conference video call with her mother and the sister in Abu Dhabi, holding the phone up to the mirror so they could see the fishtail wonder.

'It's too caramel,' I heard her mother say. 'It's draining all the colour from your face. It will just show up brown in the photos, too.'

'There are others,' Jen said.

'Try them on for us.'

Jen rested her phone on the ledge in the change room and presented her back to me to help her unzip.

'Hi, Mrs Basso,' I said. 'Hi, Camille.'

'Hello, Maggie,' they chorused. Neither looked or sounded happy at my presence. I did destroy the family heirloom wedding dress, I remembered. Oh, and there was that time I threw up a stomachful of pineapple margaritas into Camille's closet. In the dark the sweater shelf had felt a little like the bathroom sink. She had plenty of nine-hundred-dollar cashmere sweaters, though, and I only ruined two.

Jen tried on two more dresses before she found The One. It was pure white, not a sequin or bead in sight, with a bell skirt, nipped-in waist and slender shoulder straps. In my opinion it made her look like a *Vogue* princess, and by the look on her face, Jen agreed. The problem was that it cost seven thousand dollars. Actually, that wouldn't have been a problem if her mother had liked the dress. Her mother would have paid far more than that for something slinky and bead-encrusted with short sleeves, like the stick-thin models on the runway wear. But it was a traditional white dress with a bell skirt and Mrs Basso said it was unflattering, 'considering' Jen's bosom. That was the word she used, *unflattering*, a euphemism for 'it makes you look fat'. But instead of insisting that her daughter choose a slinkier dress, which Mrs Basso desperately wanted to do but knew was against the rules, she complained about the price of the bell-skirted dress.

'Seven thousand dollars,' she said. 'It's so much. And you didn't even have your engagement party at the Melbourne Club, so why do you want such an expensive dress?'

'It's exactly what I want,' Jen murmured, turning this way and that, a flush filling her cheeks.

'I could help pay for it if you don't want to, Mrs Basso,' I lied. I was in a sparkly red dress that I'd found on the discount rack. It had a low-cut neck and fringing at the thigh and it was backless, a beautifully slutty number.

'*You* could help?' Mrs Basso spat. 'You destroyed my grand-mother's dress.'

'I know,' I said. 'And that's why I'd help pay for it. Did Jen tell you about my new career?' I shook my fringing and hiked up my boobs for the benefit of the video callers.

'Yeah,' Jen said. 'Maggie's absolutely brilliant, Mum. She's killing it on the pole in St Kilda. Five hundred dollars an hour.'

'It's called exotic dancing now,' I said. 'But it's pretty much the same thing. Hey, do you like this dress, Camille? I'm thinking it's perfect for the bridesmaids. You and Freesia will look great in it, and it's thirty per cent off.'

Jen's sister made a noise that sounded like she was choking.

'Ooh, I really like it,' said Jen. 'Camille, the red will show off your tan so well.'

'You are not wearing that down the aisle!' Mrs Basso screeched at her oldest daughter.

'Mum, you don't have to tell me,' Camille's tinny voice piped up. 'Maggie's crazy.'

'Oh, you don't like it?' Jen said. 'I like it. So festive! The wedding is close to Christmas, so it makes sense to wear red.'

Mrs Basso was turning purple. 'Do not put my daughters in that.'

Jen sighed, as if to say, *Please, Mummy*. 'What if I wear a slinky dress instead? It would go better with the red bridesmaid dresses, I think. The beading and all that.'

'Wear the bell-skirt if you like,' Mrs Basso shrieked. 'I'll pay for it. But I'll have nothing to do with you if you make Camille look like a prostitute. Her husband works at the Abu Dhabi Investment Authority. If someone at his work sees a picture of her in that, she'll get arrested and he'll get sacked. He's on four hundred thousand!'

'Okay, fine.' Jen sighed dramatically. 'Go try on the navy shift, Maggie. That one will work nicely with the bell-skirt.'

The day was a great success. The navy-blue bridesmaid dresses we eventually ordered were stunning, despite the fact they were sensible shifts, with long French-cuffed sleeves in transparent silk, and Jen was practically crying with happiness over her own dress.

'If we put your hair in a chignon you'll look like a French socialite in the navy dress,' Jen said. She sounded pleased with herself, so I guessed it was a compliment.

'I just can't believe how many of those dresses were more hideous than your great-grandmother's gown,' I said.

Jen dropped me back at my caravan. She stared at one of the tyres, which was looking flat.

'By the way, I'm coming to Lisa's party,' she said.

I looked blankly at her.

'Dan's ex, she invited me to her engagement party too,' she clarified.

Something in her voice made me pause. 'Lisa . . . I thought you were better friends with Dan than Lisa.'

'Mmm.' She got out her phone. 'Remember how I said she was competitive?'

'Yeah. So?'

'She heard you were coming to the party with Dan.'

The text message from Lisa on Jen's phone was chirpy. *Hey hon, I heard your friend Maggie is coming with Dan to my engagement party. Just thought I'd say, you should totally come too! I'd luv to see you. Have been missing you guys. Xx Lisa*

'"Have been missing you guys" . . . who does she mean?'

Jen shrugged. 'The friendship group, I guess. Although, I've only met her three times, so I doubt it's me she's missing.'

'She means it's been too long since she got her erotic kicks out of seeing Dan publicly mourn their relationship. Probably. Tell me again why I'd never met Dan before your engagement party?'

'Because you ignore Biyu's texts to hang out with her boyfriend's friends and you refuse to go to barbecues.'

'Barbecues are God's punishment for inventing single-use plastics. Well . . . great. We can go together.'

She hugged me. 'Thanks for today. You really came through for me with my mum and sister.'

'They didn't seem very surprised to hear that I've become a stripper.'

'It's good to meet people's expectations,' Jen said.

I hopped out of the car and walked towards my caravan as, a few metres away, Jen's roller door slid up. She wound down the car window and leant out as she eased the car into her backyard. Her golden hair shone in the sun.

'And, um, by the way,' she called out. 'Sean's coming to the party too. And he's bringing Sarah. So you might have been right about those two.' She made a sympathetic face.

Red blazed across my vision. I kicked the caravan as hard as I could and a dull thud rang out.

'Fuck!'

My foot hurt.

# Chapter 14

I walked to work in the cool morning, wondering how things would be between Rueben and me. I hadn't seen him since we got up close in the op shop and Agnes had interrupted us. So naturally I entered the office singing Springsteen at the top of my lungs and air-guitaring the 'Ghost of Tom Joad' solo while balancing a takeaway coffee on top of my satchel. Rueben had his back to me when I walked in, but joined in singing in his throaty rasp. He had a good voice, which shouldn't have been surprising since his speaking voice was so sexy.

'How typical,' I said, after we'd finished shouting about freedom and Mom and highways. 'I bet you like Springsteen because his songs make people relate to criminals.' I sat at my computer and opened up my personal email account and a game of solitaire.

'Springsteen will make you relate to anyone,' Rueben said. 'Criminals, honest people and everyone in between.'

'But especially criminals.'

'Criminals are eminently relatable.'

'You'd know.'

He stretched his delicious arms over his head and shot me a penetrating look from those lily-pad eyes. 'The problem with criminals is a lot of them are good people. Some are better people than the supposedly honest ones.'

'Like me?'

'Look at you, stuffing around, taking money from Centrelink in the name of doing charity work, and instead of working for your pay you're snooping in your ex-boyfriend's emails and playing solitaire. I'm far more honest than you.'

I yawned and closed my solitaire game. 'Everybody loves to point out my hypocrisy. They do it all the time. But *you're* the one who suggested I hack his Gmail. I was just doing it to please you.'

'You're a martyr.'

'I am. You should be thanking me for making you feel better about yourself.' I stretched back over my chair. 'You know what my favourite word is? Milquetoast. I often catch myself muttering it on the tram while people try not to watch me. It means "a timid or submissive person", which obviously describes me.'

He laughed. So this is how it's going to be, I thought. No mention of the close encounter in the clown suits.

'I won't be taking money from Centrelink much longer, anyway,' I told him. 'They'll be taking it from me. Turns out my debt is . . . big.' I rolled my eyes.

He swivelled in his chair to face me, frowning. 'How big?'

I muttered a number.

'Seven grand?' he asked.

'Ahem . . . venty.'

'*Seventy?*'

'Yeah.'

'That's insane.'

I shrugged. 'Seven years of wrong payments.'

'Have you got a payment plan worked out?'

'Nah.'

'Get one worked out. They won't let it go.'

'Yeah, all right. Just one more thing I can boast about to my old school mates at the engagement party I'm going to this weekend. "I've got this great payment plan going with Centrelink so I don't get charged with fraud! Huzzah!"'

'Do they know you live in a caravan?'

'No, thank Blob. But maybe I should take a normal, strapping young man like yourself to the party, to appear well-adjusted.'

'I wouldn't want to make your friends fall over with jealousy,' he said. 'And I really don't like engagement parties.'

'I wasn't really asking you,' I said quickly. 'I'm already going as someone's pretend girlfriend and I think there'll be enough judgement without me turning up with an ex-con on the other arm at my pretend-boyfriend's ex-girlfriend's engagement party.'

'Well.' He turned back to his spreadsheet. 'You *do* worry about what people think, Maggie.'

'I'm a nice middle-class girl. I went to a private school. Worrying about what people think was what I ate for breakfast for eighteen years.'

I went back to my solitaire game, but I was secretly mortified that Rueben had brushed aside the hints I'd dropped about asking me on a date.

—

On the afternoon of the engagement party, Jen and I sat in her backyard letting the last rays of sun warm us through. Jen made some kind of quinoa salad with fancy leaf lettuce, while I put some hummus in a bowl and, while cutting up cucumber sticks, wondered if she was getting sick of me messing up her house.

She'd been so quiet over the last few days I wasn't sure she'd noticed the extra dishes I'd been piling up in her sink.

Jono was due back in Melbourne any minute and was coming to the party.

'You're not going to pick him up?' I asked.

'I have to get ready for the party. He's meeting us there.'

This was out of character. Normally Jen dropped everything to meet Jono at the airport. Halfway through dinner she put down her bowl, slipped her old mustard-coloured gardening gloves on and began pulling out weeds and throwing them on the compost pile. Weeding the garden was a sure sign that Jen was trying to make a decision about something. I didn't ask what she was thinking. Asking personal questions was immensely difficult, even of the people I loved. I could talk about myself all day, but asking my best friend what she was thinking about seemed like a terrible intrusion.

'Your tomatoes could probably go in now,' I said.

'Mmm.'

Jen ripped up some grass in a frankly vicious manner, her upper arms wobbling gently with the action. Abruptly, she paused and looked up at me.

'If Jono doesn't have sex with me this week, I'm . . .'

I held my breath.

She looked at the grass in her hand. 'I'm going to tell him I'm not happy,' she finished.

I breathed out. 'Not happy with the relationship? Or not happy about the lack of sex?'

She thought for a moment. 'The lack of sex.'

'Maybe you should just leave him.'

Her eyes took on the vague expression they always did when I made that suggestion and she didn't answer, but I decided not to let it go this time. The wedding was so close, and Jen's entire future was at stake. It was crucial to choose my words carefully.

'Seriously . . . are you sure he's the right person for you?'

She went back to pulling up grass, her head ducked low so I couldn't see her face. 'He's the man of my dreams.'

Was that irony in her voice? Or did she really say that in earnest?

'There are a lot of women who come through the shelter at my work who thought they'd met the man of their dreams, too.' Not that I'd met any except Hannah. Jen didn't need to know that, though.

'What are you saying? You think Jono's an abuser? Maggie, that's gross.'

'No, no. Of course not. Just that sometimes you meet a guy and think he's perfect and then six years later you realise . . . he's a butt. It's hard to see clearly when you're in love.'

'How would you know? You've never been in love.'

That shut me up. Jen took off her gloves, went inside to wash her hands and then came back out to finish her dinner.

'I'm gonna curl your hair tonight.' She chewed her quinoa, deliberating. 'Not super curly, just wavy, like an old film star. Lisa will be so jealous. Not that I don't like Lisa, she's super nice. But we have to help Dan out, don't we?'

Jen finished her meal with a slight frown on her face. It wasn't clear if she was thinking about Jono, or Dan, or my soon-to-be-film-star hair.

'Poor sod,' she said. 'He really loved Lisa.'

So that was it. 'Yeah, he said so at dinner one time.' I hardly listened to anything else she said after that. I had already started planning what dress to borrow from her.

—

Jen steered me into the correct wine shop, where among the racks of hipster brand labels she picked out a cult pinot noir from the Adelaide Hills that I could give to the happy couple as an engagement present. It was a small-run, hand-pressed wine, expensive for me but not out of reach for a divorce lawyer who knew his arse from his elbow. It was the sort of wine that said something about the purchaser, something like *I have money but I also have taste*. I made a mental note to get Dan to pay me back for it, because I couldn't afford to go around buying wine for strangers I probably wouldn't like.

Jen had also done wonders with my hair. Somehow she'd poured it into long, gentle waves, the kind you saw on models and wished you could replicate but always ended up looking like Kim Kardashian after a trip to the electric chair. She'd also done something sexual to my eyes with charcoal eyeshadow. I looked hot. My recent diet of wine and whatever food I could steal from Jen was working a treat. My butt was nicely rounded without being overpowering and I'd lost a small amount of weight. I felt pretty good as long as I could forget that the weight loss had come about from a lack of money rather than any actual effort on my part. I'd scrambled myself into a tight velvet dress that made my boobs look good and hugged my newly narrowed waist, and revolved in front of Jen as she clapped.

'You're hotter than a bin fire,' she said. 'You look expensive, like Marie Antoinette.'

'Hark, I may fucketh thine peasant tonight,' I said.

She curtseyed. 'Ho, let us sexeth in yonder crops.'

Jen looked gorgeous too, in an aqua 1960s-style silk dress with long sleeves and a high neck. The short hemline showed off the perfect skin of her tanned legs. Her curls were high and tight and her lips were red.

'You put in a little extra effort tonight?' I asked her as we walked out the door.

'Gotta keep up with you.' Subtext: *Gotta get laid.*

We met Dan on the corner of Smith and Johnston. He was pale and nervous. He'd obviously shaved that morning and it made him look younger, and his flannelette shirt appeared to have been ironed.

'You look nice,' he said.

Nice? I looked steaming bloody hot, but okay. 'Thanks.'

'And so do you,' he added, kissing Jen on the cheek.

'Thanks, Dan. All the moral support you need tonight, okay?' She squeezed his hand.

He blushed. 'Yeah, no worries.'

Lisa and her fiancé lived in a warehouse conversion in Fitzroy, just behind Smith Street. It was the kind of apartment building that was perfect for yuppies with too much money and not many interests outside of drinking coffee and wearing lycra. The door was made of heavy industrial steel, artfully rusted.

'You ready?' I said to Dan.

'I'll go on ahead.' Jen walked up the polished concrete stairs.

Dan faced me, his blue eyes wide and nervous. 'Look, if it seems like I'm about to punch the guy, just drag me outta there.'

'Maybe we should have a jailbreak signal. Like, I could start dry-humping you on the couch, or you could call me baby.'

He laughed. 'I'd love to see Lisa's face if you dry-humped me on the couch.'

'I think calling me baby would be worse.'

'You don't like baby?'

'It's almost as bad as schnookums.'

He put his arm around my waist. 'Okay, schnookums, let's do it.'

We walked into the apartment and it was like we'd opened up an issue of an architecture magazine, blown up a page filled with expensive objets d'art and stepped inside a languid, Instafamous model's apartment in New York. Except the architects hadn't been able to put in more windows, so one wall was floor-to-ceiling glass with views of the city and there was not a single other window in the whole place. Not even in the bedroom, and I know because I looked. Actually, the bedroom didn't have a door. Just an archway.

We hung our jackets on hooks in the hallway. A crowd of people was gathered around the space-age kitchen bench and a beautiful woman stepped towards us immediately. She matched the apartment. Long, honey-coloured hair, a tall, slender body and skin like a porcelain doll. She was almost enough to make me believe in God, because nothing on earth could have created facial features as symmetrical as hers. Her cheekbones were basically chiselled out of marble. Holy shit, this couldn't be Dan's ex.

It was.

She cracked a huge smile, showing white shiny teeth.

'Dan!' The embrace she wrapped him in went on a few seconds longer than was appropriate, but her eyes were squeezed tight to my curious look. Finally she released him and turned to me.

'You must be Maggie.'

Her teeth were so white I thought they might blind me.

'Yes. Hello.' The noise that came out was slightly strangled but she appeared not to notice. How had Dan managed to have sex with this unearthly creature without crying out of sheer awe? Maybe he did. Maybe that's why she broke up with him, because he cried during sex, or made little voodoo pictures of her face to worship at an altar. My confidence shrivelled up like a dry, sad prune.

'Simon, come and meet Dan and Maggie,' she called to a man behind her. 'Dan, Maggie, this is Simon O'Mahony.'

Dan stiffened beside me. This was the divorce lawyer.

He was an odd-looking man, between thirty and thirty-five, not strictly handsome, with the palest eyes I'd ever seen. His hair was close-cropped and he was shorter than Dan, who wasn't that tall to begin with. He offered a broad and veiny hand to Dan to shake.

'Nice to meet you,' said Simon.

'Yep,' said Dan.

Simon looked Dan up and down, assessing him, then offered him wine with polite formality. He was looking too closely at Dan's baby face and shirt. *Bumpkin*: you could almost hear the sneer from Simon's brain. He knew that Dan was not wearing the flannie in nostalgic irony like a Smith Street hipster. He was wearing it because it was useful, kept him warm, and had pockets.

I was suddenly invested in Dan's happiness. I wanted to impress Lisa and her new guy in a way that had nothing to do with my ego. Well, only a little to do with it. I smiled stiffly at Lisa and she wrinkled her nose and cheeks into a smile so enthusiastic it nearly ate her face. Neither of us could think of anything to say.

'This is good wine,' Simon informed us, as he poured some into Dan's glass. I was momentarily confused, because the bottle he was pouring from was the same brand as the wine I'd brought, and I thought he was complimenting my present. But no, I was still holding my wine in a brown paper bag, and he was congratulating himself on his own good taste. I plonked my bottle on the counter.

'Think you'll like this one, then.' We'd probably bought it from the same shop. I felt dirty.

The room was full of glittering people. Even the men were shiny. The kitchen was all stainless steel with hints of marble here and there. Jesus, what would the rent be on this place, eight hundred a week? Clearly they weren't short on cash. Simon and Lisa must have visited Mid-century Modern for their furniture because I recognised a 1960s couch and coffee table set I'd been eyeing off about six months earlier. I tried to remember what had been written on the price tag to make me leave the shop in such a hurry: maybe three thousand dollars? The sight of three issues of an architecture magazine artfully fanned out on their coffee table nearly made me laugh out loud. There was no substance to the place: no lived-in mess, no awkward family photos, no books. I guess that would have spoiled it. You can't have any sign of actual human life in a warehouse conversion, because they're not made for humans to live in. Warehouse conversions are for display purposes only.

Simon poured me a glass of the good wine and I felt him assessing me, probably feeling smug because I was such a poor replacement for Lisa. Jen's amazing make-up couldn't alter the fact that I had round cheeks instead of high cheekbones.

Even among my own friends I was known as the Local Failure, the girl who bounced back to her mother's house so often the Jehovah's Witnesses left extra pamphlets when they visited just in case I came home the week after. So what did that make me now, among all these conspicuously successful people? Any minute someone might announce that I lived in a caravan. Where is Sarah Stoll, I wondered? Is she behind me? Is she waiting for the right moment to strike? What if she hears about my living situation? I tried to stifle the fear. I have nothing to be ashamed of, I told myself. It was bullshit, though. You don't grow up middle-class in Australia and go to a private school without learning that it's not okay to be poor.

Simon turned to Dan without breaking eye contact with me. 'And when are you two going to take the plunge and move in together?'

At the condescension in his voice I exchanged a look with Dan, who was too outraged to answer.

'You'll find out what it's like,' he continued. 'Word of warning, the first year is hell. You'll need two bedrooms. Trust me, you need your own space, don't you, Lisa?'

Lisa giggled, a little self-conscious. 'Oh my God, yes.'

'What could be worse than being in the same room as the person you love, right?' I said.

Simon pretended not to hear me and switched his gaze to Dan. 'You need to make time once a week to sit down and formally discuss the issues you're having. Really hash it out. Basically, you just need an hour a week in which to argue.'

Well, now that I knew how to make it in the world according to Simon, the Successful Divorce Lawyer, I felt like going home, getting completely smashed and maybe eating a kebab. Lisa began talking to me about her dress. Apparently it was new and she'd had to hide it from Simon so he wouldn't know she'd been shopping.

'And then I said, "Oh this old thing? I got it ages ago!"' She laughed that nervous, breathy laugh.

Lisa and Simon were slippery. I couldn't figure out how to act. Lisa didn't seem to mind my lack of speech; she had the art of one-sided conversation down. As she chattered, I realised with something like horror that Jen and Dan were right: Lisa was nice. She was making an effort to include me and make me feel welcome. When she smiled at me, it was a genuine smile. Devoid of character, perhaps, but genuine. She kept patting Dan on the arm as she spoke. She cared about him. Holy crap, maybe she really did want to be friends.

I excused myself and found the bathroom. Weird that it was so hard to acknowledge that Lisa was nice. I liked Dan, but I wasn't in love with him. I half wanted to date him because living in a caravan didn't seem like a long-term prospect, but that was all, so it couldn't be jealousy, right? Is that why I wanted to hate her and was frustrated because she was harmless? I scoured the bathroom for some sign of life, a hint of freak show, but I found nothing. They didn't seem to own shampoo, deodorant, razors or dodgy pills. Just some expensive Aesop hand wash. The chitter of the party filtered through the walls. Simon and Lisa don't like each other, I decided. It was his staginess, her high-pitched laughter that decided the point. The way he derided her subtly with his little jibe about needing space. Was that what marriage was like when you only did it so you didn't have to be alone?

But Lisa didn't have to be alone. She'd had Dan. He might have been beneath her socially and in terms of appearance, but he was a good person. She seemed to have real affection for him, whereas Simon and Lisa didn't seem to enjoy each other's company. Dan had said they'd only been together for six months but Simon was exactly the type of man Lisa had always wanted. Wealthy, confident, slick. Dan claimed bitterly that he was just an amusement for Lisa while she waited for the real thing to come along.

Four years was a long time to wait for the real thing.

I walked out of the bathroom and further into the party, as far from Simon and Lisa as possible, heading towards Dan and Jen at the window. Jen was elbow to elbow with women who were wearing almost identical sparkling cocktail dresses, their faces unfamiliar to me except for Biyu, the one college friend I actually liked, even though I avoided her dull barbecues. Biyu had lived in the room between mine and Sarah's at Barff College, and had often taken it upon herself to correct people who gossiped that I had slept with nine of the guys who lived on my floor. It was only seven.

'Maggie!' Biyu called out as I approached. She had short hair and a round, pleasant face, the kind of face that didn't judge you, and she could be relied upon to wear the same banana-yellow nylon jacket no matter what the occasion. She'd earned the nickname Signature ever since she'd once referred to the jacket as her 'signature piece'.

'Have you met Dan?' I asked her.

'Of course! How do you know Dan?'

'Maggie's my date,' Dan said quickly.

Oh, that's right, we were pretending.

Biyu's eyes widened. It could have been joy, but it was more likely surprise. 'Oh my God, I had no idea you two were together. Maggie, you lucky thing. Dan is my favourite person in the world.'

I smiled. 'It's kinda recent.'

Dan leant in to mutter quietly in my ear. 'I work with Biyu's boyfriend, Joe. He's a sparky.' I often forgot about Biyu's boyfriend because he was exceptionally boring, though really I should have remembered him because he had the misfortune of being named Joe King.

'Have you seen Sarah yet?' Jen asked me, equally quietly, while Biyu was distracted by another friend.

'Haven't had the pleasure.'

Jen's eyes flicked to a spot a few feet behind my head. 'Then don't turn around.'

The smooth, lullaby voice sang in my ear. 'Hiiii Maggie.'

I turned. Sarah was dressed in a flowing, glittering muu-muu and high heels that jangled when she walked. Tonight, the violence in her aura was less scorching and more simmering. Smug. Her lips were pulled into what she clearly knew was not a smile. If she hadn't been so unpleasant I might have mentioned the lipstick on her front tooth.

'Sarah. How's Sean?'

The circle of people around me fell silent. Somewhere beneath the honking laughter and the din of clinking glasses in the kitchen, I heard the intake of breath – from Biyu, probably. It wouldn't have been Jen, because Jen would have known that I wasn't going to lie down tonight.

'Taking the high road,' Biyu said quickly. 'Wonderful, Maggie, just wonderful.'

Sarah ignored Biyu and licked her teeth, but it didn't remove the lipstick. 'Sean's great.' She let the vowels drag. 'Where are you living now?'

A touch on my arm alerted me to Dan's presence. 'Another wine?' he asked.

'Yes.'

He pressed the already-poured glass into my hand and took the empty one. What a man.

Biyu, sensing danger, took the opportunity to distract Sarah. 'Did you end up buying that lovely house in Prahran, Sarah? I saw it on the internet. Two bedrooms?'

'Yaaas, I did.'

I took a large gulp of wine, shooting Dan a grateful look over the top of the glass. Jen was standing too far away to put her arm around me, but I recognised the urge in her. She made a face and rolled her eyes while Biyu and Sarah talked about Sarah's amazing house at a volume intended to be heard by those within a two-metre radius.

'My mortgage is, like, so massive,' Sarah drawled. 'I mean, owning my own home is amazing, *so* much better than renting, but paying *all* that money each month is *so* depressing.'

Biyu nodded in sympathy. 'I know, how annoying is it? Joe and I can't have any fun. We never go out anymore. The mortgage eats up all our cash.'

Sarah snorted into her wineglass. 'Huh. I think my mortgage is bigger than yours.'

Sarah, Dan and Biyu all fell silent. Biyu's cheeks turned red, clashing horribly with the yellow jacket.

'Well,' I cut in, 'I think my penis is bigger than yours, so I win.'

The silence stretched into a void. Dan began to shake beside me. For a moment I thought he was choking until I saw the corners of his eyes were creased and realised he was trying not to laugh. Instantly the desire to giggle overtook me as well. I stifled it valiantly for about two seconds, until it burst out of me in a little sheet of snot and wine that landed on Sarah's sleeve.

That was too much for Biyu and Jen. They burst into hysterics as Sarah gave me a disgusted look.

'Sean,' Sarah called out, her voice full of malice. 'Come and say hello to Maggie.'

I followed Sarah's look and saw Sean talking to a smiling brunette who I vaguely recalled from school as Sarah's best friend, Morgan Something. Sean was dressed in a baby-blue shirt and trousers that followed the tall, slender line of his figure. His dark eyes met mine and he smirked. What next? Was Sarah going to call him 'dahling' in front of me? Dan put his arm around my waist and squeezed. Jen stared at Dan's hand, then met my eyes as if to say, *Wait, are you dating Dan for real?* I felt my cheeks flush and willed myself not to knock back the whole glass of wine while Sean lazily strode over to us. I busily inspected my wine glass.

'Maggie,' he said, eyes fixed on Dan's arm around my waist.

'Sean,' I said. The circle of people around us was quiet, no doubt waiting for an explosion of some sort.

'How's Dot?' he asked.

'Traumatised.'

'Where are you living?'

'With Jen.'

'No she's not.' Jono had slid into the group between Biyu and Dan, fresh from the mines, his hair still wet from the shower. 'Sean! Nice to see you, mate.'

The uni girls all said hello in unison. Jono was grinning, oblivious to the tension in our little circle. I could see Jen miming at him, *No, No!* He frowned at her, uncomprehending.

'Lisa!' Biyu called out shrilly. Lisa, who had been walking past the group, presumably to greet a latecomer, jumped, but rather elegantly, like a doe. Biyu waved her over.

Poor Biyu didn't like conflict. She could sense the hatred humming between Sean, Sarah and me like a power station humming at fifty thousand volts. Calling Lisa over was a fraught act, considering Dan and I were standing there, but she must have been desperate.

'Yes,' Sarah called out. 'Come and tell us about the proposal.'

Lisa did her best impression of a doe in headlights, smile frozen on her face, clearly panicking at the prospect of telling the story of Simon's proposal in front of Dan. She came over slowly, though, and stood by us, smiling awkwardly.

'Excuse me,' Dan said, and headed towards the bathroom.

I couldn't blame him, but the loss of his warm hand from my waist was a blow. With him there, I only felt like my back was against the wall. Without him, I was standing out on a shaky platform over a long drop. I considered following him to the bathroom.

Sarah grabbed Lisa's hand. 'You look so beautiful tonight, Lisa. And your ring! Stunning. So jealous.'

'Thank you, Sarah.' Lisa turned to me and put her hand on my arm. 'I'm so glad you came, Maggie.'

'Oh, thanks,' I said lamely. 'Thanks for inviting us.'

'Well, I wasn't sure about it, you know? I didn't know if it was the done thing, to invite your ex to your engagement party. But then I thought, I really want Dan and I to be friends. He's so special to me.'

'Oh, yes. Special.' Uh. Idiot.

'I had no idea he had a new girlfriend! I mean, I am so happy for him. But he only told me last week that he was bringing you.'

'Oh. Sorry.'

'No, no! I didn't mean – I was just surprised, that's all.' Her hand was now gripping my arm ever so slightly. 'But I'm glad he's found someone.' She crinkled her face into that huge, perfect smile again.

'He's a good bloke.'

'He *is. Such* a good bloke.'

Sarah was watching us with the hint of a smirk on her face. Smelling blood, I thought. Jono had started talking to Sean, who clearly wanted to listen in on our conversation but couldn't find a way to shut Jono up.

'The proposal!' Biyu prompted.

Lisa smiled, then put a delicate hand over her mouth. 'Well, Simon kept it a big secret. It's a good thing he did, too, because

I'm a massive snoop and I totally would have found out otherwise.' She giggled and her ring flashed under the downlights.

'Oh, so am I, massive snoop.' Biyu leant in and made sure that her boyfriend was nowhere near to hear her. 'Totally check my ex-boyfriend's Facebook messages,' she confided.

Lisa, Jen and Biyu laughed together and I made a noise like I was trying to join in, but I was wracked with confusion. I thought hacking your ex's private messages was something you were supposed to keep secret – I wasn't about to quote from one of Sean's emails to Sarah – but no one else blinked an eye. Had social convention changed so much since I had moved into a caravan and been cut off from the internet?

'Well, we were in the restaurant,' Lisa continued. 'That special duck place on Smith Street, and Simon had ordered Peking duck for us to share. Anyway, when it came out he offered to wrap me a Peking duck pancake and I was like, this is weird, he never offers to do that kind of thing. And I swear he must have learnt some kind of sleight of hand trick because next thing I know I'm picking up this pancake and a ring falls out! And it was, like, covered in sauce but so beautiful, and then he got down on one knee in front of everyone.'

It was a breathless monologue, punctuated occasionally with giggles.

'Aw, so cute,' said Biyu.

'How adorable,' said Jen.

'Ngnh,' I said, or something to that effect.

Sarah put her hand on Lisa's waist. 'Lisa, I can't get over it, you look amazing. Look at your waist! It's so tiny. You are'—she looked at me—'the most beautiful girl in this room by a long, long way. Simon is so lucky.'

'Thanks, Sarah. You look gorgeous too.'

'And this apartment! Amazing. Warehouse conversions are so glam. And spacious. I'd hate to live in a little shitbox, something you can't swing a cat in.' Sarah looked at me again, testing the water. 'Or in a share house.'

Lisa broke in, talking fast as if to fill the air with sound to paste over the nothingness. 'I hate the way Simon arranges the couch!'

I stared at Lisa as I contemplated this outburst and wondered what arranging a couch might entail. Plumping cushions? Draping a throw rug? Hiding your sensual collection of spanking paddles under the seats? She was a beautiful, chattering, slightly nervous girl, and I realised she would have been perfect for Dan. His calm earnestness would have settled her nerves and insecurities, while her sweetness would have been enough to keep him happy forever. I guessed if he wasn't a builder – if he was a divorce lawyer – they'd still be together. She kept looking over at Dan, quick glances in his direction. He was now standing by the fridge, looking morose. Lisa's beautiful grey eyes glittered. She was lucky to have had him, I decided. Jen was looking at Dan, too, a vague expression on her face. Or maybe she was just avoiding looking at Jono, who was staring at Sarah Stoll's cleavage.

Dan caught all three of us watching him and walked over as if he'd been summoned.

'Ring story's all over,' I whispered in his ear. Lisa watched my lips move and took a sip of her drink, not even pretending she wasn't keeping tabs on him.

The group fell silent again and poor, flustered Biyu felt the need to say something pleasant.

'Well, isn't this nice? Dan, Lisa, Simon; Sean, Maggie, Sarah, all together at a party and getting along—'

'So, Jono, what were you saying about where Maggie lives now?' Sarah said sweetly. 'You said she's not living with Jen?'

'Maggie's living in a caravan in the alleyway behind our house.' Jono grinned. 'It's a ten-foot heap of shit.'

# Chapter 15

My facial muscles seized up one by one until I wasn't sure if I was smiling or frozen in an Edvard Munch-style scream. A tic pumped under my left eye. Sarah's face, on the other hand, became unusually expressive. She beamed. She actually beamed. One hand let go of her wineglass stem and extended outwards, as if she was flexing a set of claws.

'A caravan?' She said it lightly, as if it was nothing. 'A caravan. An apartment didn't appeal to you, then?'

Biyu leant in and lowered her voice, a hand over her mouth. 'Oh my God, Maggie, I didn't realise you were so hard-up. I would never have brought up the mortgage thing earlier if I'd known. I'm so sorry!'

Somehow, that was worse than Sarah's delighted expression. The last thing any sane person wants to be is an object of pity.

'Biyu, don't worry. I basically live with Jen. It's only temporary, since I broke up with—' Sean raised his eyebrows. 'I mean, I'm moving in with Dan soon.'

Dan flinched. Lisa turned white.

Relief flew across Biyu's face. 'Ohhhh, congratulations. Isn't love grand? You two are gorgeous together.'

Dan was beginning to sweat beside me. I could tell he hadn't meant for the charade to go this far. He only wanted to act as if we were casually dating, so he wouldn't seem so pathetic turning up to his ex-girlfriend's engagement party alone. Sean looked Dan up and down, sizing him up, obviously trying to think of something vaguely insulting. Luckily Sean's brain worked at half-speed, and all he could think to say was, 'Is that right?'

Sarah narrowed her eyes. Somehow, my performance hadn't quite fooled her. She ran her tongue over her teeth. Going in for the kill?

'Funny how you two have moved so fast. Didn't you meet at Jen's engagement party?'

Sean frowned. Then it hit him. Dan was the guy whose pants I'd been caught inside. He stiffened. Straightened right up, like a pole had been rammed up there.

'We did,' I said. 'It was an instant love connection. Wasn't it, Dan?'

Dan was staring uneasily at Lisa. I elbowed him in the ribs. 'Uh, yeah,' he said.

This didn't suit Sarah, so she changed tack. 'Well, that's great news. I guess Centrelink will want to know about it, though.' Her smile was innocent. 'When you move in together, I mean. Don't you have to report that kind of thing?'

I seethed, but before I could say anything Dan pulled me away. I wrapped my arm around his waist firmly enough that he couldn't shake me off and blow our cover.

'I think you're having too much fun with this game,' he hissed.

—

What would Rueben do if he was here? I wondered. Would he pretend to listen to the conversation around him, or would he let the impatience show on his face and make the clean-cut legal types uncomfortable? Something tightened up in me when I thought of Rueben. He made me more aware of my breath and my shadow, the blood in my veins. *You do worry about what people think, Maggie*, he had said, and he was right. My cheeks were still hot from Sarah's jab about Centrelink.

Jen followed me to the fridge, where Dan had deposited me with instructions to stop telling everyone we were moving in together. I thought she would have something to say about how well I'd carried myself; with what dignity and grace I had pretended not to care that my ex-boyfriend was screwing the enemy, but nada.

'I think your pretence is working too well,' she whispered. 'Lisa keeps staring at Dan. Simon's gonna notice.'

'Yeah, she's clearly not over him.'

'Look at them.' She nodded towards the floor-to-ceiling windows, where Lisa had walked over to Dan and was now standing close to him and talking, touching him on the arm occasionally. 'She left him for someone else and now she's flirting with him at her own engagement party. She's going to keep stringing him along, even after she marries her rich divorce lawyer.'

'Probably. How are things with you and Jono?'

She took a sip of her drink. 'Sometimes, when he talks to Sarah Stoll's cleavage, I imagine shoving my thumbs into his eye sockets.'

I was startled. 'What?'

'Nothing. Let's go talk to Biyu.'

Jono interrupted by putting his hands on Jen's shoulders.

Her cheeks turned pink and I could see her wondering if he'd heard the thing about his eye sockets.

'You keep springing up behind us like a spare dick at an orgy,' I said.

'You want another beer?' Jen asked quickly.

'Nah, I'm pretty knackered,' Jono said. 'Wanna head home?'

'We just got here!'

Jono shrugged. 'We've said our hellos, now let's go.'

—

At the end of the night, Dan walked me back to the corner of Smith and Johnston streets.

'Lisa's in a gilded cage,' he said. 'It's what she wanted, though. She probably went after him for ages, even while we were together. Scoping out how much money he made, what kind of shoes he wears, going to parties and talking to his friends. But she hates him.' He hit the button for the pedestrian lights and we waited, watching the cars go by at the intersection. 'She loves him, but she hates him.'

'You reckon?'

'She complains to me all the time about what a jerk he is and all the shitty things he does.'

'What, Lisa calls you to complain?'

'Yeah, every now and then.'

'What will happen when the love runs out? If she doesn't like him as a person?'

'Oh, they'll have affairs.' He waved his arm. 'She's the kind of person . . . some people don't want to be happy. Some people have to be unhappy. They seek out people they don't respect to start relationships with, so they don't have to worry about losing someone they actually love.'

Something about his speech made me uneasy. I met his eyes and he was watching me thoughtfully.

'I worry about you too, you know, Maggie. Jen says you go into things seeing the end before it begins.'

'Jen said that?'

He smiled. 'None of my business. I guess if you date worthless people like Sean then it never matters if you lose them.'

I stopped dead. 'Ouch.'

'Sorry. I'm feeling kinda burned, seeing Lisa and Simon together for the first time.'

I wondered if I would be doing Dan a favour by pointing out that Lisa clearly still had feelings for him, or if he'd be better off staying away from her and the potential heartbreak. Give him all the information and let him make his own mistakes, I decided.

'Lisa was definitely jealous tonight,' I said.

He flushed. 'You reckon?'

'She kept touching your arm and following you around the room.'

'She always used to do that when we were together.'

'Yeah, but you're supposed to stop doing it when you break up.'

'Oh.'

'So?' I said.

'So what?'

'So what do you want to do? Do you want to keep fake-dating and see if she goes mad with jealousy and leaves Simon?'

'That seems a bit evil,' he said.

'It is a bit evil. Do you want to do it?'

'Yeah, okay.'

'Great. Thing is, I need something from you if I'm going to keep up this ruse.'

He sighed. 'What now?'

'Do some work on my mother's house.'

'Maggie, I'm trying to make a living here, I can't work for free.'

I waved an arm scornfully. 'I don't mean fix the whole place up. Just do a bit of tinkering here and there, so she's pleased with me and writes me back into the will.'

'Won't I be the one she's pleased with, though? I'll be doing the work. Maybe she'll write *me* into her will.'

'If she does, I'll marry you. Don't worry, you can still have affairs with Lisa.'

Dan kissed me on the cheek. 'I'll think about it. Goodnight.'

I waggled a finger at him. 'You owe me for tonight. Putting up with Sarah Stoll and my ex, getting outed as a caravan-dweller. You owe me a fixed front gate at my mother's house.'

He crossed the street to catch the last tram.

'Oi,' I shouted after him. 'What were you whispering to my mother about the other day?'

He waved as the tram doors creaked open for him but didn't answer. I watched the tram leave, the red glow of taillights crawling down Smith Street like a caterpillar.

—

That night I heard the sounds I'd been dreading since Jono arrived.

I woke at four in the morning, stomach churning with the good wine, mouth dry as a sock. The caravan smelt musky, that earthy, urine-y smell that rabbit warrens get when there are too many rabbits and not enough warren. How had I managed to create that smell all by myself? I had no water in the caravan, so, floor creaking, I slipped on an oversized T-shirt and thongs and opened the door into the cool night air. The pedestrian gate to Jen's backyard was sagging on its hinges and normally made a racket when it scraped along the concrete, so I opened it as slowly as I could, pushing it gently and lifting it off the ground.

They were making so much noise I needn't have bothered.

Jen sounds like Minnie Mouse getting rammed by a rhinoceros when she has sex. It's all high-pitched squeaks and gasps. Jono wasn't making much noise aside from the occasional grunt, but the cool breeze floated it right over to my delicate ears. They'd left the windows open.

I quietly unlocked the back door just as a hand spanked a warm, fleshy thigh with an audible *slap*. In the moonlight I saw that the door to her study was ajar. I walked to the bathroom as quietly as I could and filled a glass of water at the sink.

By the time I left, the sounds had stopped, hopefully of their own accord and not because they'd realised there was an intruder in the house. I snuck out softly and quickly, eager to get back to the caravan, although the rabbit-warren smell seemed even stronger now. I put the glass of water next to the bed and thought about what Dan had said at the end of the night. *If you date worthless people, it doesn't matter when you lose them.* I guess he could have been talking about Sean, or Jono, or Lisa, but he could also have been talking about me.

My memory skipped to the moment Sarah had repeated the word *caravan* and I had to close my eyes. Even in the dark, my face burned. By the end of the night, everyone would have known that I lived in a caravan, and in the morning Sarah would get busy texting people, telling them the news about Maggie and her pathetic life.

—

Jen was overjoyed the next morning. She burst into the caravan and climbed on top of me, her hair coiling about her head in strange shapes, like the miniature stone gargoyles in her parents' backyard.

'I had sex!' She wrapped her arms around my neck and flopped there.

'With who?' Jen had brought unwelcome sunlight with her when she'd burst through the door, and my head was already pounding.

She gave me a playful tap. 'Jono! Finally!' She did a little horizontal dance, knocking the breath out of me, and her dressing gown fell open to reveal wrinkled pink pyjamas with love hearts on them. 'I told him how sad I was that we hadn't had sex, so we did it over my desk.'

'Awww, how sweet.'

'And now we get to hang out for a whole week before he goes home!'

'Wonderful.'

Jen rolled off me, smiling and stretching her arms over her head. She was in no hurry to leave, and her good mood would make her generous.

'What do you want for breakfast? Let's go out somewhere. My shout. Or I'll make something.'

I rolled into her and buried my nose in her shoulder. 'I don't care. I'm a loser, I'll eat anything.'

'Oh, sweetheart. What happened?'

'Don't you remember? Sarah Stoll knows I live in a caravan. Everyone knows. I have a Centrelink debt the size of Alice Springs that Rueben assures me is not going away any time soon, and I nearly pass out from the horn every time he speaks, even though I'll probably lose my job to him. I may as well give up and become a sex worker now, but no one's going to want to pay me for sex so I'll have to become one of those girls who wears a sandwich board advertising a coffee and sausage roll for six dollars. Sean and Sarah will come by every day to take pictures and taunt me, and when I'm forty I'll try to kill myself but fail, and all the cats I ever own will run away.'

She patted me on the shoulder. 'There there. Dot won't run away, and if she does I'll replace her with a cat that looks just like her and you'll never be able to tell.' She rolled out of bed. 'I'll go get dressed, come round in ten.'

———

I waited in Jen's kitchen while she threw on some clothes. Jono greeted me with a nod and a yawn.

'Woke up with a really sore left ball this morning.' A sweaty hand emerged from his boxer shorts. He looked at the kitchen bench, then at me. 'Make me a coffee?'

'Make your own,' I said.

'You know, you're practically living in Jen's house for free, you could at least make coffee. Or put a dish in the water and scrub it,' Jono said, as he took a bite of a muffin that Jen had presumably made. He didn't wash his hand before he took it and I imagined the muffin now tasted of ball sweat.

'You know, you're also living in her house for free, you could make *her* something for once,' I shot back.

'I don't see you turning down her scrambled eggs.'

'Well, at least I don't yell at her to get me a coffee when I'm hungover.'

'Guys, please!' Jen hurried in to break up the argument. 'I'm right here, there's no need to bicker. Maggie, let's head to brunch. Jono, we'll be back in an hour.'

Jono blew Jen a lazy kiss as we left. Something about the gesture was uncomfortably familiar. His muffin-eating entitlement disturbed me, and I realised it was because he reminded me of myself. Someday soon, I promised myself, I would repay Jen for all the times she'd looked after me.

# Chapter 16

'Mum, you know that list of my old boyfriends you wrote . . . who was your favourite one on it?'

'God, you're just like your father,' she snapped.

I swivelled in my chair and cradled the office phone between my neck and shoulder. I could feel Rueben watching me out of the corner of his eye but I didn't care. Agnes was paying a morning call to the teenage mothers at the shelter and I'd run out of mobile credit, so the Angels would have to pay for this phone call.

'Why am I like Dad?'

'Because he's a selfish prick,' came the instant answer.

The sound of her favourite soap opera was audible in the background, the one with a magical-realist plot element involving a puppet that came to life. Mum had every Friday off work and every Friday she watched the soap without fail.

'So you're saying I'm a selfish prick?'

'I know why you're asking me about the list. You're getting desperate and you want to look up one of your old boyfriends to see if any would be foolish enough to let you use him for money again. Your father doesn't have a conscience and neither do you.'

'Are you calling me a sociopath?'

'Sociopaths are charming.'

'Is that a yes?'

'No. You're just a run-of-the-mill cheater.'

'I think that's a bit unfair, really. Maybe I'm too nice to end relationships that I know are on the rocks, so I just . . . pop on over to the next one.'

Mum burst out laughing. Even Rueben snorted. I shot him a dirty look.

'Too nice? Stop deluding yourself. How is our agreement going?'

'Swimmingly. I love the caravan and I love my job.' It wasn't until I said it that I realised I *had* come to like working at the Angels.

Mum didn't even try to keep the meanness out of her laughter. 'And Jen's wedding planning? Have you found her a new dress yet? If you had any money you should have offered to pay for it, since you destroyed an heirloom.'

'The wedding dress will be amazing. Leave me alone.' I hung up.

'Wedding dress?' Rueben asked. 'Are you getting married?'

I rolled my eyes. 'My best friend is marrying a douchenozzle and I had to help her choose a dress to wear while she ruins her life.'

Rueben merely raised his eyebrows.

'Maybe you should be my date to the wedding. You'd look great in a powder-blue suit,' I said.

'I don't do weddings,' he said. 'Marriage is possibly the worst cultural institution ever invented.'

'I agree, but we could at least have sex in a bathroom or something. You should have come to the engagement party on Saturday night. You might have helped me avoid humiliation, plus the bathrooms in converted warehouses are really something special. This one smelt like frangipani.'

'How were you humiliated?'

'Someone I utterly hate discovered I live in a caravan and gleefully broadcasted it to everyone I know.'

Rueben smiled. 'Always worrying about what people think.'

'It's a valid pastime. Humans have evolved to worry about what each other thinks. Social exclusion can be deadly in the wild. If nobody likes you enough to protect you from bears or share their food in a famine, you're pretty rooted, aren't you?'

'Guess that's why you're making a list of wronged boyfriends. I imagine there are a few people out there already who don't much like you.'

'Idiots, all of them.'

He grinned. 'I agree.'

A little thrill ran through my body from head to toe when he said that.

At lunchtime I borrowed five dollars from Rueben and bought a bacon and egg sandwich from the corner store. Butter ran down my chin as I ate it at my desk.

'So why'd you go to jail?' I asked through a mouthful of egg.

'Mind your own business.'

None of the grannies had turned up for their shifts in the op shop that afternoon so Agnes ordered us to cover for them, since the office was quiet anyway. In the absence of any customers, we sorted through clothing from the donation bins, tagging and pricing clothes and hanging them on the racks. As we idly sorted the Italian loafers from the vinyl pants, I kept up my line of questioning.

'C'mon. Why did you go to jail?'

He ignored me and kept working, tagging a 1980s puffball wedding dress at forty dollars and hanging it up.

'Why? Whyyyyyyy?'

'Will you shut up if I tell you?'

'For a good ten minutes.'

He sighed and straightened a pair of sandals. 'When I was eighteen I stole a car to impress my mates and got caught. Normally you don't go to prison for stealing a crappy car, especially if it's your first time, but my court date was at lunchtime and I guess the magistrate was hungry and didn't like my naughty face. He put me away for thirty days, said it would sort me out.'

'So that was the first stint.'

'Yeah. Problem is, it's hard for ex-cons to get jobs. I just hung around smoking pot for about a year. Then I got the munchies one night and didn't have money to buy chips, so I grabbed a butter knife out of the kitchen drawer and tried to hold up the service station. I was high as a bear on acid. The stupid guy behind the counter wouldn't hand over the cash. I got a bag of frozen peas from the freezer and threw them at his head.'

I burst out laughing. 'What, and they did you for assault?'

'Well. Unfortunately the peas knocked him off balance and he split his skull open on the counter. So I got done for assault occasioning serious bodily harm as well as armed robbery. I was lucky to only get two years. They could have sent me away for a lot longer.'

I couldn't help sniggering. 'Frozen peas.'

'Poor bastard needed staples in his head.' He was half smiling.

'Was he all right?' I started sifting through an inordinate number of rhinestone brooches, which had burst out of a tortoiseshell jewellery box. They were just begging to be fixed to a woolly yellow cardigan.

'Yeah, he was all right in the end. He sent me a Christmas card while I was in jail.'

'A Christmas card, when you nearly turned him into a vegetable?'

'You're hilarious. I think he's religious. Forgiveness, et cetera.'

'Give peas a chance, and all that. Got it. What did you do after you got out of jail the second time?'

He paused. A brief look of sadness crossed his face. 'Not much. Worked as a removalist for a while. Did a lot of the kinds of jobs that are okay in your twenties but start to hurt in your thirties.'

'So you gave up on that, and now you do your twenty hours a week volunteering and Centrelink pays you the Newstart, right? Same as me?'

'Yep. I'm looking forward to the day I never have to deal with Centrelink again, though.'

'You mean, the day you get offered a permanent job here and I don't?' I narrowed my eyes at him.

'You want a paid job here?'

'If it ensures I never set foot in a Centrelink office again, yes.'

'Stop blathering to your mother during work hours and maybe they'll give you a job,' he said.

I huffed and opened up a cardboard box. 'For an ex-con, you're a goody two-shoes.'

He lobbed a lacy white bra at me. It caught on my shoulder and flopped over my boob like a bulbous snowflake.

'Oi,' I said, trying to disentangle the hooks and eyes, which had caught in a hole in my T-shirt. 'You're ruining my look. Who donates their old bras, anyway?'

Rueben looked at the clock. 'It's Prayer Time in ten minutes,' he said. He gently lifted the bra from my shoulder and put it back in the box.

'I've gotta make a phone call first,' I said.

—

I should have known better than to try to call Centrelink with only ten minutes to spare. After eight minutes in the hold queue, time I spent trying to decode a piece of graffiti on the wall next to the op shop that said *a one-eyed donkey stole my wife* and coming up blank, I gave up and joined Rueben on his way to Prayer Time.

It was strangely quiet in the prayer room. Agnes, Josephine, Christine, Boris and Bunny were sitting in a circle with their heads bowed when Rueben and I walked in.

'Are we late?' My voice echoed through the silent room and Josephine shot me a dirty look.

'We're praying,' she hissed.

'What for?' I asked, stupidly. Everyone's heads lifted. 'Sorry, I mean, is this a group prayer, for something specific?'

Agnes folded her hands. 'We're praying for the charity's finances. We had some bad news today, which I will outline at the end of today's session.'

My stomach dropped. Was this the moment my job prospects folded for good? Not wanting to poke the bear, I took a seat, and Rueben slid into a chair next to me. After an interminable prayer from Boris, which had an oddly rhythmic quality to it, like a Dr Seuss book, Josephine read a 'motivational' poem.

'On a dark and gloomy night
With no end to trouble in sight
When I was sad and crying a river
God said, "Child, I am your giver
Your pain will soon be at an end
Because I will always be your friend
You will rise again like Jesus
And all your good works will please Us."'
I strongly suspected she'd written it herself.

'This is a very special getting-to-know-you Prayer Time,' Bunny said. 'I hope you've all come prepared to spill a little secret – something most people don't know about you!'

I'd forgotten all about Bunny's special Prayer Time and hadn't given a moment's thought to the little-known fact about myself that I could share. All I could think of was the time I slept with a roadie for Kings of Leon when they did the festival circuit ten years back, probably not an appropriate factoid to share at work, or the time I drove into my mother's front fence when I was sixteen, hungover and driving without a licence. I decided to lie and say I'd been born with six toes on each foot, or that my middle name was Muriel.

Josephine read a passage from the Bible, something about men trading sheep for wives.

'Now,' Agnes began, looking uncomfortable, 'I hope that by the end of this special Prayer Time we feel closer and more connected to each other by sharing something about ourselves that may surprise our colleagues. Today was Bunny's idea, so perhaps we will ask her to go first.'

Bunny cleared her throat. I looked at the clock and hoped this wouldn't take too long.

'My story's not about me so much,' she began, and I didn't

believe her for a second. 'But it's about life. The sacredness of life. I support the freedom to be born – that is, I'm part of what people refer to as the pro-life movement.'

I knew there was a reason this girl gave me the creeps.

'I believe in direct action to influence people's choices in this important decision – and I'm proud to say that just last week at the East Melbourne clinic, we saved a baby's life by convincing the mother to ask for God's help instead of killing her unborn child.'

Direct action? I nearly lost my cool. Jen and I had gone with our friend Siobhan to the East Melbourne clinic when she was twenty-one and needed an abortion quick-smart after her boyfriend had done a runner. The street had been lined with Bunnys, shouting and holding pictures of dead babies. Someone filmed us walking into the clinic, trying to block our path. Siobhan moved to Tasmania not long after.

Bunny picked up her guitar. 'I hope you don't mind, I've written a song about life in all its preciousness and glory. I'd like to sing it for you because I think music is the best way to open hearts and change minds. It's called "Every Heartbeat".'

Of course, Bunny. Of course. We'd love to hear your song. She strummed the guitar and broke into her ode to embryos.

'*Every heartbeat is precious*
*Tiny as it seems*
*We're all children in God's hands*
*You're a sacred seed . . .*'

I had to give it to her, it wasn't quite as bad as 'We All Love Jesus', but then she went for a high note and missed by a long shot. By the time she'd finished we were ten minutes into Prayer Time.

'Right,' Agnes said. 'Uh, thanks for sharing that, Bunny.' She had the look of a woman who'd recently eaten a dodgy oyster. 'Boris?'

Boris's voice was so soft I could hardly hear about how he used to work for a bank in New York before the Global Financial Crisis, and subsequently had a nervous breakdown and found God. When did bottling things up go out of fashion? I wondered. I shifted slightly in my chair. It squeaked as if I'd dragged it across the room, and Bunny shot me a withering look. Slowly, I inched my leg towards Rueben's and pressed it ever so gently against his jeans.

Christine went next, fiddling with the beads in her necklace and blinking hard.

'My ex-boyfriend murdered his wife,' she blurted.

Holy shit. This was too much for me. I took a pen from my top pocket as Boris started to rub Christine's shoulder. All eyes were locked on Christine, so no one noticed when I started writing on a scrap of paper.

*I need to get out of here. Changed mind re: bathroom bang?*

As I wrote, Christine was detailing how she found the wife's bones in a hard-shell suitcase in the garage after living with the guy for four years.

'I thought he was a nice man,' she finished. 'He seemed like a really nice man.'

Well, I thought. If even nice men murder their wives, how do you tell who to sleep with? Might as well go for the sexy ones if you're risking your life either way.

I passed the note, hidden in a dirty tissue I found in my pocket, back to Rueben. His fingers brushed mine as he took it, lingering just a little longer than necessary. The room was silent. He didn't unfold the tissue.

It came to my turn and I flicked a look in Agnes's direction. She seemed anxious, as if she was expecting another heavy story.

The faces on either side of her were attentive, the minds behind them ticking over, desperately thinking of the saddest story they could tell. They all wanted those sympathy sighs and pats, too.

I knew my lie about six toes wasn't going to cut it.

'Um, you may not know that I live in a caravan.' A few eyebrows raised. 'Yeah, um, it's a 1962 hand-built aluminium ten-footer and it's shaped like a trapezoid. And it has a speed stripe. I used to have trouble from the police wanting me to move along because I park it on the streets of Collingwood, but now they're used to me.'

'Wow,' Bunny said. 'That's amazing. Does it have a shower?'

Hey, no one else had questioned the confessors. This wasn't *60 Minutes*.

'Uh, I park behind my friend's house and shower there.'

'Does it have a toilet?' asked Josephine.

'No. Same deal.'

'What if you have to go in the night?' asked Bunny.

'Don't ask.'

'All right, thanks for sharing, Maggie,' said Agnes. 'We better keep moving. Rueben?'

'My mum was runner-up in the Miss Australia pageant in 1979,' Rueben said.

Everyone *ooh*ed. That explains his good looks, I thought. The gratitude on Agnes's face at such a short and pleasant secret was heartwarming.

'Well, thank you, everyone, that's the end of the getting-to-know-you session,' she said.

'Wait, what about you?' I asked.

Agnes shifted irritably. 'Well, I'm a member of the North Fitzroy yarn bombing association,' she said. 'We knit colourful covers for telegraph poles and trees.'

Aw, how cute. My appreciation for Agnes's sensible shoes and plain manner went up a notch. I stretched, hoping she would wrap things up. Work would be a relief at this point. Rueben had unfolded my note and read it, but he hadn't written a reply.

'And now we come to the business end of this afternoon's session,' Agnes said. 'I want to update you all on the financial situation that I mentioned earlier.'

Uh oh.

'It's not so good at the moment,' she continued. 'There's a lot more competition in the non-profit space. Those fashionable water charities and thousands of cancer fundraisers are eating into our market share. To be quite frank, we need to bring in more revenue, or cut back on our costs. Both, preferably.'

My heart sank. No question, she was talking about job cuts. Not that I, as a volunteer, would be booted from the Angels, but I had been banking on landing a paying job soon to clear my Centrelink debt.

'The shop is spending too much money and time sorting through donated junk and having rubbish removed. We're going to have to install security cameras and prosecute anyone who dumps waste in the op shop bins.' Josephine sucked in a breath at the word 'prosecute'. I supposed it was unchristian. Agnes ignored her. 'Bunny, how are the letterbox drops going?'

Bunny looked startled at the question. She opened her mouth but before she could·invent something, Agnes continued.

'We need to be more aggressive in the lead-up to next year's winter campaign. This year's was a complete bust; we didn't even reach half our target. I have here samples of the Salvos' mail – direct mail, mind you, not unaddressed mail. I know it costs a bomb and we don't have the budget for it – but look at the ideas behind their letters. Why aren't we doing anything similar?'

The Salvos had a million-dollar marketing budget at their disposal, and the direct-mail pack boasted a fold-out paper blanket, colour pictures of cold homeless people, personal stories, coupons and a return envelope. We could never afford something like that.

Josephine piped up. 'Agnes, I worry about this talk of money-making. We're not a business, we're a charity doing God's will. We need to look to our roots and find that passion. What would Jesus say about competing with the Salvos, who do God's work too? Would he approve of us trying to take "market share"?'

'This is not a halfway house for lost Christians!' Agnes snapped. 'We're here to help the poor, not save our own souls. Our purpose is to get results for people living in poverty, and that means reducing our overheads and increasing donations. Efficiency! If you're not on board with that, you should question why you're here at all.'

Rebuffed, Josephine sank back into her chair, red-faced. Silence in the room. My mind started ticking over, and I thought of my Centrelink debt. I shot Bunny a sideways glance. Her mouth was hanging half open and I realised that, although she was in the office three days a week, she did absolutely no marketing for the Angels at all. All she did was get kudos for working in a charity while she wrote bad songs about Jesus. Her job was there for the taking, if someone was canny enough to take it.

'Agnes,' I asked cautiously. 'How much money, exactly, do we need to raise to cover our expenses?'

'We need an extra twelve thousand dollars by the end of the year to cover our running costs or we'll have to close one of the shelters, probably the men's shelter. Next year I want to aim to increase our revenue by sixty thousand dollars.'

Nobody spoke. I suppose no one except Agnes ever kept

account of how much money it actually cost to run the shelters and the op shop.

'How many times a year do we ask our supporters for money?' I asked. 'Like, send them letters?'

Bunny looked at me like I was an idiot. 'Agnes just mentioned our winter campaign.'

'But . . . is that it? Is that the only time we contact our donors?'

'They support us through the op shop at other times of the year,' she said defensively. 'And it's very expensive to send letters.'

'What about emails? How often do we email them?' Silence. I persisted. 'Do we even collect email addresses?'

'That's a very good question, Maggie,' Agnes said.

Holy shit, what century was this charity operating in that they didn't even collect email addresses?

'Well, why don't we send another letter before Christmas?' I said. 'I don't mean a fancy direct-mail pack like the Salvos, I mean just writing a plain old letter to our supporter base. I can write up something similar to the Salvos' winter appeal – just change it to make it a Christmas theme – and we can mail it in bulk to save on costs. And then we can think up some ways to increase our supporter base. Maybe have a look at the average income of our supporters and see how we can target people with higher incomes who have more to give. Like, Camberwell types.' Like the guy next door to my mother who sold his gold mine in 1996 for two hundred million dollars and now collects vintage Ferraris as a hobby. We need to target him, is what I didn't say.

I waited with bated breath.

'That's an excellent thought, Maggie.' Agnes beamed. 'If you could write a draft letter, that would be fantastic. Can you have it ready to show me next week?'

'Yep.' Phew.

'I'll add an email sign-up to the website and online donation forms,' Rueben said.

'Wonderful.' Agnes beamed at him.

Bunny looked mutinous but I didn't care. I needed a job more than she did, and if people didn't donate to the Nicholson Street Angels then I wouldn't even have a volunteer position. Prayer Time disbanded and we returned to our desks, some of us more sprightly than others.

'Nice suggestion,' Rueben said in a low voice. 'Did you think that up on the fly?'

I grabbed him by the sleeve. 'I have no bloody idea what I'm doing,' I hissed. 'Help me.'

He laughed. 'Of course I will. We'll bring the Angels into the twenty-first century together. Watch out for Bunny, though, I thought she was about to stab you.'

'Hide the butter knives,' I said.

At five to five I shut down my computer and packed up. 'So your mum was a beauty queen?'

'Yep.'

'Makes sense.'

'You think I'm hot.'

'Don't get ideas.' I slung my bag over my shoulder.

'I'm already having ideas.' He winked.

'*I gave* you those ideas,' I said. 'And I notice you didn't respond to my bathroom suggestion. You better watch out or I might give up on you.'

'So do you want me to have ideas or not?' he asked, as I left.

'Peas out, man,' I called over my shoulder.

# Chapter 17

Over the next week and a half, Rueben and I put our heads together to write the fundraising letter. We brought in as many examples of other charities' imploring letters as we could find, brainstorming ways to plagiarise them without being too obvious about it. Even my mother helped, sending me letters she received from animal charities with cute pictures of bandaged koalas and skinny dogs. Rich people loved to give to animal charities, I discovered. I suspected in my mother's case she didn't believe poor human beings deserved her money. People must have done something to land themselves in a mess, whereas animals were always innocent. I raised these suspicions with Rueben and Agnes.

'Pretty sure your theory is correct,' Rueben said.

'Can confirm,' Agnes added. She had come into our office to drop off an example of an Oxfam fundraising letter.

'The women in the shelter didn't bash themselves up,' I said indignantly. 'And the dudes in the men's shelter haven't exactly had the best chances in life.'

'You don't have to tell me,' Rueben said. 'But it wouldn't kill you to pander a little if it brings in the money we need.'

'You need to get across that they're victims of circumstance,' Agnes said.

'Like this.' Rueben pointed to one of the Salvos' emotive personal stories.

'I can do that.' I cracked my knuckles and got to work.

It took days of drafting and re-drafting just to write two pages. Meanwhile, Rueben told me about the time he drove to Tamworth and streamed an American country music special that counted down the Top 40 on the charts.

'I had no idea it was so bad over there,' he said. 'There was a song that went something like, *I love God, my mama and you.* That was the chorus.'

When he sang *and you* a little shiver went down my spine.

'That's not as bad as "Truck You",' I said. 'Every time I hear that song I get dumber. I'm putting together a playlist for my best friend's wedding and I'm tempted to put it on there. Jen's fiancé is an idiot, he probably loves it.'

'I've got a great playlist for weddings,' he said. 'I'll send it to you.'

'Not all country, is it? Jen's already put the hard word on me to make it mostly pop.'

'Hardly country at all.'

'Does your band play at weddings?' I felt suddenly shy asking about his band, like I wasn't cool enough to talk about it. I had to remind myself that they were in their thirties, playing dingy pubs, and were never going to hit the big time. But the music had been good, I remembered.

'We don't usually, no. Blues and country's too dreary for weddings. It's all about break-ups and going broke.'

'You played at Jen's engagement party, though.'

'That was coincidence. We were already booked to play when she hired the bar.'

What about wedding rehearsal dinners?'

'Yeah, I guess.'

'Because I'm supposed to organise the rehearsal dinner too.'

'Have you chosen a venue yet? The owner of The Fainting Chair has just opened a restaurant behind Smith Street,' he said. 'I know for a fact there's going to be a band area, and he's hired a good chef.'

'Lock it in,' I said.

He smiled. I wanted to keep him talking, so I asked who his favourite musician was.

'Lucinda Williams.'

'Nice.'

'Yours?'

'Gillian Welch.'

'My second-favourite,' he said.

—

On my way home from work, with sixteen per cent battery on my phone, I finally got through to a person called Fifi at Centrelink. She asked for my case number, which I read out from a line of numbers I'd scribbled on my forearm in biro earlier in the day, and then asked for the reason for the call. I explained that I had a debt the size of China and I wanted to contest it.

'It was your mistake,' I insisted. 'I just kept lodging my student payment claims and you – meaning you people at Centrelink – kept paying them. How was I supposed to know that I wasn't meant to get the money anymore? Seventy grand is insane.'

Fifi was sympathetic. 'It is a sizeable debt,' she said. 'But it's also your responsibility to familiarise yourself with the rules.'

'Seriously? Seven years of mispayments and it's all my fault?'

'You can lodge a formal appeal,' she said. 'Go to the website, download the Review of Decision form. Fill it out, lodge it and wait thirteen weeks for a decision.'

'Thirteen weeks. Do I still get my Newstart payments in the meantime?'

'Tick the box on the form that asks if you need to be paid while your case is being reviewed,' she said. 'Good luck.'

I hung up and scuffed my shoe on the pavement as magpies called in the wattle trees above. The debt had lodged in my solar plexus like a piece of undigested stale bread, winding me every now and then with the reminder that my life was rooted.

—

In the supermarket, I chose food that didn't need to be cooked and could be kept out of the fridge for a couple of days. Salad, bread, fruit, peanut butter, chips, boxed wine. The next stop was the laundromat, where I watched my clothes spin in the washing machine. Following the spinning drum was addictive, like looking through a kaleidoscope. With each rotation, I repeated my mantra. *This is fine. This is fine. This is fine.*

I took the food and clean clothes back to the caravan and tidied up. Made the bed, put the clothes away in the minuscule wardrobe, lit the candles on the table. Home sweet home. Killer Friday night. My phone was dead and I couldn't be bothered stealing power from the neighbours. I would charge it tomorrow. As it got dark I settled onto my bed to read by candlelight. I missed having electricity twenty-four hours a day, temperature control, hot water from a tap. I missed having more than half a metre between my bed and the kitchen counter. Dot was coiled around my legs, purring like a motorised heater because I'd just fed her tinned tuna to lure her away from roaming the mean streets of Collingwood. After a while, I rolled over to blow out the candles.

'Maggie? Are you asleep already?' It was Jen's voice, coming from outside the caravan.

I got up and opened the door to find her bearing a steaming, foil-covered dish that I desperately hoped was lasagne. As if she'd read my thoughts, she pulled back the foil: cheese, cheese and more cheese, golden brown. A hint of white bechamel. Definitely lasagne.

'I was hoping we could do some wedding planning.' She was practically shivering with enthusiasm.

'Sure, come in. What does wedding planning involve?'

'Spreadsheets.' Great. She placed the lasagne on the table and eased her laptop satchel from her shoulder. 'Where can I set up?'

'There's only one table in here, and the lasagne has priority,' I said.

'Well, of course, I knew I'd have to feed you if I wanted to get any work done.' She threw the satchel on the bed and got to work cutting slices of lasagne and putting them on plates. 'Do you have any lettuce to make a salad?'

'For once, I do.'

After we ate, I cleared the table and Jen opened her laptop to show me her spreadsheets. Her wedding spreadsheet contained six tabs and was nauseatingly detailed. The current projected cost of the wedding, not including the engagement party and the honeymoon, was $56,000. 'But I haven't even thought about lighting yet,' Jen sighed, as if it was a given that the lighting would blow out the budget.

'What do you want me to do?' I asked.

'Well,' she said, immediately businesslike, 'we're having a cake at the wedding but we're not going to be serving it for dessert, so I want you to research take-home cake bags and bag ties, so each guest can take a piece home with them.'

'Bag ties,' I repeated.

'Yes. I'd prefer if the bags aren't too cellophane-y, because if they are everyone will crackle on their way home. And I don't want crappy ribbons for the bags but I also don't want super-expensive ribbons.'

I scratched my head. 'Is there anything a little less detail-oriented that you can get me to do?'

She thought for a moment. 'Help me choose the wedding dance song? I don't trust my own taste, and I definitely don't trust Jono's. He'll have us dancing to "Pony" by Ginuwine.'

'I know exactly what you want,' I said. 'I've been preparing for this moment my entire life. I've already been making a song list to send to the DJ. Get a load of this.' I showed her Rueben's playlist.

Twenty minutes later Jen and I were slow-dancing to Buddy Miller's version of 'How I Got to Memphis' and she was showing me a two-step move while I tried to convince her that it was a perfect first-dance song.

'But it's about a woman leaving,' she said, twirling me in the tiny space between the sink and the wardrobe.

'Exactly.'

Jen narrowed her eyes at me.

'And the man *following* her,' I added, bumping my elbow on the edge of the bench. 'A small but crucial detail. He follows wherever she goes.'

'I'm marrying a man, not a dog.'

'Are you sure?'

'Careful! You nearly knocked over the wine.'

I'd opened a bottle of cleanskin red to assist in our important wedding-planning tasks. To avert disaster, I topped up Jen's and my glasses, took a swig from mine, then placed them out of reach of clumsy elbows. An hour later we'd nearly finished the wine and I had eight 'absolutely definitely' songs, five 'maybe' songs and three 'I'll-convince-you-when-you're-drunk songs' on the list to give to the DJ. Jen switched the music on my phone to Beyoncé and turned it up.

'Okay, this has to be on the list,' she shouted, flinging her arms in the air.

'A wedding's not a wedding without "Single Ladies",' I replied. We jumped around, rocking the caravan dangerously.

'Is that someone knocking?' Jen asked, still dancing.

'What?'

'Someone's knocking!'

I opened the door and leant against the cold aluminium frame to steady myself.

'Hello,' said a young but authoritative voice.

It was dark outside, but a streetlamp shone down on a man standing arms folded, legs spread, a slightly podgy Bruce Willis with faintly familiar rosy cheeks like soft pillows. It was the police officer who'd tried to arrest me for public urination.

'Hello again,' I said. 'What is it this time?'

'The neighbours have registered a noise complaint. It sounds like a bunch of elephants thundering around in there. I thought I told you to move on.'

I decided to lie in the hopes of moving him to pity. 'But where will I go? I told you I have no one to stay with.'

He sighed and adjusted his uniform, which looked a little

tight. 'Look, you can't just park this on the street and sleep in it. I can arrange for a social worker to get you a bed, if you don't have anyone to stay with.'

My heart skipped a beat as I imagined him dragging me into the Nicholson Street Angels shelter as a client. I didn't know what street the shelter was on – only Agnes and Josephine had access to that information – but they would instantly see my name on the list. Christ. This guy really needed to be more of a hardarse if he wanted to perform the Bruce Willis stance. Now I had to slink out of the pity party I'd created.

'I have every right to live in a caravan!' I stuck my finger in his face. 'People used to live under a pile of leaves in caveman days. You can't intimidate me. I will live however I want!'

He folded his arms, a new, contemptuous line about his full mouth. 'Fine. *But you have to move on.*'

'Excuse me?' Jen had finally stopped dancing. She stuck her golden head out. 'Is there a problem, officer?'

Jen was wearing her house pants, silky purple floaty things. Earlier, when she'd got too hot dancing, she'd taken off her jumper. Now all she had on was a white tank top with a built-in shelf bra. You could see her nipples through it just a tiny bit. Perfect.

PC Pink Cheeks tried not to stare at her headlights.

'Ahem, ah,' he said. 'I just, ah, need you to turn down the music and move the caravan somewhere else. There's been a noise complaint.'

'Of course we'll turn down the music,' she said, soothing him. 'It's this broken window, it must be seeping out and disturbing everyone. Is it eleven o'clock already? I had no idea. We should wrap this up anyway, I have to work early tomorrow. I'm a nurse.'

Pink Cheeks was nodding along with her words, probably without realising it. He looked so freshly scrubbed it was almost cute.

'Have you met Maggie before?' Jen asked.

'Yes, er,' he said.

'He tried to arrest me for peeing in the gutter,' I said. 'Allegedly.'

He tore his eyes away from Jen reluctantly and fixed them on me. 'I just need you to move on,' he repeated. 'This is a residential area and the neighbours don't like it.'

'I'm a neighbour and I like it,' said Jen.

'Er, what?'

'I live in that house.' She pointed. 'And Maggie has my permission to park her caravan here. What's your name?'

She must have caught him by surprise because he opened and closed his mouth like a fish for several seconds before replying.

'Tommasio,' he finally managed.

'Oh, you're Italian too!' Jen exclaimed. That was my cue to go inside. I busied myself with packing up the laptop as she charmed him. 'My father's from Castelrotto. Are you Northern or Southern?'

Tommasio cleared his throat, flustered. 'Um, yeah, I've got some family in Campania.'

Within minutes, Jen was regaling him with stories of her nonno sun-drying tomatoes on his roof. By the time I cleaned a plate to serve Tommasio up a piece of her lasagne they were comparing war stories of their Catholic fathers. The end result of Jen's charm offensive was an agreement: I could stay in the caravan as long as I kept quiet, behaved myself, and promised to move the caravan at least as far as Abbotsford the instant I got a third complaint. PC Pink Cheeks left the caravan in a daze, still gazing absent-mindedly at Jen's golden curls as he threw one leg over his police motorbike. She waved, and he almost fell off the bike in his hurry to wave back.

# Chapter 18

Jen's charm and quick thinking had got the police officer off my case, so to thank her I went around on Sunday night to shower her with compliments as she cooked me a roast chicken dinner. Jono was in town but thankfully had gone out with friends, so Jen and I settled in front of the television with plates of chicken, peas and potatoes and a bottle of wine each. One of the reasons I love Jen: despite the fact that ninety per cent of brides go on a diet, she steadfastly resisted. The wedding was three weeks away but she was already perfect and deserved roast chicken with extra gravy.

'Do you want the last potato?' she asked, eyeing the last golden gem.

'You have it.' A fine example of the self-restraint and generosity that nobody ever gives me credit for.

After dinner it was time for *The Bachelorette*, a mud face-mask for Jen and choc chip cookies for me. Maybe she was on a diet after all, because she refused the cookie I offered her.

'Are your sisters going to be in town for the wedding

rehearsal?' I asked. 'I have to give the restaurant firm numbers this week.'

'No.' Jen's eyes were fixed on the sexy magician onscreen, juggling bowling pins for the blonde bachelorette. 'That was one of the reasons I wanted to have the rehearsal a week before the wedding, so they'd miss it. They're getting in the day before the wedding.'

'Won't they need to practise their duties?'

'They've been in hundreds of weddings. You walk down the aisle, hold flowers, cry and smile. You'll be the one holding my train, anyway. You're the only one who needs to practise. It's actually a good thing you're here, because I have some wedding stuff I want to go over with you.'

I sighed. 'The price I pay for roast chicken.'

She gave me the finger and took a cookie. Guess she'd decided to have one after all.

'So you've booked the venue for the rehearsal dinner,' she said. 'What else?'

'I've hired you a band, too. Rueben's band.'

'So you can shag him afterwards? Good thinking. Listen, I want to invite more people to the dinner, not just the bridal party. My sister told me the bride never gets time to hang out with her friends at the actual wedding, so can you ask Biyu, Dan, my book club, everyone?'

'Yeah, sure. Do I have to invite Jono, though?'

'Oi,' she said.

'Seriously, Jen, you could do a lot better.' I may have drunk too much of Jen's wine, and it may have been the exact wrong moment to hit her once again with the hard truth – three years ago might have been a better time – but no one else was going to take one last shot at helping her see the mistake she was careening towards. Besides, indiscretion looks so good on me, I wear it like a fancy top hat. I drank up and let rip.

'For God's sake, can't you dump Jono and marry Tommasio the cop instead? He loved you. I've already thought ahead to what your children will be called.' I counted on my fingers. 'Traditional Italian: Maria, Giuseppe. Modern Italian: Adele, Antonio. Modern Australian: Mia, Joshua. Modern celebrity: Apple, Blue. I'll even be godmother. I can totally pretend to be Catholic in the ceremony. In fact, I'm ready to take your daughters out shopping and corrupt them completely.'

Jen's face closed down as if someone had drawn the shutters, and she put her wineglass on the coffee table. 'Can you stop saying things like that, Maggie? I know you don't like Jono but it's pretty awful for me. Especially when you're the only person I've got to help me with the wedding. You're telling me to marry some red-faced cop I just met the other night? I had to sweet-talk that guy to get *you* out of trouble. Jono is the person I'm marrying. I'm going to spend the rest of my life with him, and if you want to be my kids' godmother you have to get along with him.'

'Get along with him? Get along with the guy who's wasted half your youth, blind to the fact that he's the luckiest tool in Melbourne? I'm supposed to get along with a man who's got an intellect the size of an ant's dick and an *ego*—'

'Maggie!' Jen's sharp interjection and pained look over my shoulder made me turn.

Jono had entered the room at some point during my speech and was staring at me, mouth open. I hadn't heard him come in over *The Bachelorette*'s skydiving date. Jen gripped the edge of the coffee table as if for balance. There was a wariness in her expression I didn't recognise.

After a long silence, Jono pointed at me. 'Get out of my house.'

'It's Jen's house. She decides who comes in.' Limp comeback. Blame it on the wine.

'Jono,' Jen said. 'Maggie didn't mean it. She's had too much to drink.'

He turned slowly to Jen but kept his finger directed at me. 'I'm going to stay at Rob's house. If I see her face in this house between now and the wedding, there won't be a wedding.'

'Oh, hell no,' I said. 'That's manipulation. Jen, don't fall for his crap.'

A soft tone entered Jono's voice, like he was speaking to a child. 'You really think she's going to choose you?' he said to me, half smiling. 'Which one of us can give her kids, you or me?'

He walked out, slamming the front door. Jen put a shaking hand to her forehead and blinked too many times.

'Jesus Christ, Maggie, I can't believe you've put me in this position.'

'I didn't realise he'd come in,' I said lamely. 'He just . . . pops up.'

Jen began cleaning up our dishes and I had a bad feeling that it was just so she didn't have to look at me. I tried to collect the wineglasses and take them to the sink but she waved off my help.

'I could put up with you using my place like a hotel,' she said, 'and being cavalier with Jono – you've been treating him like an afterthought for years – but I thought you'd be able to keep your actual bloody opinions to yourself, if only to keep the peace during the most important time of my life.'

'Oh right, of course, because I'm such a fucking train wreck and you're a saint for putting up with me, is that the subtext?'

'Subtext? No, it's the freaking text. You think Jono sponges off me, but you're so much worse! You come into my house and make yourself at home and reprogram my Netflix and open my letters and eat my steak and borrow my money, and tell me what's wrong with everyone, including me, including my fiancé—'

'You mean I tell the truth.'

'You have no boundaries!' She was shouting now.

'You're going to have a go at me for sleeping around, too, aren't you?'

'No! That's literally the only thing I'm *not* having a go at you about. If you're going to screw everyone in Melbourne at least stop being so sensitive about it.'

'There it is. You're judging me.'

'I am not!' She slammed the cutlery into the dishwasher with such force that bits of chicken flew off the forks and landed on her cheek. 'I have never judged you. I didn't even judge you the time you ended that poor bastard's eight-year relationship when you slept with him in Ios.'

'That "poor bastard" got the best blowjob of his life. He made his bed.'

'Good for him!'

'Exactly, good for him.'

'Christ.' Jen wiped her face.

Through the window to the backyard I could see Dot, illuminated by the streetlight beyond, kicking up dirt in Jen's vegie patch, presumably to cover the unwelcome fertiliser she'd just added to the tomatoes. Jen had her back to me now and was running hot water over the roasting dish. I was convinced she was cleaning with force in order to induce guilt in me, to hammer home the point that she was always the one looking after me and never the other way around.

'Every time,' I began, 'every single time I want to do something that feels good I have to be reminded that everyone else thinks it's bad, and that if I'm going to do it I'll have to contend with everyone else's need to preserve their reputations, which they insist on projecting onto me as well.'

'You tell yourself whatever you need to get by.' Jen shut off the water and leant back against the kitchen sink. Her voice was quiet. 'I reckon, in sex, we forget who we are. And I think you want to forget yourself more than anyone I've ever met.' She looked down at her hands. 'He's asked me to choose, and it's not easy, but then again it kind of is. I need a break.'

Her words hung in the air.

'A break from me?' I said.

'A break from you.'

I watched her, trying to ascertain how serious she was. Her cheeks were flushed, her eyes pink from holding back tears. There were things I wanted to ask, like, am I still your maid of honour? Am I still invited to the wedding? Am I still your friend? But I was afraid of what the answers might be. So I left, creeping back to the caravan in the cold, reassuring myself that by tomorrow night we'd have made up and everything would be all right.

The caravan that night felt more solid, its walls thicker, the squares of carpet under my feet heavier, as if in the wake of Jen's rejection it had suddenly become my permanent living situation. I went to bed without showering or cleaning my teeth, worrying about what I would do in the morning when I couldn't walk into Jen's house like I was its third occupant and refusing to think about what I'd do if Jen decided she wanted me out of her life forever.

# Chapter 19

I woke at three in the morning, sweating and uncomfortable, feeling exposed, a squatter on a street full of prying yet invisible neighbours, more alone than I'd ever been.

Jen and I sometimes went to the Japanese bathhouse in Collingwood, luxuriating in front of other women, competing with each other over who was the more comfortable with public nudity, who could spread her legs widest without putting a hand over her crotch to cover it, who could put her arms behind her head and lean into the wall as if she'd never noticed her own cellulite. Being in the caravan without Jen as my safety net felt like sitting spreadeagled in the bathhouse in front of a bunch of people with magnifying glasses.

I reached for the boxed wine. The weight of it was comforting in my hand. I've heard that people make plans for their lives: where they're going to be in five years or ten. What jobs they're going to do, where they're going to travel, who they're going to marry and how many shares in oil companies they're going to buy while they're ticking the ballot paper to vote for the Greens.

I don't know what I've been doing with myself while they've been planning; probably I've just been drinking. Even the cheapest boxed wine will help you see warmth in the streetlights.

I took a sip. It wouldn't do me any good, since I needed to go to the bathroom. I reached a hand out and stroked Dot, who was asleep on the pillow next to my head.

'We're moving on again, Dot,' I said.

Half an hour later I was idling the panel van one street parallel from my mother's. She never went down this street, and wouldn't notice the caravan. I switched off the engine, sat back in the driver's seat and thought hard. What could I say to convince her to let me sleep in my old bed? I'll never ask for money again. Or have irresponsible sex. I'll get married before I turn thirty. That's right, I'll get married in the next three months and have two babies and buy a nice little weatherboard house in Brunswick. I'll have handrails installed in your shower when you get old and decrepit. No, take out decrepit. Take out old, too. I'll get handrails installed in your shower if you ever need them.

There was no way it was going to work. Mum wouldn't come around this time. I looked at the clock on the dashboard. It was just past three-thirty in the morning, so it wasn't like I could knock on the front door, anyway. I locked Dot in the caravan with bowls of food and water, and fresh kitty litter, then walked around the block to Mum's house. I tiptoed past the broken gate and across the verandah. My bedroom window was easy to open. I'd never told Mum the lock was loose and could be turned from the outside, because it had come in handy when I was a teenager and needed to sneak out to a party or roll around with a boyfriend. I took off my shoes and eased the window up. It squeaked slightly, but Mum's bedroom was a long way from mine, across the courtyard on the other side of the house, so I wasn't worried about her hearing it. Holding my shoes in one hand, I swung my legs over the ledge and landed on the soft carpet.

My bedroom was neat. I found an old pair of pyjamas in the closet, wriggled into them and snuck down the hall to the bathroom. This was the tricky part. Her bedroom was far enough away that she wouldn't hear me in the bathroom if I was quiet, but she might hear the toilet flush, so I had to avoid that. On top of that, our water pump was old and the pipes squealed when you turned the taps on, so I couldn't wash my hands or even get a glass of water. Still, the big bathroom, the pale blue Art Deco pedestal sink, the privacy of an old, dark, womb-like house and the soft carpets in the hall all combined to settle a sense of relief over me. I snuck back down the hall to my bedroom. Mum always kept the bed made and I slid under the covers in gratitude. I had to stifle a giggle at all the times I'd snuck out of the window growing up; it had never occurred to me that one day I might be sneaking in.

—

The squealing of the pipes woke me at seven-thirty. Mum had her own bathroom, so I didn't have to worry about her noticing that mine had been used. Instead, I lay in bed, thinking about how to arrange things. I could call Mum today while I was at work and ask myself around for dinner, pump her full of wine then pretend to leave. She was shuffling around the house now, getting ready for work. I heard her in the kitchen, clinking plates and cutlery. She was taking forever. Finally she left the house, footsteps crunching on the gravel front path.

I got out of bed, straightened the covers carefully and put my pyjamas back in the closet. After a shower I helped myself to a snack from the fridge, rearranging the food so that it didn't look like anything was missing. While I did my make-up I dialled Jen's number, put the phone on speaker and rested it on the bathroom counter. I ran through phrases in my head to offer Jen as the phone rang. The word *sorry* wasn't one I dropped often, but I could stand to say it for Jen.

I didn't get a chance, though, because she didn't answer.

Before I left for work I checked on the caravan. It was still safe, parked in front of the only house on the street with uncut grass. I opened a window for Dot so she could roam the streets while Mum wasn't there to spot her.

—

Mum was surprised when I called her at work to invite myself over for dinner that night, but didn't object.

'Did you get fired or something?' she asked.

'No, I just want to see my dear mother. Also, I could use a steak.'

'Think I've got some rump in the fridge.'

'Perfect. See you at six-thirty.' I hung up.

Rueben was fixing something that had gone wrong with the Angels' website, frowning into his computer, his stubble longer than usual.

'Do you want to get lunch on Victoria Street?' I asked. 'I could go for some pho.'

He looked up, surprise showing on his quiet face, and smiled. 'I would, but I brought my lunch today. Thanks, though.'

At least I got a smile with today's rejection. I took myself off to Victoria Street but bypassed the pho restaurants. Nothing sadder than spilling noodles on yourself while eating alone. Instead I ordered a takeaway salad at a cheap lunch spot. When I went to pay, however, my card was declined.

'That's weird.' I smiled nervously at the cashier and waved my card at the machine a second time. 'I'll just, er, check my balance and come back in a sec.' I left the salad on the counter and darted out of the shop, avoiding the cashier's irritated glance.

When I checked my bank balance on my phone, there was $4.70 in my account. That couldn't be right. Centrelink should have paid me yesterday. The hum of Victoria Street smeared my senses, dizzying me with the smell of fried food and the rattle of a passing tram. I walked back to work, sweating and panicky, thinking back to the form I'd filled out to contest my debt. I'd ticked the box to keep getting paid while they assessed my claim, right? I definitely had.

I sat at my desk, stomach squirming from fear. And hunger, as I didn't get my bloody salad. Rueben was at his desk, chewing a white-bread sandwich.

'Ham salad?' I guessed.

'Mmhmm.' He looked up. 'Ate your pho already?'

I hesitated. 'Weird thing happened. Centrelink forgot to pay me this week. Couldn't buy my lunch.'

He frowned. 'Mistake, or deliberate?'

'Dunno.'

His chewing slowed as he took in the information, then he wheeled his chair over to me. 'Have this.' He held out the other half of his sandwich. 'I don't need it.'

'Thanks, it's fine,' I said, but he'd already left the sandwich in front of me and wheeled himself back to his desk.

'I feel like that kid at school,' I said. 'There was always one skinny kid who'd eye off your sandwich. I just thought they had a fast metabolism.'

'I used to be that kid at school,' Rueben said. 'Only I'd take your sandwich without asking.'

I dialled Jen again after lunch. No answer. A feeling of panic and loss welled up in my chest, and I pushed it back down again. She's probably at work and can't answer, I told myself.

—

At Mum's house, I ate my steak in a state of misery. It had been nearly twenty-four hours since Jen and I had fought and we still hadn't made up.

'Why are you pushing your food around like that?' Mum asked.

'I'm too tired to chew,' I said.

'Poor darling. Having a part-time job is just that exhausting, huh?'

'Save the sarcasm, Mum.'

After dinner I said goodbye to Mum and walked around the block to sleep in my caravan.

The next morning I waited for Mum to leave for work, then broke in to shower and eat after she was gone, trying not to think about how low I had sunk, having to sneak into my own childhood home. I spent the day on Mum's couch, watching television and trying to memorise where every cushion had been placed so that I could leave the room exactly as I found it. At 4 pm I made a sandwich and took it back to the caravan. I repeated the exercise the next morning, waiting for Mum to leave so I could shower.

I was out in under twenty minutes and took another sand-wich to avoid Monday's lunch disaster. The traffic was bad and I was late for work, but I promised Agnes I'd stay late to make up for it. At my desk, I dialled Jen again, who didn't answer, and daydreamed about how sweet it would be to climb back into the womb and just hang out there for another nine months. Maybe that was part of the caravan's appeal. It was tiny and stuffy and smelt kinda funky, like what I imagined a womb might smell like.

I dropped my head onto the fern on my desk and sighed into its leaves. One frothy tendril tickled my nostril. My life was screwed.

'What's wrong?' Rueben asked when he came back from a meeting with Agnes about the website.

'I did a Bad Thing,' I said.

'How bad?'

'Bad. Worse than saying *meaty thighs* in public. Almost as bad as clocking someone with a cannonball of green vegetable matter.'

'Let me guess, you pissed off Centrelink again.'

'Worse. Much worse.'

'Annoyed your mother? Got arrested for giving someone a wristy?'

'I exhausted Jen's patience.'

'That doesn't sound too bad.'

'You don't know Jen,' I said. 'She's the most patient person in the world. I could steal the very last piece of food in her pantry and all she'd do is offer me the sauce.'

'Well,' he said, 'when I have a problem, I make lists. You know, write down all the individual steps you have to take to achieve something.'

'What was on your list to get this job? "Boast about expertise boosting cash registers?"'

'You don't "boost" a cash register. You get the shop attendant to open it up and give you what's inside.'

'Duh.'

So, I made lists.

### List One: Get Jen to forgive me.

*Steps:*

- *Apologise for being too truthful about Jono.*
- *Learn how to make coffee.*
- *Make her said coffee.*
- *Pay her back her steak money.*
- *Be a better bridesmaid. (How?? Feign interest in chair covers?)*
- *Offer to assist with tomato-sauce-making day.*
- *Actually assist with said tomato-sauce-making day, instead of drinking all the wine and telling her she hasn't reduced the sauce enough.*

God, this list was getting long.

Since I was on a roll, I wrote another list.

### List Two: Be kind to Mum.

This one was even harder. After thinking for a minute, I wrote *Remember her birthday.* Phew, that took some effort. I moved on to the next list.

### List Three: Be less of a failure.

Okay, this was harder still.

*Steps:*

- *Pay off Centrelink debt (get permanent job at the Angels?).*
- *Never say 'meaty thighs' in public.*
- *Get more sex.*

### List Four: Become a nicer person.

*Steps:*

- *???*

# Chapter 20

'Someone broke into my house,' Mum said.

'What?' I twirled the phone cord, smelling the hot plastic from the overworked kettle in the office kitchen. It was nearly six and I was about to pack up.

'Someone broke into my house while I was at work.'

'Shit, what did they take?'

'That's just it, they didn't take anything! They had a shower in your bathroom.'

I cleared my throat. 'Uh, what? How do you know? Did you hear them?'

'No! I was at work.'

'Then how do you know someone had a shower?'

'Because I got home just then and the bath mat's on the ground, and it's still damp. There are drops of water in the shower, too.'

Fuck fuck fuck. I slapped myself in the forehead several times with the palm of my hand. Of course my mother would notice something minuscule like the placement of a bath mat.

'Could it be a leak?' I asked.

'It's not a leak!' She was practically shouting.

I decided to come clean. Mum sounded freaked out. 'Mum—'

'I think it was your father,' she said.

'What?'

'He used to do that. After he left. His girlfriends would kick him out, he'd come back to the house while I was out and eat the food in my fridge. Rearrange it badly to pretend he hadn't been there. Then he'd leave again. I always knew he'd been in, though, because I could smell his horrible aftershave.'

'Could you smell it today?' The chair I was sitting on suddenly became uncomfortable. Guilt can do that – make furniture gain sharp edges in an instant.

'No, but it's been years. He's probably too poor to afford after-shave now. Bloody loser.'

I was about to confess that the shower-taker was me when she broke in again.

'I want to change the locks. In fact, I'm going to get security doors.'

'I know someone who can do that for you,' I said quickly. 'Maybe for free. Or just for the cost of the security doors, not the labour.'

'Is it that nice Dan person?'

'Yes.'

'Are you having sex with him?'

'No.'

'Why not?'

'I thought you didn't like me having casual sex.'

'It wouldn't be casual sex if you were going out with Dan.'

'Well, I'm not going out with Dan.'

'He still running after the engaged girl who's prettier than you?'

'Did I say she was prettier than me? That doesn't sound like me.'

'No, you said she had nice hair. I just assumed.'

'Give me a couple of days,' I said. 'I'll see if I can get the security doors for you. Oh, and can I come round for dinner again tonight?'

'Yes, all right. It's just pasta, though,' she said.

'Sounds good.' I hung up and put my head in my hands.

'Who's Dan?' Rueben asked.

'Never mind. And stop listening to my conversations.'

'I'm two metres away from you, how can I not listen? Besides, they're so fascinating, what with the casual sex and the shower talk.' He stretched back in his chair with his arms over his head and his T-shirt rode up, exposing a hint of skin above his belt. Christ, he was looking fine today. Every day.

'Get back to work,' I said irritably. 'Fix the website.'

'It's home time,' he said, but he turned back to his computer anyway. I picked up the phone again and dialled Dan. He answered on the sixth ring, sounding sleepy.

'Hey Dan, how's things?'

He sighed into the phone. 'Fine.'

'Are you in bed? It's five-thirty.'

'Just a nap. No work today.' In the background, I heard the dulcet tones of a woman asking if Dan was lying on top of her undies.

'Whose voice is that?'

'No one,' he said.

'Is that Lisa with you?'

'Uh, no.'

'Didn't she have to work today either?'

'It's not Lisa.' I heard footsteps, like he was walking out of the room, and the sound of a door closing.

'It really sounded like Lisa's voice. Light. Very attractive. Like the breath of a unicorn.' The image of them in bed together irritated me. I couldn't even get my pretend boyfriend to stay interested in me.

Dan coughed. 'Bloody hell, you hear like a bat. Don't tell anyone, okay?'

'Does she still think we're going to move in together?'

'Nah.' He lowered his voice to a murmur. 'I let her think you were just really, really into me and that I wasn't really into you. Somehow it worked to get her back.'

'Wow, thanks for that. Another hit to my reputation.'

'Sorry. But you were right.' He was whispering now. 'It made her super jealous.'

'You seriously owe me for this. Can you fix security doors to my mother's house?'

'No.'

'No you can't, or no you won't?'

'Can't, won't. It's specialty.'

'And you've already achieved your goal, since Lisa's in bed with you, so you don't need me anymore. Great.' I sighed.

'Bye, Maggie. Thanks for your help. Don't tell anyone about Lisa.'

He hung up. I furiously dropped the phone back in its cradle. What a fairweather friend. As soon as Lisa dumped him again he'd come running back, whining for more help to make her jealous. Still, I was happy for him. Kind of.

Rueben didn't look up from his computer. 'If that was your boyfriend in bed with someone else, you sounded pretty calm about it.'

'Dan's not my boyfriend, he's just the guy I, uh, you know. We're friends now. I helped him get back together with his ex.'

'Ah. Saving the world, one sexual encounter at a time.'

'That's me.' I stood up, the better to pace out my frustration across the threadbare carpet. 'In other news, I'm totally fucked,' I continued.

'Why?'

'I needed Dan to help me fix stuff at my mother's house because – long story – I accidentally freaked her out, but Dan's shot his load and is too satisfied to get out of bed and do it.'

Rueben looked as if he wanted to smile at the non sequitur but managed to keep his usual cool. 'I'm not even going to ask. This is too much.'

I stopped pacing. 'What do you know about security doors?'

'Something, I s'pose.'

'Something?'

'I know a guy who sells them wholesale.'

'Would he do me a deal?'

'No,' Rueben said, 'but he might do *me* a deal.'

'Can you fit them to my mother's doors?'

'I'm not qualified.'

'But could you do it?'

'Yeah, probably.'

'Great. How's Saturday?'

'What's in it for me?' he asked.

'C'mon. Do it out of friendship.'

He deadpanned me.

'Okay, fine, do it and I'll have sex with you,' I said.

'You already want to have sex with me. You propositioned me the first time we met.'

I threw my hands in the air. 'Jesus, dude, why don't you want to have sex with me?'

He sighed and rubbed his face. 'Maggie. I can't accept sexual favours from you in return for handyman jobs. That's . . . I dunno, that's at least workplace harassment, isn't it?'

*I'll give* you *a handyman job*, I almost said. I put my hands on my hips. 'Who said anything about sexual favours? I was talking about good old-fashioned dirty sex. Now you're just embarrassing me. You should do the doors to put me out of my misery. Or have sex with me. Either one is fine.'

He laughed. 'You have to measure them first, though, get a quote . . . I'll give you the guy's number.'

———

Luckily, my mother's doors were a fairly standard size and she only wanted a fairly standard type of security door. The doors weren't cheap but I convinced Mum she'd nabbed a great deal from Rueben's mate and that we were saving on labour costs by having Rueben fix them to the doorframes. They would be ready by the weekend, and in the meantime, I was eating dry cereal for dinner every night, because it seemed like a bad idea to try breaking into her house again before the security doors were put in. I spent the three intervening evenings reading at the pub around the corner, nursing a lone cider paid for with mouldy coins I found in the panel van's centre console. At 10.30 I went to the bathroom one last time, cleaned my teeth with a toothbrush I'd stashed in my handbag, and went home to bed. I had not showered in three days, but the less said about that the better.

When Saturday morning rolled around, Mum stood on the verandah with her arms folded, appraising Rueben, taking in his tatts, stubble and poised, wiry body, while I shifted uncomfortably in the silence.

'I hear you need some extra security, Mrs Cotton,' he said in that gravelly voice. I nearly shivered at the sound of it. Then he got to work.

My mother watched him with narrowed eyes.

'How come he knows how to install security doors?' she whispered to me, her voice masked by the sound of the drill. 'I thought you said he worked in IT.'

*Prison*, I nearly said. 'He's one of those guys that can do stuff.'

Later, while Mum was making sandwiches, I asked him where he got his skills.

'It's just a drill and a screw gun.' He lifted a hand to wipe his forehead. Rueben made sweat patches look good. 'Any idiot can buy them at Bunnings and read the instruction booklet.'

I merely stared.

Rueben smiled. 'You're like Dora the Explorer discovering opposable thumbs.'

'How have you even heard of Dora the Explorer?'

'I have a niece.'

I brought him dry ginger ale and tried to look sexy sucking on an ice cube while he tested the new lock.

'The band's been practising for the wedding rehearsal dinner,' he said, and I was hit with a visceral sadness at the thought of being left out of Jen's rehearsal dinner and wedding. The best thing to do, I decided, was to act as if the fight had never happened. Even to Rueben.

'That's great,' I said. 'I'm glad someone will be prepared for this dinner. The planning is doing my head in. I can't decide if there should be a theme. What's a good theme? You know, that will liven up the party.'

'The inevitable heat death of the universe,' he suggested.

'Come on.'

'Moving to Tasmania and getting a mortgage and having a few kids and dying a country death.'

'What's a country death?'

'Falling off a tractor. Getting bitten by a snake. Eating a diseased rooster.'

'Getting face cancer from kissing a Tasmanian devil,' I added.

'That's the spirit.'

I sipped my ginger ale. It was flat. 'I could hang cut-outs of diseased roosters from the ceiling to remind Jen that she's marrying a rotten cock.'

After he'd attached security doors to the front and back of the house, Rueben disappeared around the side, looking for other possible entry points through which sneaky ex-husbands could wriggle their lazy, worthless selves. Did Mum really believe it was my dad breaking in? She had sounded pretty convinced on the phone. While I was sitting on the verandah waiting for Rueben to return, Mum brought out curried egg sandwiches on a tray.

'Where did you meet this guy?' she asked.

'I told you, at work. He's our IT guy.'

'But all those tattoos. Young people these days do such strange things to their bodies. He looks like a criminal.'

'But a handsome one, right?' I said.

Mum licked her upper lip. 'Damn straight.'

I couldn't help laughing.

'I suppose you're sleeping with him, too,' she said.

'I wish.'

'Well. Hide your wallet if you have him around to the caravan, that's all I'm saying. Although I suppose it's not necessary, since there's nothing *in* your wallet.' She went inside again.

Rueben and I sat on the verandah eating the egg sandwiches.

An awkward silence fell between us – at least, I felt awkward, trying not to stare at his sensational collarbones – and I felt the need to fill it.

'I have a theory that people who eat their egg whites runny are nasty in bed,' I said.

'Why would that be?' he asked.

'Runny egg whites are disgusting. If you're into that, you're probably into gross stuff in the bedroom too. Like fish-shaped butt plugs and stuff.'

'Fish-shaped?'

'Haven't you noticed that butt plugs are often fish-shaped?'

'Maybe that's their natural shape.'

'I swear they've got little plastic scales sometimes.' I made an O with my fingers. 'Little round open mouths and bulbous eyes.'

Rueben finished his sandwich and wiped the crumbs on his jeans but didn't answer.

'So, how do you like your egg whites?' I pressed. 'Personally I could stomach them runny once, for you.'

'That's so romantic,' he said.

We said goodbye to Mum, who was eyeing Rueben with a little less suspicion and a little more admiration, and walked down the path towards our cars. Rueben drove a surprisingly boring black Honda, which I found disappointing.

'Would have picked you for a Valiant man,' I said, stretching in the afternoon shade of the plane trees.

'I'd be a Valiant man, if they weren't such a bastard to run.'

'They do break down a bit,' I admitted. 'But this doesn't seem to suit your personality.'

'Do I have to express my personality through a car? Can't I just express it through a grey T-shirt and a non-committal stare?'

'It makes you harder to understand.'

He took a step towards me. 'Maybe it makes me more fun to get to know.'

Holy shit, he was flirting with me. Finally. My mouth went dry and I couldn't think of a single thing to say, except, 'Hey, where's my copy of the key?'

'I didn't know you wanted one. You'll have to ask your mum to get you a key cut.'

'I can't ask her, I don't want her to know I'm staying at her place.'

'How is that even possible?'

'Jen kicked me out, Mum won't let me move back in. I've been going through the window but I'm starting to worry about the neighbours calling the police. I need a key so I can get in the back door without her knowing.'

Rueben looked up at the sky, as if it could explain my idiocy. 'So you freaked your mother out by breaking in, and now you're fixing the problem by having her pay for expensive doors to keep you out . . . except you want a key. That's not only very strange, but also illegal. I can't give you a key without the homeowner's permission.'

'But it's my mother, and you know me!'

'Doesn't matter. Not going back to the can for you.' The flirtatious look had disappeared. Just as I was making headway.

'As if they'd put you in jail for it.'

His face was set. 'I'm serious, Maggie. You have no idea how straight I'm willing to play it to stay out of there. Don't ask me to fucking jaywalk.'

He got in his car and drove off without saying goodbye.

# Chapter 21

I hovered in the work kitchen, making tea and checking my bank balance on my phone, just to see if it had grown over the weekend. Nope. I dreaded another interaction with Centrelink, but I'd have to call them at some point, since I'd worked the whole of last week for no pay.

'What's up, Maggie?' Agnes asked as she made her instant coffee.

'Just thinking about, uh, rent,' I said.

'Are you having financial trouble?'

I considered whether or not to tell her the truth. 'Well . . . nah, not really.'

'You can tell me.'

'It's kinda awkward 'cause you're my boss.'

'Sure, but I'm not paying you.'

Most of the time, Agnes was in a rush to do something and her voice had a breathy, nervous edge, but when she was relaxed and in the mood for talking, her tone took on a brussels sprouts quality. No nonsense, wholesome, somewhat bland. She was a master in the art of giving orders in a deceptively casual tone so you didn't resent it, but with just enough authority that she couldn't be ignored. I felt healthier just by listening to her. After a brief hesitation, I decided that, judging by her voice, she was the right person to fix my life by proxy.

'So,' I said, 'I was kind of using my mother for money for a few years, but recently she got sick of it and cut me out of her will. Said I had to prove I could be independent before she'd ever help me again. Part of the deal was that I couldn't move in with another boyfriend – I'd been doing that for a while, too – or a friend, or I'd lose the bet. She wants me to support myself, work full-time, get my own place. But instead of getting an apartment and a real job – I mean, a full-time one, like, a paid one . . .' Whoops, I hoped she didn't take offence to that 'real job' comment. But she didn't look offended, just kept listening intently. 'Anyway, instead of that, I started living in a caravan and doing the Centrelink volunteer program.'

'You're doing good work here.'

'Yeah, well, Mum thought I just wanted to stick it to her. But I kinda like it. The job and the caravan, I mean. It's just that there's no bathroom or electricity or running water.' I sighed, maybe a little too dramatically, and leant against the wall, stirring my tea. 'I thought I could live free and society would make room for me. But it doesn't. The police keep hassling me because the neighbours don't like it. And now I'm breaking into my mother's house at night to use her bathroom and sleep in my old bed, because it's all too hard, and my best friend isn't speaking to me, because . . . well, she has reasons.' Reasons like, I'm as considerate as a tooth cavity.

Agnes sipped her coffee, seemingly in no hurry to dispense wisdom. Finally, she settled her cup back on the sink and wiped her mouth.

'You'll sort yourself out,' she said. She looked at her watch. 'I have to organise an electrician to fix the wiring in the men's shelter. How are you going with that fundraising letter?'

'Uh, good. I think I'll finish it today.'

'Great.' She walked away.

Jeez, Agnes. Thanks for your help.

—

I opened up the fundraising letter file on my computer. I'd done six drafts but was still reluctant to call it finished. It was going to cost nine hundred dollars to mail the letter out to all our supporters, but what if it didn't even bring in that much in donations? We had to keep our overheads and administration costs below twenty-five per cent of our income, Agnes had told me, otherwise our donors would get annoyed and stop giving us money. So, if the letters cost nine hundred dollars to mail, they needed to earn . . . four thousand dollars, give or take.

I went over the wording of the letter for the thousandth time, then read through yet another blog about how to write good fundraising copy. 'Copy': it had taken a while to figure out what that meant, and when I realised that I was essentially doing the same job as Sarah Stoll, Premium Bitch of Advertising Copy, I had been momentarily disconcerted. Now, though, I was all business. I had learnt to write the word 'you' – as in you, the generous donor – instead of 'we', the needy charity. I had learnt to write an emotional story about just one potential recipient of the donor's generosity instead of many, I had learnt to tell the donor exactly what they could achieve with their donation. What interested me most was that you were supposed to ask the donor for an exact amount, specify exactly how that amount could help, and then offer two options to donate higher amounts.

As in, give $50 and keep four people warm and fed for the night, give $100 to outfit and train three women for job interviews, give $250 and Maggie will hump you.

Which got me thinking. Agnes insisted that the bulk of the Angels' donors were people living close to poverty themselves.

'You'd be surprised how many of our donors are on Centrelink benefits,' she'd said. 'They don't have much money but they're generous with it because they know how it feels to worry about how they'll get by. They can relate.'

'Fine,' I reasoned, 'but if we can convince a few people with a lot of money to give larger donations, surely that would bring our overheads down and mean less effort for us?'

'Yes,' she said, 'and we've tried, in the past. We've got through to a few, but to be honest, it's just not worth the effort. Most of them aren't interested. They give money to other causes, but not to relieve poverty.'

I was determined to try anyway.

'Rueben.' He looked up from his ramen noodles, but slowly, to show he was still annoyed with me for deceiving my mother. 'Can you find out if it's possible to buy a list of names and addresses of people in Victoria whose incomes are over a certain amount?'

'I think it's possible,' he said coolly. 'Are you thinking of targeting certain people in the fundraiser?'

'Yeah.'

He tapped on a few keys, scrolled a bit, ate a forkful of noodles and put the fork down. 'There are lists, but it's expensive,' he said. 'Too expensive for us.'

'How expensive?'

'For targeted stuff, thousands.' He showed me the screen.

'Dammit. Can you hack them?'

'What?'

'Can you hack the companies that sell the lists?'

'No, and I wouldn't try. They're heavily protected, and do I have to repeat that I'm not going to jail for you?'

'I wasn't being serious.'

'Sure you weren't.'

I went over the letter again, thinking. 'What if I just scatter-gunned people in certain suburbs? Like, Toorak, Hawthorn, Brighton. I could research the five or ten richest suburbs in the state and grab names and addresses from the phone book.'

'That would take hours. Days, maybe.'

'Yeah, but it's not costing the Angels anything, is it? We're volunteers.'

He shrugged. 'You're right.'

'Admit it. Sometimes my ideas aren't terrible.'

'Sometimes your ideas aren't terrible.'

—

It was time to accept that further tweaking and proofreading would not improve the letter. It was done. I hit print and stretched. The office was quiet. Agnes was out, Josephine was off work for the day, Rueben was busy improving the back end of the website to make it easier for supporters to donate online and for us to collect their email addresses. It turned out we did have about a thousand email addresses, we just never bothered to email our supporters. I opened a spreadsheet with our supporter contact list, added a column for email addresses to collate all the information in the same place, then started a new spreadsheet called '5 Richest Suburbs', ready to plug in names and addresses from the phone book.

A noise at the door drew my attention. It was Bunny, slinking into our office. Her hair was piled on her head in coils, which were arranged around a flower crown of all things, tiny rosebuds made of pink and white ribbons with green wire leaves, and her legs were encased in annoyingly enviable cat-print tights. Bunny rarely entered the office where Rueben and I worked. Her work-days only overlapped with ours on Mondays and Fridays and I tended to avoid her whenever possible, especially since my plan to steal her job occasionally brought on a slight twinge of guilt in my throat. She lingered in the doorway and twirled a red curl at the nape of her neck.

'How's it going?' she asked Rueben.

He looked up. 'Fine, thanks. Nice flower thing.'

She pushed off from the doorframe and walked over to his desk. 'Rueben, you are such a sly one, you never mentioned that you're a musician! I only discovered it from Christine just now.'

'Right,' he said.

'What do you play?'

'Guitar.'

She was around the other side of his desk now, eyeing his computer screen. 'What's this?'

'The back end of the website.'

'Amazing.' She leant over him. 'I've never seen it before!'

That's because you don't do your job properly, Bunny.

'Do you sing?' she asked.

'A bit.'

'Self-taught?'

'Yeah.'

'Me too. Hey, why don't we do a duet next Prayer Time?'

The thought of Rueben roped into a duet with Bunny was exquisite, but the pained expression on his face forced me, out of humanity, to intervene. 'What have you been up to, Bunny? How's the marketing going?'

'Wonderful,' she said. 'You know, I think right now the most important thing is office morale.' She put on her Concerned Face. 'After that meeting about the finances, I think people are feeling really down, so I've been talking to Agnes about redecorating the office to brighten everyone's spirits.'

'Redecorating?'

'I've ordered some wall decals.'

'Of what?'

'Bible quotes, butterflies. I think we need to look upon the beauty of God's creation. Once we can do that, we'll really turn things around for the Nicholson Street Angels.'

'Hmm, good thinking, Bunny,' said Rueben.

By now she was at my desk, looking at my screen.

'Spreadsheets,' I told her. 'Pretty fascinating stuff.'

She shot me a false smile and sauntered out of the room.

'She's such a fucking weirdo,' I said.

Rueben smiled. 'You're jealous.'

———

Rueben and I were having a tea break in reception late in the afternoon, refreshing our memories of Shane Warne's text messaging scandal by reading aloud from the stack of decade-old women's magazines on the coffee table, when Hannah wandered through the door, a box of chocolates tucked under one arm. She seemed alert, nearly sober.

'Got given them,' she said. 'They're for the sheilas.' The sheilas meant the women currently staying at the shelter. Hannah delivered messages from them to us, kind of like Moses. 'Jackie wants to know if her psych appointment's tomorrow.'

I had no idea who Hannah was talking about. 'Josephine will know about that, but she's not in.'

Bunny bounced out of her office and into reception at the sound of Hannah's voice, creaming for some songwriting inspiration, no doubt. I suspected it was the main reason she liked to be near the Vulnerable. 'Hannah! Have you brought those chocolates? You're so lovely.'

'Hi, Your Majesty,' Hannah said.

Bunny self-consciously touched her flower crown.

The bell on the door jingled again, and Belinda arrived.

'Saw you from the op shop,' she said, giving Hannah a hug. They'd first crossed paths at the shelter, before Belinda was allocated a safe house. Belinda turned to Bunny. 'The women need better shoes!' she burst out. 'I want you to put up posters about the kinds of donations we want.'

'We can't do that,' Bunny replied, taken aback. 'I mean, we can say we need good-quality items, but we can't just say "give us better shoes".'

'People judge you by your shoes,' Belinda insisted. I looked down at hers; they were pale-pink pumps in soft crocodile skin. Fabulous. 'You wear shoes made of pleather, you may as well be a psychopath.' Bunny was slinking backwards, nodding and smiling, so Belinda turned to me instead. 'Some of the women in the shelter are trying to get jobs. How can they get jobs in shit shoes?'

'I don't know,' I said. But the thought filled me with motivation to finish the spreadsheet. Making sure the women didn't have to wear psychopath shoes was something to work towards. It was time for those wealthy donors to cough up.

At quarter to five, Rueben got up to take his coffee cup to the kitchen and took mine to wash as well.

'Can you grab the draft letter off the printer while you're up?' I asked him. 'I want to proofread it once more before I give it to Agnes.'

'All right.'

He returned a few minutes later, carrying only the clean mugs. 'Didn't print.'

'Didn't it?'

'There was nothing on the printer.'

'Oh.' I hit print again, walked over to the printer to collect it, and then took it back into our office.

'It's five o'clock,' Rueben said. He started packing up.

'I took this comma out in the last draft, but now I'm thinking I should put it back in,' I said.

'Maggie, if you've got to the taking-commas-out-and-putting-them-back-in stage, the letter is done. Give it to Agnes in the morning, it's home time.'

'I'm going to stay here and go through the phone book,' I told him. 'I'm still on Toorak.'

I pulled the White Pages website up on my screen, and started copying and pasting names, addresses and phone numbers into the '5 Richest Suburbs' spreadsheet. Like Rueben had said, it was painstaking work. My hand was going to get sore from clicking.

'I told you, it's going to take forever.'

'I know.'

He sat back down. 'Okay, I'll do Brighton,' he said. He turned his computer back on. 'Send me a link to the spreadsheet in Google Docs.'

'Really?' I knew he was probably doing it because he cared about the work, but a small, selfish part of me hoped that he wanted to stay late with me, too.

'Yeah. You want to order pizza?'

'You don't have to stay, this was my dumb idea,' I said.

He smiled. 'I told you, it's not dumb.'

'You said it's not terrible. It is pretty dumb.'

'What do you want on your pizza?'

'Salami.'

Bunny stuck her head back in to say goodbye. Christ, three times in one day?

'Bye, guys.' She wiggled her fingers at Rueben.

'Bye, Bunny,' he said, resignation in his voice.

———

By 10 pm I had a headache and a violent cramp in my hand, and the room was full of the odour of empty pizza boxes. On the plus side, I'd finished all of Toorak and some of Portsea, and Rueben had finished Brighton. I wanted to have the spreadsheet completed by Wednesday, so I had decided to do the unthinkable: email myself the spreadsheet and finish it the following day, when I didn't have to go to work. I took a deep breath and pictured it: every woman in the shelter with a pair of pale-pink crocodile-skin shoes.

'God, I'm sore,' I complained.

Rueben looked up from his spot on the floor. He had taken to stretching every twenty minutes or so, contorted in strange yoga poses. Right now, he was on his knees with his arms reaching in front of him. Pose of the child, I knew that one.

'Why don't you stretch out your spine a little?' he said.

'Rueben Blackwood. Criminal, IT guru, yogi.' I got down beside him and copied his movements. 'Hey, that actually feels amazing. But the carpet smells like wet dog.'

'Separate your fingers, too. Like this.'

'This?'

'No.'

He took my fingers, just the ends, and spread them out one by one, like daisy petals. Then he brushed his thumb over them. Sparks might have shot from my fingertips, I don't know.

I couldn't stay in child's pose after that. I rolled onto my back, aware of Rueben's body next to me. I breathed in and out slowly, as if I could train my heartbeat to not betray me just by concentrating hard enough. The carpet scratched the skin of my shoulder blades and I suddenly felt cold, like maybe I needed a warm man to lie on top of me. Rueben was breathing deep and slow too, like a cat. I blinked against the harsh fluorescent lights above us, and when I looked back at him there were patches of bright white against his eyelashes, and even though I knew it was just the afterglow from the fluorescents, it still made him look like he was made of silver. He was all raw nerve, or was that me? I smelt salt and butter as he leant down to brush his lips against my cheek. Why didn't he go for my waiting mouth? I was frozen, wanting more, not able to speak in case I ruined it.

An unwelcome noise broke in from beyond the reception desk, the sound of a key in the front door and the confused rattling of the knob. Rueben and I rolled apart. I was just pushing myself up off the floor and dusting my knees when Agnes entered the room. I could tell it was Agnes without even turning around because of her distinctive shuffle, usually quite pleasant to my ears because she was one of the few sensible people in the office, but tonight I was so angry at the interruption I wished she'd fall flat on her face or choke on a mouthful of dry Milo. When I turned around, my hand reaching unconsciously to check my hair, Agnes's face said it all. She was not fooled by the faux nonchalance. She glanced from me to Rueben and back again.

'What are you two still doing here? It's past ten.'

Rueben recovered faster than I did. 'We're targeting a new group of donors for the fundraiser. Thought we'd stay late to put the list together.' He sat down at his desk as if nothing had happened.

'Well, all right.' As if to fill the awkward silence Agnes began telling us about her ordeal with the electrician at the men's shelter and how she thought she'd just pop back to the office to collect her thoughts and her folders before she went home for the night.

'I'm off too,' I said. 'I think we've almost finished here anyway.'

Rueben and I busied ourselves shutting down computers while Agnes loitered, as if she was a chaperone who shouldn't leave us alone. We all walked out into the evening air together.

'Goodnight,' Rueben said. He smiled a crooked little smile and a river of desire flowed through me.

'Yeah, night,' I replied, and walked off as if my thighs weren't burning.

—

The next day was warm and sunny. I spent the entire morning working on the spreadsheet, burning through my phone's data and sweating in the caravan. A bedroom, air conditioning, a functioning kitchen with running water, and Lord, dear Lord, a full-size bathroom with a shower and bath: these all seemed like unfathomable luxuries. I kept banging my head on the ceiling above the fold-out table – it was lower there than in the centre of the caravan – and tripping over clothes on the floor, and I had to walk to the pub every time I needed the bathroom. But I promised myself I would finish this spreadsheet and find the Angels a major donor.

At lunchtime, I bit the bullet and called Centrelink again.

'There's been a mistake,' I said, 'another one,' and explained that I'd filled in the form correctly to contest my debt but hadn't been paid my Newstart Allowance for the fortnight. There was a long, uncomfortable pause while the woman on the other end of the line clacked some keys to look through my file.

'About that,' she said. 'We've rejected your claim to continue receiving Newstart while we process the paperwork. You've also been removed from the volunteer program. If you want to claim Newstart, you'll have to go online and put in a new application. And, of course, you'll have to look for a full-time job.'

'But I have a job,' I said faintly. 'I mean, I like my volunteer position at the Nicholson Street Angels, and I'm working on a big campaign for them right now.'

'Sorry,' she said. 'That's the way it is.'

'But . . . do I still go in to work tomorrow?'

I could almost hear her shrug. 'You won't be paid for it, so if I were you, I'd use the time to start looking for a job.'

I felt sick. All that work I'd put in for the Angels, and Centrelink could just pull me from the program with one swipe of a pen? Since Agnes hadn't said anything yesterday, I assumed that no one from Centrelink had bothered to inform her that my period of volunteering was up, and given the amount of clerical errors they'd made so far, I decided to operate on the assumption that I had some time. Just a little bit of time to prove beyond a doubt that I was essential to the Angels' financial wellbeing, so they'd offer me a paid job. As long as I didn't tell anybody, even Rueben, about the extent of my Centrelink problems, I might be able to hang on long enough. I got a weird sensation in the torso area from thinking about Rueben. I imagined it was a similar thing to what dogs feel when they get so excited they pee on your feet. Either I was becoming incontinent, or I wanted to impress him.

In the early evening I called Jen and left her a message.

'It's been a week since we last spoke,' I said, 'which is, like, a year in Jen and Maggie time, so to fill you in on what I've been doing: writing in spreadsheets, breaking into my mother's house, trying to get Rueben to sleep with me. I'm working hard, it's a new thing I'm trying. To be honest, I think it's barbaric. Hard work is terrible, I don't know how you stand it. Anyhow, I'm so desperate for a lasagne I'd almost buy one, except I don't have any money. Um . . . call me? Oh, and I'm parked on Bradley Street, near Mum's. In case you're looking for me. Bye.'

I had intended to say *I'm sorry*, but apologies don't work too well over voicemail.

—

I was as crusty as a picked scab the next day, aching all over from sitting in one position while working on the spreadsheet, but I rolled into work on time just the same. I had real hope for once, the kind that wasn't predicated on someone giving me something I hadn't earned. This hope was founded on the fact that I thought I'd done a pretty good job with the letter and my extra research. The Angels were going to make a killing out of it, I told myself, and I nearly believed it. The men's shelter would have proper heating put in; women fleeing abusive relationships would find decent job training and work outfits. The potential for success was there, I just had to make sure everything lined up. I would hand Agnes the letter as soon as I walked in, and just as she was ready to heap praise on me for that – *Wonderful, Maggie, you're amazing, you've saved us!* – I would hit her with the next thing, the list of rich potential donors and the specially targeted letters that asked for $500 instead of $50. We had over two thousand names on the rich list and even if only one per cent responded, it would still bring in ten grand.

I settled in at my desk, waiting for the right moment to talk to Agnes, which was after she'd had her coffee. Rueben wasn't in yet, which was unusual. Normally he got to work ten minutes early.

At nine-thirty, I detected the chemical waft of instant coffee floating in from the kitchen and I knew it was time. I casually slunk into the kitchen, holding the pink folder containing my fundraising letter.

'Hi Agnes. Is Rueben sick today?' I asked her, trying to sound nonchalant.

'Yes, he called this morning. Gastro. I thought you'd know about it already,' she said, eyeing me meaningfully.

'No, I didn't know.'

'Ah. Perhaps I misunderstood Monday night's little escapade.'

I felt my cheeks grow hot. 'No, ah, we're not . . . together.'

'Uh-huh.'

'I've finished the fundraising letter.' I held out the pink folder. 'I'm really interested to know what you think.'

She didn't take it. 'Bunny already wrote a letter.'

'What?'

'Bunny wrote a fundraising letter. She gave it to me on Monday night. It's good, actually. I have to admit I was surprised. It didn't even contain her usual choice phrases, like "reach into your heart for the homeless" – it was very matter of fact.'

I was dumbfounded. My mouth opened and closed like a fish for a couple of seconds. The ceiling fan whirred quietly.

'I don't—' I began, then stopped.

Agnes checked the time. 'I have to go. Just focus on collecting those email addresses for the follow-up. It was a good idea of yours, this letter. Haven't forgotten that.'

She smiled briefly, picked up her coffee and left. The temperature in the kitchen seemed to have risen by a few degrees. I ran a hand over my forehead and came away with sweat.

That bitch *stole my idea*.

I almost followed Agnes into her office to demand she read my letter, which I was sure would be better than Bunny's, but I stopped short when I realised that I had absolutely no credibility at the Nicholson Street Angels. All Agnes knew about me was that I was the idiot who tried on sunflower-print onesies in the op shop and rolled around on the floor with the sexy IT guy late at night. Bunny had worked at the Angels for a lot longer than I had and had presumably never done such things. She was also the marketing coordinator, so even if my letter was objectively better than hers, Agnes would probably assume Bunny's would bring in more dough.

'Fuck fuck fuck,' I whispered. This was a bad day for Rueben to come down with gastro. I really needed his advice. I was struck with a wild, paranoid thought: what if Rueben was faking his illness to get out of work, and had conspired with Bunny to steal my thunder? Were he and Bunny at a prayer meeting somewhere right now, clapping hands and swapping notes on how to spice up the missionary position?

I looked up Rueben's address in the personnel files, then shut down my computer and left the office without saying goodbye to anyone. I needed to do some serious drinking.

# Chapter 22

I drove to Smith Street, knowing the right anaesthetic was waiting for me among the clean-skinned bottles that populated the new American-South-style bottle-o that was manned by a bearded hipster. Smith Street was quieter, calmer and cleaner than usual; the street sweepers had been through this morning and the sun was out. The bottle-o rose up from the pavement like a perfect, pink erection; a beautiful, neon-lit specimen touting the specials. The sign could have added, 'Just for you, Maggie, you hot mess.' I parked the car, sidled in like a dog in heat and dry-humped the display case of discounted wine. White wine was cheaper than red by a dollar so I bought white, never minding that it wasn't refrigerated. Six dollars to forget my life. Especially to forget that I had gathered that six dollars together by cleaning under the mats of my car for the first time in three years, and that I was paying in five-, ten- and twenty-cent pieces.

Maybe Rueben really was with Bunny. Maybe she was a good option for him, what with her musical inability and her upswept red hair and her earnest commitment to Doing Good Deeds. Maybe jail had warped his mind, maybe those grey halls and right angles and echoing noises of steel on steel had made him want a woman who was soft and lovely, if an idiot. I knew my reasoning was ridiculous, and that Rueben thought Bunny was a numpty, but I drank down the lukewarm acid in the bottle all the same. Bunny had well and truly screwed me. I could do her job with my eyes closed, but she was going to get all the credit. Agnes might have offered me a job if my fundraising letter was a success, but now I was going to have to start collecting cans out of bins for cash.

I left the car on a side street and rode the 86 tram to Northcote, hugging my bottle. Taking the tram wasn't just to avoid drink-driving. I was also down to a quarter of a tank of petrol and couldn't afford to refill. When the cute second-hand stores and good bars on High Street appeared, I pulled the string and the doors creaked open to let me out. It was hot, not a blade of grass to be seen anywhere. This was asphalt city, teeming with dingy mid-rise buildings painted blue and black and grey.

The street I wanted was a few blocks past the Northcote Social Club. It had an eclectic mix of done-up weatherboard houses with huge steel extensions on the back, sagging bunga-lows owned by old nonnas whose grandchildren were waiting to fight over their inheritance and subdivide the land, and blocks of cream-coloured 1960s brick apartment blocks with concreted front yards. I checked the number I'd scribbled on a piece of paper and stopped in front of one of the low cream brick complexes. It was reasonably well kept. Someone had tried to green the concrete yard with a raised garden-bed of vegetables.

I knocked on number three, a ground-floor flat on the side of the building, facing the driveway. A cafe table and two chairs sat outside the door, alongside a pot containing a healthy fern. After a moment came the sound of a latch turning, and a face darkened by the security screen door peered out at me.

'Maggie?' Rueben opened the screen door. He was wearing tracksuit pants and a Rolling Stones T-shirt with a hole in the neck, and he looked pale. 'What are you doing here?'

I did my best not to sway. 'Just checking on you. Agnes says you're sick.'

Without waiting for an invitation, I pushed past him into the kitchen. The cupboards were light green and the linoleum floor was peeling at the edges. Dated but clean. I rested the nearly empty bottle of white wine on the counter and tugged my cotton dress down over my thighs to make sure I was covered, then wondered why I did it. As if my dress would fall off at the sight of Rueben. Well, maybe.

Rueben eased himself down onto a kitchen chair and passed a hand across his forehead, where a slight sheen of sweat had broken out, most likely at the effort of coming to the door. I felt relieved; he really was sick.

'Bad prawns,' he said. 'It's nice of you to come, but I really don't think wine is going to help.'

'The wine is for me, obviously.'

'How thoughtful.'

I leant against the counter for balance.

He frowned. 'Are you drunk? It's barely midday.'

'No,' I replied.

'You *are* drunk.'

'I'm not drunk. My shoes have been drinking. They keep falling over.'

He raised his eyebrows.

'Bunny stole my idea,' I told him.

'What idea?'

'She wrote a fundraising letter and gave it to Agnes before I could hand mine in.'

Rueben rubbed his face. 'Let me guess. Instead of talking to Bunny, or talking to Agnes, or thinking of an actual solution to the problem, you left work, got drunk and came here to whine? I thought you were checking up on me.' He looked hurt.

'Well, I mean, that too,' I said. 'And I kinda wanted to snoop around your apartment.'

'Go ahead,' he said. 'There's not much to see.'

I snooped. The apartment had one bedroom and was small and clean and unexpectedly filled with pot plants. The guy liked ferns. The living room was set up as a music practice room, with a couch squashed into the corner and no television. Three guitars hung on the wall, including the fancy steel slide I had seen at The Fainting Chair.

'Nice place,' I called. 'How do you afford an apartment on Centrelink money?'

'My sister owns it,' Rueben answered. 'She rents it to me cheaply.' Back in the kitchen, he was still sitting pale at the table. I felt sorry for him.

'You look bad,' I said. 'And kinda blotchy, like you're dehydrated. Do you have any Hydralyte tablets?'

He shook his head. 'I'd get some, but I don't think I can walk that far.'

'Lucky I'm here. Where's the pharmacy?'

He gave me clear directions but I still got lost. Fifteen minutes later I found the pharmacy and bought Hydralyte, Gastrolyte and paracetamol for good measure. When I returned to Rueben's apartment he was in bed, but had left the front door open for me. I mixed him up some Hydralyte and brought it to him, along with painkillers. I pulled up a chair and sat by the bed as he sipped the drink.

I liked sick Rueben, I decided. He was less sexy, more help-less, more cute.

'So tell me what Bunny did,' he said.

'I told you pretty much everything.'

'And what are you going to do about it?'

'What can I do? She's worked there longer than I have. I've got no cred. I just have to suck it up.'

'Okay, first things first. You can't copyright an idea, you know that. You spent a long time on that letter – too long, what with taking out all the commas and putting them back in – and I'm sorry that you won't get the glory for it. But remember, you haven't just come up with the letter idea. You've also spent hours and hours finding potential new donors, and together we've sorted out the email address problem.'

'You sorted it.'

'We both did. The letter is going to bring in a lot of money for the Angels, and you were mostly responsible for it.'

'I'm depressed,' I said. 'The bitch outsmarted me, and it burns. I *know* I'm smarter than her.' I banged my fist on his bedside table.

'You are. And that's why you live in a caravan.'

'Because I'm eschewing materialism.'

'Exactly.'

'Because I don't judge people by the size of their mortgage,' I went on. He grinned. I grabbed the bottle of wine from the kitchen and sat down again. 'You know, I could be just like Sarah Stoll. I could tan myself tandoori orange, bleach my hair until it fell out, date a few tennis players and talk about my massive mortgage and how many pairs of shoes I owned and the whole world would consider me a completely acceptable human being. "*Daaahling*, I heard you fucked Roger Federer,'" I mimicked. "'Well done. I know he's won more grand slams, but personally I find the curve of Rafael Nadal's cock more elegant." But me, I live in a caravan in Collingwood for five minutes and I'm a pariah.' I took a swig.

'Slow down, Maggie. You'll be passed out by dinner time.'

'Well, stop driving me to drink.'

'Who's driving you to drink?'

'Bunny. Sarah. My mother. You, with your sexy eyes.' The bottle slipped out of my hands and landed on the floor with a clunk, but didn't break. I picked it up before it could spill and wiped my mouth with a wet hand.

'Maggie, go home. Watch some television. Take a Valium.'

'Don't try to drug me into submission.' I could feel my body gently rocking, like waves lapping at the seashore. Or like a large, slow pendulum. 'I will not numb my mind with television. The revolution will not be televised!'

'Okay.'

'Also, I don't have a television. Or electricity, unless I steal it.'

'I need to sleep,' he said.

'Oh.'

I waved goodbye and left his apartment, even remembering to lock the front door from the inside before I shut it.

The tram took me back to Collingwood and my car, which was still parked off Smith Street. I climbed into the back, flopped down like a dead fish onto my old jacket, and passed out. When I woke up, it was just past six in the evening and the car was roasting. Angry red lines on my skin from where the jacket lay crumpled under me told me that I was dehydrated. The world spun slightly when I sat up. I staggered outside and locked the car, feeling aimless, only wanting to get into the fresh air. I walked along Wellington Street and turned onto Keele Street, imagining what I'd plant in the front garden if I owned any of the houses. The sun was easing down along the horizon and the squeals of children playing in the last light of day on a corner playground followed me down the street. A jacaranda flower dropped into my hair as I passed a showstopper garden. The blossoms had coated a section of the footpath in a purple bowl.

I was at Jen's front door before I remembered I wasn't allowed in there. Her absence the past week and a half had hit me like a sledgehammer. It was becoming clear that I had never appreciated her as much as I should have, or considered that she might be the only person who could decide what was best for her future. I couldn't quite stop my fist from knocking on her door, and when I heard Jen's footsteps in the hall, anxiety and relief rose in me at the same time. I needed to tell her I was falling apart, and that she was the only one with the right kind of glue.

Her face when she saw me was sad, and tired.

'Can I come in?' I asked.

She looked down the hall as if there was someone there who might tell her what to decide, but I knew that Jono had already left to go back to the mines. When she looked back at me, I knew what she was going to say.

'Nah,' she said.

'We still on a break?'

'Yeah.'

I said, 'Okay,' and turned to walk away, half expecting she would call me back, but as I reached the top step I heard the door close behind me.

—

Biyu called as I was walking back to my car.

'Jen asked me to take over the rehearsal dinner logistics,' she explained awkwardly. 'I'm so sorry about you guys.' She was sympathetic, apologetic.

'It's okay,' I said dully. It really wasn't.

I sent her the plans so far. There wasn't much left to organise, anyway.

At this point, I either needed to get laid or listen to Leonard Cohen and mourn. A post-post-modern art exhibition in an old motorcycle garage on Keele Street blared neon lights into the dusky afternoon, leaving pink worms in my vision when I closed my eyes. A small group of hipsters sipped beers on the footpath, no doubt discussing whether the gold slippery dip and fluoro children's carousel had a deep, sexual meaning. Everything came back to sex. If I couldn't get sex tonight, or at least a full-sized bed to sleep in, or at least a bed that wasn't made of vinyl, it would be some kind of tragedy. I tried to catch one of the hipster's eyes. He had a bushy beard and his jeans were a size too small but I could forgive that. The look he shot me out of the corner of his eye said that he didn't feel the same way about me.

'What the hell is wrong with you people?' I shouted, electing to take the silent rejection poorly. 'You!' I pointed at the group and they stared back, wide-eyed. 'Do you know how stupid you look? With your haircuts?'

They exchanged smirks. 'Uh, what's your problem?' The guy who spoke had a cultured, lilting voice and a thick, luscious moustache. The requisite bare ankles peeked out from his beautiful brown leather brogues. He held out a forearm as if to fend me off, even though I was at least three metres away.

'My problem is that you're all overdressed little boys who don't know how to root.'

Luscious Moustache laughed. 'I don't think we're the problem you're not getting any, lady.'

Ouch. They turned in towards each other, closing ranks against me to chuckle behind their hands, and I staggered backwards as if I'd been pushed.

'Yeah, well, you probably admire Ayn Rand!' I shouted.

All right, things were desperate. I was too drunk to drive, so I abandoned my car and took two trams to Camberwell, one eye open for ticket inspectors. It was dark and cold as I made my way down Bradley Street. I was looking forward to putting on a jacket when I got to the caravan. The street's fences were festooned with cats, including Dot, who was perched on top of the brick fence belonging to a palatial modern house next to the one I usually parked in front of. She swung her tail like a pendulum, watching me.

Something was wrong. I turned my head left, right, centre. Cats, cars, fences. An oil slick on the asphalt in an empty car space.

No caravan.

—

It's the things you don't see coming that hit you hardest. The carpet had been ripped out from beneath my feet and I stood in the street shivering from the cold and something worse. I grabbed Dot. I had to keep hold of her, and not just because she was warm. But I held her too tightly and she squirmed under my arm, clawing my bicep in protest as I walked to my mother's house, squeezing back tears. At least Dot hadn't been in the caravan when they stole it, or I would have lost everything. My beautiful caravan. All my complaints about its tininess, lack of bathroom, its wobbliness disappeared. It was the perfect home, and it was gone.

As soon as I walked through the broken gate, Dot shot out of my arms and straight to Mum's front door, scratching to get in. She was familiar with the house; she knew that high-grade tuna and kangaroo meat were on the cards here.

The surprise on Mum's face when she opened the door was mixed with annoyance and just a little resignation: *Oh, it's you.* With the greatest effort of my life, I smiled: everything was fine.

'We've come over for dinner,' I said, and pushed past her into the hall. Dot sprinted ahead of me to the kitchen, where she would paw at the spot on the floor where her dish usually went until Mum fed her.

'Lucky me,' Mum said. 'I have some leftover pasta.'

'You've already eaten?'

'I eat at six-thirty when you're not here,' she said. In the kitchen, she plonked a bowl of spaghetti in front of me, gave Dot some roo meat and went back to doing the dishes. She watched as Dot inhaled her food and then sat back, waiting for more. 'You're not feeding her Whiskas, are you? Dot needs fresh food.'

'You think I'm made of money? Dot's lucky to get the home-brand stuff.' Almost everything I owned had been in the caravan, and I had no money to buy cat food. I swallowed a brief surge of panic.

'Hmph. So what's the occasion?'

'Nothing, I just wanted to visit my dear mother. And Dot has been hanging out for some roo meat.'

'Uh-huh. Your caravan is messy. You can't be bothered cooking. Jen is out somewhere and can't entertain you. Am I getting warmer?'

I almost told her about the fight with Jen. She wouldn't have been able to help, but perhaps she would have sympathised. No, who was I kidding? She wouldn't sympathise with me, only with

Jen. And no way would I tell her about the caravan. Mum would probably laugh, and I couldn't bear ridicule just now.

'A girl at work stole a great idea I had for a fundraising letter and got all the credit for it,' I said.

Mum stopped scrubbing. A wet hand emerged from the bubbles in the sink and rested on her hip.

'And you're letting her get away with it?'

I shrugged. 'Rueben says I just have to bide my time or something. Because I'm smarter than her and I'll win in the end.'

'Not like you to roll over so easily.'

*My spirit is broken, Mum,* I wanted to say, but I just sucked up a piece of spaghetti and wiped the sauce from my lips.

After dinner, we watched *The Bachelorette* and rated our favourite contestants from one to five. Mum, predictably, liked the magician with big muscles who didn't seem to have an actual job, while I preferred the finance guy who was kind of short but had a sweet way of talking with his mouth to one side.

At ten o'clock she stretched and yawned. 'Time for you to go back to the Shangri-La. Can't have you breaking our agreement.'

'No worries,' I said, 'I'll just go to the bathroom first.'

I snuck into my bedroom to check that the window was unlatched, and found it had a big new fancy lock attached to it. There was a key resting on the windowsill. Rueben's work from Saturday. I unlocked the window and eased it up slightly, pocketing the key for good measure, then went back into the kitchen and gave Mum a pat on the shoulder, the closest to a hug we ever got. Some families cuddle and say I love you and give each other birthday presents, we pat.

I was hoping Mum would forget that I'd brought Dot with me, but of course she didn't.

'I think Dot's in the garden,' Mum told me.

'Okay, I'll grab her.' I didn't know what I was going to do with her, and hesitated. Dot was used to being moved and had never run away yet, but if I deposited her back on the fence on Bradley Street instead of into a warm bed she might be confused enough to try wandering back to Collingwood.

'See you next time you're hungry,' Mum said, as I went out the back to look for Dot. I found the cat in a tree and carried her around to the front yard, where I set her on the doorstep. She sat, looking up at me in irritation.

'Wait here for me,' I whispered.

I went for a walk around the block to pass the time, waiting for the lights in Mum's house to go out. It didn't take long. The yellow glows in the windows ticked out and I checked the time on my phone and walked around the block again. Mum usually had no trouble sleeping but, in case this happened to be the night she decided to lie awake worrying about her dreadful daughter, I made an effort to wait at least twenty minutes before I slipped by the front gate and snuck through the grass to the side of the house.

As I slid the window up all the way, I had to stifle a giggle. Cat Burglar Maggie. Breaking into her mother's home for a warm bed and cold pasta in the middle of the night. This time I'd remember to hang the shower mat up in exactly the right location to dry before she got home from work. I swung my legs over the windowsill, still thinking about the cosy bed I was about to climb into, when something hard slammed into the side of my head and I went down like a sack of beans.

'I *knew* it,' my mother shouted. In the moonlight, I could see her silhouette hopping furiously. 'You lazy scumbag son of a bitch!' Whack, whack, whack, she hit me across the shoulders with what felt like a small cricket bat.

'Mum!' I shouted. 'Stop hitting me.'

She reeled back. 'Maggie?'

There was a slight pause, during which the side of my face began to throb like crazy, and then she found the light switch and the room flooded with brightness. Mum was clutching a rolling pin and wore a confused expression.

'What the hell are you doing?' she asked.

'My caravan got stolen. I needed somewhere to sleep.'

'Well, why didn't you bloody say so?'

I rubbed my face, which was swelling rapidly. 'You said I couldn't stay here! Who did you think was breaking in? Dad? He lives on the Gold Coast now. I spoke to him two months ago.'

'You are unbelievable. Unbelievable.'

I raised my hands, palms up. 'I know.'

'Why didn't you stay at Jen's house?'

'Jen and I had a fight.'

'What about?'

I swallowed. 'Jono came home while I was badmouthing him to Jen. He said she had to choose between us.'

She flung up her hands. 'I don't blame him. You think you have the right to badmouth *anyone*? You've spent ten years failing the same degree and coming round here to complain about how none of your boyfriends will put up with your cheating.'

'I've spent ten years cultivating my talents.' Self-defence mode: it's my automatic response, but tonight exhaustion was wearing away at the facade, and my voice sounded drained and weary.

'Talents? Blowjob artist is not a career!' She breathed out, as if to try to stop herself from shouting. 'I worked hard. I was never a bloody genius but I worked hard, and if I'd married the right man I'd be on a cruise ship right now, deciding where to take my next overseas holiday and planning upgrades to the beach house. But I had to marry a lowlife gambler like your father. And then I had to go and have a daughter *just like him*.'

I took a step back but she moved forward, jabbing a finger in my face.

'Even so,' she continued. 'Even so, I cared for you and loved you and tried to help you see that you had to take some responsibility for your life.' She dropped her head, ferreted around in the pocket of her bathrobe, and pulled out a fifty-dollar note. 'Here.' She shoved it at me. 'This should get you a night in a youth hostel.' She turned and took one angry step towards the door. Then came a loud crack, and a shriek, and half of her disappeared.

'Mum?'

My eyes had trouble adjusting to the sight: my groaning mother sprawled in a ditch that had opened up at the end of the bed. The floorboards had given way. She was spreadeagled in a mess of sagging, shredded carpet, splinters of wood sticking through it like castle spikes. She groaned again, dazed and blinking, arms flapping like an upended turtle, one hand still wrapped around the rolling pin.

'I think I've broken my ankle,' she said.

# Chapter 23

'It was your fault, really,' I said. 'You made me agree to an impossible deal, and I needed somewhere to sleep.'

I was sitting at the end of Mum's hospital bed at 7 am, munching on her cheese and pickle sandwich left over from the night before. My CT scan was all done, and aside from a slight concussion and a black eye, I was fine. My mother, on the other hand, had a fractured ankle and a mean expression. She'd narrowly avoided needing surgery but the cast would have to stay on for six weeks. Half an hour ago, I had taken the opportunity to text Jen with the news: *Mum broke leg. In hospital.* I added the ward number as an extra hint.

Mum tapped her fingers on a blue blanket that smelt distinctly of washing powder, sucking in her cheeks as if to inhale the sour words she wanted to spit at me.

'So you let me waste money on new security doors.'

'You got the security doors so cheap, it was practically a steal. And you'll be safe from real robbers!' I brushed crumbs from my lap. 'Now that I've broken the terms of our deal, can I stay at your place again?'

Fast as a snake, Mum snatched the open container of jelly from her table and pitched it at me. The tub bounced off my forehead and cool jelly splattered over my face, leaving green blobs in my vision. I wiped a couple of green flecks from my eyelashes and licked my finger.

'I take it that's a no?' I asked.

'You are permanently struck from the will, and – and'—she clenched a fist—'you are uninvited from family dinners!'

—

I left to get Mum a coffee and as I returned, I heard hushed voices coming from inside her hospital room. I peeked through the door. Jen was perched on the end of Mum's bed with her back to me. She must have rushed to get to the hospital, because she was still dressed in one of her Jono-is-away-so-I-don't-have-to-try outfits: faded black trackies with a hole in the left butt cheek and a T-shirt that I'd given her a few years ago with 'Kill All Men' scrawled on the back. She was gabbing away to Mum about how Dan was measuring up one of the bedrooms in her house to put in shelves and a wardrobe for when she and Jono had their first baby. My chest filled with dread at the thought. I hung back, listening at the door.

'With all the dust and paint and VOCs that get stirred up when you renovate, I think it's better to get the room set up before, so that I'm not inhaling all that stuff when I'm actually pregnant,' she was saying.

'Good idea,' agreed Mum.

I imagined Jen was wearing a faraway smile as she pictured a little peach-coloured blob that smiled at her when she kissed it, instead of the screaming goblin in a cot that she was far more likely to be stuck with.

'Also,' she continued, businesslike now, 'it's a good distraction from the wedding planning. I was going mental choosing chair covers. Did you know there's like, ten different coloured sashes that you have to choose from to go with the chair covers?'

'Can't you just get chairs that don't need covers?' Mum asked.

'Well, that's what I finally figured out, but they're much more expensive. Like, those nice bentwood chairs cost nearly twice as much to hire as the ugly ones with the sashes.'

Mum finally spotted me lurking, and crooked a finger to tell me to come in.

'Hi, Jen,' I said.

She almost fell off the bed when she saw my black eye, which was now shiny, purple and swollen enough to blur my vision.

'Maggie! What happened to you?'

'Didn't Mum tell you? She clobbered me with a rolling pin before she fell through the floor.'

'You deserved it,' Mum grunted.

Despite the pain in my face, the loss of my caravan, the dread of the Centrelink debt and the four dollars in my bank account, my heart bloomed at the sight of Jen's face. Now that she's here, we'll make up, I thought.

'I'm glad you're still getting my texts, even if you're ignoring them.' I put the coffees down and threw my arms around her.

She seized up like a tin can and put her hands on my shoulders to gently ease me back.

'I just popped in to see how Valerie's doing,' she said awkwardly. 'But I've gotta go now.'

'What? Jen, how long is this going to go on?'

Mum buried her nose in a magazine, pretending not to listen.

'I just . . . need some space,' Jen said. She turned to Mum. 'Bye, Valerie. Call me if you need anything.'

After she was gone I sat in the chair next to Mum, feeling numb. She reached over and patted my knee.

'She'll come around,' she said. 'She'll realise men aren't worth anything, anyway.'

'I don't know,' I said. 'She's got some pretty low standards when it comes to men.'

I could see Mum thinking, *And when it comes to her friends*, but at least she didn't say it.

—

By the time Mum was discharged, it was late afternoon. We'd spent all day listening to the rattle of gurneys across linoleum floors while the nurses popped in and out of Mum's room, giving us conflicting information about what time we'd be able to leave. I'd drunk a bucketload of cafeteria-grade bitter black coffee and was full of nervous energy, despite the aching face. Finally we signed the papers and left the hospital, Mum hobbling before me on crutches. Out the front of the hospital, smokers lined the wall in their surgical gowns, puffing away.

'I can get home by myself,' Mum snapped.

'No you can't,' I said. 'You can't even carry all your pain-killers by yourself. Look at them.' I held up the pharmacy bags containing super-ultra-paracetamol-with-codeine.

Mum and I shared a cab in silence. When we got to Camberwell, I let her pay the driver while I carried her things inside the house. I arranged the painkillers in a tower beside her bed and got her a glass of water, then checked the fridge to see what there was to eat. I brought her reheated spaghetti in bed and put a stainless steel bowl on the floor in case the painkillers made her feel queasy.

'I've put a plastic garden chair in the shower because you're supposed to shower sitting down like an old person,' I said. 'And maybe you should tell me where you're keeping the unfair will, so if you overdose on painkillers and die I can tear it up before anyone knows about it.'

'Never.'

While Mum ate her spaghetti, I sat on the other side of her bed and called PC Pink Cheeks to report the caravan stolen. He sounded genuinely upset and asked if I had somewhere to live.

'Yeah, I'll probably move in with Mum.' Mum frowned at this.

'So, not your friend Jen?' He was trying desperately to sound casual.

'Maybe. You know, if you find my caravan you should bring it round to her house. She'll probably be so happy she'll make you another lasagne.' I figured giving him some motivation was my best shot at getting the caravan back.

'Right, yeah! I mean, sure thing, I can bring it there if I find it.'

I hung up on Pink Cheeks and turned back to my mother.

'Here, Mum,' I said, and held out the rolled-up fifty-dollar note she'd shoved at me the night before when she told me to sleep in a hostel. 'Take it back. I'm moving back home and now that you're on crutches you're physically unable to stop me.' Mum made no move to take the fifty, distracted by Dot, who had padded into the room, jumped onto the bed and was purring in her face.

'Dot,' I patted her, 'I don't believe in God, but you'll do.' I put the fifty on Mum's nightstand instead, where it unrolled and promptly fluttered to the floor. 'As Dot is my witness, I hereby renounce my sins. I shall stay in this house and look after my dear mother, who is injured because her lowlife daughter broke into her house and startled her into falling through the floor.'

'That will work in the short term, but not for much longer.' Mum sighed into the pillow. She looked old and pale. 'That day your friend Dan came over, he told me I needed to get the floors and the roof fixed urgently. Oh, and there's rising damp every-where. Needs new wiring. Walls sagging. It's going to cost two hundred thousand.'

'Is that what you were whispering with him about?'

'Yes. I asked him not to tell you. The mortgage is maxed out and I can't cover it.'

'The house is mortgaged?' I said faintly. 'That's impossible, you inherited it from Granny and Grandpa. It was paid off.'

'It was,' Mum said, 'before your father took out a loan against the house so he could gamble and then skipped out on it, and before I started going into debt to pay the seventy thousand dollars a year it costs in maintenance and rates. But I can't refi-nance again, because I have very little equity left.'

'So you're saying . . .' I couldn't finish.

'The mortgage is nearly equal to the value of the house, and my salary will not cover this year's maintenance, taxes and water bills, let alone any major repairs. I am, as you might say, dead fucking broke.' She pronounced each word like a BB gun pellet hitting a target. 'I suppose I need that.' She nodded towards the fifty-dollar note on the floor.

'The house has to be sold,' I said, 'is that what you mean?'

'Yes. The bank hasn't made a move to repossess it yet, but it's only a matter of time. A year, maybe. I should put it up for sale before the market falls further.'

A small scritching sound, probably a mouse, came from underneath the floorboards, as I tried to think of something positive to say. 'You might get more than you think for it.'

'I might have enough left over to buy a one-bedroom

apartment, if the auction goes well. Hopefully the police will find your caravan, because I won't be able to afford a bedroom for you. You've still got your job, I hope?'

I swallowed. I couldn't tell her about Centrelink, or that my plan to get the Angels to hire me full-time had failed. 'Yeah, it's going well.'

'Good. You're a late bloomer, but you're all right.' It was the closest she'd ever come to saying *I'm proud of you*, and I felt dirty lying to her.

'I should have started making money earlier,' I said.

She stroked Dot's chin. 'A wise man once said, all the money you've saved won't buy your youth again. At least you've had fun.' Her voice was tired and thick. 'I suppose you blame me for everything. You probably wish you had a different mother.'

'I don't. I mean, that was quite the manipulative move, letting me think there was money to inherit just so I'd go and get a job, but still. I don't.'

'I bet you wish you had Jen's mother instead of me.'

'Jen's mother is even more awful than you.'

'But she bought Jen a house.'

'True. Still wouldn't trade.'

———

I psyched myself up before stepping through the front door of the Nicholson Street Angels. It had been a whole two days since Bunny had gazumped me and I'd skived off before lunchtime to get drunk and embarrass myself at Rueben's place. I was a new woman now. A worse woman. A woman with a shining purple bruise that covered half her face. Mum had really done a number on me with the rolling pin. I was dressed in one of the finest outfits I'd found at the back of my closet at Mum's place, a black silk jumpsuit I'd bought online with Sean's credit card when we first started dating. It was a little low-cut for work, so I'd slipped a black singlet top underneath to tone down the cleavage and paired it with flat black canvas shoes.

I trudged to Agnes's office door, feeling like a dog playing poker in my silk suit. She was at her desk, staring at her computer with her hands steepled before her and glasses slipping down her nose. Her grey hair was up in a bun and she radiated severity.

I knocked on the doorframe. 'Hi, Agnes.'

She looked up. 'You're early. What happened to your eye?'

'It's kind of a hilarious story, Mum and I fell through the floor at her house. Well, she hit me with a rolling pin because she thought I was my dad – I mean, an intruder – and then she fell through the floor.' I was blathering. Nervous. Stop, Maggie. 'Anyhow, I just wanted to give you the list.'

'List?'

'Of wealthy addresses.' I explained the concept. Separate letters to wealthy potential donors, asking them for higher dollar figures. 'It's a spreadsheet for now, but Rueben has figured out how to automate the letters to print different amounts.'

I sensed a warm presence at my back. I didn't have to turn around to see who it was, because the rush of heat in my under-wear told me it was Rueben. Probably my vagina recognised his scent or something.

'She's written a great follow-up letter as a reminder to donate, too.' His voice sent shivers down me. 'And we've worked out how to automate a thank-you email, and a reminder email to those who don't donate within two weeks of the mail-out.' Nice of him to say 'we' – I had had absolutely nothing to do with the email automation.

Agnes flashed a rare smile. 'Well done, you two.'

Rueben nodded and slid away. I hung about for a moment, hoping for more praise. Instead, Agnes tilted her chin to indicate my black eye. 'Still on the outs with your mother, I take it?'

'I can't seem to do anything right in her eyes,' I said.

'We all disappoint our parents. Mine wanted me to marry a successful Pakistani man.'

'And?'

'Well, my Greek-Australian wife is very successful.'

'But they weren't happy?' I asked.

'Not at first.'

'What made them come around?'

Agnes tapped the papers on her desk. 'We just gave it some time. Eventually they got to know Ruth and now they love her. It helped that we installed air conditioning in their house.'

'I knew it!' I blurted. 'All parents can be bribed with house upgrades. Although . . .' I thought of Mum and her mortgage. 'It's going to take a lot to fix my mother's house. Turns out she's broke and mortgaged to the eyeballs.'

'I'm sorry to hear that.'

'And now someone's stolen my caravan. This isn't fun anymore.'

'You only liked being poor when you had a rich mother.' Agnes stood up. 'Suck it up, princess. Now, I have to go and do damage control. One of our clients stabbed a social worker in the eye with a pencil this morning.'

—

'Thanks for letting me take the credit in front of Agnes,' I said to Rueben at lunch.

'The credit's all yours,' he said, biting into a sandwich. 'Nice shiner, by the way.'

We were sitting at the kitchen table, and I was hoping that Bunny wouldn't come in and bring the singers with her. For now, all I could hear was Hannah shouting and singing in the op shop next door. A new felt hat had come in, and Belinda had put it aside for her.

'She's happy,' Rueben said, as we listened to Hannah. 'Her daughter invited her to Christmas.'

'So she found her daughter? I never asked in case she hadn't.'

'The adoption agency wouldn't release the files, so Agnes paid for her to do one of those tests where you send away a DNA sample. Turned out her daughter had done one a while ago, hoping to find biological relatives.'

'That's amazing.'

My mind went back to Monday night, and the moment when Rueben almost kissed me, and I decided to say something sexy.

'Do you ever wonder who invented hairdryers?' I asked.

He thought for a moment. 'Nope.'

'Me neither.'

Back at my desk, I did what had recently become a depressing routine: took out my wallet and examined every crevice, pouch and card slot in case I found a spare note tucked away in there. Nothing.

Nothing, except for a small cream card embossed with Mrs Fitz-Hammond's details. I suddenly realised I had the best hope of saving the Nicholson Street Angels' finances sitting right there in my hand.

'What the hell,' I muttered, and dialled her phone number.

Mrs Fitz-Hammond answered, which surprised me a little – I was half expecting a butler to pick up the phone.

'Mrs Fitz-Hammond? It's Maggie Cotton calling from the Nicholson Street Angels. I'm the one who was there that day you dropped off the Yves Saint Laurent.'

'Ah yes, the one who taught me the phrase "camel toe". Such a useful saying.' She sounded like she was three brandies deep.

'That's the one. I'm just calling because we're running a fundraising drive for the Angels at the moment. Both the shelters are in urgent need of maintenance and—'

'How much do you want?' she interrupted.

'Ah . . .' I coughed. 'Well, that's up to you, I suppose.' I really should have practised my pitch before I picked up the phone.

'Hmph.' It sounded like a noise of irritation, as if I wasn't being straightforward. 'Why don't you come around for afternoon tea? I had UberEats deliver doughnuts this morning from that delightful place in Brunswick East. I couldn't choose between the flavours, so I ordered rather too many.'

For a moment I freaked out at the thought of knocking on the presumably giant door of her presumably giant house and asking for a donation. But then I thought of the doughnuts, and my stomach rumbled.

'I'd love to,' I said. 'When?'

'Well, what are you doing now?'

I excused myself from work without telling Agnes or Rueben where I was going. If this gamble didn't pay off, I didn't want them knowing I'd annoyed our best source of designer clothing. I drove to the address on her card, which was in Toorak, of course. My fuel light had finally come on but I decided I could probably make it there and back without emptying the tank completely. The house was a large Victorian stone villa with an enormous garden packed with every type of dahlia that could possibly exist. I parked near the wrought-iron gates and trudged up the gravel path to the front door.

She seemed even smaller when she answered the door, and impossibly thin. If she wore sunglasses she could probably be mistaken for Joan Didion.

'Hi Mrs Fitz-Hammond,' I said.

She craned her neck to look behind me, then frowned. 'You didn't bring that handsome man?'

—

'This is a Qing dynasty vase,' Mrs Fitz-Hammond said, 'though sadly not the rare kind. And this,' she gestured to a man's anguished portrait, painted in rather violent strokes of colour, 'is a Sidney Nolan. My second husband chose it.'

I had a salted-caramel doughnut in my mouth, so I couldn't utter much more than 'Mmm' at each of the expensive items she was showing me in her darkly furnished rooms.

She was taking me on a tour of the house, which was bigger on the inside that it had appeared from the street. Her walk was elegant but lacked the bounding quality she'd demonstrated in the Angels' shop, which I attributed to her disappointment that Rueben hadn't come. It seemed she only bounded for handsome men. If I'd known, I would have brought him, as I suspected she might have been freer with her chequebook.

'My first husband left me. Men do that, you know.' We were coming back towards the front sitting room, where she had shown me her collection of Danish mid-century glass vases. She settled on a sofa upholstered in blue and cream striped silk and crossed her spindly legs at the knees. She was wearing cropped orange and black trousers and a matching jacket with a popped collar. It was a fetching outfit.

'Men leave,' she reiterated. 'Either they find someone younger, or they die. Just pop off. Pop!' She flicked her fingers.

'It's a useful thing to learn early in life. Don't get too attached to any of them.'

'Gotcha,' I said. 'See, I don't get good advice like this from my mother.'

'Now.' She folded her hands and I thought she was going to introduce her chequebook. 'Why don't you try another doughnut?'

It dawned on me then that she might be lonely. All at once it felt manipulative to mention the fundraiser, like I'd be one of those people who trawl old folks' homes for affection-starved oldies and weasel themselves into their wills. I selected a strawberry doughnut and, instead of delivering the pitch I'd planned, leant back into the sofa. 'How old are you, if you don't mind me asking?'

'Eighty-seven,' she said promptly. 'Why, do I look close to death? I plan to be cryogenically frozen when I die, in case they find a cure for death in the future.'

'Not to be rude or anything, but did you have a lot of lovers? I mean, I saw that photo of you in the hallway – the one in the bikini – they must have been all over you.'

She smiled, beatific. 'Oh, hundreds. I've outlived all the wimps I loved in the sixties, though.' She waggled her finger at me. 'Girls these days waste all their time on one lousy man. I want to shake them!'

She had a lot of opinions on modern relationships, and when she discovered I knew nothing about her other interest – theatre – she stuck to the topic at hand. When it got close to five-thirty, I stood up to leave. She tried to press another doughnut on me but I shook my head.

'I'm going to my mother's house for dinner,' I said, trying to give the impression that I was a good daughter.

'Well, come around again soon. And bring that nice man from the Nicholson Street Angels shop, if you like.' She sighed at the memory of Rueben. 'Men are like beautiful flowers. So fragile, in so many ways. My fourth husband . . .' Her eyes moistened. 'He was a good one. Such an ego, but ah, when he was in a good mood, he would light up a room. Come over next week and I'll tell you about him.'

—

I knocked, then remembered that Mum was going to have trouble coming to the door.

'Mum,' I shouted through the letterbox flap in the front door, 'don't get out of bed, I'm coming through the window.'

No response.

After checking that no one was lurking in my darkened bedroom with a rolling pin, I slid up the window and eased myself in, then went to the front door to let Dot enter, since she was too haughty to climb in through windows and had simply sat down on the verandah to wait.

'Mum?' I called, creeping towards her bedroom.

'In here.' She was trussed up in blankets, one arm flung across her forehead like a fainting damsel from the Victorian era.

'Are you all right?'

'I don't feel well.'

'It's the painkillers,' I said. 'I'll make dinner.'

I made the Maggie Special, scrambled eggs on olive bread, and brought it to Mum in bed.

'Ever considered adding something green to the food you eat?' Mum said, eyeing the plate.

'Sorry, Your Highness,' I said. 'Tomorrow night I'll cook you up an Ottolenghi salad with freaking pomegranate seeds.'

Then it hit me: tomorrow night was Jen's wedding rehearsal dinner. Mum noticed my face fall.

'What's wrong?' she asked.

'Tomorrow night,' I said. 'I organised it and now I'm not even invited.' I burst into tears and sat down hard on the bed. Mum put the plate aside to pat me on the shoulder.

'There, there,' she said. 'If it's any consolation, you'd look absolutely terrible in a dress with that black eye.'

———

The next morning, I woke to the sound of my phone ringing, muffled because it was buried under some dirty socks on the floor. I rolled over, blinking in the morning light and debating whether to answer, but when I pushed the socks aside and saw Jen's name on the screen I nearly fell out of bed in my haste to pick up the phone.

'Hello?'

'Hey. Can you come over?' Jen's voice sounded weird.

'Uh, isn't Jono there?'

'He . . . went out.' She cleared her throat.

'Sure. I'll be there in a sec. I mean, I'm at Mum's, I'll be half an hour.'

'What, you're not in the caravan?'

'Caravan's stolen,' I said.

'Shit,' Jen replied.

'Tell me about it.'

I had a micro-shower and threw on a pair of jeans and a ratty T-shirt. Mum's old Ford was sitting unused in the garage, since she couldn't drive with a broken leg, so I borrowed it to avoid having to stop for petrol, which I couldn't have paid for anyway. The Saturday morning traffic wasn't too bad and I reached Jen's house a little after ten. Collingwood's birds were tweeting in force on this bright morning and my spirits lifted with them. Tonight was Jen's rehearsal dinner. She'd finally cracked and realised she didn't want to celebrate without me.

Her face when she opened the door was slack and pale. 'Hey. Come in.'

There were no smells in her house; no morning coffee, no scent of bacon, no perfume or lingering shower gel. She shuffled down the hall in her trackies and slumped down at the kitchen table.

'Shall I make coffee?' I asked hesitantly. She nodded.

It was the first time in my life that I'd made coffee for Jen instead of the other way around. I couldn't remember if she took milk or sugar so I surreptitiously placed them on the table for her to fix it how she liked. I watched her pour a splash of milk into the mug and ignore the sugar, and noted it for next time.

'So what's happened?' I asked.

She cleared her throat, like she'd done on the phone. 'Well, nothing really. I mean, I don't want to make a big deal out of it.'

'Okay, what's not a big deal?'

She sipped her coffee slowly, fiddled with the sugar bowl and looked away.

'Jen, come on. What is it?' I asked again.

'Could you . . . do you know . . . anything about the previous owners of your caravan?'

Not a question I was expecting. 'The previous owners? Of my caravan? Aside from the fact that they were called Shane and Sheila or something?'

'Is it possible – I mean, did they look like the sort of people who . . .'

'Who what? What is this about?'

She clenched her fists. 'I have crabs.'

Silence. 'Crabs. As in, the kind you eat?'

'No, Maggie, not the kind you eat. Pubic lice.'

'Whoa.' Jen had never had an STI before, but, as a nurse, she'd seen them all. Me, I'd had a stint of chlamydia as a reckless twenty-three-year-old and had been vigilant about condoms ever since.

'That piece of shit,' I said. 'I'm gonna kill him.'

'Jono says it's not him!' she said desperately. 'Says he doesn't have any crabs. He stormed out this morning when I asked if he'd been with anyone else. That's why I thought . . . maybe I caught them from your caravan. I rolled on the bed once. Have you been itchy at all?'

I shook my head slowly. 'No, I haven't been itchy. No crabs. It's not the caravan.'

'It must be.'

'It's Jono. He's lying to you.'

She pressed two fingers to her forehead, as if to ward off the words.

'The wedding rehearsal is tonight,' she whispered.

'What, you're going ahead with it?'

'I can't call it off,' she said. 'I have to believe him. He says he didn't cheat.'

'Remember how he was avoiding sex with you for a while back there?'

She shook her head. 'No, no, I trust him.'

I decided not to press the issue. 'How do you get rid of crabs?'

She waved one hand, eyes closed, like she was too embarrassed to look at me. Tears shone on her cheeks. 'It's easy. There's a shampoo. I'll shave, too. I have to get all my sheets and blankets treated, and wash all my clothes in hot water. It's the best

STI to get, as STIs go. No long-term damage.' She sniffed and wiped her eyes. 'I'm gonna go and tidy up.'

I looked around. The house was spotless, but I let her go. She shuffled into the bedroom. I wondered if now was an inappropriate time to look in her fridge for something to eat for breakfast. I could really go some bacon, I thought, and maybe a hash brown.

I had a pan of bacon sizzling and was about to crack an egg into it when Jen came rushing back into the kitchen, brandishing a purple and white bottle.

'That bastard!' she screamed. 'Look what I found in his suitcase.'

It was a bottle of crab shampoo.

# Chapter 24

'I knew he was average,' Jen said. 'I knew he was just another lump of a man who did remedial maths and spent his time shuffling between the top of the rig and the bottom of his beer glass. That he dropped his dacks to dance to "Eagle Rock" and knew all the words to every song on every Hunters and Collectors album and went to titty bars with his mates and would die without ever having read a novel and thought that a good holiday was going to Bali and drinking in every bar in Kuta in his Bintang singlet.'

Sirens from Hoddle Street floated into the kitchen, while shards of porcelain crunched gently under Jen's boots and turned to dust. They were the remnants of a bowl painted with dainty roses that had been an engagement present from her Aunt Jennifer, who Jen was named after. Jen had thrown the bowl to the ground in anguish three minutes beforehand.

'But he was *my* average guy,' she said, 'and I loved him. Because I'm average, too. I like yoga and my job and watching dating shows, and if the Starbucks near work hadn't closed down

I'd probably drink pumpkin spice lattes with every other basic white girl and I wouldn't even be embarrassed about it. I didn't care how he voted or whether he pronounced my father's name correctly or whether he cared about climate change. All I asked was that he behave like a halfway decent person, and not screw somebody else and – give – me – crabs.' She selected a glass jug from the engagement presents she'd lined up on the table and was about to toss it to the ground to join the remains of the bowl on the tiles when I stopped her.

'You're not average,' I told her.

'You're the only one who thinks I'm special.' She wiped her eyes. 'Everything I thought I was going to have has just vanished.'

I knew how she felt. Her whole future was spiralling away into a distant galaxy. All the dots on her timeline – cutting the cake on the dance floor, giving birth for the first time, celebrating wedding anniversaries – were spinning off to become stars that lit up someone else's planet; whoever was unfortunate enough to end up being the future Mrs Jono instead of Jen. I opened my arms and she crumpled into them, the warm, shuddering friend I loved more than anyone else.

'I'm sorry,' she said into my shoulder. 'You knew he was no good, and I didn't want to hear it.'

'I shouldn't have been such an arse about it,' I said. 'I should have been more sensitive.'

She straightened up, shoulders back like her mother always instructed her, and then knelt to pick up the shards of the rose-painted bowl. 'You'll become sensitive when the Pope turns Protestant. But there was an obvious solution to the problem that I ignored the entire time I was with Jono.'

'What's that?' The air was thick with the smell of salt, regret, and just a hint of next door's homegrown weed.

'I should have listened to your reasons for hating him,' she said quietly. 'I shouldn't have written off your opinion just because you're crap at relationships. Because you're not a bad judge of character.'

'I did know two years before you that Sarah Stoll was Margaret Thatcher in a private-school hockey uniform.'

'And you were right.' She dumped the broken porcelain into the bin.

—

'Jen, slow down.' I hurried after her, tripping over a mattress that someone had dumped on the street.

The sun was setting over Collingwood's former factories, and Jen was stalking by them in a tight white lace minidress. She strode ahead of me, Miss Havisham bent on revenge, and I scurried to keep up, adjusting my dress.

After we had cleaned up the mess in the kitchen, I'd run her a bath and set up a small speaker on the edge of the vanity to play heartbreak songs, then left her to cry because she'd said she wanted to vent and wallow in sadness. When she emerged an hour and a half later, pink in the face and red in the eyes, I timidly asked if she wanted me to start calling people to cancel the rehearsal dinner. She shook her head and instead motioned for me to follow her into the bedroom, where she rummaged through her closet and pulled out a black silk dress.

'Get dressed. Act normal,' she commanded.

As usual, the clothes she lent me were excellent but didn't fit properly. I was in a low-cut minidress that was loose in the bust and tight in the hips, and black satin-covered Karen Millen spike heels. I kept rolling my ankles trying to keep up with Jen.

'Are you . . . are you going to do something vengeful?' I asked, breathless.

'I'm going to scoop out his eye with a sharp spoon,' she said.

'Wow.' I rolled my ankle for the fourth time on the uneven asphalt. 'I think I should call my mother. She loves revenge missions.'

'Valerie's coming,' Jen said. 'I already invited her.'

'You know, you can still cancel tonight. I'll make the phone call. I can say it's my fault – I didn't book the restaurant or something. You won't have to explain anything, just quietly call off the wedding this week.'

Jen ignored me. Her mobile rang and she slowed down to look at it. 'It's Jono.'

'What are you going to do?'

She smiled a smile so false and perfect it was as if it had been buffed onto her face with wax and a soft cloth. 'How's this?' she asked. She swiped her phone to answer the call. 'Hi Jono.' Her voice sounded dead, but calm. She put him on speaker and pressed a finger to her lips to keep me quiet.

'Babe,' he said. 'Are you almost here?'

'Five minutes away.'

'Did you ask Maggie about . . . the thing?'

'Yeah, it's the caravan. Definitely.'

I stared at Jen.

Jono laughed too loudly. 'She better not be coming tonight.' There was too much relief in his voice.

'She is coming, actually. After all, she *told the truth and accepted full responsibility for what she did*.' Jen stressed every word, rather ominously in my opinion. 'She would never *lie* to me, so I've decided to forgive her. Forgiveness is a wonderful thing. She's back in the wedding party.'

'Uh, okay.' He sounded uncertain.

'See you soon, babe,' Jen said. 'Is the band there yet?'

'Yeah,' Jono said. 'Some guy with prison tatts showed up. Did Maggie book these people to play music?'

———

Jen drank like a fish and swore like a sailor throughout the wedding rehearsal. She recited her lines before the celebrant and deliberately screwed up his name – 'Josh, I swear to love you always' – then laughed hysterically while Jono stared in confusion. I felt like a child whose parents had decided to have a mid-life crisis. Jono's mate Sammy pretended to hand over the rings and I pretended to hold Jen's train, and all the while Rueben sat in the corner with his bandmates, nursing a beer and watching us from the other end of the restaurant's private function room, waiting for the farce to finish so they could begin playing. Rueben looked like heaven, like the kind of man you'd wait ten years for, the kind you might win if you were really, really good at something, the kind that, if you were a tiny, thin violinist with great tattoos and wild hair who could play the fiddle solo in 'Amarillo By Morning', then just maybe you'd have a shot with him. I hadn't talked to him yet. I needed about three more drinks. What would I say? Hi Rueben, I'm rethinking my opposition to marriage, if only so I can divorce the guy and take his house? Be with me, because I'm even better in bed when I'm desperate?

The celebrant finally closed her folder. 'And then I'll say, "Ladies and gentlemen, I would like to present—" and call out your full names, and then everyone will clap,' she told us.

Jen burst into hiccupping sobs.

'Babe, it's just a practice,' Jono said.

She stared up at him, her face twisted. 'I'm just so . . . happy.'

I swallowed. 'How about we get you some food?' I gestured wildly to the waiter to let him know we needed nibbles, stat. The celebrant backed away, smiling tightly, and packed up her things.

'I need another drink.' Jen sniffled. 'Turpentine, preferably.'

—

Guests started trickling in for the dinner part of the evening, and since Jen was busy leaning over the bar flirting with the fifty-something-year-old bartender and downing mojitos, I took it upon myself to greet and seat them, even the ones from Jen's book club who I didn't like. (Anyone who reads a Christos Tsiolkas novel and says they related to the characters is not to be trusted.) The four book club women looked pleased when they figured out I was twenty-nine and single.

'Don't worry, you only look twenty-six,' said a tall woman in a brightly coloured Gorman jumpsuit, which was basically a clown suit for professional adult women.

'Yeah, what's your secret?' That was from an exhausted-looking mother with a smidge of baby vomit on her dress. Listen, lady, the secret is not having kids.

'A cooler full of human organs,' I said. 'A lack of adult responsibilities. And babies' blood. Just a few sips a day.'

Biyu pulled me aside. 'Jen's acting a bit strange,' she whispered. 'Is something wrong?'

'She's nervous,' I replied. 'Should I try to draw the attention away from her, do you think?'

'You usually do,' Biyu said, sounding a little apologetic. 'You could tell Sarah you have a large penis again, or something like that.'

'Sarah's not here tonight,' I said. 'Jen didn't invite her.'

Biyu put a hand to her mouth. 'Oh. Was I not supposed to tell her about the dinner? I thought you said Jen wanted everyone to come.'

My heart sank. 'Biyu, tell me you didn't take it upon yourself to invite Sarah Stoll to Jen's wedding rehearsal dinner.'

Sean and Sarah were standing by the bar. He wore suit pants and a blue striped shirt unbuttoned at the collar to show his dark chest-hair, while Sarah was poisonous in red lipstick and a black and white long-sleeved body-con dress. I became acutely aware of how tight Jen's black dress was around my hips.

Sarah and her spray tan were sipping a chardonnay. Sean looked me up and down, handsome as ever but inspiring in me nothing but loathing. All I could think about was what I would say when I talked to Rueben. His band was halfway through their first song, a slow number. Rueben wasn't singing, although there was a microphone in front of him, so I hoped that meant he would sing backup vocals. The rhythm guitarist, a young, skinny, black-haired guy, was crooning into his own microphone, but I didn't recognise the song. Rueben caught my eye and winked, filling me with a rush of heat.

Love is insidious. It creeps up on you like a spider, bites you in the back of the neck and slowly spreads its poison while you're scrambling around for an antidote. There isn't one, of course. There's no one better than me, I told myself. I'm sex-faced. I'm open-minded. I'm good with a spreadsheet. I'm as elegant as the dandy with the shih tzu. Rueben would have to be crazy not to love me back.

I downed my drink.

Jen barrelled over. 'Excuse me,' she said to the bartender. 'That pavlova I ordered? We're going to need it wheeled out before the main course.'

My mother hobbled in late on her crutches and gave me the evil eye, so I stuck out my tongue at her. She was in a 1980s Ken Done toucan-print dress that was outrageously tight on her but looked surprisingly cool overall. Her flyaways had been smoothed into a chignon and her lips brightened with hot-pink lipstick. She sat down at a table with Jen's uncles and aunts, who were already working through their third tray of canapés. Jono tapped his glass with a teaspoon to get everyone's attention and I wondered if the spoon was sharp and if I should keep it away from Jen in case she really did gouge out his eye. Or maybe I should let her do it, I thought. A sympathetic judge would only give her a few years in the slammer if they heard about the crabs. Was provocation still a valid defence?

Jono coughed and began his speech. Jen had slid into the chair next to him and snapped open a lipstick, smacking her lips as he spoke, peering into her hand mirror. We all stared. No one ever saw Jen applying make-up; she was always already perfect. She had a glass of red wine in front of her, the colour of a bloodstain.

'Thank you all, friends and family, for being here for us,' Jono said, opening his arms.

*Here for us*, I repeated to myself silently. Ah yes, next he'll say *supportive*.

'Jen and I have the kind of amazing, supportive relationship I'd never thought I'd have.'

Doctor, we have here a terminal case of abuse of language. I suppose he heard that stuff on television. *Married At First Sight*, *Dating Naked*, the kinds of shows where they talk about relationships and support and utilising every moment to catalyse dreams while getting drunk and crying about how they never thought their search for love would lead here, to a bearded sex therapist with crystal-enhanced genitals, who is trying and failing to add meaning to their lives.

'I literally can't wait to commit to this beautiful, gorgeous, sexy woman,' Jono said, and in a parallel universe somewhere Maggie Cotton dry-retched, though in this universe she just gagged a little and asked the guy next to her to grab the waiter for a refill.

'To Jen.' He raised his glass, and we all did the same.

'To Jen,' we chorused. People cheered and clapped. Two tables over, I noticed Dan drape a hand across Lisa's shoulders. Sarah nuzzled into Sean's neck. A cute waitress delivered beers to the band, bending down to whisper something in Rueben's ear. I stuffed a spring roll into my mouth and almost choked.

Jen stood up and my heart started pounding.

'Jono,' she said, swaying a little on her feet. 'When I met you I was twenty-three, and to be honest, pretty insecure. You didn't quite fit the pattern I had expected my life to take, but you looked good in a V-neck T-shirt, and isn't that what it's really all about?' People laughed; a little nervously, perhaps. Jono smiled awkwardly. 'And you know what? You made me happy. You really did.' Claps. *Awwws*. A few nods and whispers. Jen picked up the glass of wine from the table and held it close to her chest. 'And I made it my business to make you happy. Cooked for you. Gave you a home, rent-free. Did that thing in bed you like with the Minnie Mouse noises.'

Jono coughed. 'Uh, babe, maybe you've had a bit too much to—'

Jen raised her glass in the air. 'To Jono. The guy who took six years from me and never once paid an electricity bill. The guy who gets text messages in the middle of the night from people who are saved in his phone as "Goldilocks" and "Fire Crotch".

The guy who gave me crabs and told me I'd caught them from my best friend's caravan.'

She dumped the whole glass of wine over his head.

In the restaurant's deathly silence, I searched for Rueben's gaze and caught it. Those lily-pad eyes crinkled slightly, and he smiled.

Jono was wiping red wine from his face, shaking his head as if to wake up from a dream. Jen looked my way and nodded.

I had waited six years for this moment. I stretched, wiggled my fingers. Cracked a few knuckles. Strode over to the giant pavlova on the silver tray behind Jen and Jono's table. Picked it up, tray and all, and dumped the lot over Jono's head. Pieces of meringue and gooey cream slid down his face. I popped a piece of kiwifruit in my mouth and licked my fingers. It would be a shame to waste it all.

'Maggie!' My mother's shout echoed across the room, and she hobbled towards me, a frown creasing her forehead. When she reached us, she gathered both crutches in her right hand and, with her left, leant on the table for support. 'That was a pathetic effort,' she told me, and raised her crutches.

*Whack.* She cracked Jono around the shoulders.

'Hey!' He held up his arms to fend her off.

'Shut up and take it, you cheating dog,' she said, and hit him again. 'How dare you. How dare you!' *Whack.* It was as if Mum, because she'd never had a chance to take revenge on her own cheating dog, had transposed my father's face onto Jono's, and was feverishly beating the shit out of a goo-covered guy whose hands were flailing about like little seal's flippers.

'Go for it, Mum,' I said.

She rested back on her crutches for a moment to take a breath. 'The pavlova was a start,' she said, 'but it won't leave bruises.'

'I hear you.'

*Splat*. Something warm hit the side of my face and exploded. I wiped my hand across my cheek in shock and came away with chunks of arancini. I looked around wildly and saw Sèan standing a few feet away, pointing a righteous finger at me.

'If anyone gets done for cheating here, it should be her,' he said.

'But you cheated on me first with Sarah!' I cried.

'No I didn't!' he yelled. 'I was only flirting.'

'Hey!' Dan interrupted. 'Leave her alone.'

'Oh, that's right,' Sean said, furious. 'Lover-boy from the alley.' He picked up a plate of rocket and beetroot salad and chucked the whole thing at Dan. The plate shattered at Dan's feet and little ribbons of lettuce landed across a pair of pink high heels belonging to Lisa.

'Oi!' Lisa said. 'These are my favourite shoes.'

There was silence, like a break in the clouds, while the guests held their breath and waited to see what I'd do. Dan stepped towards Sean but I put a hand on his arm to stop him. This was my moment. My problem was that both Sean and Sarah were before me, and I wanted to get revenge on the two of them but couldn't rely on throwing something with each hand and hitting them both. I imagined a window into my soul: it was filled with hot spring rolls, sharp like darts, directed at their targets. Slowly, I reached down to the platter on the table and gathered a spring roll in each hand.

'Don't you dare,' Sarah warned.

I narrowed my eyes and unleashed. The one I threw at Sean with my left hand fell short. My right hand had more power. Sarah tried a sideways avoidance manoeuvre, which only helped my arrow hit its target, since I'd aimed badly to begin with. The spring roll hit her torso, leaving a greasy smear on the white section of her dress.

'That's for dobbing me in to Centrelink,' I said. There was a collective intake of breath from Jen's aunts at the next table, possibly because dobbing someone in to Centrelink was so deeply dishonourable it was tantamount to taking a hit out on the person.

'I'm calling the police!' Sarah shrieked.

A loud crash distracted us. Jen had upended the entire bridal table with one hand, and with the other was chugging red wine from the bottle. Jono, on his knees, wiped pavlova from his forehead and reached a begging hand to Jen.

'Babe,' he was saying. 'Babe.'

In the middle of the frenzy, I felt a warm, rough hand settle on the back of my neck. I turned and looked into Rueben's eyes. It was like the sound had been turned down. All I could hear was my own breathing, all I could see was Rueben's green gaze, all I could feel was the heat where his hand connected with the back of my neck. He was smiling.

'Do you think it's too late to reinvent myself?' I said. 'I've decided I want to be Gandhi.'

'I hear Gandhi was a bit of a jerk.' He stepped close enough that I could see the fine lines fanning out from his beautiful eyes. I wanted to run my fingers down his wiry arms and over the tattoos etched there, but I knew people, especially my mother, were looking at us.

'This is a bit forward,' he said, 'but would you be interested in having sex in the bathroom?'

'I should probably help stop this mess,' I said.

'Maggie, you're the epicentre of this mess.'

'That's true.'

Rueben took me by the elbow but, instead of leading me to the bathroom, led me out the front of the restaurant, where the streetlight added a russet quality to his dark hair. The night felt long again, minutes dripping like candle wax, and I waited for him to say something.

He closed the distance between us, took my upturned face in his hands and kissed me. His kiss was warm and soft and I tasted salt and could smell the waxy lemon of the magnolia blossoms above us. There was hardly any space between us, like we weren't two people but one and a half, as if we'd met in the middle and spread into each other like butter melting into hot bread. My hands were trembling and I grabbed the back of his shirt to steady them. He pulled away too soon but kept his hands on my neck.

'What's changed?' I asked, breathing hard. I felt boneless, senseless. 'You've been knocking me back so long I assumed you'd taken a vow of celibacy.'

'I liked you from the start,' he said. 'But I thought it was a bad idea to go out with someone from work.'

I pulled him back towards me and kissed him again, long and slow.

'Now,' he said when he finally broke away. 'We should go and stop this mess.'

I pulled a magnolia blossom from the bottom of my shoe and we turned to go back inside.

# Chapter 25

'Okay, who's responsible for . . . this?'

Two police officers stared around the food-smeared restaurant in disbelief for exactly ten seconds, then decided to question the oldest people in the room not covered in food, who happened to be Jen's uncles and aunts. No way they were going to rat on Jen. A tiny, shrivelled woman in black raised a trembling hand and pointed a bony finger at me.

The police officers, a man and a woman, descended on Rueben, who was standing next to me with an arm slung around my shoulders. The man's eyes dropped to Rueben's tattoos.

'Name?' he said.

'No.' I waved a hand in front of their faces. 'It was me.'

'Okay,' the woman said. 'We'll take both of you in.'

Behind the officers, I saw the aunts and uncles gather around a weeping, wine-soaked Jen and drag her out of the room.

'What's your name?' the police officer asked Rueben again.

'Rueben Blackwood.'

'Got any priors?'

I could practically hear Rueben gritting his teeth.

—

At midnight, I capitulated and took the blame for damage to the restaurant. At 1 am, just as I'd finished making my statement, I remembered I was broke and couldn't pay for the damage, so I began to insist that Jono had started it. At 3 am, Jen showed up at the police station in her ugg boots and mascara-smeared eyes to claim that she was responsible for the whole thing. At 4 am Jen's father phoned the station from Saudi Arabia to confirm that he would be paying for the damage. Fifteen minutes later, they let us go.

Jen and I stood outside the Collingwood police station, breathing in the cold air, not looking at each other.

'Sorry I left the restaurant,' she said finally. 'Aunt Rosa shoved me in a cab before I knew what was happening.'

'It's okay,' I said. 'You don't argue with Aunt Rosa.' I rubbed my shoulders and neck, which were aching from sitting in a hard-backed chair for so long. 'Do you think they let Rueben go earlier?'

I heard a noise behind us and turned to see the station door open. Rueben stepped out, looking grey and worn. He saw us but kept walking.

'Hey!' I trotted after him. 'How come they kept you so long? I told them you had nothing to do with it.'

'Why do you think?' His face was bleak. 'I've got priors. They were trying to pin something on me.'

'That's so unfair.' My voice broke a little on *fair*, full of right-eous indignation. 'Hey, stop walking. It's not my fault they kept you in there.'

He stopped and put out a hand to fend me off. 'Maggie, I can't see you anymore. This isn't going to happen.'

The moon was flat and bright, a silver disc. Perfectly suited to romantic encounters, not so good for getting dumped before you've even begun a relationship.

'But we kissed,' I said. 'We haven't even had sex yet and you kissed me. That means you like me.'

'Yeah, I like you, but I like walking down the street without an ankle monitor more. You don't know how easy it would be for those cops to write me up for something and send me down again. Resisting arrest, drunk in public, anything. I can't be around someone like you.'

'Why not?'

He waved his hands. 'Because you're a walking disaster and you're made of Teflon. You blow things up but the shit doesn't stick to you. It lands all over everyone else.'

He walked away.

'But I like you,' I called after him. I almost said *I love you*, but that would be crazy, even for me. Anyway, he didn't turn around.

It was no time to fall apart. Jen was taking care of that side of things, swaying uneasily beneath the police station's fluorescent sign as if she'd lost her anchor. I took her home.

—

Someone was banging on Jen's front door. I unwrapped my legs and my poor pounding head from the blankets, stumbled out of the bedroom and stood blinking in the light. Ugh, everything was too bright. I flung open the door to find PC Pink Cheeks standing on the doorstep, smile also bright. Offensively bright.

'I found your caravan!' he said. He was dressed in plain clothes: jeans and a T-shirt. I looked him up and down. 'It's my day off,' he continued, 'but there was a note on the file to call me if it came in. I collected it from the impound lot this morning. It was in Mentone, someone put a ding in it and left it by the beach. No bad damage, though. Is Jen here?'

I stepped outside and pulled the door closed, putting a finger to my lips. Not because I didn't want to wake Jen up, I just wanted him to talk softer because my head hurt.

'Oh,' he whispered. 'Did she work a late shift?'

I nodded. It's not a lie if you don't say the words out loud.

'Here it is,' he said, still whispering. 'See? Hardly a scratch. Just a little dent.'

We walked over to where the caravan was parked by the kerb and inspected it. It looked the same, almost. Same patched-up window, speed stripe with paint flaking off, small round brake lights at the back. My beautiful, familiar aluminium dream.

'About Jen,' I said, 'she likes cats, but her ex would never get one. She wants three kids and soon, so don't waste time. You have to laugh at her dirty jokes but have a very traditional sense of right and wrong.' I grabbed him by the upper arm and stared into his wide eyes. 'She likes a man to be independent but she thrives off kindness. Do you get my drift? Do you?' I shook him a little.

He looked slightly overwhelmed. 'I've only met her once. You make it sound like I want to marry her or something.'

'Frankly, you'd be crazy if you didn't. She's as faithful as a warhorse, cooks like Nigella and those tits are real. Plus she's kind and smart and all the rest, and she works hard.' I put my hands together to plead with him. 'Please, deliver her from the walking V-necks she usually dates, and ask her out.'

He paused at the door of my caravan. 'But . . . what if she's not interested?'

'A risk, but worth it. Now, let's see the damage.'

'You didn't even check if I was single.'

I raised an eyebrow. 'Tommasio, I know you're single. It's written all over you.'

On the outside, the caravan looked fine. A couple of scratches and one dent in the side, which could be beaten out. Inside, however, the cupboards had detached from the walls and splintered. My clothes and sheets were spread over the floor and my crockery had smashed.

'Holy shit,' I said.

'Whoops, I didn't check inside,' Tommasio said, gazing in at the mess.

'What the hell happened?'

'You said it was hand-built, didn't you? Maybe the cupboards weren't fixed to the wall properly. The crash must have dislodged them.'

I sighed. 'Well, thanks for bringing it back to me.'

'Can you fix it?' Tommasio looked anxious.

'I dunno. Yeah, sure.' I said it to appease him. I had absolutely no idea how to fix it.

'Whoa, what happened?' Jen had joined us without either of us realising. Tommasio jumped and blushed. Jen was dressed in her purple house pants, puffy-eyed, her golden hair in wild corkscrews. She poked her head around the caravan, lifting pieces of cupboard and holding them in place as if that would magically fix them. 'Did someone smash it up deliberately?' she asked.

'I think they had a little crash and it dislodged the cupboards,' Pink Cheeks said.

'Or more likely the tow truck that brought it back from Mentone didn't have proper suspension,' I said.

'Maybe.'

Jen caught Pink Cheeks staring at her. 'Excuse my appearance,' she said, touching her hair. 'Last night I discovered my fiancé was cheating on me. At our wedding rehearsal dinner.'

'Oh!' he said. 'So . . . does that mean you're single?' She stared at him, dead-eyed. 'I mean,' he continued hurriedly, 'here are the papers for the caravan. Just sign and it's all yours. And again on this page. Okay. Great. Nice to see you. Bye.'

A second later he popped his head back in. 'Did you say at the wedding rehearsal dinner? Because apparently there was a huge bust-up at one last night. Was that yours?'

'Yeah, that was hers,' I said. 'I got questioned for hours.'

'Oh, wow. That was you.'

'Yeah. And they tried to pin something on a guy I like, just because he's been to jail before.'

Jen brushed past us and shuffled back into the house. Pink Cheeks's eyes followed her with longing.

'Hey, Pink – hey, Tommasio, can you check on something for me?' I said.

'Like what?'

'Make sure they're not going to try to accuse Rueben Blackwood of doing any of the damage last night. He wasn't involved.'

'I can check, but I can't do anything dodgy.'

'Of course not.'

—

The birds were singing in Jen's lemon tree when I came into the kitchen, and my spirits rose with the steam that floated up from the coffee pot. Jen was morose at the table, not yet able to consider that Jono had given her a get-out-of-jail-free card.

It would take some quality time on the couch to realise this, and for the pain to fade. I handed her a cup of coffee.

'I was faithful to him for six years,' she said, 'and now I have to start again. At twenty-nine. Twenty-nine with pubic lice.'

'You have a house and a career.' I patted her on the shoulder. 'You're beautiful and a wonderful person, and you don't live in a caravan.'

She wiped her nose with the back of her hand. 'I don't know what to do. What do I do?'

'You just keep going.'

'Who will I have kids with now?'

'You'll meet someone right away. They'll be lining up at your door.'

'My ovaries are going to shrivel. How will I have four kids if I don't start until I'm in my thirties?'

'You want four? I thought you wanted three.'

'I might want four! I want the option of four!' She lifted her T-shirt and pressed it to her face to soak up the tears.

I stayed with Jen all day. It was like old times, watching bad movies and eating mac and cheese with potato gems. She cuddled into me on the couch and told me more of Jono's secrets until I was convinced he was the King of Arseholes. Not that I had needed any more convincing. Apparently he would refuse to touch her if she let her leg hair grow out for more than a day.

'Jen, that's not normal.'

'I know.' She sniffed. 'I was just in denial.'

I refilled her bowl with mac and cheese and she took a bite, chewing thoughtfully. 'What was the name of that accountant you dated for five seconds at uni? I wonder if he's still single.'

I thought for a second. 'Wrestling deer guy? I can't remember his name. He'd probably be more steady. No fly-in fly-out.'

'How come you can't remember his name?'

I threw a potato gem into my mouth and burnt my tongue. 'Because I didn't date him.'

'Oh, right. Just cheated on Salvatore with him.' Jen became quiet. 'Why do you find it so easy to cheat on people? You and Jono are alike.'

'I was. Not anymore.' I rolled my head back, ready for divine inspiration to shoot down from the ceiling and help me phrase this properly. All I got was bright spots in my vision from the light. 'From now on, I'm ethically non-monogamous.'

'What does that mean?' Jen sounded suspicious.

'It's like legal cheating, you agree on it beforehand. I read about it in an article.' Before she could voice an opinion, I motored on. 'Also, I'm gonna do stuff for you now, not just eat your food and borrow make-up.'

'You did make me a coffee,' Jen observed.

'And that's only the beginning! Now that you and Mum are talking to me again, that makes two people I'm going to be consistently nice to. And this rich old lady gave me good advice about not relying on men, which, when I remember her exact words, I'll pass on to you. She was all about ethical non-monogamy, too. Spreading your eggs between many baskets.'

'What are you going to do for money?' Jen asked.

'Maybe I'll ask the guy at The Fainting Chair for a bar job.'

I popped a potato gem in my mouth, thinking about how I'd come across in a film. Maybe they'd cast someone with big tits and tattooed eyeliner.

'Do you think I could date a rich man?' I asked Jen. 'Like, not just an accountant or something, but a guy rich enough to be an angel investor for start-ups?'

'Why do you ask? Did you meet an angel investor?'

'No, I just wondered.'

She scrolled through Netflix, contemplating the question with an absent gaze. 'You've always dated men who made little or no money. I thought it was so you could say you weren't relying on a man.'

'Yeah, I relied on my mother instead.'

'I think you could date a self-made rich man,' she said. 'But not family money.'

'I wouldn't fit in with a Toorak mother-in-law.'

'Exactly.'

'Maybe I should go to San Francisco to meet an angel investor,' I said. 'Then in two years I could be a pregnant thirty-something popping chia seeds and coconut water and talking about co-sleeping.'

'I'll come with you.' She ran her finger around the now-empty potato gem bowl, collecting the salt, and licked it.

—

'We shouldn't have watched *When Harry Met Sally*. That was a mistake,' I said. 'No happily ever afters allowed from now on.'

'The movies are a lie. No one can trust anyone.' Jen's voice was thick.

I sat up. 'Right. Jen. We have to get drunk. You need to get drunk. No more crying and wailing and mourning.'

As afternoon turned to evening, I emptied a bottle of red wine into her, and began hating the world with a feverish fury. Nothing could be more unfair than Jen, dearest Jen, getting pubic lice from the King of Arseholes. And me! I was hard done by too. I had a shattered caravan and a broke mother and a seventy-thousand-dollar debt and a future filled with dole queues. And I was in love with a handsome criminal who was too sensible to date me.

'We have to get out of here,' I said.

Jen looked up at me with pink, puffy eyes and sniffed. 'What?'

'We have to get out of this house. What are we doing here, crying and wailing? It's six pm!' I swung the empty bottle around to accent my words. 'It's happy hour. We should be out having sex. Sex!'

'Sex with who? The latte-loving hipsters of Collingwood? No thanks.'

'What's wrong with hipsters? They wear great shoes.'

'They're not real men. If we want men we'll have to go somewhere else. Like St Kilda, or Chapel Street.'

'You're kidding me.' Two years beforehand I'd made a public vow never to set foot on the south side of the river again, and in particular never to walk down Chapel Street, with its gangs of roaming footy boys, or to frequent the bars of St Kilda, with the possible exception of seeing a band at the Esplanade Hotel.

'I'm the one who's got crabs!' Jen shouted. 'I'm the one who's been cheated on! I can't even sleep with anyone until I've got rid of them, so I think I will dictate where we go looking for sex!'

'Okay. You're right. We'll go to St Kilda.' St Kilda, spray-tan mecca. Where we would be surrounded by deep V-neck T-shirts showing hairy man-cleavage – or heavage, as I preferred to call it – and pomaded hair attached to too-groomed, too-plausible jerks.

We prepared ourselves in silence. I slathered on mascara with gritted teeth while Jen patted concealer under her eyes to hide the dark circles. She lent me clothes again, a loose but short purple dress and gold heels. I looked almost too plausible myself.

'I don't know how to do this,' Jen said. 'I don't know how to pick up in a bar.'

I placed my hands on her shoulders. 'I know exactly how you feel. You feel destined to be alone and celibate, like a monk but with none of the advantages of monkdom, like moral superiority and self-control and spiritual emancipation. You need to work on your aura. It's always easier to get laid when you're already getting laid. Your aura needs to exude a sense of: I don't need it but I know *you* want it.'

She sniffed. 'God, how do you manage to sound so confident when you don't know what you're talking about? All right, call a taxi.'

Jen was screaming drunk by the time we arrived at the beer garden. She threw the bottle of wine we'd been drinking in the taxi into the gutter and it smashed, leaking cheap red onto the asphalt. The bouncers looked us up and down as she marched past with her nose in the air and smirked before parting to let me through after her.

The bar was dark and clean, decked out with glossy subway tiles and hanging lightbulbs dimmed to offer a bronze glow. It was packed with rich, tanned people. Jen found the guy nearest to the bar, who also happened to be quite good-looking, and grabbed him by the shirt collar.

'You,' she said. 'Have you ever given your girlfriend an STI?'

Alarm flashed across the man's face and his eyes went wide, as if she'd asked him if he was into pegging.

'Er, excuse me,' he said, shuffling backwards.

'Bastard,' Jen called.

A woman – presumably the man's girlfriend – shot Jen a filthy look and muttered the word 'psycho' as she took him by the arm and turned her back.

'Watch out for him! He can't be trusted!' Jen shouted as I dragged her away.

I plonked her on a sofa in a dark corner and pushed a large glass of water towards her.

'Okay, new plan,' I said. 'We'll just sit here and try to be normal for a while.'

'This was your idea,' she hissed. 'We're finding a man.'

'Why? You can't even have sex! You'll pass on the . . . you know.'

'I can still give blowjobs.'

'And what will you get out of it?'

'I'll get revenge on that bastard. I'll text Jono now and tell him I'm about to suck someone's salami.'

She whipped out her phone and I tried to grab it out of her hand.

'Jen! There's no point. Don't contact him now. Just act as if you don't even know or care who he is, it will drive him crazy.'

'The bastard gave me crabs!' she shouted. 'So shut up!'

A few people turned around, in amusement or horror, I couldn't tell which. Too much botox.

'Jen, I think you're the one who needs to be quiet.'

I wrestled the phone out of her hand and threw it in my bag. Jen dropped her head into her hands and began to weep softly.

'I want my mum.'

I stroked her hair. 'I can't bring you your mum, she's still in Sardinia or wherever. But I could probably get you my mum.'

'Yes, please,' she said.

I bundled her into a taxi and gave the driver my mother's address.

# Chapter 26

'Here you go, darling.' Mum put a bowl of Moroccan chicken in front of Jen, who was still swaying from the wine. It was only eight-thirty but Mum was already wrapped in her fluffy robe. She turned to me. 'I had a check-up at the hospital today. I'm going to need rehab because of you. I'll probably have a limp forever. Look at me, I'm hobbling around like an ancient.'

'Don't worry, the hobble is very endearing,' I told her. 'In fact, I bet you'll attract a man because of it, someone with caring instincts. Don't you remember Britz, Dad's friend who lost his eye playing squash? He got heaps of ladies. They loved his pirate patch.'

'He got the sort of ladies who carry their dogs around in their handbags.'

I gasped. 'Remember that girlfriend of his who had a miniature poodle? And he accidentally ran it over with his golf cart because his depth perception was off?'

Mum glared at me. 'How would you like it if I gave you a hobble?'

'I'd work it, baby. I'd get a silver-tipped cane.'

'You're hilarious.'

'I know.'

'Don't reproduce, will you?'

'I thought you wanted grandchildren?' I asked innocently.

'I've decided that your brother will give me grandchildren. You can look after me in my dotage.'

'You better put me back in your will if you want me to look after you in your dotage.'

'That will be decided on a weekly basis, when I assess your performance.'

'Man, you are one tough nut,' I said.

'It's a poodle-eat-poodle world, isn't it?'

Dot padded into the kitchen and jumped up on the table to headbutt me. She was unofficially living with Mum now and seemed quite content at having tuna on tap. Silence fell, except for the sound of Dot purring and Jen chewing her chicken. Red sauce coated the corners of Jen's mouth.

'Are you all right, darling?' Mum asked her gently.

Jen swallowed her mouthful. 'I never want to mention Jono's name again. Just then, that was the last time. I'm starting my life over and it will be as if he never existed. If we ever have to refer to him for any reason, which I hope we don't, he shall henceforth be known as Shitballs.'

'Okay,' I said.

'Good plan,' said Mum.

'So keep talking,' Jen ordered. 'Talk about something.'

'Okay.' I nodded. 'Anyone want to hear my theory about how to talk to a therapist, if you ever get one, to demonstrate how sane and sensible you are?'

'No,' Jen and Mum said simultaneously.

'Fine,' I said. 'How about we come up with a back-up plan for my life.'

'There's no such thing as a back-up plan,' Mum said.

'But – and please don't throw jelly at me this time – everything's fucked.'

Mum sighed. She didn't even tell me off for swearing. 'What is it, specifically, among all your stupid problems, that is bothering you?'

I thought over all my problems. The Centrelink debt, the broken caravan, Mum's will. Everything came down to money. Almost everything.

'I can't make people love me.'

Jen snorted.

'Of course you can't make people love you,' Mum said. 'I've tried myself. It never works.'

'Do you mean Dad?'

She refilled Jen's bowl. The chicken slopped in, red and steaming. 'Before he left, I did everything I could. I let him waste my entire inheritance. But you can't force someone to love you. If anything, you push the person away by trying.'

'That's so depressing, Mum. I thought you taught me to be persistent.'

She rolled her eyes. 'Persistent in what you do, Maggie, not persistent in trying to force other people to bend to your will. And you have a hell of a will. If only you applied some of your admirable work ethic for soliciting sex to other aspects of your life, you might actually have a career by now. And quite possibly a husband.'

'I don't want a husband. I just want him to—'

'Who?'

I shut my mouth. Jen smirked at me.

'I bet it's that man who looks like a criminal,' Mum continued. 'I saw you drooling over him at the rehearsal dinner. All right, when are you going to pop out some babies with him?'

'I thought you didn't want me to reproduce?'

Mum considered that for a bit. 'He's a bit of a handsome dog.'

'You would have good-looking babies,' Jen agreed.

'His mother was a beauty queen,' I told them.

'Ahhh,' Jen and Mum said, nodding together like puppets.

'I suppose if you're going to get knocked up it may as well be by him,' Mum went on. 'Do you think he would stick around, though?'

'I'm not getting knocked up!' I said. If they moved on to baby-talk, it was time to leave. 'Jen, do you think it might be your bedtime?'

'I'd drive you home, but this idiot buggered up my driving foot,' Mum said, gesturing to me.

I took Jen home in a taxi and tucked her into bed.

'You might as well stay over,' she said sleepily.

I didn't need asking twice. I removed my bra and cuddled in next to her. 'Don't wake me tomorrow,' she said. 'I don't have to work until three.'

I was just dozing off when my phone buzzed with a text. Rueben's name flashed on the screen.

*Hey Teflon girl. Tomorrow's my last day at the Angels. Make sure you get to work on time so I can show you how to run the new website.*

Rueben was quitting? My throat closed over like a hand had grabbed it and squeezed.

—

It was a beautiful December day and I was miserable. I trudged down Nicholson Street, crushing fallen blossoms under my feet, muttering a string of expletives. The first person I saw when I crossed the threshold of the Nicholson Street Angels' office was Bunny, which didn't improve my mood one iota. She'd paired a gypsy skirt with cowgirl boots this morning, and had stuck chopsticks through her bun.

'I think you're needed in the op shop today, Maggie,' she announced by way of greeting, smiling through perfectly white, gritted teeth.

'No,' I replied.

'Excuse me?'

'No, I'm not needed in the op shop today. Rueben is showing me how to run the new website.'

'No need for that,' she said. 'I'll be running the new website.'

I counted to three. My options were: turn around and leave the Angels, never to see Rueben again. Spend the day in the op shop and sneak out to see Rueben at lunchtime. Ignore Bunny and sit down at my desk as usual. I chose option three.

'Uh,' Bunny said, stepping back to catch her balance as I pushed past her to the inner sanctum of the office. She was lucky I didn't grab a chopstick from her hair and shove it down her throat.

Rueben was looking badass in his grey T-shirt and jeans that hugged his slim hips. He was at his computer and didn't acknowledge my arrival. I wondered if he was trying to play it cool. I threw my bag down and nosed my way in between him and the desk, hands on my hips.

'Did you really resign?'

Rueben's lily-pad eyes met mine. I stared into them: the heavy eyelids I was now familiar with, the slight downturn at the outer corners. Fine lines fanning out, the skin otherwise smooth and tanned.

'Yes,' he said.

'Because I'm El Bitcho de Teflon?'

He put his head back and laughed. 'Because I got another job.'

'What job? What could possibly be better than working with me?'

'A paying job,' he said. 'Full-time. Nothing amazing. I'll just be doing low-level database management at a software development company that my sister's friend owns, but it's something.'

It felt weird standing over him. My knees were touching his, and they were growing warmer by the second.

'Well. Congratulations.' My words were devoid of feeling. I hardly wanted to stay at the Nicholson Street Angels if Rueben wasn't going to be there. I dug my nails into the palm of my hand to stop myself saying something stupid.

'It's a good job,' he said. 'I'm happy.'

'Sounds like it.' I cleared my throat. 'I'm happy for you.'

'Shall I show you the back end?'

'Excuse me?'

'The back end of the new website. It's easy. I've switched us over to WordPress. Any monkey can run the site now.'

I pulled up a chair and sat next to him, my heart thumping. 'I guess that means this monkey can do it.'

He smiled. 'Here's the login URL, the password is—'

'Bunny's trying to steal this off me, too,' I interrupted. 'She wanted to handball me into the op shop today and get you to show *her* how to run the site.'

'It makes sense to have more than one person know how to do it,' he said. 'For the days when you're away, or in case you leave the Angels sometime.'

'You mean in case Bunny has me fired.'

'She can't fire you. You're a volunteer.'

'You know she could get me booted.'

He swivelled to face me and put his hands on my shoulders. 'What's wrong?' he asked gently.

'You know what's wrong.'

He didn't take his eyes off me. 'Why don't you say it?'

For a moment I nearly did: *Rueben, I love you.* I even opened my mouth. Then I shook my head.

Agnes chose that moment to pop her face through the doorway.

'Come on, you two. We're posting out the fundraising letters today. All hands on deck to stuff them in the envelopes.'

I was half relieved, half frustrated. We both jumped out of our seats like jack-in-the-boxes and followed Agnes. Ahead of us, I could see thousands of letters already stacked in neat piles, presumably according to dollar amounts, on the meeting room table. Rueben walked ahead of me into the room but Agnes stopped me outside the door, her face stern.

'I need to talk to you later,' she said. 'I had a phone call from someone at Centrelink this morning.'

So Centrelink had finally got around to telling her that I'd had my Newstart Allowance cut off and was being forced out of the volunteer program. Numbing dread filled me. My time at the Angels was up.

Bunny bounced towards us, blocking me from coming near the meeting room table, all up in my face with her buoyant red hair and glittering teeth.

'Agnes, we really need someone in the op shop today,' she said, still nose to nose with me as if I was a wild animal trying to escape. 'I already asked Maggie to do it once. There's only one volunteer in there and it's Olga – she can't operate the till.'

Agnes sighed. 'Fine. Maggie, do you mind?'

Fucking Bunny. 'Yeah, all right.'

As I turned to leave, I saw Rueben pick up a copy of the letter on the table and frown.

'Wait,' he said.

Bunny practically shoved me out the door. I batted away her hand and held on to the doorframe with my fingertips, peering over her shoulder.

'What is it?' I said.

'This is your letter.' He looked up. 'Agnes, this is the fundraising letter that Maggie wrote. I proofread it for her six times. Did Bunny tell you she wrote it?'

Bunny's hands went slack on my shoulders. I shoved her out of the way, picked up the letter and scanned it. It was my fundraising letter, word for word. Bunny hadn't just stolen my idea, she'd stolen the whole damn thing.

'Whoa,' I said. 'Bunny, how did you get this?'

'She must have taken it off the printer,' Rueben said. 'You printed it out about a hundred times before it was finished.'

'I don't know what you're talking about,' Bunny said. Actually, her voice was a screech. 'Agnes, it's a conspiracy. They're obviously in on it together to undermine me. They're liars!'

Agnes sighed and adjusted her glasses. 'God, this is a huge pain in my arse. The letters are good. Can we just stuff the envelopes and discuss it later?'

Nobody moved.

'Maggie,' Agnes said. 'I will talk to you about this at lunchtime. Go and cover the volunteers in the op shop.'

—

'The lack of clichés and spelling errors should have alerted me that it wasn't Bunny's work.' Agnes sighed and leant back in her chair. I was seated opposite, fiddling with the toy cats on her desk.

'Because she didn't write "Every dollar is a holy gift"?' I asked.

'What a huge pile of donkey shit this is,' she said, and I stifled a giggle, valiantly turning it into a cough at the last second. Agnes swearing was like a ballet dancer farting. She took off her glasses and pinched the bridge of her nose. 'I've asked Bunny to resign. I've long suspected that girl does nothing, and the last song she wrote made me want to swallow arsenic. It looks like you'll have to do her job for now. You'll be on probation for three months before we make it permanent.'

I did an internal happy dance. I didn't feel bad for Bunny. She'd suck some idiot into giving her another job.

'Does that mean I'll get paid?' I asked. 'I mean, like a salary?'

'Yes. Good timing for you, I imagine?' She gave me a knowing look. I nodded. 'It's still three days a week, but you'll earn more than you're getting now.' Which was currently zero. 'Bunny is finishing up at the end of the week. I've asked her to show you the ropes of the marketing job but I doubt she'll do it. She really hates you.'

'I'll add her name to the list,' I said.

Agnes stretched. 'Don't screw it up,' she said. 'My idiot fuse is getting shorter and shorter. I'm tempted to fire every last worker in this place and do it all myself.'

'You'd probably do an all right job,' I said. 'But just think, you'd never be able to take a holiday.'

'That's true. My wife would kill me.'

—

I practically skipped into the kitchen, where I found Rueben making a cup of tea. I did a Sucked-In-Bunny dance. It involved holding the kettle in front of my crotch and pumping my hips at Rueben.

'*Bow down, Bunny! Bow down, Bunny!*' I sang, channelling Beyoncé.

'Maybe you should, uh . . .' Rueben cleared his throat and nodded in the direction of the doorway. I turned. Bunny. Crap.

'*Excuse* me?' Bunny said. She flushed and looked from Rueben to me.

'Hi, Bunny.'

'Were you just singing about me?'

I decided to unleash the fury. 'Yeah, yeah, I was. It's called "Bow Down, Bunny". Hit single in the making.'

Bunny drew herself up, nose high in the air. 'You will drag everyone in this charity down into your pit of sin,' she told me. 'I've worked here for three years. I'm a believer. You won't last ten seconds in my job. What will you do for office morale?' She shook her finger at me. 'I know about you. I know you don't know the difference between the Anglican church, the Catholic church and the Baptist church. I heard you once call a Reverend "Father".'

'Who the hell cares?' I said.

'I care. Where do you worship? What church?'

'I have an altar to Beyoncé in my caravan.'

Bunny huffed.

'Is that true?' Rueben asked me. 'I thought Gillian Welch was your favourite musician.'

'I can't believe this,' Bunny said. 'I do the Lord's work. You're just a volunteer from Centrelink!'

I grinned. 'Not anymore.'

Bunny turned pale. 'This circus is a sign. My talents are being wasted. I should have an audience. I should be singing for Jesus in front of thousands.'

'You should, Bunny,' Rueben said smoothly. 'You have so much talent. Anyone who's heard you sing can't talk of anything else afterward.'

It was true, kinda.

'Thank you, Rueben.' She sniffed. 'You're the only one here who's nice to me.' She turned on her heel and flounced out.

'And why are you wearing chopsticks in your hair?' I called after her. 'They're eating utensils. What would you think if a Chinese woman walked around with a fork stuck through her bun?'

Rueben shook his head at me.

'Why *are* you nice to her?' I asked. 'She's the devil.'

'Yeah, but she just lost her job.'

'Ah, she'll be fine. I'm sure she'll sell tens of copies of her next album.'

He sipped his tea, offering a slight smile. I put the kettle on for my own tea, humming to myself. The kitchen seemed brighter, cleaner somehow, the grey lino floors almost jaunty now that I knew I'd never see Bunny step on them again. I wanted to keep Rueben talking, to at least cement our friendship before he left for another job. It was obvious I had to play the long game if I was going to bring him around. I turned the conversation to a subject that I knew would hook him: Americana and alt-country greats. I already knew he loved Gram Parsons, Emmylou Harris and Townes Van Zandt, so I asked him what he thought of David Allan Coe's 'Revenge'.

'Perfect songwriting,' he said.

'I agree. But I bet you just love David Allan Coe because he's an outlaw, so you think you've got something in common.'

He shook his head. 'He's far more outlaw than I ever was. I think he spent time on Death Row, and it wasn't for throwing a bag of peas at someone. Do you just like him because he lived in his car?'

'It was a hearse.'

His smile stayed in place. I stepped closer. *We can work this out*, I was thinking. I took note of every detail of Rueben's person. The stubble on his cheeks that was one part silver, three parts rust. The whites of his eyes, turning to blue around the edge of green irises. The curved outline of shoulder blades beneath his T-shirt, which I noticed when he reached to get the carton of milk out of the fridge and handed it to me for my tea.

'Okay Rueben,' I said. 'I'm ready to say it now.'

'Say what?'

'Come to my caravan after work.'

He shook his head. 'Don't.'

'Don't what?'

'I don't want anything from you.' His mouth was set in a line.

'But it's your last day. We need to . . . we need to celebrate,' I said lamely.

He bent his head towards mine and I felt his breath on my cheek. 'You know exactly what will happen if I come to your caravan.' I felt a shot of fire head south. 'But I told you, I'm not getting involved with you. I'm gonna go on eHarmony and match with an accountant or something. Someone safe.'

'I practically *am* an accountant,' I said. 'I have a diploma of accounting from the University of Melbourne. Only took me ten years.'

He shook his head again.

'I'm very safe,' I called as he left the kitchen. 'I'm a prophylactic.'

—

Clouds rushed to cover the sun in the afternoon, and the first drops of rain tapped on the roof and darkened the asphalt outside. Typical. Agnes sent me back to work in the op shop after lunch, probably so I wouldn't run into Bunny in the corridors. I didn't get a chance to talk to Rueben again until I was locking up the shop and saw him leave the office and get into his car. I ran out of the shop and knocked on his window.

'Charlotte Court, Collingwood,' I yelled through the window. 'That's where my caravan is parked. Come round at seven. I'll have dinner ready.'

He mouthed *No*, and put the car in gear.

'I'm a changed woman!' I shouted as he pulled away from the kerb. 'I have a paid part-time job!' I cupped my fingers around my mouth as his tail-lights disappeared around the corner. '*I'm ethically non-monogamous!*'

# Chapter 27

I was full of nervous energy after work so, despite the rain, I walked to the supermarket, armed with fifty dollars I'd borrowed from Jen – the last loan, I promised her, seeing as I would get paid next week. I made phone calls as I walked. I had a plan.

PC Pink Cheeks was down for it.

'Shall I bring wine?' he asked.

'Sure,' I said. 'Now, the important thing is for Rueben to know *I* got you to make sure the police wouldn't harass him in future. Can you remember that?'

'Of course! But you know, we don't harass people, generally.'

'And let me do the talking – you just back me up afterwards.'

'Sure, sure, can do.'

I returned to the caravan soaking wet, lugging supermarket bags. The interior smelt weird, as if whoever had stolen it had rubbed their creepy underarm scent all over the place. Incense would cover it. I took a stick of sandalwood from a drawer and struck a match to light it.

Smelling the sandalwood, I became twenty years old again, in my second year of university, lying on a single bed in my college dorm with Salvatore, my old boyfriend. He had large, dark eyes courtesy of his Maltese mother and big, soft hands. There was nothing hard or mean about him, nothing unnecessarily tough. We never talked about anything important – neither of us cared about politics at that stage of our lives, and we'd never experienced much beyond school, university, parental divorce and minor heartbreak – but we could talk all night about whatever it was that wasn't important. I remember we exchanged *I love yous*, but I don't remember ever thinking that love was a permanent state, or at what point in the relationship I grew restless. Maybe two years into it. Acting on my restlessness, of course, was what ended the relationship and broke Salvatore's heart. I had no excuse, except that I never realised quite how much he loved me, or how I felt about him.

When we broke up, he moved everything he had out of my room at college; 'everything' being his Grand Theft Auto games and PlayStation console, his Clint Eastwood films and his bike helmet. I saw him from my window, wheeling his bike back to his own residential hall with the bulging cardboard box under his arm, passing between the shadows of the trams along Royal Parade. It's easy, when you're nineteen or twenty, to believe that there will always be a new person to love you. But that break-up cut me deeper than I expected. And no one had loved me like that since.

When the rain eased, I opened the windows to further air out the caravan. It took a few minutes to stack up all the splinters of cupboard and ease them under the bed, brush out the dirt on the floor with a dustpan and broom, and wipe down every surface. Jen arrived with a pile of clean sheets and gathered the dirty ones to be washed. She had somewhat excised Salvatore from her catalogue of Maggie stories, or at least sidelined him in my history, turned him into a minor character. He didn't fit the narrative of Carefree Maggie, who'd never been in love. I wonder if she ever suspected my twinges of regret about him.

'Are you sure you want to sleep here tonight?' she asked, holding the dirty sheets at arm's length. 'You can stay at my place.'

'I plan to get laid tonight, Jen,' I said. 'But yeah, if that doesn't happen I'll stay over.'

'Good luck, comrade.'

'So you're coming back at seven-fifteen?' I asked.

'On the dot.'

Clean clothes were few and far between, but I dug out a pair of jeans and my vintage Meatloaf T-shirt, bought online in a fit of irony. It was from the Bad Attitude tour of 1984–5 and featured a picture of a sexy red-lipped skank leering from a motorcycle. The shirt was completely ridiculous, but also soft and delightful from thirty years of washes. It rubbed against my breasts like a kitten. There was no way Rueben could resist the T-shirt, I told myself. I put on mascara and lipstick, checking myself out with a hand mirror.

When the rain started to come down again harder, it dampened my mood. If Rueben was undecided about coming, this would really put him off. I made a beef stew on the camp stove and opened a bottle of red wine to go with it, then sat down to wait.

Sometimes, on a really bad day, I'll list all the terrible things I've never done to another person. Like, sure, maybe I've been unfaithful a few times, but I've never stabbed anyone, thrown acid, sabotaged a condom, blabbed a terrible secret to someone's mother, or deliberately listened to U2, so I can't be that bad. But. Sitting and waiting is a bad idea. Inevitably, after you've listed all the reasons why you're not a monster, you can't help but catalogue all the reasons why you'll never be happy anyway.

I suspected that I was madly in love with Rueben.

I suspected it was the deepest thing I'd felt since Salvatore.

I suspected that Rueben didn't love me back.

I went over the history of our friendship. Borrowing money for sandwiches, email hacking, time wasting, general complaining, and getting him arrested. Half the glass of wine somehow found its way down my throat. I had displayed weakness, assuming that his attraction to me would ensure he overlooked the things I did and said.

Seven o'clock came and went and there was no sign of Rueben. Fifteen minutes later, Jen knocked on the door again.

'He not here yet?'

I shook my head.

Pink Cheeks knocked soon after.

'I brought the wine,' he said. 'I forgot to ask if you wanted red or white, so—'

'Great, come in, he's not here yet,' I told him. Pink Cheeks sat down at the table opposite Jen and smiled nervously. There wasn't enough room for three of us at the table, so I sat on the bed.

I texted Rueben.

*I'm really hungry, are you coming over?*

*I told you I'm not coming,* he wrote back.

*Fool,* I wrote back. *Heartbreaker. I made a stew for you.*

No response.

'Tell him you have something important to show him,' Jen said.

'You mean like my vagina?' I asked.

Pink Cheeks coughed.

I texted him again. *I have something important to show you and it's not my vagina. Seriously, I'm not trying to sleep with you, just have to tell you stuff.*

I took out three bowls and tore a piece of bread in half, dipping it into the stew as I scooped out three serves.

'More wine?' Pink Cheeks asked.

'Fill me up,' I said.

I replaced the lid on the pot and lay down on the bed with the bottle beside me. At the table, Jen poked at her stew doubtfully.

'Have you read all those novels?' Pink Cheeks asked, pointing at the books stacked at the base of the bed.

'Of course not,' I said. 'What I really need is a guide to celibacy, preferably written by a monk.'

Outside, the rain had settled into a dull rhythm, heavy drops splashing up from the gutter, flashing in the yellow streetlight. I sat up and dragged a brush through my hair while Jen and Pink Cheeks watched awkwardly.

'There's probably no point waiting, guys,' I said. 'I'm doomed. I met the man of my dreams and then let him see the real me. Error of the century.'

'The real you is wonderful,' Jen said. 'If he lets a little food fight and minor police questioning stop him from grabbing onto the greatest love he'll ever know, he's an idiot.'

'You're a loyal friend, Jen.'

I poured another glass of wine, thinking that if the fund-raiser was successful then at least I would still have a job and be able to pay off my Centrelink debt in about hundred years, even though I wouldn't have Rueben. And wasn't I a survivor? Wasn't I always the one who came through relationships unscathed, with only a Hawthorn scarf and a few sad memories to never speak of?

But the more I drank, the more I felt.

At a little after eight, Jen stood up. 'Maggie, do you love Rueben?'

I nodded.

'Then what are we waiting around here for?'

Tommasio looked at her with adoration in his eyes. 'You're right,' he said. 'You're so right.'

'What's she right about?' I asked.

'We're going to his house,' she announced. 'We're gonna get this guy.'

—

I hooked the caravan up to the tow bar and we all piled into the panel van. Tommasio sat in the back, holding the stew carefully between his knees so it wouldn't spill, and Jen had the wine with her in the front passenger seat. She was firm in purpose, her mouth set in a determined line.

'Is that, uh, an open container of alcohol?' Tommasio asked her cautiously. 'Because—'

'I'll put the cork back in,' Jen said, and Tommasio shut up.

'Here we go,' I said, as I put the car into gear and eased it out of the parking space. The little caravan rattled and wobbled but followed faithfully. 'We're taking the party to him. Are you ready to play your part like a champion, Tommasio?'

'Never been more ready for anything in my life,' he said.

I parked the van across the street from Rueben's flat and the three of us got out. Jen and Tommasio took the stew and wine into the caravan while I walked across and knocked on Rueben's door with a shaking hand and a pounding heart. The latch turned with a soft click and my mind went blank. It was as if my body was frozen solid. Then the outline of Rueben's face appeared in the dark doorway and I melted again. The light from next door's living room bathed him in soft light that suited his casual grace.

'Hi,' he said.

'I've come over,' I said.

'I see that.'

'Actually, I haven't come over.'

'Oh?'

'I've brought my house to you.' I stepped back and waved a hand towards the caravan, a silver turd beneath a Northcote gum tree. 'Would you like to come in?'

There was a pause the length of eternity. Then he smiled, and I saw his white teeth and those laughing eyes, and without thinking I smiled back.

'I have wanted to see the caravan for a while,' he admitted.

We crossed the street and I flung open the door, before remembering that Jen and Tommasio were inside. Jen stood up to greet Rueben as if the caravan was a palace and she was the butler.

'Hi, Rueben,' she said. 'We didn't quite meet properly the other night. I'm Jen. Come in.'

'I liked your speech at the rehearsal dinner,' he said. He ducked his head as he came in and flicked me a quick curious glance but didn't say anything more.

'This is Tommasio,' I said. Pink Cheeks jumped up, smiling, and held out his hand. 'Tommasio is a police officer.' Rueben's expression became slightly grim, but he shook Pink Cheeks's hand anyway. Before I could start my speech about how I stood up to the police for him, Pink Cheeks blurted out triumphantly,

'We're not charging you with damage to the restaurant. I checked to make sure.'

'I already knew that,' Rueben said. 'They let me go with a warning.'

'Well, I mean, I got the warning struck off. Maggie asked me to.'
'Okay.'

I ground my teeth. Pink Cheeks had jumped the gun and stolen my thunder. And now that Tommasio had said it out loud, asking the police not to harass Rueben was not quite the heroic act it had been in my head.

'So,' Rueben said, looking at me, 'what was it you wanted to show me?'

'Uh, that was it. Tommasio just kinda blurted it out.'

'Well, it's not just that,' Jen said indignantly. 'Maggie did all this stuff for you. Called Tommasio, made a stew. She's never done anything like this before.'

'Thanks, Jen,' I said.

Rueben's mouth twitched. 'You're right,' he said. 'My standards are highly unreasonable.' He took the glass of wine Pink Cheeks offered him. 'Are you here as a witness, Jen? To Maggie's good deeds?'

'I'm here to make sure you're good enough for my best friend,' she said. I nearly covered my face with embarrassment, and tried to signal to her to stop, but she didn't notice. 'Maggie is tops. She tried to tell me that my ex was a dud, and if I'd listened I might have saved myself a case of—' She almost said 'crabs', I could see the words form on her lips. 'A case of a broken heart. So I want to make sure you know her value.'

Perhaps Jen had missed the point of this exercise, which was to convince Rueben that I was good enough for him. My grand gesture was rapidly turning out to be a mediocre gesture.

I appreciated her sentiments, but they were poorly timed.

Rueben smiled. 'I know her value,' he said gently. 'Couldn't have missed it if I'd tried.'

—

Jen and Pink Cheeks, winking and smiling ostentatiously at me, left to walk to a bar on High Street, with Pink Cheeks dropping clumsy hints on their way out about how Jen's ex obviously hadn't appreciated her. Jen nodded vaguely at this while she said goodbye. Rueben sat on the bed beside me. The rain drummed gently on the aluminium roof. His hand rested between us on the bedsheet, his fine, brown fingers tracing lines on the cotton. There was only twenty centimetres between us but it felt like a kilometre. I was petrified of screwing up. All of a sudden I wanted to be sitting at the table instead – wanted even more distance between us. It would be safer.

His wineglass was empty. He picked up mine and held it to the light, and when he ascertained that it was freshly poured he sipped it.

'Well, this is my caravan,' I said.

He touched the wall beside him.

'It's nice,' he said.

He shifted closer. I tried to keep my mouth closed, as if I didn't want to tear Rueben's T-shirt from collar to base and bite the skin above his bellybutton. I could smell his soap and the laundry powder he used, and it occurred to me that I'd hardly seen him wearing anything else.

'Do you just have a wardrobe full of grey T-shirts?' I asked.

He didn't blink. 'Six. I wear my Stones T-shirt when I'm not working.' He started humming 'You Can't Always Get What You Want'.

'You should take over from Bunny. Sing at the next Prayer Time.'

'I'd rather fuck a lamprey.'

He put a hand on my waist. I felt an upwards rush of heat from my stomach to the top of my head.

'I'm not a lamprey,' I said.

'You're pretty jumpy for someone who's been harassing me to come over.'

'You said no.'

'But now I'm here.'

'The word "no" is not to my taste,' I said.

'Clearly.'

'So I had to come all the way here and now the stew's cold. And you've taken my wine.'

'Any other complaints?'

'Yes,' I said. 'You're always going on about my character defects.'

'When have I ever mentioned your character defects?'

'In my head you bring them up all the time.'

He bent his head and kissed me, hard and slow, tracing lines down my body with his fingertips, sending my blood into a roaring, pumping torrent in my head, in my ears.

'So what made you decide to come over instead of slamming the door in my face?' I asked when he broke the kiss. 'Was it because I promised not to show you my vagina?'

'I was looking online at eHarmony profiles. Lots of accountants.' He stroked my shoulder. 'Not many of them looked like they had a Meatloaf T-shirt hidden in their bottom drawer.'

He put down the wineglass and held out his hand. I took it without thinking and he eased me gently onto the bed.

'Are you glad I'm here?' he asked.

'Yes.'

He wrapped his arms around me and I felt my legs give and become tangled up in his. He slid his body onto mine, slow and supple. I drew his T-shirt over his head and unbuckled his jeans. God, his body was fine. Two birds tattooed on his chest looked like honeyeaters in flight, the yellow in their wings faded almost to nothing. Below his navel, next to a small white scar, a wattle branch traced its way down to his left hip bone. There was a patch of dark hair on his chest. He was exactly the right ratio of lean muscle. My neck burned where his lips touched and it felt hot in the caravan as he dragged my T-shirt over my head and kissed his way down my chest to my belly.

'I promise I won't get you arrested,' I murmured. 'But I'm pretty sure it's illegal for someone to be this hot.'

He rolled onto his back and pulled me on top of him and by then I was completely naked. Somehow he'd made my clothes disappear; my jeans were in a crumpled heap by the bed and my tits were brushing his chest as I bent over him and kissed him and eased him into me, and then there was nothing left but the hot air and his body and my body and the sounds of his breathing as I rocked myself on top of him, tracing designs on his hips with my fingertips. His hands were exactly where they had to be, and when I lost my grip on time and place I braced my own hands on the cold wall and cried out.

—

'When did your beard start going grey?'

He had his eyes closed but was smiling a little as if he knew I was watching him. We were lying on the hard vinyl bed, clinging to each other, and I was almost ready to believe in the existence of a divine creator because I'm pretty sure a man as beautiful as him couldn't come into being by accident.

'Young,' he said. 'Late twenties.'

'How old are you now?'

'Thirty-six.'

'Huh. The grey makes you look older.'

He put his hand on my shoulder and pulled me in to rest my head on his still-hot chest, rising and falling with his breath. The chest hair under my cheek was coarse.

'Earlier today you said you had something to tell me,' he said. 'What was it?'

'I've been thinking about wallpapering the caravan,' I blurted quickly. 'Getting some pretty William Morris wallpaper like in my mother's dining room, the kind with the hummingbirds, just like your tattoos.'

'Uh-huh.'

'I think my cat would like new wallpaper.'

'You're terrified, aren't you?'

'No.' Liar. My heart was pounding. 'Well, it's just that my cat used to love me, but now she loves my mother more. So I don't know about the whole thing.'

'That's life, isn't it? Cats come and go. People sometimes leave, too. No way to stop it happening.' He kissed me. 'Never mind, we'll just give it some time.'

His calm self-assurance no longer infuriated me the way it had when I first met him. I felt elation and fear in equal parts, as if I was holding a rare and beautiful butterfly and the only way to stop it from flying away was to keep my palm open and pretend it wasn't there.

'If we're going to start a relationship,' I said, 'I should tell you about my warning bell. The pre-emptive strike.'

'Go ahead.'

'I learnt it from my first boyfriend.' I checked his reaction.

Nothing but mild curiosity. So I took a breath and barged on ahead. 'His name was Jeremy, it was when I was in high school. He cheated on me and I didn't see it coming. He hooked up with the prettiest girl in our year at a party and I was devastated, because I'd been faithful to him. Now it's just what I do. I run off.'

'I bet he regretted it. What's he doing with his life now?'

'He's a banker in Switzerland. Married to Switzerland's only female rally-car driver, who also used to be a model.'

'Oh.'

'So I try to live like Tilda Swinton and have lots of lovers. More eggs in my basket.'

He kissed me. 'High school was twenty years ago, idiot. Get over it.'

I slapped his chest where I'd been fondling it moments before. 'Twelve years ago. I'm younger than you, old balls.'

He kissed me again to shut me up, then sat up. 'Where's the bathroom?'

'Yeah, about that.'

# Chapter 28

'Mum, remember Rueben?'

My mother appraised him, while assuming her favourite power stance behind the kitchen bench. She'd taken to using my great-grandfather's carved walking stick instead of her crutches, and had paired it with a red scarf and tall brown boots. I suspected she felt like an outlaw or pirate, clomping around the house with her frizzy grey hair and hard stare and mahogany walking stick. The house was due to go on the market in March, flaws and all, and I'd agreed to help her clean it up as soon as her cast came off in a few days.

The kitchen was filled with the smell of Moroccan chicken simmering on the stove. She gazed at Rueben's tatts, facial hair and poised, wiry body, while I shifted uncomfortably in the silence.

'Hm. Hello.'

'Nice to see you again, Mrs Cotton,' he said in that gravelly voice. I nearly shivered at the sound of it, as I had been doing every day since I'd met him. 'How are the security doors holding up?'

Rueben had finished up at the Nicholson Street Angels with only Agnes the wiser about our relationship, and the new job at the software company was going well so far. Two nights earlier, lying next to me in the caravan, he'd suggested dinner with my mother.

'That's a bad idea,' I said. 'She thinks tattoos are trashy and will spend the entire night comparing you to my ex-boyfriend.'

'I bet I can get her to like me.'

I secretly enjoyed the thought of bringing him to dinner with my mother, but couldn't decide whether I took greater pleasure in the thought of irritating her or showing him off.

'Fine.' I shrugged. 'Brace yourself.'

Rueben set the table, while I stood next to my mother as she stirred the pot and fired questions at me in a low voice.

'What about that Dan fellow?'

'He's back with his ex.'

'And Sean?'

'Mum, give up.'

'And what's Jen doing with this policeman?'

I grinned. 'They haven't gone on a date yet, but he's working on it.'

'Rueben,' Mum called, 'would you please take this pot to the table? I can't carry anything heavy anymore because of this young fool.' She nodded to me.

Rueben obliged, carrying the cast-iron pot between oven mitts, while I poured the wine. Mum sat down, doled out the chicken onto our plates and went straight in for the kill.

'So, those tattoos. I take it you've been in jail?'

Rueben looked like he'd been expecting it. 'Yes. I went in for eighteen months when I was twenty and I've been out for fifteen years.'

'Hmph. What were you in for?'

'Mum,' I cut in.

'Armed robbery,' Rueben said smoothly.

'And?'

'Assault.'

'Domestic violence?'

'No, I hit a guy with a bag of frozen peas and he needed stitches.'

Mum didn't even smile. 'Any sexual assault convictions?'

'Mum!'

'No,' Rueben said.

She narrowed her eyes. 'Any *accusations?*'

'No.'

'Fraud?'

'No.'

'Gambling addiction?'

'No.'

We all paused while Mum thought of more worst-case scenarios. I took a giant gulp of wine.

'Mum, he's a very clean-cut sort of person now,' I said.

She ignored me. 'Drugs?' She snapped.

'Not anymore.'

'Dealing drugs?'

'Never.'

She sat back in her chair. 'All right. But don't go dragging my daughter down. She's a bit useless already, she doesn't need any help with her downward mobility.'

Rueben squeezed my shoulder. 'She's pretty talented, from what I can see. She brought in over twenty-five thousand dollars for the charity with her fundraiser. The lights are still on because of her.'

'Well, she's always been good at screwing people out of money,' Mum said.

'It's my main skill,' I said.

Rueben dropped his head to inspect the chicken but I caught his smile. Perhaps he was recalling how I was not so good at screwing money out of Centrelink anymore: I had utterly failed there. They were insisting I repay the debt in full, although, since it was being docked fortnightly from my meagre earnings at the Angels, I would pay it back in literally about a hundred years. At least they'd declined to prosecute me for fraud.

'And how long have you been seeing Maggie?' Mum asked Rueben.

He smiled at me. 'A few weeks. But I've been working on her for a while.'

'Have you? Why?'

'Mum!' I said.

'What?' She shrugged. 'I didn't mean it like that.'

'Maggie's my kind of girl.' Rueben touched my hand under the table. I appreciated him pretending that he'd pursued me instead of the other way around, and I squeezed his hand back to let him know it.

Mum brought out chocolate mousse for dessert, so I forgave all her insults. When Rueben got up to use the bathroom, Mum leant in and I prepared myself for a barrage of criticism.

'That man.' She paused for a moment. 'You could do worse.'

Rueben and I left at nine-thirty. He walked to the car while I hung back to say goodbye to Mum on the verandah and Dot did figure-eights around my feet, purring in the quiet evening.

'So now that I have a boyfriend,' I said, 'am I an acceptable daughter?'

*Thud.* She whacked the side of my head. 'You've always been acceptable, idiot.'

'Yeah, right.'

'Come here.' She gave me the tiniest of hugs: arms only, wrapped around my shoulders, not too firm. It was miraculous, the first hug she'd given me since I was a child. 'Boyfriend or not, I'm proud of how you've got your life together.'

'I haven't exactly got my life together. I still earn less than minimum wage and I stay at Jen's place half the time.'

'True.' She turned to go inside. 'But you've done better than I expected.'

—

I ran my hands over the racks of poufy dresses: pink silk, yellow polyester, a 1990s purple sequinned fishtail. The dresses looked sort of overgrown, like shiny shrubs, sometimes stained under the armpits, and fragile beneath the fluorescent lights. They loosened their musty scents when I brushed past them. I came upon a flowing 1970s maxi dress and pulled it out to show Jen.

'Too fancy,' she said. 'It's just a date, and I might even cancel.'

'Jeez, doesn't Pink Cheeks deserve a nice outfit?' I asked. 'Ooh, this looks like a Collette Dinnigan.'

Jen whirled. 'You found a Collette Dinnigan?'

'No, I said it looks *like* one. It's made of polyester. This is an op shop, remember? We sell the good stuff to expensive second-hand stores.' I looked at the clock on the far wall. 'I'm going to have to get back to work soon.'

'Work is next door, it's not like you have far to walk. Look, there's Agnes, she doesn't mind.'

Jen waved to Agnes, who was talking to one of the grannies,

and Agnes waved back, seemingly unconcerned that I was taking a long lunch break. I was currently Agnes's favourite person, ever since Mrs Fitz-Hammond had written a cheque for ten thousand dollars in response to my fundraising letter. Mrs Fitz-Hammond and I had started having regular doughnut sessions. During the last one she'd shown me love letters sent to her by some famous French director in the early seventies, which contained the kind of explicit sex talk that made sticking one's hand down a stranger's pants outside The Fainting Chair seem like a chaste Victorian romance in comparison.

'You haven't *lived* until you've had a foursome,' Mrs Fitz-Hammond informed me.

At the last afternoon tea she'd promised to write the Nicholson Street Angels into her will, and I hadn't even had to ask her.

The grannies of the op shop smiled sweetly at us as they re-racked purple sweaters and polyester pants while Belinda stood motionless beneath the glowing exit sign, watching over her employees like a queen looking down upon her subjects.

'You're not really going to stand Pink Cheeks up, are you?' I asked Jen. 'He booked a table at Cumulus! That's expensive, you know.'

'I guess I won't.' Jen re-racked a horrible early 2000s tube dress and tugged a golden curl. 'It's just, Tommasio's sweet, but he's earnest. I mean, really earnest.' She looked over her shoulder to see if anyone was listening, and dropped her voice. 'Did you know he acted in student films during his arts degree, before he entered the police force?'

'Really?'

'He sent me a link to one of his short films. He was showing off, I guess.'

'Did you watch it?'

'Yeah. It was awful. He beat his wife to death with a telephone. And then he cried. It was really melodramatic. He and his on-screen dead wife were wearing fake wedding rings from the two-dollar shop.'

I held back a snort of laughter. 'I suppose there's a fine line between dweeb and man of your dreams, but I believe Pink Cheeks traverses it adequately. Here, this dress would look nice on you.' I held out a short cream dress with a crocheted hem. 'Empire line, 1960s, very Jen.'

She took one look at it and burst into tears. 'It looks like a wedding dress.'

Crap. Weeks ago, on the day that Jen had been supposed to get married to Jono, I'd whisked her out for a pedicure and she spent the whole time doubled over in the chair, sobbing into the pedicurist's hair as the poor woman tried to keep Jen's foot still so she could paint her toenails. Since then, the only sign of Jen's pain was the thick concealer she used to hide the dark circles under her eyes.

'Right. Sorry.' I re-racked the dress and handed Jen a tissue. She waved it away and wiped her eyes.

'I'm okay, I'm okay,' she said. 'It's not really about Shitballs, just the . . . the symbolism of the white dress.'

'Uh-huh. Listen, I know Tommasio's earnest, but he's not dumb. And he's not at all like J— like Shitballs. He likes to help people.'

'I know.'

I wrapped her in a tight hug. 'It's up to you. You don't have to go on a date if you're not ready,' I said. 'But if you do, can you get him to stop making me move the caravan? He hassled me twice last week.'

'Yeah, all right.' She sniffed. 'You know what, it is a nice dress.' She pulled the cream dress out again and held it up. 'Besides, it's cream, not white.'

'Much less symbolic,' I agreed.

'Maybe it would be good for me to just face my fears.'

'You don't want to indulge a terror of cream dresses forever,' I agreed.

She ducked into a change room and I helped her zip it up at the back.

'Cute,' I said.

'How about you bring along Rueben and we make it a double date?' she asked hopefully.

'Hell no. Besides, Rueben and I are going away this weekend, to the Otways. We're gonna celebrate my birthday early by banging in the rainforest.'

She whirled to face me. 'You're going away together? That sounds serious. Don't freak out, Maggie.'

'I'm not going to freak out.'

'Yes you are. Look at you, you're all antsy at the thought of a relationship. You're going to run out on Rueben while he's lighting the candles and go bang someone in the pub.'

'I'm not!'

'At least get the sexy times in before you run.' Jen mimed vigorous hip-thrusting. Over her shoulder I caught the grannies staring, wide-eyed. 'And then tell me all about it, 'cause Rueben is hot.'

'He is hot.' I got lost for a moment in the thought of Rueben shirtless, mentally tracing my fingers over the honeyeaters.

'How are you getting to the Otways?' she asked.

'We're taking the caravan.'

# Acknowledgements

I am so grateful to everyone who helped bring this novel into the world, especially my agent, Catherine Drayton, and publisher, Beverley Cousins, as well as Claire Friedman and Genevieve Buzo. Without them, Maggie really would have gone nowhere.

Various people helped along the way, including my teachers at the Clarion Writers' Workshop: Karen Joy Fowler, Chris Barzak, Saladin Ahmed, Maureen McHugh, Jim Kelly and Margo Lanagan, and my mentors Kaaron Warren and Sophie Hamley. Thank you also to Varuna, the Writers' House, Manning Clark House, Arts South Australia, and everyone at Writers SA past and present, especially Sarah Tooth.

Thank you to the writing friends who never let me down: Liana Skrzypczak, Vanessa Len, Mike Reid, Pip Coen, Travis Lyons, Zack Brown, adrienne maree brown, Lilliam Rivera, Eugene Ramos, Tiffany Wilson, Melanie West, Becca Jordan, Nathan Hillstrom, Dayna Smith, Jess Barber, Bernie Cox, Evan Mallon and Sara Saab (who lets me borrow her jokes).

My parents, who are the most patient people in the world, my brothers, and Al McKinnon, Lil Ellis, Georgie Clark, Tessa Wood, and Zoe Gibbs, for treating the writing of fiction as a legitimate life choice. Bonnie Grant, for always coming up with the best lines. Emily Calder, for making up stories with me since 1990, give or take.

# About the author

Rose Hartley is a graduate of the Clarion Writers' Workshop. She lives in Adelaide with her cat, Doris, and her 1962 caravan, Cecil. *Maggie's Going Nowhere* is her first novel.

# Discover a
# new favourite